BLOOD IN THE WATER

BLOOD
IN THE
WATER

Tom Meredith

T

The manufacturer's authorised representative in the EU for product safety is Authorised Rep
Compliance Ltd, 71 Lower Baggot Street, Dublin D02 P593 Ireland
(www.arccompliance.com)

Troubador Publishing Ltd
Unit E2 Airfield Business Park,
Harrison Road, Market Harborough,
Leicestershire. LE16 7UL
Tel: 0116 2792299
Email: books@troubador.co.uk
Web: www.troubador.co.uk

ISBN 978 1836281 672

British Library Cataloguing in Publication Data.
A catalogue record for this book is available from the British Library.

Printed and bound by CPI Group (UK) Ltd, Croydon, CR0 4YY
Typeset in 10.5pt Adobe Garamond Pro by Troubador Publishing Ltd, Leicester, UK

1

Three months since a recorded case of COVID-19 in the UK

The sound of gunfire echoed off the rolling valleys and awe-inspiring summits of the surrounding hillside, sending the soldiers scurrying for cover beneath the foliage in the bracken and gorse-adorned countryside. Their approach to the farm that lay in the lip of the valley couldn't have been better coordinated, as they moved stealthily in pairs, covering one another, as they crept and crawled forwards. They moved carefully, flanking the long gravel driveway that snaked its way down into the collection of buildings spread out below them.

With their SA80 rifles raised in their hands, they inched forwards, fanning out over the fields that flanked the gravel. Once Red Team were positioned at the first building, a ramshackle barn housing nothing but a number of broken tractors, they signalled to the rest of the men to swing round from the right. The others vaulted the fence leading out of the field and slunk into the farmyard. Simultaneously, Red Team checked the barn was clear and proceeded the final few yards to another gate, which led to the back of the farm and the largest of the outbuildings.

Meanwhile, Blue Team had finished clearing the small outhouses and were moving swiftly across the yard, passing disused quad bikes and dilapidated sheds. As they sneaked forwards, there was suddenly a rattle of gunfire from the remaining building, and they were forced to duck behind the burned-out shell of an old model Volvo. They returned fire and signalled to Red Team to move in, whilst one of them scanned the barn for the possible hostile. After ascertaining quickly that the only vantage point was an alcove to the left of the building, the soldiers focussed their fire on that spot. A figure stepped out momentarily, only to disappear in a hail of bullets; a haze of smoke rose gently over the dusty farmyard. There was no return fire, and both teams moved onwards in a pincer formation. Within seconds, the barn had been cleared, and the exercise had been pronounced a success. It was time to return to the barracks.

As they trudged back, the sun beat down on the weary members of the 1st Battalion Rifles (the Rifles for short), causing sweat to mingle grimly with the camo face paint they wore. This had been a punishing ten-day training-exercise deployment, and the men had been pushed to their limits – although they'd expected nothing less. Even hardened troops such as the Rifles didn't enjoy their visits to Senta Barracks, positioned close to the sleepy village of Sennybridge in the heart of the Brecon Beacons. There was little opportunity to marvel at the spectacular rolling hills and sweeping farmland that lay between the undulating peaks of the countryside. Instead, they were subjected to days on end of gruelling intensity, both physical and mental, to replicate combat situations as closely as possible.

Over the past few days, the temperatures had soared in the Brecon Beacons, and the heat, combined with the sheer savagery of the training, had seen many collapse through exhaustion.

Their plight was real enough, as were the dangers the soldiers faced in these conditions. It was only two years prior that the last soldier had lost his life on an exercise in this very camp, succumbing to a cardiac arrest in extreme conditions whilst partaking in an SAS selection test. The tragedy of his death had been amplified by the fact that he'd previously been deployed in combat under the extreme heat conditions of Afghanistan, had distinguished himself honourably and was one of the fittest men in his regiment. The sight of his distraught parents at the subsequent inquest into his death had shaken the military community to its core.

He hadn't been the first and no doubt wouldn't be the last. Several army reservists had died some years before in almost identical circumstances. Both inquests had shown that the army had failed in its duty to adhere to certain health and safety requirements. The reality was that some mistakes had been learned, yet others had not, and implementing the necessary amendments hadn't been considered practical. There had to be an element of risk to the training; a fear for survival had to be instilled in exercises such as these, else the troops wouldn't be as well prepared as they needed to be on the day they were called to fight on the front lines for real.

The controversy that had surrounded those inquests had largely been forgotten. The members of the British armed forces had been shown as true heroes in the recent pandemic crisis, second only to the NHS and care workers when it came to being hailed as national heroes. They were rightly lauded for their efforts during the crisis, which were many and varied. From ferrying vital protective personal equipment to hospitals and care homes across the UK to helping set up mobile testing facilities, all whilst maintaining the security of the country, their endeavours had been crucial in helping the country to come through the crisis.

As the rate of deaths had flattened and life gradually began to return to normal, the troops had swiftly been redeployed to training barracks around the UK to increase the country's state of readiness once more. There was an expectation that, in the wake of the pandemic, the months would see an increase in the number of threats to the country's security, both at home and abroad. Several regiments had already been despatched to foreign nations that had fallen into tyranny in the wake of the crisis or whose governments had collapsed, leaving dangerous insurgencies to fill the void of recognisable authority. It had seen an upsurge in British and NATO operations around the globe, but so far, none of these threats had reached British shores.

The Rifles were soon to be deployed on a peacekeeping operation abroad, and although the location of this mission had so far been kept from them, they all knew where they'd be going. Every member of the battalion had also known what that had meant– a stint at a training camp in the Brecon Beacons. It just so happened that they weren't the only ones in Sennybridge at the moment. Training alongside them was a crack squadron from 22 SAS, the active regiment of the Special Air Service. Unfortunately for the Rifles, this meant they were partaking in several exercises in tandem with the SAS, adding to the intensity and gruelling nature of their time in Wales.

Only yesterday, the men had been dropped in pairs at preselected points in the Brecon Beacons, with very little in the way of orienteering equipment to help guide them to the next rendezvous point. Their starting position had been predetermined to ensure there was no avoiding the highest peaks, with the cone-shaped summit of Pen-y-Fan crossed twice in a punishing climb. With bergens strapped to their backs, which seemed to hold a steadily increasing weight as they strove to reach this rendezvous point, they attempted to avoid the sharpest cliffs and quarries. Their muscles were screaming at them to stop, but they pushed themselves onwards and returned to the barracks some hours later, exhausted and grimacing from the pain of the fresh blisters they'd accumulated.

A few members of the Rifles aspired to join 22 SAS one day, and that aspiration had only been heightened over the past few days. There was a reason it was one of, if not the, most accomplished and formidable special forces units in the world. During several of the drills, the men of the Rifles had experienced the disheartening yet inspirational sight of being routinely outstripped by the members of 22 SAS. Their exceptional reputation had grown in prominence, particularly in the Troubles in Northern Ireland and both Gulf Wars, with their missions ranging from counterterrorism operations to covert reconnaissance and operations behind enemy lines during active conflicts.

Corporal Ross Matheson wasn't one such aspiring SAS recruit. He'd been full of ambition when he initially applied to join the British Army, but after two failures to make the grade during officer training, he'd joined as a private – the lowest military rank. He'd served with distinction on several combat tours, as well as on several peacekeeping operations in Africa. There had been a time when he would have pushed to make the step up from corporal to sergeant, which is typically a soldier who's second in command of a platoon, or perhaps even forcing a move to another battalion to gain promotion. As it was, he was content to remain with the men who had become his family as much as the wife and young daughter he left behind when on deployment.

With a long face that characterised his family heritage, he looked almost waxy and gaunt in the winter. His short, dark-brown hair matched the patchy stubble which made his wiry chin scratchy, with eyes so dark a grey they seemed almost black.

Despite being in his late twenties, he appeared much older and tougher. Much of that was due to being battle-hardened from his years of service to his country, but some of it was more recent. Those stormy-grey eyes seemed to be fading, and the haggard complexion that haunted him throughout the winter had returned over the past two days, despite the scorching heat. His breathing was more desperate and rapid than that of an experienced soldier who was accomplished in composing himself and staying calm.

He knew this would be his final exercise in the scenery that had become almost a second home to Ross over the years. This was his fourth exercise in Sennybridge, and on each visit, he'd fallen more in love with the sleepy village and rolling hills surrounding it, despite the sometimes-torturous training he endured whilst there. He could recall few details from his first posting to the Brecon Beacons a decade ago, other than the extreme conditions that had dogged the training. Battling through firmly entrenched snow and swirling blizzards, with the cold biting his face, he'd hiked for dozens of miles with little in terms of orienteering equipment. They'd spent nights lying on the frozen ground, devising ambushes.

*

The cold had been piercing, as though icy blades were stabbing every area of his body, and the hands holding his rifle had been numb with pain. It was an oppressive, inescapable sensation that kept him in a heightened state of alert. That had been a good thing, at least. His body had flexed beneath the undergrowth, eager to spring into action and send the blood pumping around his body once more. The first gold glint of dawn was overhead, the hills and undergrowth basking in its sovereign beauty, and yet he and the other members of his platoon had remained invisible to the naked eye. The hours had passed by until a flicker of movement near the treeline 100 yards ahead of him had caught his attention.

Five figures had been emerging stealthily into the designated kill zone, the rippling of their camouflage smocks almost imperceptible to the untrained eye. The lead figure had been scanning the area, his eyes darting over the undergrowth, but he'd failed to notice the tripwire hidden ahead of him. He was just a few steps from it now, and Ross had been counting down the steps, his finger stiffening over the trigger of his assault rifle. For a second, his eyes had deceived him, and he'd believed the figure had taken the crucial step to trigger the trip wire, which was their signal to fire. He'd been a fraction too early, and the burst of gunfire from his weapon had shattered the still air into a thousand pieces. The lead figure had fallen to the ground, and Ross had suddenly been flanked by the other members of his platoon, with the crisp double-taps from their weapons joining his own until all five figures lay motionless on the ground.

He'd known instantly that he'd made a mistake, and so he'd moved quickly to rectify it. He'd stumbled clumsily over the fallen ground and attempted to drag one of the bodies out of the undergrowth. He'd realised immediately that he was compounding his error, and his hasty efforts to move the body had rendered him vulnerable to any booby traps the enemy bodies might conceal. The captain in charge of that particular exercise – a sinewy, humourless northerner whose black hair was streaked with grey – had torn a strip off him in front of the entire platoon. At the time, he'd feared he'd be thrown out of the army with immediate effect, but it had been the making of him. He didn't put a single foot wrong in the week that followed and had excelled at every available opportunity, determined not to be singled out again for the wrong reasons.

Not since that day had he felt as unsettled as he did today, however. He'd always coped well with the heat, but today, he'd struggled to keep up in the exercise and had fallen off the pace during the morning's hike. Only sheer grit and willpower had helped him make up some ground on the rest of the men. That hadn't saved him from the wrath of Major Pollard, who – despite having served alongside Ross for several years – wasn't a man to make allowances. He demanded and achieved high standards from all the men under him and was one of the most feared but respected officers in the British Army. He'd served with the SAS in the past and was still capable of leading highly skilled covert operations abroad. The major had made it clear, in no uncertain terms, that Ross had to up his game.

The subsequent gas-mask exercise had left him struggling to breathe, aggravating the cough that had plagued him for the past two days. The smallest cough still inspired a universal fear in the wake of the pandemic, and he'd been subjected to plenty of grief from the other members of his company in the barracks overnight. It had led to many jokes that he was the new patient zero for a further wave of the virus, and when he entered the mess for dinner, he was greeted by the sight of the whole battalion wearing face masks.

Swearing at each of them in turn, he'd collected his food – ignoring the cook who'd recoiled at his approach – and sat next to his long-time friend Corporal Dawkins. 'Don't you start,' he muttered darkly as Dawkins slid further up the bench away from him, grinning as he did so.

His fellow corporal was several years his younger, with boyish features and a natural charm that many experienced veterans lacked. He was one of the shorter members of the regiment, at about five feet seven inches tall, with light-brown hair and not a scrap of fat on his well-conditioned body.

'You'll wake up dressed in nothing but a gas mask if the lads have their way,' quipped Dawkins.

He wasn't wrong. Ross had often seen such treatment dished out to his fellow soldiers, to the hilarity of the regiment, and he'd suspected such a plan was being formulated behind his back. Being stripped and handcuffed to his bunk with just a gas mask strapped to his face was the least of his worries, however. He'd been scanning the mess daily for any new faces or suspicious activity in the past few days, but so far, nothing had jumped out at him.

Private Faye, the baby-faced assassin – aptly named for his love of Manchester United, youthful features and sharpshooting prowess – was still the entertainer of the group, cracking jokes and holding poker sessions nightly. Nor had there been any change in behaviour from any of the other men, including those from 22 SAS. He'd trained with them all before, and they blended in seamlessly with the Rifles men, despite the slight air of superiority emanating from them.

*

The next morning, Corporal Matheson awoke, mercifully fully clothed but sweating profusely. It clung to his entire body and his head was pounding with pain. As he pushed himself into a sitting position on his bunk, he knew he'd been transported back to the terrifying place in his dreams once more. Shaking slightly, he looked around, grateful to see he was alone, and he hastily began to dress for the morning's exercise. He reported to the barracks as normal to find the grim-faced Sergeant Hiscock awaiting his arrival.

Hiscock hadn't been blessed with either good looks

or a kindly face; his was more the sort of complexion that would scare rather than calm others. He was a rugged man with unkempt stubble; sallow, unhealthy-looking skin; and uneven, yellow teeth that parted into a leer, even when he was attempting to smile. Although he'd been a trained army man for the past twelve years of his life, he walked with a stooped back akin to that of a particularly ugly gargoyle. This had earned him the nickname of 'The Hunchback of the Cotswolds', on account of the barracks he was normally stationed at.

The unpleasantness extended beyond his mere physical appearance. He was a man it was impossible to trust, and in a role where togetherness and camaraderie were so essential, this was an especially unpleasant trait. There was no denying his expertise as a soldier, though, nor his ability to have the ear of the right people. In that regard, appearances were deceptive, as the sergeant appeared to be able to influence senior officers to ensure his own rise through the ranks, often to the detriment of his fellow soldiers. He was once more in line for a promotion after filing a report on the inadequacies of the armed forces on their recent peacekeeping operations in North Africa. This was despite having been involved extensively in the discussions about how the operations would be conducted. Upon his return to British shores – and perhaps having read certain press coverage of the missions – he'd sent a detailed report to the Ministry of Defence (MOD), criticising his commanding officers and stating how he would have handled the operations differently. Unsurprisingly, this had led to further resentment towards him from those within the barracks; however, he seemed supremely unconcerned by this.

'You're very nearly late for exercise, Matheson. Timekeeping is the only thing you haven't failed on over the past two days,' he sneered, pausing to smirk at his own joke.

Ten minutes later, the members of the SAS squadron were equipping themselves, alongside the Rifles, in preparation for the morning's exercise. Ross found himself next to one of the SAS men, whom he knew only as Wolf. He was young, maybe even in his early twenties, with short, black hair; thoughtful, dark-green eyes; high cheekbones; and thin, firm lips. He had a tough, well-rounded physique and spoke with a North Wales lilt. 'Ignore the sergeant. He's a complete *drewgi*.'

Ross smiled in spite of himself. He recognised the Welsh insult after all the time spent in the barracks with men from that country, and he couldn't help but think 'skunk' was an appropriate way to describe the sergeant. 'Cheers!' He grinned before turning sharply to direct a violent coughing fit in another direction. Ignoring the fresh jeers directed at him, he clutched his throat, struggling to instil a normal rhythm into his breathing.

He felt the arm of the SAS soldier on his shoulder and heard him say something, although he couldn't discern what it was through the continuing coughing fit. After several minutes, he managed to compose himself enough to tighten the straps of his backpack and assure those around him that he was fine, but he'd just had something stuck in his throat. Nonetheless, he knew the truth, and it was with a grim certainty that he made his way back into the fresh morning air, gulping in as much oxygen as he could.

*

Bullets whizzed incessantly over their heads, indiscriminately homing in on life, despite this being an exercise. The troops jumped off the trucks, ducking their heads, and then assembled seamlessly into their attack formation, regardless of the deafening gunfire overhead.

The target today was a cottage that lay on the lip of a valley some half a mile from their drop-off point. Ross was with two of the SAS men – one of whom was Wolf – as well as five members of his own regiment, and they fanned out to the left flank. He found himself next to Wolf as they flattened themselves to the ground beneath a covering of bracken and laid down cover fire. The remaining members of the company were moving swiftly down the right flank, over the gorse-covered hillside; they were working in tandem, with one darting ahead whilst the other lay down a burst of covering fire.

'Go,' hissed Wolf, who was already twisting on to his feet and sprinting forwards.

Ross hastened to follow him, but he found himself clutching his throat, suddenly unable to breathe amongst the caramel scent of the gorse. He lost his grip on his rifle for a split second and fumbled to reclaim it in his grasp as bullets whanged dangerously close. Ahead of him, Wolf had dropped to the ground, rolling and then pulling himself forwards on his hands and knees. As the rifle tumbled to the floor, Ross's knees buckled, and he dropped to the ground, almost in slow motion, with both his hands clawing at his throat.

Abruptly, the sounds of gunfire and the thundering footsteps coming towards him were gone, as the remaining oxygen was slowly sapped from his lungs. His mouth moved rapidly as he fought to push air through his body and flush out the toxins that were winning the bitter war with his immune system. Without the oxygen they required to function, his internal organs began to fail. Within a matter of seconds, his body was simultaneously experiencing multi-organ and respiratory failure – a deadly combination from which there was no return. For a man so used to combat, his body was losing its final battle – one against itself – deprived of the vital element it needed to stay alive.

Corporal Matheson barely felt the oxygen mask being strapped over his face and his head being lifted from the ground, nor did he hear the frantic shouts and hurried movement around the spot where he was struggling to stay alive. He reached up with his right hand, trying to touch the face of his daughter one last time, and his eyes filled briefly with tears before his head rolled back and his body became limp and lifeless.

2

It was as though another lockdown had settled over the capital once more. The cobbled streets that characterised parts of London were devoid of their usual bustling occupants, and the Tube lines were only just beginning to crackle into life. The sun still lay resolutely below the horizon, waiting to make its all-too-brief appearance before retreating to its sanctuary once more and plunging the city once more into darkness. The faint chirping of birds weaving their way through Hyde Park could be heard in the cold, and a stillness hung in the misty air.

In the midst of such a scene, it seemed strange to see a man step out from the seemingly closed café that sat beside the Serpentine lake. The figure paused, briefly turning his head left and then right, as though they were checking for something or someone unseen, before setting off purposefully around the beautifully positioned body of water in the heart of the park. Almost as though it had been waiting for the man to appear, the sun summoned the courage to peer over the horizon, causing the dormant raindrops on the glass windows of the café to unexpectedly sparkle like diamonds as golden rays shone down over the capital.

Rather than pausing to marvel at the sudden beauty the sun had revealed, the figure quickened his pace, moving swiftly through the park, his perfectly polished black shoes seeming to whisper as they kicked up fallen leaves from the path. If the man had taken a moment to halt his journey, he may have been able to discern the rhythmic heartbeat of the city beginning to tick quietly like an old grandfather clock. However, the figure clearly had a destination in mind and was moving briskly towards it with no other thought in his mind than to reach it as soon as possible.

There was no doubt London had changed to a certain extent following the harrowing events of the previous year: Tube commuter numbers had fallen sharply compared to before the outbreak of the pandemic; and very few tourists lined the Mall that led to Buckingham Palace and congregated with excited chatter outside the Houses of Parliament. The atmosphere had changed, and there was a definite air of caution and suspicion, plus a feeling of not knowing who to trust – or rather who to trust to be in close proximity to. Despite the eventual relaxation of social distancing rules, it was common to see people keeping their distance from other members of the public, and face masks were still being worn by some in the busiest corners of the city.

Although it had been commonplace to question the government's handling of the outbreak and the speed with which it had reacted, there was a feeling they'd contributed to the country beginning to get back on its feet. By and large, the majority of small local businesses had survived the crisis, with governmental and charitable aid, whilst the larger industries had ground back into gear regardless of incurring huge deficits due to the pandemic. The plan to rebuild the country stronger was well under way and, notwithstanding all the criticism, there were signs the politicians were finally listening to the views of the public.

There had been a shift in policy away from austerity and nationalist-inspired isolation towards a more inclusive government that was willing to reward the heroic efforts of the health workers by introducing wage rises for nurses and increasing funding for the NHS. Likewise, those schools in particular who'd worked tirelessly to stay open and support children with learning disabilities and the families of key workers had been recognised and their budget restrictions eased. There were no longer noises from backbench MPs, or even cabinet members, about the urgent need to cut immigration, which had in the past fuelled xenophobia in parts of the country. It appeared that a more tolerant and benevolent ruling establishment was emerging from the horror that had finally relinquished its grip on the nation.

The discovery and delivery of the vaccines had healed some of the divisions and bitter squabbles, not just in parliament but also around the country. Unlike the distribution of the protective personal equipment to frontline staff during the pandemic, which had often been delayed, the vaccines had swiftly been dispensed across the country, and the UK had been one of the first countries to fully benefit from the inoculations. However, the fact that protective face masks were still to be seen in public showed a fear that another mutated wave of the virus could hit, although there had been no sign of that.

Of course, the vaccine itself wasn't infallible. No vaccine is, and perhaps that was adding to the tension and paranoia that the number of deaths would begin to snowball once more. It was something the world would have to get used to living with, and there would still be deaths – but not the vast numbers there had been previously. Although it had been one of the hardest hit countries, particularly in Europe, the UK had been able to keep a lid on the number of deaths since the vaccines had been administered.

There had been conspiracy theories, of course, about the origin of the virus in the first place, with some claiming it to have been manmade in a laboratory in China, or perhaps it hadn't even originated from the place it was said to have done. In reality, the peddlers of those theories were individuals with specific political and social agendas, for whom this narrative suited their worldview. Nevertheless, in the background, the public and even some political leaders were unaware of the attempts being made to exploit the opportunity that the pandemic had provided.

The figure striding across London on this cold, dewy morning was one such individual. To a casual passer-by, he looked like any other businessman on his way to work in the city, and a first glance at him wouldn't warrant a second. A man in his mid-forties with receding, greying hair; a wide jawline; and a medium height and build – he was dressed in an expensive navy suit and tie, with a brown overcoat and shiny leather briefcase in his hands. Upon closer inspection, his cold, grey eyes were darting nervously around in their sockets, scanning the ground around him, and his grip on the handle of the briefcase was slippery with sweat.

As he turned on to Constitution Hill, he glanced over his shoulder and paused briefly. At that moment, a cyclist came swinging round behind his left shoulder, causing the man's body to tense as though he were braced for impact. The bike and its rider veered away from him, and within seconds, it was vanishing up the Mall and out of sight. After shaking his head slightly, the figure continued his journey, though his pace had quickened even more. He was covering the ground in large strides now, perhaps shaken by the encounter with another member of the public. He turned left on to the Mall, passing in front of Buckingham Palace, where the royal standard was fluttering gently in the first morning breeze, signalling the Queen was in residence.

More cyclists and pedestrians were visible now, appearing from the entrances to the Royal Parks that flanked the palace and continuing onto the red-coloured surface. The figure cursed under his breath. He knew he should have set off earlier, but there was nothing he could do about it now, and besides, he hadn't set the time of the meeting. Perhaps he should have disguised himself, but he'd thought that wearing business dress would help him blend in with his fellow commuters if – as had happened – he hadn't been able to walk the streets of the capital alone. He fumbled with the clasp of his briefcase, which it had become unbuckled again, tightening it once more and holding it even more firmly.

He glanced down at the handsome TAG Carrera strapped to his wrist and noted the time. As expected, he was right on schedule, but that did nothing to ease the tension he felt. His breathing was getting faster, and he willed himself to remain calm. Nothing could go wrong. He'd timed everything to the last second, and he trusted the man he was due to meet – as much as you can trust any politician, that is. There was always the faint possibility that someone had found out about their meeting, but there was no way anyone could know the reason it had so hastily been arranged.

For a moment, a flicker of doubt passed through his brain, but he dismissed it. He just needed to get this done and then, just maybe, he'd at least have a clear conscience. A new life was what he hoped to obtain in return for the intelligence he had to offer, but it was always possible that they'd insist upon him going to prison. That prospect didn't thrill him, and it was what had pushed him to the point of fleeing the country altogether, along with his secrets, or else embracing the offer that had come his way from a certain foreign power.

In the end, a sense of duty and a flicker of patriotism had led him to contact an individual within the government and arrange this meeting. No matter what he'd done – whether that was with or without political approval – he'd served his country for over two decades in various roles. Of course, there was an element of self-preservation as well, and he had no desire to take total responsibility for what was to come.

He was nearing the end of the Mall and passing the sweeping lake that ran through the heart of St James's Park to his right. He paused, deliberating whether to turn right. Downing Street was almost visible across Horse Guards Parade, and the sandy earth that had once hosted the Olympic volleyball tournament was heating up in the rapidly rising sun. The impulse faded as soon as it had arrived, and he turned off the main straight of the Mall, briefly looking back towards the royal residence standing at the end, and for the first time in his life, he appreciated the red-carpet effect the coloured road surface created, as though visitors would really be met at the end by royalty.

It was only as he passed underneath Admiralty Arch that he paused once more. He should have taken extra precautions, doubled back along his route and made sure he wasn't being followed. For the past three weeks, he'd been employing those exact counter-surveillance measures, so why had he not done so this morning? It had been a conscious decision, of course, being safe in the knowledge that nobody could have known where he'd spent the previous night, and yet something had happened to make him doubt that decision. It was too late. The meeting was arranged, and he was exactly on schedule. This was no time to question himself.

His hand slipped on the handle of the briefcase yet again as he passed under the magnificent Edwardian architecture commissioned to commemorate the life of Queen Victoria. The central arch was only ever opened for ceremonial occasions, such as a royal wedding or a coronation, and it remained closed the rest of the time. Work had begun to turn the curved, stone, Grade I listed construction into a luxury hotel, providing an iconic full stop to the processional Mall and offering sumptuous views of the parks beyond.

He glided beneath the right arch and stepped into another world. From the serenity and quiet beauty of the royal estates, he'd entered the already bustling heart of the capital. Despite the sun barely having risen, black cabs and cyclists were careering between lanes, and the first blares of angry commuter horns could be heard. He found the sudden noise unnerving and quickened his pace after a further swift glance at his wrist.

He never made it another step, however. Through the morning air, he heard a faint whistle as a final warning. A split second later, the .50 high-calibre bullet slammed into his chest and came to rest nestled just above his heart. He fell backwards onto the tarmac and looked down to see that his suit and overcoat were steadily darkening. His eyes scanned the neighbouring rooftops, even as the grey colouring was leaving his irises and his face was turning increasingly waxy.

The leather briefcase tumbled from his grasp as the blood seeped beneath his left sleeve and over his wrist. There were screams in the surrounding air, but they were growing ever more faint. He tried to cry out, but no sound left his throat. A single tear dripped from his left eye, mingling with the blood now trickling from the side of his mouth. He reached out a pathetically limp hand and clawed at the asphalt, his eyes now sliding rapidly in and out of focus. For a second, he found the strength to pull himself into a sitting position against a nearby pillar, but then the shadow of death loomed over his defeated body.

With a desperate realisation crystallising in those flickering eyes, he raised his head feebly to look up at the man now towering over him. A look of shock flitted across his dying features for a split second, and he tried frantically to crawl along the pavement to get away from the nightmare now smiling over him. His body failed him, however, as it was unable to obey his instructions, and he jerked violently as fresh blood oozed from the corners of his mouth. Despite the certainty of his fate, his hand opened and closed as though trying to grab something out of reach. Even as he did so, the shadow above him crouched down and swept up the briefcase in their left hand before striding off into the panicking swarm of people, their face hidden from the cameras by a baseball cap fitted tightly over their head.

The only man capable of identifying the individual slipped further down the pillar, with the final colour receding from his waxy features as the last trickle of blood dripped onto the pavement. Atop a neighbouring rooftop, the sniper began to disassemble the lightweight aluminium housing of the Steyr Scout rifle. As they removed the scope and placed the weapon inside a toolbox, they reached into the waistband of their hi-visibility trousers and checked the M9 semi-automatic pistol they'd stashed there. Without a backward glance at the motionless body or the gathering crowd around it on the pavement below, they turned and made their way speedily towards the fire escape.

Meanwhile, a special Westminster-edition Range Rover swung into Trafalgar Square. The back door opened for the briefest of seconds to allow a man in a baseball cap to jump deftly inside before it was slammed shut; its blackened windows blocked out the glare of public scrutiny. Smiling slightly to himself, Henderson placed the briefcase on the seat beside him, discarding the hat as he did so. It was time to move on to the next phase of the operation.

3

The two men met near the Old Royal Naval College in Greenwich, both dressed in dark clothing that made them almost invisible against the backdrop of the black canvas overhead. It had been a strange choice of venue, but the shorter man had insisted upon it. He was nervous, and his small, watery eyes were darting across the road in the cold morning air. His face was horribly disfigured – the result of an accident at a waste disposal plant in Ukraine many years ago – and the short, black hair of his eyelashes and eyebrows had been burned away, exposing his black pupils in their hollow sockets and disguising the true extent of his age.

The Old Royal Naval College itself was an extraordinary collection of buildings located in the heart of the Maritime Greenwich UNESCO World Heritage Site. The spectacular buildings had originally been constructed to serve as the Royal Hospital for Seamen at Greenwich, the designs of which had been laid out by Sir Christopher Wren, but after the hospital closed in 1869, it had become the Royal Naval College, Greenwich. From the other side of the river, it was possible to make out the former royal residence Queen's House in amongst the striking buildings of the college, whilst the Royal Observatory looked down on the whole scene from a hilltop in Greenwich Park.

There was a faint smell of rotting tobacco swirling around the two men as they met in the middle of the college grounds, with the early morning chill encircling them in an oppressive grip it seemed unlikely to ever relinquish. This wasn't the first time the two men had met, but there was something unusual about this particular meeting. Each rendezvous was usually scrupulously planned, down to the exact minute and location of the meet, and had been planned days and weeks in advance. The shorter, disfigured man wouldn't usually have been allowed any say in the location or time of the meeting. This morning was different; he'd made contact the day before, requesting an urgent meeting at a time and place of his choosing. The tone of the message, though not delivered verbally, had raised alarm bells at once.

Vasily Ivanovic wasn't a highly trusted asset, nor was the information he ordinarily supplied considered extremely valuable to his paymasters. Yet when an asset makes contact in such a way, requesting an immediate meet, it usually meant one of two things: their cover had been blown, and they needed to get out; or they had some extremely important intelligence to reveal regarding an imminent threat. Either could represent a major problem for the British security services. Although he wasn't a high-level asset, Ivanovic was embedded within a very prominent gas company based in London that had very close ties to Members of Parliament. If he were to be revealed as a British asset, it could be immensely embarrassing for the country.

'You have to get me out, please,' he said in broken English with a thick Eastern European accent.

The man opposite him remained emotionless. He was dressed more smartly than Vasily, in dark-denim jeans and a black Belstaff Trialmaster jacket that looked as though it had been tailored to fit his defined physique. As the coat had been originally designed to cope with the gruelling, often arctic conditions of the Scottish Highlands, the jacket's high collar and throat latch kept out the morning cold expertly. It was also more than capable of being used during physical exertion due to the breathable material with which it was made and its underarm ventilation, whilst the corduroy linings and four front pockets gave it an extra-sleek appearance. The black watch face of the Omega Seamaster Planet Ocean strapped to his left wrist completed the look.

Contained within the stylish mien was an athletic-looking man in his thirties with slightly gelled short, light-brown hair and piercing, blue eyes capable of x-raying almost anyone. He seemed totally at ease in these rather uncomfortable surroundings, with the eerily silent yet majestic naval buildings towering around them and the river rippling silently not far away from them. He'd analysed his surroundings prior to attending the meet, of course, but even upon arrival, he'd rapidly assessed three exit points he could utilise if the need arose. He was now studying the man beside him with an icy stare that gave nothing away yet probed for what had prompted Ivanovic to call this meeting.

It wasn't unusual to see an asset on the brink of being discovered behave in such a way. Nevertheless, Ivanovic had never before indicated he was on the brink of a breakdown. Something had got him spooked all right. The longer he remained silent, the more frustrated the Ukrainian became – a fact demonstrated a moment later when Ivanovic spat irritably, 'Do you have nothing to say? Spies – all the same, no matter what country.'

'Do you have something to tell us, Mr Ivanovic? I assume there was a reason for dragging me to the dockyards so early in the morning?' asked the agent in a calm, emotionless voice.

'*Don't you listen?* I need out – now.' The Ukrainian was glancing around him nervously once more, as though he were expecting to be attacked at any minute.

'I can assure you this area is secure. You're safe here, but if you want out, then I need to know what you know.' His voice was gentle, coaxing, but there was an icy edge to it. 'Or we can't help you.'

Anger mingled with fear in Vasily's black eyes at this. 'You can't leave me in there. If they find out, they'll kill me. I give you information. You protect me, yes? That was the deal. Now protect me.'

'But what from, Vasily? You haven't told me whom or what you want protecting from? Until you give me that, I can't help you.'

The Eastern European man spat an ugly word in Russian.

At this, the British agent raised his eyebrow. 'That's hardly how you refer to a friend now, is it? I speak excellent Ukrainian too – in case you were intending to trawl through every derogatory word in the Slavic languages. Save us both the time. I have better things to do than standing in the freezing cold being insulted by a pathetic little man still crying over the end of the Cold War. Either tell me what you know or I'm gone.' It was time to get tough with this wretch; it was the only way to get the information, it seemed. Vasily had to be equally as scared of them abandoning him as he was of his employers or whoever was threatening him.

'No… you can't go. They'll kill me.'

After taking a quick step forwards, the agent grabbed Ivanovic's right arm and twisted it upwards behind his back, forcing the man down onto the grass. He hissed into the man's ear, 'We've tried the nice approach, but it's not working is it, Vasily? Now tell me what it is you know.' He knew that Ivanovic wouldn't shout out in pain, for fear of alerting either those he was scared of or members of the public to their presence.

Instead, the Ukrainian whimpered faintly and gasped, 'OK... OK... I tell you.'

The agent hauled him back to his feet, released his arm and dusted down the faded leather jacket that perhaps accounted for just how much Ivanovic was shivering in the morning air. 'That's better.' He smiled. 'There's no need for any unpleasantness. Now, from the beginning, what's happened?'

'So cold...' Ivanovic said with a note of respect in his voice as he massaged his shoulder. 'You British bastards are learning, eh? You'd have fitted in with the KGB.'

'I think not,' the agent declared coldly, his eyes purest ice.

'OK, OK; there's something coming. I don't know the details, but I've been told to expect a large evacuation for our people in the next few days. London is no longer safe.'

The agent waited, studying his asset curiously. 'And?'

'That's all I know. They don't tell me why. Please,' Ivanovic said in a rush, still glancing around him.

'It sounds to me that you'll be well looked after by your own people. If they're evacuating you all as you say, then you don't need our help.'

There was a startled and alarmed tone to the Ukrainian's voice as he gabbled, 'You'd let this happen. I told you. London is not safe. You have to help me. If I return home, they'll find out. They always find out.'

'Let what happen, Vasily?' asked Agent Ben Viper coolly. 'You've told me nothing, no specifics, only a vague notion that the capital is under threat. You haven't told me how, why, when or by whom. I wish you all the best upon returning home. Thank you for your service.'

He had turned to leave when a low hiss of a single word from the Ukrainian caused him to turn around once more. There was no flicker of emotion or reaction on his face, but there was a sharpness in his tone that hadn't been there previously. The possibility that had been giving the security services sleepless nights for months – it couldn't be. 'What did you say?'

'Virus. It's the virus,' hissed Ivanovic once more. 'I don't know who or where or when, but the virus is coming. They'll release it in London.'

4

The Cabinet Office in Whitehall had always rather puzzled Aldwyn Haynes. His experience of politicians was that, by and large, they enjoyed a sense of grandeur – a feeling they were living above others. Their own lavish offices in Westminster – with their regal, velvet-upholstered chairs and expensive works of art – gave the air of a group of people who were smugly satisfied with the positions of authority they held. You'd think, therefore, that Cabinet Office Briefing Room A (COBRA) – the site of the most important committee, which handled national emergencies – would be similarly decorated and lavish.

However, the truth was that it appeared much the same as every other office briefing room housed in company buildings throughout the capital. It was a large, wood-panelled room with a sleek oak conference table in the centre and banks of computer screens arranged against the far wall, at which every attendee could pivot in their swivel chairs to observe the goings-on. The room itself was soundproof and swept frequently for listening devices to ensure there could be no high-level leaks from the meetings.

The same faces as usual were arranged around the table: the Home Secretary, Foreign Secretary and Defence Minister were all in attendance, as well as the Chief Medical Officer, the Director General (DG) of MI5 and the chief of the Secret Intelligence Service (SIS), otherwise known as MI6. In addition to the heads of both services, there were other high-ranking officers present from the intelligence services, plus the Commissioner of the Metropolitan Police (the Met). There were representatives too from the Civil Contingencies Secretariat, which specialised in contingency planning for major national emergencies. General Sir Nicholas Myers, the Chief of the Defence Staff and de facto head of the British military, sat opposite Aldwyn, who himself was there in the capacity of a section chief of MI5.

Historically speaking, the composition of a COBRA meeting's attendees varied depending on the matter being discussed; though, over the past year, COBRA had almost permanently been in session with the same figures in attendance at each meeting. The nature of the crisis had only varied subtly in detail, with the primary focus of each COBRA meeting being the pandemic that had swept the nation. Only in the past few months had there been less of a necessity for frequent convenings of the committee. Today, though, all those crucial figures were back in their familiar places around the table, the same dossier laid in front of each of them.

Each member rose from their seat as the Prime Minister swept into the room, followed by his security detail (who remained either side of the doorway) and accompanied by the Health Secretary. The PM motioned for everyone to be seated and then settled himself into the seat at the head of the table, whilst the Health Secretary took up the remaining chair immediately to his left.

'I'd hoped we'd have no further need for these meetings,' began the PM, 'and I say that not because I don't wish to see all your faces daily once more.'

There were a few shy titters of laughter around the table.

He continued, 'I'm going to hand over to the Home Secretary initially, to provide us all with the background to recent events. COBRA is now in session, and I needn't remind you of your responsibilities regarding what's discussed in this room. Please, Home Secretary.'

Before Haynes's eyes flickered to the Home Secretary – a dark-skinned woman in her forties with a rather abrasive manner and smooth, black hair that hung low over her sunken brown eyes – he studied the PM. He didn't like what he saw. The man looked tired, his usually intently scrutinising green eyes were bleary with deep-purple bags hanging beneath them, and he looked somehow simultaneously thinner and older.

It was unusual for Haynes to have genuine respect for a politician, but in this case, he'd grown to somewhat admire the man sitting at the head of the table. The same couldn't be said for some of his cabinet members, but in the case of the PM, Haynes felt he'd acquitted himself as best as he could have done during the pandemic crisis.

Perhaps some of that respect was due to the man's career before entering politics, in which he'd served with the Special Boat Service (SBS) in Libya during the Civil War conflict, assisting in evacuation of key personnel as well as conducting a series of covert operations. It was after the Libyan conflict that he turned his attention to politics, possibly because of his frustration at the orders those in command were giving whilst he was on the ground. Since entering politics, though, he'd campaigned on a humanitarian and political front, and during the pandemic, he'd attempted to focus on the human cost as well as the economic one. Inevitably, of course, he'd been forced into some concessions on that front by a militant party, many of whom had economic self-interests of their own that swayed their political decision-making. This was a time when the country would need his leadership, particularly if the worst did indeed happen. They'd need the energised, athletic figure in his characteristic tailored, blue suit with short-cropped, brown hair and eloquent public-speaking manner, rather than the exhausted man sitting before him.

'Firstly, I'd like to echo the PM's words,' Home Secretary Teresa Powell began brusquely. 'It's good to see the finest minds gathered here once more.' After swishing her black hair out of her face, she stared intently at each individual in turn with a look that contained anything but warmth. 'Like all of you, I' hoped we wouldn't be facing this problem again. In the early hours of yesterday morning, during an army exercise in the Brecon Beacons, a soldier collapsed and died shortly after presenting with coronavirus symptoms. If you open your files, you'll see the soldier in question, his background and an eyewitness report from the major on site at the time of the exercise. For more details on this, I'm going to hand over to the general.'

Despite being Chief of the Defence Staff for the past eighteen months, it was clear that General Sir Nicholas Myers had never quite got used to certain aspects of his role. He'd seemed far more comfortable during the time they'd spent together in Northern Ireland. With over three decades of combat experience across several war zones, the arts of diplomacy and public speaking hadn't always been the most essential skills. When it came to dealing with politicians in arenas such as these, Myers was clearly still learning, and he looked slightly uncomfortable as he leaned forwards in his chair, his deep-set, hazel-coloured eyes shifting in their sockets. With short, greying hair; a thick-set, muscular posture; and a lined face – he looked every inch the battle-hardened soldier that he was, and when he spoke, it was in a tough Lancastrian accent.

'Prime Minister,' he began, 'yesterday afternoon, I spoke personally with Major Pollard, the commanding officer at Senta Barracks. He told me that the soldier in question, a Corporal Ross Matheson, had been struggling during the exercises on the previous two days. He'd been experiencing bouts of coughing and shortness of breath during training assignments.'

'Sorry to interject, General,' said the Foreign Secretary (though Haynes couldn't help but notice that she wouldn't have interrupted a fellow politician in this way), 'but that isn't uncommon, is it? It's well publicised that army training exercises hardly leave one skipping afterwards. You work the men hard. Surely a little shortness of breath is to be expected?'

Samira Patel had been born to a British Pakistani family, her parents having emigrated from their ancestral homeland and settled in Birmingham during the 1960s. Since having first qualified as a doctor, she'd turned her attention to politics after her childhood friend had been deported from the country for reasons she didn't know to this day. Hers had certainly been a meteoric rise through the party to the post of Foreign Secretary, and there was no denying her talent – or her ruthless nature. Those who underestimated her – due to her inherent good looks, sultry lips and brown hair tied into a tight bun at the back of her head – lived to regret it and wouldn't make the same mistake again.

General Myers smiled slightly and inclined his head. 'That's correct, Foreign Secretary. Senta Barracks is hardly a holiday camp. That being said, Corporal Matheson wasn't a starry-eyed recruit fresh out of Hendon. He's been involved in live combat operations, and this was his fourth training assignment in the Brecon Beacons, with the others in harsher conditions than those the 1st Battalion Rifles experienced during this exercise. The major spoke very highly of him as an officer and of his physical capabilities in particular. He was always amongst the fittest members of his regiment and had never shown any difficulties in keeping up with whatever drills were devised.'

'Having read the report, though, General, there was always an SAS team training in tandem with the Rifles,' the Foreign Secretary intervened once more. 'Would that not have led naturally to an increase in intensity that soldiers like the corporal weren't used to?'

'Might I suggest you take the Foreign Secretary with you to Senta Barracks on your next visit?' sneered the Secretary of State for Defence. 'Then perhaps she can report back to us in person on the intensity of your training.'

Nobody laughed, perhaps due to the irony of the minister's suggestion. Being in his late fifties, with wispy, grey strands of hair clinging resiliently to his scalp, he was the most out-of-shape individual in attendance at the meeting. His piggy, hooded, brown eyes were watering, and his slightly crumpled grey suit suggested a man out of his time, yet there remained a shrewd political operator beneath the frail appearance.

'I'd be delighted, as long as Seward accompanies me.' The Foreign Secretary smiled, inclining her head towards the Defence Minister.

'If we could return to the matter at hand,' interjected the PM, 'before I send the whole cabinet on SAS training. General, please continue.'

'Thank you, Prime Minister,' the general said gratefully. 'The Foreign Secretary is, of course, correct that there was a squadron of 22 SAS training with the Rifles, and yes, that will have led to an increase in intensity of the training drills. As a result of that, I would expect the smallest drop-off in the performance of some of the Rifles soldiers, but you must remember that these are all seasoned and professionally trained troops. Corporal Matheson had also trained alongside the SAS in the past, and it isn't uncommon for there to be some overlap in their exercises.

'Major Pollard recounted to me that the corporal hadn't just been struggling with coughing and breathing difficulties during the exercise, but that he'd also been behaving in a strange manner. Several members of the battalion, those to which he was closest, raised question marks over his behaviour. He'd just returned from an extensive period of leave and arrived in the village a day early. Whilst that in itself isn't unusual, when you place that alongside the testimony of his fellow officers, something was wrong.'

'But forgive me if I'm wrong, the virus doesn't alter personalities.' The Home Secretary looked perplexed.

Her question was directed at the Chief Medical Officer, who had not yet spoken. She lifted her head out of her hands for the first time since the briefing had begun. Professor Elizabeth Davies had been a consultant haematologist in the Midlands, having grown up in the area, and she'd been the leading physician in that field for almost two decades before focussing specifically on sickle cell disease and other such blood disorders. She'd then taken up a post with the Department of Health before subsequently being appointed Chief Medical Officer under the previous PM – a position she'd retained under Waverley's premiership.

She was in her sixties, with bushy, dyed-blonde hair and a jovial face. Her clear, blue eyes often twinkled, but today, they were filled with a sadness she hadn't wished to revisit. Everyone around the table knew just how much of her life she'd invested in fighting the virus over the past year, and she'd felt the personal loss more acutely than anyone else present. During the outbreak, she herself had contracted the disease and had been hospitalised, even spending several weeks in intensive care. It had been touch-and-go whether she'd survive, and when she was eventually released, it was to hear the news that her youngest grandchild, who'd suffered from acute asthma, had died from the virus days earlier.

It was perhaps that memory that had triggered the solitary tear forming in that ocean-blue right eye. She swept it away, unfurled her horn-rimmed spectacles, put them on and began to address the room: 'Correct, Home Secretary; coronavirus doesn't cause behavioural changes. As you're all aware, "coronavirus" is the name given to the collective family of viruses that cause this type of disease in animals. Of those viruses, only seven so far have gone on to infect humans.

'COVID-19 spreads primarily through droplets of nasal discharge or saliva, and the transmission rates can be extremely high. Without speculating in this meeting on the origin of the virus again, we believe the original host to have been bats, which have long been host to a wide range of nasty viruses, such as Ebola. We need to bear that in mind when discussing whether we have a new outbreak on our hands. Of course, there were several strains of the virus actively spreading throughout communities in tandem, and it's able to mutate at an alarming rate.

'In terms of the symptoms, everyone around this table is familiar with the major ones: a dry cough, fatigue, fever and increased difficulty in breathing. Of course, there are others, such as a loss taste or smell, and aches in other parts of the body. Primarily, however, it attacks your respiratory system and deprives the major organs of the oxygen they need to function. It first infects the cells that line the throat, airways and lungs, effectively turning them into breeding factories for the virus to thrive. It multiples and infects more cells in your body.

'Effectively, the virus triggers an imbalance in your immune response and causes a severe inflammation of the vital organs, primarily the lungs. In this instance, the virus triggers a form of pneumonia, in which the tiny sacs in the lungs fill with water and eventually cause shortness of breath and difficulty breathing. This is one of the major causes of death, but not the only one.

'Our immune system is designed to defend us from viruses and disease, but in instances such as these where the cells are being attacked, it actually does more damage to us internally. Your blood pressure drops dangerously low and septic shock can set in as many of the vital organs begin to fail. They're being deprived of that vital ingredient we all need to survive' – she paused to wipe her glasses and fixed her eyes on the PM – 'oxygen.

'It's something we all take for granted, but it's essential to our survival. Without it, our body experiences what we call "acute respiratory distress syndrome", whereby widespread inflammation in the lungs stops the body getting enough oxygen to survive. This can lead to multi-organ failure; for example, the kidneys are no longer able to clean the blood, and the lining of our intestines is eroded. If the virus reaches this stage in a human being, their chances of survival are exceptionally slim.

'The corporal died of multi-organ failure. His lungs had doubled in size due to inflammation, and they were unable to release oxygen to his kidneys, his liver or, indeed, his heart. He'd received the COVID-19 vaccination, and we still have the test results from his antibody test last year, which show he'd built up an immunity from the virus. He stated that he'd experienced only mild symptoms of the disease, as did his wife and child. The general also informs me that he was tested upon his arrival at Senta Barracks and after he displayed symptoms, but these results returned negative.

'Unfortunately, the test that we conducted on his body last night shows he was suffering from a variation of the COVID-19 virus at the point of his death. We've compared the damage the corporal sustained to his internal cells and lungs to that of a significant number of COVID-19 patients who suffered a similar cause of death. Those comparisons show a number of differences in the way the virus seems to have impacted the corporal's body.'

It was Seward Atley who interrupted this time: 'If he was negative when he arrived at the barracks, then he got it from one of the other soldiers, surely?'

General Myers took it upon himself to answer that question: 'All the men have been double and triple tested. No others have displayed symptoms, and all are negative. Matheson only tested positive upon his death.'

The professor took off her glasses and wiped them slowly, her expression extremely grave, as she focussed her gaze on the PM once more. 'It would also appear that the virus strain the corporal was suffering from was more aggressive. The blood and saliva tests we've taken show that the virus in his system was a mutated strain of the one that caused the pandemic last time. The cells in his major organs were in a much worse condition than even those who died from the original COVID-19. His lungs were inflamed even beyond a point we'd have expected from the virus previously, and his heart suffered significant strain and swelling.'

The PM flipped open the file in front of him. 'Professor, are you telling us that we potentially have an even worse pandemic on our hands if this thing spreads? If the vaccines that have been distributed worldwide – which the corporal had in his bloodstream – aren't able to stop this new form of the virus, then just how nasty is this thing?'

'That's just the thing, Prime Minister,' replied Professor Davies, a note of confusion in her voice, 'we simply don't know enough yet.' She paused to wipe her glasses once more. 'As you all know, the incubation period for COVID-19 was up to fourteen days in some cases. Even those people who were lucky enough to only experience mild symptoms would have found it virtually impossible to compete in the kind of physical exertion that the corporal did before his death.

'The strain of the virus that the corporal was suffering from appears to have been in his system for several weeks. Unlike the form of COVID-19 we've been used to dealing with, which immediately begins to slowly attack the cells and starve the body of oxygen, this strain appears to have lain dormant in his system. Death from COVID-19 was often a slow process, with the initial symptoms appearing within days and then more severe effects developing over days and weeks before death, whereas this strain seems to have stayed in the corporal's body for weeks without him developing any symptoms. Once he started developing symptoms, the time between the initial signs appearing and death was significantly shorter. This would indicate a mutated strain of the virus that kills with very little warning. All I can say is that, given the way the virus behaved in the corporal's body, it would suggest a strain of the virus capable of lying dormant within a host for weeks before attacking in a quicker, more aggressive fashion than we've seen previously.'

There was a collective intake of breath around the table.

'There's something else,' she said tentatively 'which is the main reason I'd suggest that this soldier wasn't simply unlucky and the vaccine failed. Preliminary tests would suggest that this mutated strain isn't entirely naturally occurring. It shows evidence of being tampered with by humans.'

There was no mistaking the confused and fearful looks exchanged around the table this time.

'Somebody cultivated this thing in a lab somewhere?' A bead of sweat ran into the Home Secretary's sunken, brown eyes.

'It would appear so,' replied Professor Davies, before adding quickly, 'but these are just the preliminary findings. We'll learn more as we conduct further in-depth testing.'

The inevitable question hovered in the air over the table as the PM looked between the various representatives of the intelligence community before asking, 'Who do we think could have done this?'

It was the chief of MI6 who answered: 'Prime Minister, since the outbreak of the virus, we've been tracking dozens of individuals and groups attempting to harness a strain of the virus and meddle with it – to pimp it up, if you will. We've been working particularly closely with the Americans with regards to this and have conducted a number of covert operations to apprehend those responsible. To our knowledge, only one terrorist organisation has succeeded in tampering with a strain of the virus.'

'Could any of the individuals from this group have entered the UK and thus be responsible for this?' queried the Home Secretary.

'No, ma'am; we've been monitoring all arrivals, and there's no chance that a member of this group could be responsible,' Sir Jocelyn Bower replied instantly in a silky voice. A man in his late fifties, with short, grey hair; sharp, green eyes; and an impassive shaven face – he was impossible to read. This was just one of the reasons that made him so good at his job, as the chief of MI6. 'Of course, we can't rule out a foreign government being behind the strain. We know the Russians have been working extensively in their underground laboratories for months, and it wouldn't be the first time they'd attempted something like this on our soil. Then you obviously have the North Koreans and the Iranians, the latter of whom have their own underground laboratories deep beneath Tehran. They could be developing anything down there. We simply don't have the intelligence to be sure.'

'I can't risk accusing a foreign government or agency of tampering with a strain of the virus,' the PM said robustly. He directed his next question to the DG of MI5, who appeared to have been expecting it: 'What about threats at home? Have you heard anything that might explain this?'

Dame Nicole Brennan shook her head slowly. 'There has been no significant chatter relating to an attack of this kind. Indeed, none of the groups or individuals we're monitoring would have the resources or capabilities to pull off something like this.'

'Work up every lead you have, no matter how insignificant,' replied the PM instantaneously. 'In the meantime, we need to lock this story down from a press perspective. The Home Secretary will liaise with the press; this corporal died tragically because of an undiagnosed heart condition. General, you may need to take some heat from journalists regarding your training methods, but I'm sure that's something you can handle. We can't have it leaked to the public that we could have another outbreak on our hands; there would be mass panic of the kind that's impossible to control.

'There's only one other matter I wish to discuss right now. It pertains to the shooting that took place in the capital this morning.' He turned to address the Met Commissioner, who had thus far remained quiet. 'Jamal, I wish you to hand over all your initial papers over to Aldwyn's section. Seward has alerted me to the fact that there may be certain defence implications, and I'd prefer MI5 to handle the investigation from here.' The PM then shifted his attention, speaking to Aldwyn for the first time: 'I trust you can handle that on top of your efforts to find the perpetrator of this attack?'

'Of course, Prime Minister,' Aldwyn responded, not voicing the unease he felt at this now involving the Defence Secretary, who had a rather too smug expression on his face for Aldwyn's liking.

'I don't suppose you could be the one to tell Detective Ambrose could you, sir?' Jamal quipped dryly, and Aldwyn turned his head briefly at the sound of the name. 'She won't like it. You know how these young, stubborn detectives can be; they never let anything go.'

The PM laughed. 'I'd expect nothing less from a prodigy of yours, Jamal. Tell her it's an executive order. The number of my private secretary is freely available should she want to discuss it any further.'

There were several other murmurs of laughter at the table at this, as the PM stood to leave.

5

Aldwyn Haynes raised his pass in the direction of the security guard on the fourth floor of Thames House, who immediately reached beneath his curved wooden desk and pressed a control button. As he did so, the seemingly ordinary whitewashed wall behind him slid back to reveal three cylindrical pods, which were identical to those in the entrance hall floors below, each with its own biometric scanning device stationed before it. Placing his right hand under the scanner of the central pod, Aldwyn waited for barely a second before the entrance to the cylinder portal slid back and he stepped inside; the door closed behind him with a hiss. Two seconds later, the retrofitted biometric scanners had done their work, and the door on the other side of the portal slid open, releasing its temporary prisoner.

The open-plan office beyond was a hive of activity, with officers scurrying between desks, passing paper files to another colleague or else pressing them for specific information they may have gleaned from their sector or various sources. There were a dozen individually spaced desks, each comprising a sleek computer monitor with accompanying wireless keyboard and mouse, all in matching black; a multi-functional scanner; and a specialised encrypted and adapted Yealink IP business phone. There was a large meeting room hidden from view behind a sliding wooden door, as well as two technical analyst rooms and Aldwyn's own office.

As though she'd been waiting by the pods all morning, Maya Chowdhury was pressing a file into his hands as soon as he stepped out of the pod. 'Morning, Mr Haynes, I have your morning briefing here. Helen and I have highlighted the highest profile threats for you to look over. There has been increased chatter amongst the extremist terror cells that we've been monitoring in London, but nothing that suggests an attack is imminent. We also have low-level intelligence regarding three potential cyberattacks and threats relating to key structural targets, plus a request from two government agencies for increased intelligence personnel, but they were all in yesterday's briefing also.'

'In short, bad people want to kill us,' quipped a handsome, young officer of Pakistani heritage as he passed by.

'Yes, thank you, Zafar,' Aldwyn replied before turning to his young analyst once more. 'Thank you, Maya, but I think there's only one threat I shall be concentrating on today.'

'Of course, Mr Haynes; we've already upgraded surveillance in a couple of areas. Are you happy for us to go ahead with our suggested action plans?' Maya responded in a fast, excitable voice.

Aldwyn smiled. 'I'm sure your recommendations will be appropriate. Have you got any update for me from your contacts over in defence?'

'My contact in the MOD had this file couriered over to me. It's the personnel file of the major onsite at Senta Barracks, as you requested.'

'I assume you've read it?' Aldwyn knew his enthusiastic analyst all too well. He raised an eyebrow as she spluttered to find a lie. 'I'd be disappointed if you hadn't. So anything of interest?'

Blushing slightly, Maya answered, her voice slightly breathless due to the pace at which she spoke: 'He has an exemplary service record, as you'd expect for a soldier of his rank, but he's been active politically. On three separate occasions, he's lobbied the Chief of the Defence Staff and the government directly for better equipment for his troops, as well as filing extensive reports on that subject with the MOD. He's also argued for increased pay for current servicemen and injured veterans, and he's worked with several charities on the subject. His men love him, sir.'

'As I'm sure you would if I argued for extra pay for you lot.'

'No chance of that,' joked Senior Intelligence Officer Ben Viper as he appeared from one of the technical suites. 'You've thought I'm overpaid for years.' A man in his early thirties with short, light-brown hair that was slightly gelled and piercing, blue eyes, he was athletic and fit, with a relaxed manner that was capable of putting people at ease, but there was calculation behind the charm, and he was like a coiled spring waiting to leap into action. He always appeared well dressed, despite the often-casual clothing he wore, but he was an expert in disguise and as adaptable as a chameleon.

'I mean, compared to analysts, intelligence officers are...' began Maya nervously before stopping herself, as though she were reluctant to join in the banter.

However, both men simply laughed at the apprehensive look on the face of their junior analyst. This short and slim woman – with shoulder-length, brown hair and brown skin – had a pretty face with attractive hazel eyes that blinked rapidly when she was nervous, as she was at this very minute. She was wearing her preferred outfit of a professional pencil skirt and blouse. She'd only been with the division for six months, having been fast-tracked through the Civil Service recruitment scheme, with her first-class psychology degree and analytical background contributing to her first posting. Although she was deemed a little naïve with regard to operational matters, she was bright and eager to impress, with a keen mind that was able to cut through extraneous detail to identify crucial pieces of intelligence.

'Shall we?' Aldwyn gestured towards the briefing room, ignoring Ben's elaborate dive to grab a file from the nearest desk, and registered his senior officer beckoning for the rest to join them. As Ben caught up with him once more, Haynes muttered, 'No more word from your source?'

'Nothing,' Ben replied in a low voice. 'He hasn't reported for work today yet either; I checked.'

'Let's keep that particular source of information to ourselves for now. I declined to mention it at COBRA for a reason. The last thing we need right now is further prying into our assets. Keep me updated on his status.'

Ben nodded in response as they crossed into the briefing room.

Within a minute, the team was arranged around the conference table. The widescreen plasma monitors arranged across the back wall were displaying an image of Corporal Ross Matheson, as well as the layout of Senta Barracks. There were seven team members in all, including Aldwyn, Ben Viper and Maya Chowdhury; the others were Senior Intelligence Analyst Helen Robinson, Technical Analyst Simon Wynn-Jones, Senior Intelligence Officer John Bromley (who was on temporary secondment from MI6) and Junior Field Officer Zafar Hussein.

'Morning one and all,' greeted Aldwyn sardonically, his fingers interlocked before him and his elbows planted on the table as he looked around at his team. 'I think we'd all hoped we'd left the murky world of viruses and pandemics behind us and returned to the much simpler matters of terrorist organisations and espionage against foreign governments, but here we are once again.' As a man in his forties with receding, mousy-coloured hair and close-set, deadened, grey eyes – he might once have been an attractive man, but the stress of his job and the lack of a family any more had taken its toll on his weathered skin and sagging, jowly cheeks. Despite these facts, an assurance and air of inherent leadership emanated from him, which instantly garnered respect.

'As you're all aware, the PM called an emergency session of COBRA this morning in relation to the death at Senta Barracks,' he continued in a calm voice, which betrayed the slightest trace of a Yorkshire accent. 'Needless to say, this is something that needs to be contained as quietly and efficiently as possible. We need to re-examine every piece of chatter and intelligence we've had in relation to threats involving the virus. The working hypothesis is that this was a targeted attack. None of the other men at the barracks have tested positive for any strain of the virus.'

At this point, Helen seamlessly took over: 'So far, all our investigations into the corporal show nothing other than a distinguished military record and quiet home life.' Her voice was crisp and professional, as though she were delivering a public address. Standing at a little under six feet tall, she was dressed in a pristine blouse and white skirt. Her long, blonde hair fell over her shoulders, and her angular, hazel eyes and thin eyebrows peeked out beneath her trimmed fringe. She pursed her thin lips, which were coloured with a light-pink lipstick, before continuing, 'We have records from several of his commanding officers during both combat and peacekeeping operations. By all accounts, he was a dedicated if unambitious solider.'

Ben interjected, 'So far, we've been unable to trace the corporal's movements extensively in the weeks before his death. Taking the starting date of his leave, we can trace his car leaving his family's army residence in Chepstow and follow it on traffic cams as he travels east and eventually onto the M4.' She pressed the fob in her hand and the image of the corporal was temporarily replaced by a map of Britain with a dotted line shown stretching from just inside Wales across into England.

'We can see him leaving the M4 at Junction 15 and continuing along the A346 until he reaches a roundabout and passes onto the A338, shortly after which we pick him up on CCTV refilling his car at a petrol station on the Salisbury Road. We then see him leaving the petrol station, but after this, he seems to disappear from all local CCTV and traffic cams. It's like he vanishes into thin air. The next time we pick him up is three weeks later when his car is snapped joining the M4. In between those dates, we can find no trace of where he was or what he was doing.'

He and Aldwyn exchanged knowing looks.

The senior intelligence officer continued, straightening the front of his suit jacket as he did so. 'Find him. Meanwhile, draw up a list of possible locations within a twenty-mile radius that he could have been heading towards. Something happened during that time, and I want to know what it was. Zaf, I want you to investigate the MOD records of the men who were at Senta Barracks at the same time as Corporal Matheson – lean on Maya's contact over there. Offer him any incentives you can think of, although stop short of inviting him to Maya's lovely Docklands flat. That goes for you not inviting yourself there either.'

Zaf opened his mouth to interrupt, his mouth stretched in a grin, whilst Maya smiled blushingly, but Ben forestalled him: 'I also need you to look into any personal links the soldiers may have had to the virus as well as any ties to extremist groups, and I want Simon to get their financial records. Anything at all that might link them to this attack. Did any of them hold a grudge against the corporal? As unlikely as it is, we can't afford to rule out anything, even an isolated grudge that may have motivated a murder.'

The youngest of the three field operatives nodded before adding with a cheeky smile, 'Can't Maya or Helen get me the records? No offence, Simon, but you hardly offer the same service with a pretty smile.'

Maya blushed, but Helen merely raised an eyebrow and said straight-faced, 'Don't listen to him, Simon. I think young Zafar just isn't used to seeing many pretty smiles directed at him.' Her deadpan expression was softened for a second, however, as the junior field officer mimed a broken heart across the table at her.

Another cheeky smile flashed across the handsome features of Zafar Hussein. He was in his mid-twenties and had grown up in a Muslim family, although he himself wasn't particularly devout. He was clean-shaven with spiky, black hair and wholesome hazel-coloured eyes, his natural good looks adding to his easy, flirtatious manner that was so charming. As his mentor, Ben had been swift to point out that his quick wit was likely to get him into trouble one of these days and he had much to learn with regard to the risk assessment of operations in particular.

'As much as we don't need additional burdens at this time, we've been tasked with looking into the shooting that took place near the Mall this morning. I know' – Aldwyn raised a hand as Ben opened his mouth to speak – 'it should be a police matter, and ordinarily it would be. I think Ben can handle the situation with the shooting.' He had to fight back a laugh as his officer's head snapped round. 'After all, you're so keen for us to broaden our portfolio into detective work. It should be a good experience for you.'

That elicited several amused expressions around the table. Of course, Simon Wynn-Jones seemed to have a report ready.

Aldwyn continued, 'The man who was shot is Harold Morris. Morris appears to have taken up several murky roles during his time with the MOD, other than a short secondment to the Environment Agency to help with their security and a stint attached to the Foreign Office.'

He pressed a button on the remote, and on one of the monitors, an image materialised that appeared to be a long-distance photo of an open-air café with three men arranged around a circular table, and judging from the slightly grainy quality of the image, it was most likely a still captured from a CCTV camera with colour incorporated. It was towards this screen that Aldwyn directed their gaze.

'Morris is the man in the middle,' Simon Wynn-Jones pointed out awkwardly. 'The man on the left is Corporal Matheson. The third man is Peter Vallance.' He indicated the shorter of the three men, who appeared to be in his sixties with wisps of grey hair clinging desperately to his scalp and thick-rimmed spectacles perched on his rather hooked nose. 'A scientist.'

Despite their workloads generally being split, rather than overlapping, Ben knew the file and took over seamlessly: 'Vallance spent most of his career abroad, setting up laboratories in Switzerland and Germany. It was all perfectly legal stuff to begin with, looking into gene therapy and even a cure for cancer. Then one day, our scientist friend here decided that there's more money to be had in the development of biochemical agents, and he even dipped his toes into the world of nuclear physics, providing specifics for a number of terror groups.'

Another image flashed onto the screen. It showed a clearly younger Vallance, with piggy, black eyes and sunken cheeks, and very similar glasses in the exact same position, firmly in the middle of his nose.

'Needless to say,' Ben continued briskly, 'with activities such as this, he quickly was picked up on MI6's radar. They had Vallance under surveillance for a number of months back in the early 1990s, being wary of any links to the Middle East around this time, before they eventually made their move.'

'If MI6 took him out, then how was he in the country just a couple of months ago?' asked Zaf.

'It isn't the policy of any service in this country to kill off sources of good intelligence.' Aldwyn smiled. He caught Ben's eye before adding wryly, 'Unless we have no other choice.'

'They turned him,' explained Ben. 'Vallance became an MI6 asset. A very good one by all accounts. Not only did he provide details of his past dealings but he also continued to operate as a black-market scientist. He sold out dozens of his customers over the years. Naturally, MI6 was very grateful and rewarded him with the gift of his continued existence.'

Everyone laughed this time.

'The threat of selling him out to those he'd betrayed worked rather well for a number of years, but then they encountered a problem.' Ben paused, as though he were a teacher waiting for his students to answer a question. 'Vallance found God. He told MI6 he didn't want to be selling arms to terrorists any more. Whether it was religion or he just wanted retirement, it's impossible to tell,' he mused. 'However, he left MI6 with little choice but to burn him. They could have continued to threaten him, but it was felt that his remorse for his actions was genuine, even if the sudden whispering of his saviour were not.

'Naturally, he knew far too much to take up civilian life, even under a false identity. They reached a compromise: if they couldn't utilise his black-market intelligence any longer, then they could exploit his scientific intelligence instead. In the early

2000s, he was inducted into the MOD as a scientific advisor, and that's where his file ends.' Clearly frustrated, Ben pressed his knuckles against the end of the table as he leaned over it, before looking around at his colleagues.

Aldwyn got to his feet and rounded the table to stand next to Ben before addressing his team. 'I want to know why these three men were meeting, and I want to know where they went after. Simon has managed to obtain some footage of the shooting, which I'll let him explain to you all.'

After returning to his seat, Aldwyn focussed his attention on Ben's face, watching closely for a reaction. There was a slightly puzzled expression upon it currently, perhaps from the realisation that he was seeing this new information for the first time. Their technical analyst moved to rise from his chair before hesitating halfway through the motion, giving the comical image of him squatting over his seat as he second-guessed his movement. Smirking slightly, Ben ushered him to his feet before taking his own seat and smiling encouragingly at Simon.

Despite his dozen or so years in the service, there was still a certain amount of nervousness in Simon Wynn-Jones as he moved slowly round the table to stand beside the monitors, and there was an initial stammer to his Welsh accent as he began: 'I-it seems that Mr Morris was careful to avoid the cameras. I can't find, for example, where his journey originated from. In fact, I can catch only two glimpses of him on the morning of his death.' By fumbling a fob in his right hand, whilst pushing his glasses further over his eyes with his left, he was able to amend the image behind him, and it flickered over to a man walking away from Buckingham Palace down the Mall.

Several images flickered one after another, showing the body of Harold Morris lying outside Admiralty Arch, whilst a figure in a baseball cap was seen striding away from the scene with an item in his right hand.

'It would seem somebody was keen on acquiring Mr Morris's briefcase,' observed Ben.

'I managed to follow the figure in the baseball cap,' continued the Welsh analyst. 'He moved towards Trafalgar Square, and we were still unable to register his face on any cameras, but we did see this.' Another image appeared on the screen, this time showing Trafalgar Square; before one of the lions was a Range Rover with blacked-out windows, its back door ajar and the same figure clambering inside.

'So whoever took the briefcase was different to the person who fired the shot. We still haven't identified the shooter on any surrounding footage?'

The analyst shook his head.

This prompted Ben to continue, 'We're looking at a very professional operation here. Given the efficiency with which this hit was conducted and Morris's affiliation with Matheson, we have to assume they were planning something big. Were we able to pick up any images of the figure in the baseball cap prior to him taking the briefcase?'

Simon hesitated at the question and threw a nervous glance towards Aldwyn, who nodded. Ben watched the exchange, frowning, and kept his gaze on his boss until a flicker of light in his peripheral vision told him that a new image was being displayed. Aldwyn Haynes watched his senior intelligence officer – and friend – turn towards the screen, and he registered the expression of mingled shock and anger that had appeared on Ben's face. His usually handsome features had contorted into an ugly expression, and Aldwyn could see him wrestling to regain his composure.

Nevertheless, when Ben turned to face the team, his expression was calm, but the blue of his eyes had turned icy and there was a steely quality to his voice as he addressed first his boss and then the team at large: 'I can see why you didn't brief me on this before the meeting.'

These words were directed at Aldwyn, but he didn't react. He could see Helen and Simon exchanging nervous, almost frightened looks as their eyes darted between the man on the screen and their two superiors, who appeared to be scrutinising one another. Maya just looked a little confused.

After pulling his gaze from his section chief at last, Ben filled the frosty silence that his own words had caused. 'For those of you who don't know, this is Colton Henderson. An MI6 traitor.' There was a bitter edge to his voice and his sub-zero blue eyes had contracted as he tore them away from the face looking down from the screen behind him. It displayed a rather handsome-looking man in his early forties with thick, reddish-brown hair; a slim jawline; full lips; and assured smile. However, there was an eerily milky quality to his deep-set eyes that gave them an almost ghostly appearance.

'His involvement changes everything,' Ben clarified. 'He sold out everyone and everything he ever believed in – primarily this country.

'MI6 have tried to pick up a trace of him for years, but they've never got close. They heard rumblings that he was involved in political coups in the Middle East, and given his contacts in the region, that would make sense, but the last they heard, he'd become embroiled in the conflict in Syria. There were even rumours that he'd been killed during an Israeli missile strike.'

The muscles in his cheeks tightened and it was with slightly gritted teeth that he went on, 'Henderson was one of MI6's most ruthless and best field officers, with contacts throughout the Middle East. He led dozens of covert operations for the service in the region, including a raid on a high-profile Israeli government building in Jerusalem. Before that, he'd served in the SBS for six years and was involved in several clandestine assignments behind enemy lines. Make no mistake, many organisations and governments would have been clamouring to employ him after he turned his back on MI6. He could be working for anybody, but as we've already witnessed, if he's involved, then this is a threat we have to take seriously—'

It was with a slightly hesitant cough that Simon Wynn-Jones interrupted his superior. 'Far be it for me to knock our sister services' intelligence, but I can narrow down his recent whereabouts slightly. Quite how he got back into the UK, I can't tell you at this stage, but I can confirm he crossed into Syria nine months ago, using a false identity registered to a Russian diplomat by the name of Sergei Pentakov. He's made frequent trips to Syria in the past few months.'

Aldwyn cut across his analyst: 'We must remain focussed on the threat here. In the meantime, Simon and Helen, continue to work up a profile of Henderson's movements and recent contacts. I know how emotive this operation is, but we need to keep focussed. Is that clear? Right, get to work all of you. Keep me updated on all developments. Oh, and Simon, whilst you're searching our intelligence databases, see if you can track down those missing SEAL submersibles.'

As everyone got to their feet and moved towards the door of the briefing room, Haynes motioned for Ben to remain behind. Zafar Hussein shot a final mischievous glance over his shoulder as he pulled the sliding door shut.

'Directly after COBRA, I had a conversation with the Health Secretary. The man who was shot was on his way to meet with the Health Minister. He's adamant that no other members of the cabinet were aware that it was going to take place. You know Hugh; he's scared. The man he was meeting claimed to have sensitive information that he didn't want to entrust to anyone else. I'm meeting with Hugh again. Whatever has him spooked, we need to find out and deal with it immediately.' Aldwyn sighed heavily. 'In the meantime, I need you to get yourself down to the scene of the shooting. I hear the police are still investigating. Apparently, Detective Ambrose isn't a great one for taking orders.'

Ben stopped mid-nod. 'Did you just say, "Detective Ambrose"?'

'Yes.' Aldwyn absentmindedly retrieved his file from the table and moved towards the door. 'Why? Do you know them?' His evasive tone was undermined somewhat by the ghost of a smile that had crept across his face.

'Assuming it's Detective Jackie Ambrose we're talking about, then yes, I know her,' said Ben, a look of dawning comprehension on his face, 'but you already knew that.'

Aldwyn slid the door open and smiled as he replied: 'Given the fact you're already acquainted, you should have no trouble in reminding her of the PM's instruction.'

Ben nodded. He swept up his file and turned to leave, but as he reached the door he paused to look back at his boss. 'Whilst we're on the subject of personal involvement in this operation, you must have seen that the ballistics are back from the shooting. It was a .50 high-calibre bullet fired from approximately 275 yards. We've been checking the surrounding buildings, but at that distance, the sniper could have had a clear line of sight from buildings further out from the perimeter that Simon and his tech guys have been working off. I haven't shown him the findings yet.'

His blue eyes narrowed in on Aldwyn, who hadn't shown a flicker of a reaction thus far. 'The striations on the bullet have helped them narrow down the range of weapons that could have been used, and they estimate there's a high probability that the rifle used was a Barret M82. Of all people, you should realise the potential implication there. Should I look into the possibility that—?'

He never finished, as Aldwyn cut across him coolly: 'I'm aware of the findings, and I'm looking into the matter myself.

You don't need to concern yourself with this currently. There are plenty of other operational objectives that require your attention.' There was a finality to his tone that Ben dared not question on this occasion, and his grey eyes were implacable iron dots. 'Do not discuss your theories with anyone else in the team. I need them focussed on the real threats, not chasing ghosts from Operation Wolfhound.'

'Until fifteen minutes ago, Henderson was nothing but a ghost,' Ben replied curtly, 'so maybe we should start holding a séance rather than a morning briefing.'

*

Admiralty Arch, 1.30pm

The commuters had deserted the Mall and the historic streets beyond, leaving only those lucky enough to be able to enjoy a stroll in the sunshine, whilst black cabs circled the roads despairingly, attempting to find a fatigued tourist or weary shopper. A cordon had been set up around where the body had lain, and all three gates leading underneath Admiralty Arch had been closed to the public. The forensics teams had long since finished their work, whisking away samples in evidence bags for DNA and scientific analysis.

At the scene, two armed police officers remained, carrying Heckler and Koch MP5 sub-machine guns slung loosely over their shoulders, despite the commissioner's order for the police to withdraw their investigation into the shooting.

Shy and easily influenced Cedric Brown was on the verge of leaving. 'Please Detective Ambrose, I don't want to get into any more trouble. We've already disobeyed direct orders to come back to the crime scene. I shouldn't have brought you the photo, and we shouldn't have asked Roy to look into this any more,' he said fervently, with the hint of a West Indian accent.

'Go,' replied Jackie Ambrose, placing her hand on the young Constable's shoulder, 'I don't want you to get into any further trouble on my account, but I'm not coming back to the station just yet.'

The young police officer nodded before he retreated to the squad car.

Jackie watched him drive off, and she couldn't help but wonder whether the young man was right. They'd been ordered to stand down the investigation. Was it just stubborn pride that was keeping her at the scene? However, on glancing down at the photo in her hand, she knew that there was something more to this. The order from the chief superintendent to dissolve the investigation had mentioned nothing about what would happen to the inquiry now. Her green eyes darted across the photo, switching between the three faces arranged around a small café table.

Of course, there was an element of ambition here. Solving a high-profile shooting within sight of Buckingham Palace would have been a huge career boost. There were those in the station who'd be delighting in her removal from this case, and the thought of them laughing at this opportunity being snatched away from her made her angry. They had no idea what she'd sacrificed to get to this point in her career, and if it hadn't been for circumstances outside of her control, she was sure she would have been promoted once, if not twice over, by now.

People had underestimated her ever since she'd graduated from university a decade before. Her closest friend, Faye, had also remarked to her that people underestimated her because of her good looks, but Jackie didn't believe that. Despite her own self-doubts, there was no doubting her beauty, with her nougat-brown hair flowing over her elegant neck and stopping just short of her hourglass-shaped waist. Her emerald eyes had an easy talent for lighting up a room when she smiled, as though her oyster-white teeth somehow intensified her glistening, jewelled gaze, covered by languid, velvet eyelashes.

As her thoughts dwelled on her friend's words, she was transported back to her time at university. It was then she'd learned the self-assurance and confidence in herself to become one of the best detectives in London. *It should bring happiness to think of those days,* she reflected sadly, unable to shake the regret and hurt that had come shortly after graduating. That self-belief had been difficult to master, and she wouldn't have been able to summon it without help. How then had things gone so wrong just months later?

Jolted from her recollections by the screeching of tyres, Jackie tensed suddenly. In that moment, she was sure that someone was standing behind her, and yet the feeling wasn't accompanied by an uneasy prickly sensation but rather a comforting warmth that seemed to spread throughout her body. What was going on? Slowly, she moved her hand towards the inside pocket of her suit jacket, but she paused as a silky voice spoke from behind her.

'We both know they wouldn't trust you with a firearm, Jackie, particularly not if they'd seen you firing a paintball gun.'

It couldn't be. She knew that voice, but she'd never thought to hear it again. Unconsciously, her hand went to her hair before she snapped it back to her waist. Shaking herself slightly, she turned slowly on the spot and tried to keep her expression composed, despite her racing heartbeat and the shock that was flooding through her body. Determined to keep her own voice composed and emotionless, she said, 'I should have known they'd send their least-intimidating spook to scare me off this case.'

His face had changed little in the years since they'd last seen each other. His light-brown hair was still cut short and slightly spiked to one side as it always had been, and dressed in an expensive navy suit that was tailored around his athletic body and smart, gleaming black shoes, he exuded a casual confidence that had always defined him. It was that charming smile and those ocean-blue eyes that made her confidence falter for a second.

Despite appearances, there was a harder edge to him, she could tell. Looking closer, she could see a slight coldness to those eyes, and there was a calculating nature to the smile now. Although he appeared totally relaxed, she could identify at a glance that there was a reflex in him waiting to be triggered, as though he were always on alert. Even with those slightly hardened traits, it was difficult to suppress a smile, and the muscles in her face worked extra hard not to give her away. 'Seeing as you haven't troubled yourself to see how I am in the past decade, I assume that can be the only reason you're here.'

There was a pause as the man approached her, and in just a few steps, he was within touching distance. 'There was more to it than that. You knew where I was going. I couldn't bring you into that world.'

'You never gave me the chance,' she retorted instantly, losing her cool manner for a second. After all these years, how could he be looking at her as though nothing at all had happened, with his casual smile and easy charm that she refused to be sucked into again? 'You disappeared God knows where, but you'd told me you'd be back. I never heard anything from you ever again, and nobody could tell me what had happened. I thought you'd died out there.'

'Perhaps it would have been better if I'd known.' The spark disappeared from his eyes to be replaced by a haunted look. 'I made sure you knew I was alive, but beyond that, it was better for you to have nothing more to do with me.'

'What gave you the right to make that decision? Did

you stop with the self-pitying routine for a second to think about how I might feel? I wasn't naïve. I knew what you were joining, and I made the choice to follow you. Then one day, you thought you knew better. At no point in the last ten years did you think I might have needed you? You have no idea what I've been through.'

'Jackie, please.' He went to reach out a hand, before seeming to decide against it. 'I'm sorry about your dad; he was a great man. I was there; I was at the funeral, hidden at the back. I didn't want to make things tougher for you, but I wanted to pay my respects.'

'You were there?' Shock made her falter as her mind was cast back to the day of her father's funeral and the overwhelming tidal wave of grief that had engulfed her after weeks of fighting against the truth that he was gone. 'You were there, and you never thought that might give me comfort?' Anger was bubbling in her voice, but she fought to control it.

'I imagined that, if you'd seen me on that day after so long, then it would have been more upsetting—'

He never got to finish his words, as the emotion temporarily overcame Jackie, and she lashed out twice, the palm of her hand slamming into his cheek. A strange combination of vindication and shame rippled through her arm and as she drew back for a third strike, she felt his hand close around her wrist.

'I think two is deserved; let's say three is excessive.'

In spite of herself, she laughed, and that felt better than either slap. He'd always been able to make her laugh, she was reminded, and the icy edge to his eyes had been replaced for a second by the twinkle that had resided there permanently in his youth. 'Laughing doesn't mean you're forgiven, especially as I guess this is a one-off visit.'

'Only if you do as you're told. Besides, I wouldn't have thought there was enough room in your life for me and Tiggy.'

Jackie laughed once more. 'Well, as much as that is the ultimate incentive for me to drop the case, I'd have thought you knew me better than that.' She paused, the playfulness in her face fading as she added, 'Maybe you did once. Knowing details about my life doesn't mean that you know me.'

A flicker of something approaching sadness flashed across the face in front of her for a moment. In that instant, she breathed in and felt goose pimples erupt over her neck and arms. Working for MI5 might have changed Ben in a lot of ways, but clearly not his aftershave. His grip on her wrist had loosened slightly, and she was reminded of how gentle his touch could be, almost as if he were caressing the hand that had struck him.

'I wish I'd done things differently. I never meant to hurt you. When I left for Tehran, I was so excited – not just because it was my first operation abroad but also because we were beginning the lives we'd talked about for so long. I never dreamed I wouldn't come back to you.' His voice was low and soft, but there was a sadness to it she could only remember hearing on one occasion in the past.

Reaching out, she closed her eyes as her hand pressed his reddened cheek tenderly. 'What happened out there?'

Slowly, Ben lowered his eyes to look deeply into her own, and for a fleeting moment, Jackie fought the urge to pull him into a tight embrace. Despite all the anger and hurt she felt, the obvious pain in his eyes was something she yearned to cure. But the spell was broken as quickly as it had been cast. 'I can't tell you,' Ben breathed, after absentmindedly running his hand across his neck. 'It's national security.'

Withdrawing her hand, she took a step backwards and wrenched her eyes from his gaze. 'They do have you well trained. I was never afraid of the secrets, but you were excited by them. I'm glad you got the life you wanted. How lonely it must be.' She could see from the expression on his face that the words had hurt him much more than marks already fading from his cheek, but she felt only a tinge of regret. 'Tell your masters I'm not giving up on this case.'

'Walk away, Jackie,' implored Ben, and there was an earnest look in his eyes that she believed. 'The PM wants us to handle this one. You'll only be jeopardising your own career if you ignore his orders.'

Seized by a sudden impulse, she pushed the photo in her left hand against his chest. 'Who's the third man at the table? What is it you're all so desperate to hide here?' She watched as Ben lowered his gaze to the photo, and she could tell by the impassive expression on his face as he raised his head that she was right about this case. Snatching back the CCTV capture, she pressed on: 'You hadn't seen that before. I know you, and even after all those years of training, you can't lie to me as easily as you can to the rest of the world.

'I'm going to find out why these three men were sitting around a table last month and why two of them are now dead, and I'm going to find out who the third man is. Whilst I'm doing that, I'm going to work out exactly who this man was and what he knew that was so important he needed to be shot from a rooftop before ninety percent of this city had even woken up. If you want to stop me, then I suggest you get a warrant for my arrest.'

As she turned to leave, she felt her forearm grabbed roughly from behind, and she was forced to turn on the spot.

'Don't make me go through you on this,' whispered Ben, and there was a threatening nature to his voice that she didn't recognise.

She attempted to twist out of his grasp, but he merely tightened his grip.

'You don't know where this might lead. Leave it to us.'

'Let me go.' Much to her own surprise, her voice was both fierce and authoritative.

After a long look, he relinquished his hold on her arm and threw his hands into the air slightly in a gesture of resignation.

'I appreciate the concern, but it's a decade too late.' It was with a twinge of regret that she watched him turn on the spot and stride away from her, and her mind flashed back to the last time he'd vanished from her life. *Why should I listen to anything he has to say?* And yet his appearance had unnerved her, there was no denying that, but as Jackie dropped her gaze back to the photo clenched in her hand, she was filled with a renewed resolve to uncover the unfolding mystery that this shooting had left behind.

6

Senta Barracks

The last twenty-four hours since Corporal Matheson had been pronounced dead had passed in a blur. The men of the 1st Battalion Rifles had been told they must remain quarantined within the barracks whilst they were all tested. They weren't told what the tests were for, but they all knew perfectly well. The corporal had been suffering from symptoms of coronavirus in the hours leading up to his death. The men had even joked with him about that very topic, but there had not been a single laugh uttered in the past day – not even from the usually bubbly Private Faye.

As each member of the battalion had received their results, there had been a growing sense of confusion amongst the men. How could none of them have tested positive when they'd been in such close proximity to Ross in the days leading up to his death? The collective conclusion had been that he must have been suffering from some other condition that mimicked the symptoms of the virus or had a similar effect on the human body.

Just as the men had been trying to make sense of the corporal's death, a blacked-out Range Rover had appeared at the entrance to the barracks. A single stooped figure had exited the vehicle and been ushered inside the major's quarters, and within an hour, all the men had been made to sign the Official Secrets Act and instructed not to recount the events they'd witnessed to anyone until they were given the all-clear to do so. There had been a clamour of questions, which the major had been unable to answer, and then he'd pronounced that Ross's widow would be visiting the barracks that very afternoon.

*

Major Pollard stood to attention as the chauffeur-driven Mercedes SLK swung into view. Behind him, the Rifles did the same, giving a silent salute to their fallen comrade. It was with a composed air that Amelia Matheson stepped out of the car, the door now held open for her by the major himself. She was thin, tall and elegant, with curly, blonde hair and a slim figure dressed in a matching black blouse and skirt. As the major closed the car door, she seemed to lose her composure for a second before stepping forwards and shaking the man's hand.

'Mrs Matheson, I can only express my deepest condolences to you and your daughter. Corporal Matheson was a fine soldier; I had the honour of serving with him on many occasions,' the major said sincerely.

'Thank you, Major. My husband always spoke most highly of you,' the woman replied evenly, with the trace of a Liverpudlian accent.

'Please allow me to introduce some of the men your husband served alongside. They'd all like to pay their respects.'

'It would be my privilege, Major.' Amelia smiled as she was introduced to several members of the Rifles in turn, pausing in front of some to exchange a few words. There were a couple of men she recognised from the poker nights that had been held at their family home. As she reached Private Stephen Faye, she reached out and gave him a brief hug. 'I was so pleased to hear that none of you were ill with whatever it was Ross had inside him. You look after Jane, Stephen; make sure you do.'

An uncharacterised look of solemnity had stolen over the private's youthful face. 'She would have wanted to be there for you. We're both here if ever you need anything,' he said in his Mancunian accent. 'I promised Ross that if anything ever happened to him whilst we were on tour, I'd look out for you both.'

'I know.' A sad smile wreathed her face. 'He told me you and Adam had that honour of watching over us. I just hoped that you never would. I'd be honoured if you and Adam would be two of the coffin bearers at his funeral. It's what Ross would have wanted.'

'It would be an honour,' Private Faye responded humbly.

Amelia nodded weakly and moved on, shaking hands with each member of the Rifles until she reached Corporal Adam Dawkins – at which point, she swayed slightly on the spot. The major leaned forwards and steadied her arm for support, to which she gave a quick note of thanks before embracing the man who'd grown to be her husband's best friend over the years, though he was several inches shorter than her.

'Amelia, words cannot express how you must be feeling right now,' began Corporal Dawkins in his characteristically well-spoken manner. 'If there's anything I can do, anything at all, please let me know.'

The two of them hadn't always seen eye to eye. Amelia had found the corporal to be arrogant and condescending when they'd first met, but once she'd got behind the private-school façade, she'd realised he was quite an insecure but loyal man. He and Ross had formed a tight bond over the years, and it had given her comfort knowing they'd be fighting side by side in whichever conflict they were deployed to. Tears had begun to form in her beautiful, green eyes, and she felt Adam Dawkins grip her by the shoulder, as she murmured, 'Please be one of the men carrying Ross's coffin at the funeral.'

Dawkins nodded, and the two embraced once more.

As they broke apart, the major noticed a further look between them. 'Mrs Matheson, if you'd care to follow me? My quarters are this way.'

With that, the Major led Amelia across the tarmacked yard to a small, square building. He opened the door for the woman and then followed her into a little, circular office with several doorways. There was an oak desk in the centre of the room, with two wooden chairs arranged either side and a solitary painting hanging on the wall behind the desk – a copy of Caton-Woodville's famous depiction of the *Charge of the Light Brigade*.

In all his years of service, this was perhaps the moment he'd dreaded most. The introductions to certain members of the battalion had clearly shaken Amelia; tears were rolling silently down her cheeks, streaking her make-up, and her shoulders were beginning to shake.

'Mrs Matheson, I'm truly sorry for your loss. From what I gather, Ross was a good father, and he certainly loved both you and your daughter very much. I want you to know you'll both be looked after by the army, and if there's anything I can do personally, then please don't hesitate to ask.'

'Please.' The major helped her into a chair and leaned on the desk as he replied, 'I have a daughter myself. She was three when her mother died.' He suddenly looked older and greyer; the sadness stretched tight across his tough, soldierly features and his dark-blue eyes were small oceans of sorrow. 'It's OK,' he murmured, as Amelia raised her head to speak. 'It was an IRA bomb. I wasn't even the intended target. We lived next to the Chief of the Defence Staff at the time, and Suzanne just happened to be in the vicinity of the blast when the car exploded. My daughter saw everything.'

A shocked silence hung sorrowfully in the air. There was a shared grief between the two that neither wanted to break, but it was the major who spoke next, his voice remarkably even and emotionless: 'I went mad after it happened. I was a bad father, more intent on revenge than protecting my daughter. I left it to Suzanne's parents to tell her what had happened.' He paused, and when he resumed, there was a slight croak to his voice, 'And there isn't a day goes by that I don't regret it.' He leaned closer to the woman, who raised her tear-stained face to look at him. 'Whatever you decide to tell your daughter, she'll be hearing it from her mum, whom she loves and feels safe with. Nothing can make up for losing a father, but if anything can, then it's a mother's love for her child.'

'Thank you, Major,' croaked Amelia, eventually stemming the tears. 'Your daughter, how... how is she now?'

Major Pollard pushed himself off the desk and strolled around to the chair behind it, opened a drawer, and withdrew a bottle of Penderyn whisky and two glasses before he replied. 'We don't see so much of each other these days. I wasn't there for her enough as she was growing up. I could blame the army for that, but the truth is there are plenty of soldiers who are good fathers. Your husband was one of them. I guess I just found it easier to be a father to troops than to a frightened little girl who needed me.'

After pouring two glasses of the peaty amber liquid, he handed a glass to Mrs Matheson, raising his own. 'To your husband. A fine man, a loving husband and father, and a damn good soldier.'

A curious expression had stolen over the widow's face, as though she were weighing up whether to trust him. 'Major, do you know where my husband has been for the past month?'

The look of confusion on his face was all the answer she required, and she pressed on. 'The general who informed me of my husband's death mentioned that he'd just returned from three weeks' leave and had told his commanding officer that he was spending it at home with us. I hadn't seen my husband for a month.'

'Mrs Matheson,' the major began hesitantly, 'if you and your husband were having difficulties, that's hardly my concern.'

'We weren't having difficulties,' snapped Amelia at once. 'I knew my husband, and he wasn't a cheat, but he went somewhere during those weeks. He told you he was at home. I went through all his clothes this morning, and there was a rolled-up receipt deep in an inside jacket pocket from a petrol station in Wiltshire. The last time I saw him, he was acting completely out of character. He packed a bag and left, telling me he had a month-long training exercise to attend, and this jacket was one of the things he took with him. I didn't see him from then until he' – she choked slightly on the word before finishing – 'he died. I haven't found any of the other clothes he took with him that night, except that jacket. He snuck back into the house and left it there for me to find. Then you say he turns up here acting strangely. What's going on?' There was more than just beseechment in her eyes; there was belief in them too.

The major opened his mouth to respond, but at that exact moment, there was a sharp rap on the door leading back out to the yard, and without waiting for a response, the grim-faced Sergeant Hiscock had stepped through it and into the room.

He snapped to attention, and as Amelia spun round, slightly bewildered, he said gruffly, 'Major, Mrs Matheson, we were wondering if the corporal's wife will be joining us for dinner?' His mouth had contorted into its leering grin, which he focussed on the widow.

'Get out, Sergeant,' ordered Major Pollard, 'and don't think about entering my quarters again without my leave to do so.'

'Understood, Major,' the sergeant barked fiercely in response and in a second, he'd turned and left, the door clanging shut behind him and his stooped back disappearing into the rapidly fading light.

Before the major had a chance to say anything, Amelia had risen from her chair and made her way to the doorway. 'I won't take up any more of your time, Major. Thank you for the drink and your sympathies. I hope you'll consent to be one of the coffin bearers at Ross's funeral service.'

*

Sennybridge, 8pm

Less than an hour before, the sky had been emblazoned with a glowing orange hue above the Brecon Beacons National Park, but the colour had drained away, leaving only a black canvas behind, with only a handful of stars flickering in the gloom. A thick, foreboding cloud was visible in the distance as a biting, chill air swept through the night, making it difficult to breathe, and the darkened canyon above seemed to channel the cold and obscure the moon from sight.

As the cold tightened its grip on the night, there was barely a figure to be seen in the sleepy village of Sennybridge. A solitary Jackal 2 army reconnaissance vehicle – designed to protect personnel against roadside explosions and mine attacks, although this specific example not equipped with the customary general-purpose machine gun – was parked in the local service station. There was no sign of an occupant or indeed anyone inside the petrol station. The wind whistled over the naked streets before finding a human victim to feast upon, as a hooded figure stepped out from behind the local pub and into the open.

As she exited the narrow alleyway and passed the open doorway of the white-brick Abercamlais Arms, Amelia Matheson heard a chorus of raucous singing from within and was reminded of the army socials she'd attended with Ross over the years. The two of them had drunk long into the night with other members of the barracks, and she remembered one such evening where half a dozen of them had staggered back to their army residencies supporting a paralytic Stephen Faye, who'd collapsed on leaving the local pub, Guinness still in hand. One such evening had been spent in this very pub, and rather than returning to the barracks, Ross had spent the night with her in one of the rooms upstairs.

Those nights felt a lifetime ago now, and she couldn't even recall them with a smile. In black leggings, a dark-grey overcoat, boots and a scarf wrapped heavily around her face, she was almost unrecognisable, as she'd attempted to blend into the darkness. Glancing around nervously, she began to move tentatively down the street, with the sign of the pub above her the only streak of blue light visible beneath the black canvas above.

She'd asked Adam Dawkins to meet her near the old community centre, and she began to move quickly as the chill threatened to break through her scarf's defences. There was more boisterous shouting as she passed another pub, smaller this time; the old stone building seemed to sink into the road itself, and smoke curling out from the stubby chimney added an obscuring layer to the evening air. Amelia gave a start, jumping into the road, as there was movement in the alley to her left – only to see a sheepish fox slinking away into the murk. Fighting to keep her racing heart under control, she moved onwards, her thoughts lingering on her daughter.

As a mother, she owed it to Lydia to find out what had happened to her father. Or maybe she was just imagining this whole thing and trying to construct a conspiracy where none existed, so she could put off having to tell her daughter that she'd never see her daddy again. No. She wrestled with herself. She'd known Ross better than anyone else in the world and she'd known that something wasn't right, even before the grim-faced general had arrived on her doorstep.

He'd been distant from her in the weeks before he'd taken off, and he'd snapped easily, a trait he'd never before displayed in their marriage. Even during those days after the news of his father's death in the care home in Newcastle, he'd shown her and Lydia nothing but love. Yes, he'd grieved; the dozens of sleepless nights in the past year had been evidence enough for that. His mother, she knew, had died just before he'd turned sixteen, and it had been his father who'd always been there for him; losing him in any circumstances was bound to hurt.

As the wind whistled through the bushes lining the wall on the opposite side of the road, she thought of Lydia. Tonight, her brother was looking after Lydia, but Amelia hadn't been able to shift her daughter's face from her mind all day, and even now with adrenalin pumping through her body, that round face, rosy cheeks and clear, bright-green eyes filled her mind. As the road bent round to the right, and she approached a row of whitewashed stone houses, Lydia's high-pitched laughter seemed to ring in her ears.

Momentarily losing track of her surroundings, Amelia was blindsided by the figure stepping out from the alleyway before the row of terrace houses. Before she had a chance to react, she'd been seized roughly from behind, her mouth suddenly full of leather and her nostrils overwhelmed by the smell of her attacker's putrid breath. As her heels were dragged backwards over a small area of gravel, she fought to free herself, her nails digging into the flesh beneath the gloves of her attacker. She felt warm blood crawling underneath her scarlet-painted nails, but a second later, the serrated edge of a knife was at her throat, and with its cold bite, the darkness seemed to close in around her.

*

London, 2pm the following day

John Bromley was making his final preparations for the assignment he'd been tasked with. After hoisting the sling of his duffel bag over his right shoulder, he closed the back door of the safehouse behind him and scampered down the metal fire escape that ran down the side of the building in North London. He knew Camden well, having grown up in this very suburb, and many of the friends who belonged to his old life still lived and worked in the surrounding area. That life felt a world away now, as though it had belonged to a different person.

He wasn't sure what made him stop, nor why the thought had occurred to him when it never had before. On an impulse, he began to walk in the opposite direction from where he should be going, and he turned off down various side streets that sent flashes of memories echoing through his brain. Instinctively, he doubled back on occasion, or else made sharp diversions, but there was nobody in sight. Nobody could be following him. It was second nature to him to avoid CCTV cameras; he didn't even need to think about where they were, such was his memory for the area. Would he still be there? Of course, he was. Where else would he have gone? He had nowhere else to go. As he turned the corner beneath the shadow of the famous market, he caught a glimpse of the shadowy side street opposite, which he headed towards.

As he got closer, John considered turning back. What was he doing here? There was nothing that could be gained from this. He'd tried in the past. How strange it was that his heart seemed to be beating faster than ever and he realised in that moment that it was caused by fear. Fear of all things. He hadn't felt fear like that in years, despite the obvious perils his line of work posed. This was madness; there was nothing that could be done. The morning glow seemed to evaporate as he drew closer, consumed by the depressing darkness of the alleyways and the lives of their inhabitants.

However, his legs seemed to move of their own accord as they turned down the side street, and there was the shadowy figure he'd expected, huddled in a filthy mass of blankets, a stained sleeping bag zipped up over his legs, which were balled up as though he were afraid to release his knees. Beneath the outer layer of rags were clothes that were once fashionable but now hung loose and grimy. His face, sunken and waxy, cowered away from the world. The hair that had once attracted so much ridicule in the barracks for its wavy nature was now a tangled mop of grey and brown.

Yet it was the smell that was worst of all – the pungent stench of dried urine and ancient grime forming a toxic mix that would have been enough to repel many – but John had grown used to such assaults on his senses. This was the smell of neglect; neglected by himself and by everyone who'd ever claimed to love him. Despite him being prepared for the odour, John paused briefly before taking a further tentative step forwards, recoiling slightly as it filled his nostrils.

At the sound of John's footsteps, the man raised his head slightly, and the grimace that flickered across his face indicated that the movement had cost him a great effort. John had seen some terrible things in his life, both during war and from images that had been shown in Thames House, but nothing had shocked him quite liked this. He took a step back in consternation and horror. What had he expected? Not this. He should have expected it, he knew, but this wasn't the man whom he remembered.

The man before him could have been in his late fifties; his face was haggard, and there was a greasy mane of filthiest grey intertwining with the spiky, grey whiskers that protruded from beneath his upper and lower lips. The eyes that had once been so full of life were sunken and turned colourless to the world, and there was an ugly, purple bruise forming over his right eye. This couldn't be the same man. When he spoke, it cost him great effort, and the croaky sound sent a shiver through John that had nothing to do with the morning chill.

'John, is that really you?' rasped the figure in rags, sending an all too familiar whiff of alcohol towards him.

Stiffly, John jerked his head forwards, but he found himself lost for words.

A flurry of diseased coughs rent the air, and the rattle they left behind echoed through the alleyway. 'One of us turned our lives around, then.'

Anger seemed to bubble in the pit of John's stomach as he looked down at the figure who'd once been his colleague and stood beside him in the battlefield. He closed his eyes to the pain of the memories, as the clatter of machine-gun fire seemed to echo back through the years, whilst the two of them hauled another fallen friend to safety. 'How did you end up like this? What happened to you?' He couldn't keep the contempt from his voice.

Those sunken eyes seemed to narrow rather feebly, as the reply came: 'The same thing that's happened to you, except you're able to wear a mask to face the world. The rest of us can't do that.'

Fighting an overwhelming urge to lash out at the filthy figure that had consumed his friend, John spat, 'I wear no mask. I just didn't give up like you did.'

A ripple of anger flittered across his friend's haunted face, and the man attempted to get to his feet, but the effort was too much, and he collapsed once again into the mild comfort of his sleeping bag, a clanking of bottles breaking the morning silence. 'You can't fool me, John. I was there after Afghanistan, remember? We came home together, went to the same meetings together and went to the same dark places together. You might have lied your way out of that, but you can't lie to me.' The pain of speaking seemed to overwhelm him, and he clutched the sleeping bag and rags closer around him, his hand massaging his throat as though the movement would return the power of speech.

The screams that he tried to oust from his memory began to echo distantly in John's ears, and he closed his eyes tight shut for several seconds, hoping to block them out. 'We are *not* the same,' he said defiantly. 'Look at you. This isn't a life.'

'You think there's much difference between the two of us?' croaked his friend. 'It could easily be you sleeping here. How many of our friends are like me?'

'The difference is I chose to live, to help, not to give up,' retorted John, realising as he said this that the anger he felt coursing through his veins was triggered by the truth he was hearing. It could easily be him lying in an alleyway, abandoned by his friends, his government and his family. He'd seen that future for himself and resolved to avoid it at all costs. One of those costs was lying at his feet now, and John had to bite back the tears that had formed behind his eyes. He'd abandoned his friends, his men, to save himself. And this was the consequence.

'I'm not angry with you, John. I know why you left me, why you left us. You wouldn't have been able to keep up the lie when you were surrounded by living reminders of what you're running away from.'

'I didn't run away,' replied John through gritted teeth.

'Yes, you did.' The figure now descending into shadow as the morning sun passed from view temporarily. 'You thought it was the only way to save yourself. Yet the truth is you still need more help than the rest of us. I can see it in your eyes, John. You can't escape what we did. None of us can – especially you. And you can't escape how you felt about me either, and what we had.'

'Don't,' John snarled, clenching his teeth in the vain hope that it would stop the avalanche of pain that had begun to tumble towards him. The small, lifeless bodies, crumpled and bloodied – those that had haunted his nightmares and that he'd tried so desperately to block out from the waking world – were before his eyes once more.

'We all needed help, but we were abandoned and left to deal with our own damaged minds. How can you work for the same people who did that to us? Don't be angry with me.' The figure raised a feeble arm into the air towards John, as one of the dying Afghan children had once done, and the gesture was too much for John to bear.

His eyes closed to the rage and pain, John swung his boot through the air. He barely felt it connect with his friend's head, nor did he register the cry of pain. It was as though he was in an insulated bubble of pain and memories. He couldn't feel the hot tears sliding from his eyes and down his cheeks, let alone the continued blows that he rained down upon the man he'd once loved. Memories flashed through is brain, blinding him to what he was doing in the present, so consumed was he by the smell and sickening scene of the battlefield and the meagre counselling sessions that had been offered thereafter. When he stumbled from the side street five minutes later, his shoes and hands slippery with blood, John looked down at them, unable to remember what he'd done.

7

'I must say I'm surprised to see a detective up here,' the major said gruffly.

Jackie noted how forced his smile was. Ever since she'd arrived at the barracks and been greeted by the major himself, she'd been under the impression he was seizing her up, perhaps deciding how much he could trust her. His dark-blue eyes seemed to be x-raying her, as though he were the detective and she was being interrogated.

For a split second, Jackie wondered whether this was a good idea after all. She was sure to be disciplined upon her return to the station, having been ignoring calls from her superiors all morning. She had no desire to return to London, however. What awaited her there was another case of a body being found washed up in Woolwich. This was much more exciting. There was no way she was going to drop this case.

Upon her arrival at the base, Major Pollard had greeted her and introduced her to several members of the 1st Rifles Battalion company. Unfortunately, the SAS squadron that had been training alongside Corporal Matheson had departed the previous afternoon; nevertheless, she'd spent the next three hours interviewing each of the men from the Rifles and many had left quite an impression on her. The major had sat in on all the interviews, and although he had at no point moved to intervene, Jackie had sensed a wariness on the part of some of the men to speak freely with their commanding officer present.

The first soldier she'd been introduced to was the well-spoken Corporal Dawkins, who'd been close friends with Corporal Matheson for a number of years. The news of the corporal's wife's death the night before, coupled with the loss of his friend, seemed to have taken its toll on the man. His light-brown hair was unkempt, and his green eyes were sunk low in their sockets, his voice marred with sorrow. As Jackie had watched him walk rigidly from the room, her heart had been tugged to see the grief that had stiffened the joints of a soldier in top condition.

The boyish features of Private Faye were the next that she observed in speaking to him. He spoke glowingly about the corporal, and although there was a clear solemnity to his voice, his bubbly personality was evident. At the end of her questions, he was effusive in his pleas that she should join them all for a game of cards in the mess hall that evening, and he had been told to leave by Major Pollard, who didn't seem at all amused by the private bouncing up and down on the balls of his feet. Nevertheless, it was with a smile that Jackie had watched him leave the major's office, which was more than she could say for the surly brute of a man that had taken his place.

Sergeant Hiscock had trudged into the room, his arched back and ugly features reminding Jackie strikingly of the hunchback of Notre Dame. Even before he'd seated himself, his face had split into unpleasant leer, revealing jagged, yellow teeth. Jackie inferred that he treated everyone with equal contempt, but the arrogant and condescending tone of his replies left her with little doubt that Sergeant Hiscock was no feminist. Nor did he have anything positive to say about Corporal Matheson, remarking that he hadn't been particularly close to the corporal and nor did he wish he had been.

The interview ended with the sergeant kicking his boots against the carpet and asking whether it was his bedtime yet. During those fifteen minutes, the same patronising leer had remained on his face, and it was with a rather disdainful glance over his shoulder that he departed the building. There had been something, though. When she'd questioned him about whether or not he'd known the corporal's wife, that smirk had contorted ever so slightly for a moment. What this was conveying, she didn't know, but there had been a flicker there that intrigued her.

'What a charming man,' she'd remarked to Major Pollard after the sergeant had left.

Major Pollard had smiled at that. 'Charm isn't necessarily a quality that makes you a good soldier or leader in the field.'

The next to be interviewed had been a rather young Pakistani officer with slick, black hair, who'd been by far the warmest of the soldiers Jackie had spoken to. He'd bowed low upon meeting her and even kissed her hand – a gesture that might have seemed inappropriate had it not been for the charming smile and generous, hazel-coloured eyes that had accompanied it. He'd been introduced as Private Younis, who'd served with Corporal Matheson on a peacekeeping mission the year before, and he'd spoken openly about the corporal's character, believing him to have set a good example to younger recruits. Frustratingly, he hadn't witnessed first-hand anything untoward with regards to Matheson's behaviour in the days leading up to his death.

Indeed, every man she'd spoken to had refused to speak about the corporal's death, with all maintaining they'd been on the other side of the exercise course at the time and had therefore not been witness to it. Nor had they shown the merest flicker of recognition when she'd shown them the photo of the three men outside the café and asked them whether they knew either of the other individuals. She knew why, of course. No doubt Ben and his bosses had warned the soldiers not to speak openly to the police, and she cursed them under her breath.

The thought jolted her, as Ben's face swam before her once more. She'd never thought to see him again, and yet potentially the biggest case of her career was being snatched away from her by him, just like he'd snatched away their future all those years again. Perhaps she'd been naïve to think that joining the service wouldn't change him, but the whole sequence of events confused her to this day. The first few months after he'd enrolled had been fine. Yes, he'd worked long hours and had been forced to return to work at a split second's notice, but she'd expected all of that.

No, it had been that first mission. Before it, he'd seemed nervous, which wasn't a trait anyone would have associated with him, but there had been excitement too. All his training had been leading up to that moment, and although Jackie had been a little apprehensive, she hadn't been frightened. If anything, she'd been excited for him, and she knew Ben could look after himself. She'd never thought that the last time she'd see him would have been that chilly morning in Putney as he kissed her goodbye and jumped into the back of the blacked-out Mercedes that had swung into view outside their flat.

She knew there was always the slight possibility that he wouldn't return, but not in the way that had transpired. It would have been more comforting to see him return in a coffin than for him to disappear from her life without so much as a word. One morning, two men had appeared at the flat, bulldozed their way inside and withdrawn every trace of him from her life, and all that she'd been able to ascertain was that he was still alive. What could possibly have happened in those few weeks to make him do something so cruel? It was so out of character for the young man she'd grown to love.

Jackie snapped back to the present as the major continued.

'I was told the police were no longer handling the investigation into Matheson's death. Not that it isn't delightful to have you visit us,' he added politely.

He wasn't being obstructive by choice, Jackie had decided. Everything about Major Pollard oozed military, from the way he held himself, straight-backed and to attention when standing to his hunched, stiff shoulders when seated. This was a man who was used to following orders and not questioning why they'd been given or by whom. The little research that she had been able to do on her way to Wales had told her something different, though. He'd lobbied the government personally, arguing for better pay and equipment for his troops, directly challenging the authority of those above him.

Yet she saw none of that in the man sitting opposite her. His dark-blue eyes were impenetrable, and his face was staunchly implacable. In fact, had it not been for the soft nature of his voice on occasion, she would have been intimidated by the broad shoulders, tight skin and closely cropped black hair and beard, all of which served to create an imposing figure. If the stories were to be believed, however, beneath this gruff exterior was an empathetic side that could lead him to challenge orders for the greater good – at least when it came to his men.

'Perhaps your surprise at my visit explains the identical stories and lack of answers your men have provided me this morning,' said Jackie, her voice firm. 'I didn't become a detective by just accepting whatever people wanted to tell me. I know when I'm being lied to, and I certainly know when a group of people have swallowed the same work of fiction.'

The corners of the major's mouth twitched slightly into a smile, as he withdrew a bottle of amber liquid and two glasses from a drawer. Now smiling, he placed the glasses on the desk, opened the bottle and tilted it to pour a generous measure into each. With a slight tug at her heart, Jackie noticed the Penderyn label fixed to the front of the bottle and identified the Celt variety. Tentatively picking up the glass to her right, she fingered the rim of the crystal and breathed in the peaty warmth being emitted by the whisky before draining the glass in one.

The major laughed. 'I wasn't expecting that either.'

Jackie smiled in spite of herself as the major gulped down his own measure of whisky and refilled both glasses. 'It was my father's favourite whisky. And always the Celt. He loved peated whiskies and used to drag us across Scotland and Ireland to the distilleries, but he used to take us on a tour of the Penderyn distillery every summer without fail. We used to stay in the Brecon Beacons for a week, exploring through the bracken, around the lakes and up to Pen-y-Fan.'

'Why the whisky, Major? I thought you were all set to throw me out of your office after giving me the same story your men have been fed,' she said curiously.

A slight frown flitted across Major Pollard's face for a moment, before he asked shrewdly, 'And what makes you so sure I'm not going to do just that?'

Jackie found herself laughing. 'You wouldn't need the whisky for that. I can't imagine army majors are accustomed to letting people down gently. So why the change of heart?'

The major leaned forwards in his chair and placed his glass back on the desk. For a moment, it seemed as though he was going to dial back on an open approach, but after weighing up the situation for another moment, he said carefully, 'Yesterday afternoon, another woman sat in the same seat you are in now, drinking the same whisky, and I didn't answer her questions either. This morning, they found her body in the village, dumped like a sack of rubbish.'

The anger in his face was real enough, and in that moment, Jackie saw the man who'd fight for what was best for his men. There was pain and anger in those ocean-blue eyes.

'Amelia Matheson came to me for help, but I just parroted her the MOD party line – even though I knew it didn't make sense. I've always tried to put the safety of my men and their families above anything else, and yet when one of them needed me most, I let them down. I owe it to the family of both of them to help you now, even though it comes a day too late.'

After replacing her own glass on the table, Jackie leaned towards him. 'The image I showed your men earlier this morning. You and I both know that whatever was leaked to the press about Ross Matheson having an underlying heart condition and him being pushed too hard in training is just a cover story. Having met you, Major, I know you'd never have endangered one of your own men in that way, and for the army medics to miss a heart condition on every screening they conducted would be negligence of a level I can't believe. What is it you aren't telling me?'

Pollard sighed heavily. 'I've been a soldier for more years than I care to remember. I don't do politics, Miss Ambrose, and I hate underhand secrecy. I like things kept simple for me: black and white. I leave the scheming to others and gladly keep well out of it. Let other people gather intelligence, assess and have agendas. We're soldiers in the field, and my whole life, I've followed orders. Yes, there may have been occasions where I challenged them for the good of my men, but never have I questioned the politics or agenda behind any assignment I've been given.'

Jackie waited patiently. There was clearly conflict in the man; this was still evident in his eyes, which seemed to hold clashing tidal waves of purest blue. Inside, however, she breathed a sigh of relief. The smallest part of her had been concerned that she was imagining the entire thing and perhaps that the reappearance of Ben in her life had clouded her judgement. She'd often relied on instinct when it came to her cases, where an inkling had frequently led her to the correct outcome.

'Corporal Matheson was a good solider,' continued the major, replenishing his own glass of whisky, 'I never had to worry about him, either as a soldier or a man. People think that commanding a platoon of troops is about leading them in the field, but in truth, it's more important to judge their mental wellbeing away from the barracks. They know how to fight; Lord knows we train them to within an inch of their lives on exercise. That instinct never leaves you, but it only takes the slightest drop in mental readiness and you're dead.

'I'm not even talking about the effects of war on a man here. Problems at home, injury and a raft of other things can come into play. The pandemic hit a lot of people hard, and that includes soldiers. They lost loved ones, but not only that, they were also suddenly in the midst of a conflict where the enemy couldn't be seen or shot at. That fear of not being able to see the enemy surrounding you, killing your friends or family, is more terrifying to a soldier than you can imagine.'

Silence followed this solemn pronouncement, and for a few seconds, Jackie dared not break it. Eventually, she prompted tentatively: 'I read Corporal Matheson's file. His father died in a care home during the pandemic. Did that not affect him?'

The major smiled ruefully. 'If it wasn't for the fact that I study the file of every soldier before each training deployment, then I wouldn't have known. Like I say, he kept his private life separate, and he never gave me reason to question his mental state of readiness.' He paused, and Jackie noticed the crease that had appeared between his eyes. 'That's until this training deployment.' There was a bitter note of regret to his voice as he continued to speak. 'From day one, he wasn't with it. I should have sent him back to barracks to take no further part in the exercises, but it was so uncharacteristic, and I didn't want to make an example of him in front of the other men.'

The guilt was weighing heavily on his shoulders, she could see now. Perhaps it was that sense of guilt that had finally made him open up to her. Against her natural instincts, Jackie realised the last thing the major would want to hear would be words of comfort. Yet she wished she were able to reach out and help the man whose eyes were clouded with guilt and whose shoulders had dropped slightly from their military pose.

'Even before we started training, there was something wrong.'

'What do you mean?' asked Jackie curiously. 'He was struggling to breathe before you even began the exercise drills?'

Pollard seemed to be weighing her up once more, before answering, 'No. I mean, the day before the rest of the men arrived on the barracks, I saw the corporal out in the hills beyond the army range crouching down in the undergrowth. I'm not sure what he was doing. I shrugged it off at the time, thinking that he was perhaps caught short whilst going for a run, but maybe I don't know...'

What had the major witnessed? Jackie had no reason to doubt his testimony. Why would he lie about something like that? It sounded inconspicuous enough, but placed in the context of Matheson's death, everyone action was worthy of scrutinisation. 'Do you know where the corporal had been before he arrived at the barracks?'

The major shook his head. 'As far as we were concerned, he'd taken several weeks leave to spend at home with his family, but Mrs Matheson claimed he'd spent none of that time with her. Like you, she seemed to think there was some sort of conspiracy taking place. She found a receipt for a petrol station in Wiltshire on a date that coincided with the day he left their family home. Apparently, it was in the jacket that he wore the day he left, and she believes he entered their home secretly to plant it there for her to find.' He lapsed briefly into an evidently regretful silence once more. 'She wanted me to help find out what had happened to him. I hope you can help uncover that truth, but please be careful.'

Jackie nodded, swept up her bag from the floor and departed. As she did so, she pondered what she'd learned. The answer could be found in those weeks in which he'd disappeared before his death, and it sounded as though his wife had been trying to piece it together. It was because of that she'd ended up dead, and that in itself worried Jackie.

*

Two hours later, Jackie found herself rooting through a cramped hotel room in the B&B that Amelia Matheson had made home for the night. There was a single bed with a worn wooden headboard against one wall; an outdated, full-length oak wardrobe in the corner by the postage stamp of a murky window frame; and a battered desk opposite the bed. In the adjacent corner, there was a door leading into a small en suite barely big enough to house one adult.

Inwardly, Jackie was grateful she hadn't chosen to stay the night here. As if she'd not had enough to deal with, why had Amelia put herself through the ordeal of staying in such a depressing room? The peeling, faded wallpaper and low ceiling gave the room a gloomy, claustrophobic feel. Indeed, it sounded as though the widow had requested this room specifically, according to the landlord, who'd pleaded that the rest of the rooms were in much nicer condition, having recently been refurbished.

It appeared that the widow had brought few very items with her. There was a small, light-grey roll-along suitcase by the bed and nothing in the wardrobe other than a men's black leather jacket. From speaking to the major, Jackie guessed this was the jacket in which Amelia had found a receipt from a petrol station in Wiltshire. On reaching into the jacket's left inside pocket, she found the thin scrap of paper immediately and pondered what she was looking at.

It wasn't the receipt itself or the location that caught Jackie's attention immediately, however. It was the amount. Apparently, the corporal had put just £7 worth of petrol in his car that day. Of course, some people did tend fill up their car with incremental amounts, and there was always the chance he was approaching his destination and was running low, meaning he just required a small top up to the tank. Even so, Jackie had her doubts. From what she knew of the corporal's life, the journey he would have needed to make to Wiltshire would have been substantial, and he'd surely been intending to return to Chepstow, as demonstrated by his later movements. He'd been intending to make a return journey, and given how far he would have to travel, why would he not have taken the opportunity to replenish the tank entirely?

Putting the thought to one side for the moment, she checked the rest of the wardrobe after first pocketing the receipt, but there was nothing more there. After hoisting the small suitcase onto the bed, she rifled through it quickly, checking the pockets of clothing and opening pairs of socks. It seemed the widow really had travelled light, and there appeared to be no clues in amongst the luggage. Jackie glanced around the room and her eyes settled on the desk with a single long drawer beneath the top.

After crossing the room, she slid it open. There was nothing inside but an old, leather-bound Bible. She was on the point of shutting the drawer when something caught her eye. Protruding from the top of the Bible was what appeared to be a lost page of paper, making the top of the holy book's pages uneven. It was only when she opened the Bible that she realised it was in fact a loose scrap of paper that had been slipped inside the book. On it, written in rather slanting handwriting, were just three words: 'Meet with Adam'.

As she processed the message, Jackie could think of only one person it might relate to: Corporal Adam Dawkins. He'd been the closest man in the battalion to Amelia's husband. Had she arranged a meeting with him that had been where she was going when she was killed? It appeared so. That meant she'd trusted the man, but curiously, she'd left this note behind. Perhaps she'd had an inkling that something might happen to her.

Recalling the interviews she'd conducted earlier that day, Jackie remembered the sorrowful, green eyes sunk low in their sockets; the cracked voice; and the dishevelled, brown hair. She'd thought at the time that the deaths of his friend and his friend's wife had taken their toll on the man. As she considered this, another possibility occurred to her. There was a chance Corporal Dawkins had somehow been involved in their deaths – or at least that of the widow. She'd arranged to meet him and had trusted him, but she'd had been murdered before the meeting had taken place – or so it seemed.

It was unlikely she'd broadcast that the meeting was taking place. The surreptitious note crammed into the top of the Bible was evidence enough of that. It sounded as though she'd been careful not to reveal too much to Major Pollard, and when their meeting had been interrupted, she'd clammed up and refused to continue speaking within earshot of any others. That pattern of behaviour suggested a person who would have taken care to make sure that only the person she was meeting would have been aware of their appointment. That made whoever she'd been planning to meet the prime suspect in her murder, so that made *Corporal Adam Dawkins* the prime suspect.

Jackie hadn't heard the door open behind her, but a shadowy movement on the greying, mothballed carpet made her tense suddenly. As she was on the point of turning around, a pair of hands seized her from behind and swung her violently across the room. Her head crashed into the wooden wardrobe, and Jackie tasted thick blood in her mouth, as her head began to sway and her vision swam before her eyes. Unable to stand, she felt herself grabbed forcefully, and her head was slammed repeatedly against the wardrobe door.

With each blow, she felt a rush of oncoming darkness and the pain was mounting, blinding her to her surroundings. And then it stopped. Her attacker was gone. Relief and oxygen began to flood her body, and she winced as they attempted to flush the pain from her system. In the far distance, she heard the sudden rush of water and attempted to crawl towards the source of the sound. The effort was too much for her, and her body collapsed. Her arms flailed and found something to grasp. She thought dimly that it may have been the side of the bed.

The next moment, a shadow moved through the dimness, and she felt herself lifted bodily from the ground. With her arms held tightly behind her back, she felt the press of her attacker's body behind her, and she thought muzzily that they must be of similar height to her, due to the weight of pressure on her lower back. On feeling herself being pushed forwards roughly, the fog of pain in front of her eyes cleared for a moment, and she saw she was being led towards the small bathroom. The water she'd heard in the distance was them filling the sink, and with a spasm of horror, she understood what her attacker intended to do.

Although her body was still limp with pain, she tried to muster the strength to fight back, but her attacker's grip was too strong. Before she had chance to struggle any more, she found herself looking down at the basin, with water pouring over the sides and onto the floor. For a moment, she was suspended above it before she felt her head shoved roughly downwards. Her face was submerged beneath the water. Within a second, water had rushed into her nostrils and ears. She'd taken one last desperate gulp of air in the briefest of moments before her impact with the water, and it was this act that allowed her to remain calm.

Even so, the sensation was a terrifying one. With water flooding through her nose and gushing into her ears, she knew she had perhaps a few seconds before she'd have to exhale, and then she'd drown. Steeling herself, Jackie lashed out upwards with her right foot, sending her heel slamming into her attacker's groin. The impact told her she was fighting a man, and spluttering for air, she wrenched her head from the basin and gratefully gulped in big lungfuls of oxygen.

Turning slowly on the spot, Jackie saw her attacker at last. Sprawled momentarily over the loo seat behind her was Private Faye, the jovial-faced soldier she'd interviewed earlier in the day. Shock seemed to flush the water from her head, and her blurred vision began to clear just as the man got to his feet and withdrew an ugly, blood-stained knife from the pocket of his khaki army clothing that he still wore.

A horrible leer was spreading over the private's face, and Jackie half smiled at the irony. What was it the major had called him? *The baby-faced assassin.* How wonderfully ironic. There was nothing boyish and youthful in his face any more; it was alive with malice. Moving with remarkable speed, he took two steps towards Jackie, and his right arm slashed downwards, with seven inches of glinting, silvery steel slicing through the air. Remembering her training days of during her time at university, Jackie had groggily waited until the last moment before dodging to the left whilst grabbing her assailant's head as he lunged past her and thrusting it down hard onto the side of the basin.

Private Faye howled in pain, blood pouring from a deep cut to his temple, and staggered back against the shower door; the knife dropped to the floor at his feet. Jackie lunged forwards towards it, her head throbbing, but as she reached down, the soldier's boot swung upwards and connected hard with her nose. Her whole body was sent flying backwards, and she was propelled into the bedroom, with warm blood flowing thickly over her nose and into her mouth. Jackie's head was spinning once more, and she knew she wasn't in control.

The many blows to her head had left her groggy and vulnerable. She tried to get to her feet, but she swayed unconvincingly before falling back to the carpet, her legs refusing to obey the dimly flickering messages from her brain. Ahead of her, Private Faye leaned down and snatched the knife from the floor. The water that was flooding the bathroom was streaked with red as it had lapped over the blade. Jackie knew instinctively that it was Amelia Matheson's blood that was being washed off the weapon.

Of all the men she'd interviewed, she wouldn't have suspected the joking private who'd invited her into the mess for dinner and drinks. His ginger hair was now sopping wet, and blood still trickled down from the wound to his temple. He was leering again, knife in hand, and began to move towards her. Jackie fought to find her voice, to try to buy time and ask the man why he was doing this, but the water that had clogged her throat seemed to have incapacitated her vocal cords.

She closed her eyes for the briefest of seconds, and in that moment, the private had stepped across and was looming over her. The knife was still clutched in his right hand, with blood and water dripping noiselessly from it onto the carpet. He wasn't bouncing nervously on the balls off his feet like he'd done in the major's office. Had it all been an act?

Too late, Detective Jackie Ambrose felt the pain subsiding in her nose and head and a semblance of strength returned to her muscles. She watched helplessly as the private's fist swung through the air in an upward arc, the knife clutched firmly in his grasp. The slicing motion would have cut Jackie's throat if she hadn't launched herself forwards at that very moment, her whole weight slamming into the man's lower body in a rugby tackle that knocked him off his feet. Her mouth full of blood, Jackie clawed desperately at the man's right hand whilst pinning him down. Her nails scrabbled his wrist, and she dug them in deep. Although Faye shouted in pain, Jackie knew he was deceptively strong for his short stature, and with a gigantic heave, he lifted her body off his own and carried her inexorably towards the bed before dumping her on the hard mattress.

The leer on his face turned to a snarl as he pinned her wrists together above her head with his left hand, leaving his right hand free to continue the knife's path towards her throat. Even as she struggled desperately, Jackie was aware she couldn't fight off the man. She could smell her attacker now, his musty body odour causing her to gag and splutter out the mixture of water and blood still lodged in her airways. Her eyes found the knife in his fist and watched it begin its journey towards her throat.

Jackie refused to close her eyes. The man would have to look into them as he killed her, but she doubted that would trigger even the merest flicker of doubt or remorse. Private Faye had made no attempt to utter even a single word during their fight. Whatever his motivation, there wasn't a trace of hesitation in him. Even now, when her death seemed inevitable, Jackie yearned for answers, and the frustration at not uncovering the truth outweighed the fear she felt at her own demise.

The knife would put an end to that frustration – and a swift end at that. Just as the private hovered the blade into position above her throat, the door to the bedroom banged open and three figures moved into the room, the first of them in combat position with a semi-automatic pistol in his hands. Private Faye turned briefly and took them in before twisting backwards and lunging towards Jackie, his eyes alight with fear. There were two loud cracks, and a faint whistling could be heard as the bullets whipped through the air. The soldier's grip slackened over Jackie's wrists, and she pulled herself free as his lifeless body dropped to the carpet, staining it with a freshly spreading pool of blood.

For a few seconds, she stared down at the body of her attacker without really seeing him at all. She felt an arm on her shoulder and flinched out of reflex before turning slowly. All three men were dressed in khaki military uniforms, and she recognised them all. The figure in front was Corporal Adam Dawkins, and it was he who had fired the shots that had saved her. As she watched, he gradually lowered the weapon, never taking his eyes off his former friend's body as though seeing him for the first time.

Major Pollard towered over his counterparts and there was a blank look of shock on his face, as he too seemed fixated on the body of Private Stephen Faye. It was the third man who'd made to touch her shoulder, and she hazily recognised the young Pakistani officer with slick, black hair whom she'd interviewed that morning. His hazel-coloured eyes were watching her with concern, but there was a calmness about him that couldn't have been more at odds with his comrades.

When he spoke, there was none of the easy charm that he'd personified earlier in the day, but a soothing tone that inspired trust. 'Let's get out of here,' he said softly. 'Ben sent me. I'll take you to him.'

Somewhere beneath the numbing sensation that had gripped her body, a nerve twitched in surprise. When she opened her mouth to reply, she found that the power of speech had returned to her, although feebly. 'Where? Where are you taking me? Where's Ben?'

The officer smiled. 'Home to London, Detective Ambrose. Thames House.'

8

Conspiracies, plots and old adversaries whispering from beyond the grave would, in themselves, be enough to trouble perhaps every other section chief at MI5, but then again, Aldwyn Haynes had experienced them all in the past – to varying degrees, of course. But to have them all intertwined with a potentially elaborate plot was a frightening prospect, he had to admit.

He knew this wasn't a task he could leave entirely to the men in his section, however adept they may be at dealing with such threats. It was time he played his part once more from an operational perspective. One thing you accumulated during twenty-four years in the intelligence community was a list of contacts and people who owed you favours. It was time to call in some of those favours now, even if he couldn't entirely trust what they'd tell him.

Turning his thoughts to other matters, he reflected upon his decision-making that day. It had been his intention to visit Hugh Palmer immediately upon exiting Thames House that morning, but the Health Minister was still not answering his calls, and there had been other lines of enquiry he'd wanted to investigate. He'd make it his next port of call. Although he respected Hugh, and the two had developed something of a friendship over many years, this was no time to play nice. If he had information that could help with their investigations, then Hugh needed to tell him.

The meeting with Charlene McKinnon had left him somewhat confused, however. He knew her, of course, from environmental briefings and climate-change protests. Although she was very driven and forthright in her views on climate change, she wasn't the type to join those idiots gluing themselves to the road outside Downing Street today. It wasn't just her intellect but also her political savvy that meant she was granted access to the government, despite her urging them to take more action.

*

Today, her curly, dark hair had been cut short in line with the cat's-eye glasses that elegantly revealed the gorgeous hazel eyes behind the lenses. She had been dressed as immaculately as ever in a tailored, dark Saint Laurent blazer and chic blouse. There had been an impressive poise to her, which no doubt helped inflame the minds of those she wished to influence. Yet why had she reached out to Helen Robinson to arrange this meeting?

'There isn't much I can tell you Mr…?' she'd stated.

'Call me Mr Preston,' Aldwyn had replied.

'As I say, Mr Preston,' Charlene McKinnon had explained, 'I wasn't that close to Mr Morris. He was part of the security detail when this government so kindly acquiesced to an environmental inspection of the Thames Barrier. In my role advising government departments on climate change and other matters, I had contact with the Ministry of Defence, of course. We met on several occasions, yet we barely exchanged pleasantries. I don't believe our world views would have aligned.' She'd smiled, slightly sadly. 'Nevertheless, I was sorry to hear of his death.'

'But you worked with him when he was seconded to the Environment Agency?' Aldwyn had asked, curious to work out the true extent of their relationship. He couldn't quite work Miss McKinnon out. She'd volunteered herself as a source of information to Helen Robinson, yet she seemed to have nothing to offer. 'Did your relationship extend beyond the professional?' Why else would she be so eager to help?

A slight frown had crossed her chiselled features. 'I did work with him,' she had said slowly, turning away to look into the distance. Her eyes had seemed to glaze slightly, almost wistfully, all hint of crisp professionalism gone. 'We did have a brief relationship.' A single tear fell down the marble cheeks. 'I wanted more, but he broke it off.'

Aldwyn had placed a hand on her shoulder at this. 'And the last time you saw him?' he had pressed. 'Did anything seem different about him?'

It took a moment before Charlene McKinnon had regained her regal composure. 'We rather lost the little touch there had been after that, but then he sent me a message out of the blue a few days ago, warning me to keep inside for the next few days.'

Aldwyn's jaw had tightened. 'Did he say why?'

She had shaken her head.

'Did he say for how long?'

'He just said to make sure I had the latest booster vaccination and to stay inside. I asked why, but he never responded.'

After taking a few moments to thank her for her time and information, he'd begun to move off. A sound made him turn around for a second. A snigger? No, a muffled sniff. Charlene McKinnon was where he'd left her, with her face buried in her hands.

So why had the meeting troubled him so much? It wasn't just the seeming confirmation that Morris knew the virus might be about to be released. There was something else nagging at him.

Passing just beyond the Palace of Westminster, he turned into the gardens that dwelled in the intimidating shadow of the Houses of Parliament. He quickly spotted the man he'd be meeting, whose wispy, grey strands of hair were visible on the back of a balding scalp facing out over the winding River Thames. As Aldwyn moved through the Victoria Tower Gardens, he took time, as ever, to pause beside the Buxton Memorial Fountain, which had been built to commemorate the emancipation of slaves in the British Empire.

Given the powerful demonstrations of the last year in particular and deeper social scrutiny on the historical issue, the memorial had taken on extra significance in Aldwyn's eyes and served as an emotive reminder of not only the suffering that slavery had inflicted but also the work of those who'd fought tenaciously for the abolition of slavery. Although some of the decorative figures adorning the statue had been stolen over the decades and the fountain had no longer been operational by the early 2000s, there had been significant restorative work carried out as part of the 200th anniversary of the abolition of slavery.

The place held a personal connection for Aldwyn too as he'd used to meet his handler in the gardens during his early days in the service, and before that, he'd spent time doing university study in the gardens. The architecture of the fountain had always fascinated him, with its octagonal base and four massive granite basins, whilst eight bronze figures surmounted the pinnacles at the angles of the octagon. Each of these figures represented a different ruler of England – from the ancient Britons led by Caractacus, through the Romans under Constantine, through the Normans under the command of William the Conqueror, and ending with Queen Victoria.

During the anti-racism movement the year before, Aldwyn had taken some time to revisit this particular spot. He'd reflected at the time that the memorial was less of a celebration to the end of slavery and more of a pat on the back for the MPs who'd supported the movement. He must have been at his cynical best that day, and seeing the fountain again now, he regretted his previous thoughts and only hoped that the memorial would continue to be well cared for.

As he moved beyond the fountain, his eyes scanned the benches either side of the man he was meeting but the gardens seemed uncharacteristically quiet. That suited him perfectly. He'd rather nobody had to hear what he wanted to say. As he walked towards the bench, he reached inside his jacket pocket and flicked a small switch on a key fob he carried with him everywhere. Another one of Simon's devices, it served to block any surveillance or recording equipment in the vicinity. This was to be a private conversation.

'Minister Atley.' Aldwyn gave the greeting before he'd settled himself onto the bench beside the Defence Minister. In the briefest of seconds that it had taken him to pass by the man, he'd studied the minister's features. It seemed that he'd managed to escape the affliction of sleep deprivation that many of his colleagues in the cabinet had been suffering over the past couple of days. Wearing the same creased, grey, out-of-time suit that he had in COBRA the day before, Seward Atley was smiling in a rather self-satisfied manner. To Aldwyn's surprise, there was something like a twinkle in those watery, brown eyes, and the veils that usually shrouded them from view appeared to have lifted slightly.

'Ah, if it isn't the Chief Spook himself,' declared Atley, his tone a mixture of sarcasm and praise. 'I suspect the DG is already looking over his shoulder. Your department will be in charge of every intelligence operation in the country, the rate you're going.' Despite the surviving feeble wisps of hair and the heavily lined and sagging features, there was nothing frail about Atley. He was a very canny politician and a shrewd judge of both character and situation.

'It would seem that I have you to thank for the increase in workload,' replied Aldwyn, returning the smile. 'Not your way of pushing me for the top job, I hope, Seward. My team and I operate best in the shadows, and that's where I'd like to remain.'

Atley laughed – a hoarse, humourless sound that echoed through the gardens. 'I forget how fond you spooks are of those fabled shadows. There's no such thing, I find, in a modern democracy. The public would have us interviewed on a weekly basis to keep our jobs. That's when they could fit it in around repeats of *Love Island* and Euro '96!' Clearly pleased with himself, he chortled away for several moments before composing himself enough to ask, 'So to what do I owe the pleasure? There must have been a reason for you to leave those shadows you're so fond of.'

'As a matter of fact, there is,' Aldwyn said shrewdly. 'Why did you get the shooting investigation transferred over to my department? You know as well as I do that, first and foremost, it should have been a police matter.' He suddenly had the feeling he was being sized up, as the Defence Minister's watery eyes appeared to look him up and down.

When Atley eventually answered, there was a rather nasty smile playing around his lips. 'Are you telling me that the investigation should be handed back to the police?'

'I don't appreciate being manipulated, Minister. If you had information about what this operation would uncover, then you should have come to me.'

Atley shrugged. 'We're old friends, and I know you can

be trusted. Besides, I've been in politics long enough to know there are no coincidences in terms of timing. A soldier drops dead, and a man is shot in London within hours of each other. There had to be a connection, and of course' – he smiled rather sarcastically once more – 'I trusted your team to sort it out. You have a reputation for getting the job done, shall we say? And, until now, you've tended not to ask awkward questions. In return, you're afforded the same courtesy.'

Haynes wasn't convinced. 'And what uncomfortable truths are you unwilling to tell me?' he asked, his eyes narrowing.

'Ah, now that's an open-ended question.' Atley laughed. 'Government is full of uncomfortable truths, I'm afraid. Most of which, I'm sure your ingenious bugging devices have learned already.' Then, with remarkable agility for a man his age, he sprang to his feet and attempted to straighten his crumpled suit. 'We'll talk again, but for now, Aldwyn, you must excuse me. Perhaps next time you might honour me with your presence at the club over a glass of port?' He held out his hand, which Haynes grasped, but before the minister turned to leave, he fixed his watery eyes upon Aldwyn once more and fired a parting shot: 'One more thing: I'd be much obliged if you'd call off your little surveillance team of terriers. It's most inconvenient trying not to step on them accidentally.'

And then he was gone, walking away through the gardens, as the sun beat down reflecting off the octagonal base of the Buxton Memorial Fountain.

Cursing under his breath, Aldwyn turned to face the river once more, glancing to his left and watching the London Eye turn almost imperceptibly, its booths moving gradually around its axis. The movement was almost hypnotic, much like the story he'd been spun by Seward Atley.

On every occasion he'd met with the Defence Minister, he'd been reminded of a giant spider spinning its enormous webs and catching political opponents and officials alike in its midst, like overripe flies. He was being lied to; Aldwyn was sure about that. Atley had perhaps known about the meeting that had taken place between the three men at that café, but might he know more than that? Aldwyn had the most uncomfortable feeling that he was being manipulated, and he was no nearer knowing what the final play was here. The two of them had come a long way since South Armagh, that was for sure.

It was time to get some answers, and he knew where to find some. He could no longer mollycoddle Hugh Palmer. The Health Secretary would have no choice but to answer his questions. His flat was situated just across from Parliament Square, Aldwyn knew. With one final look out over the river snaking past before his eyes, he rose from the bench and began to walk briskly back across the gardens. This time, he didn't pause to admire the fountain; instead, he strode past it, out of the gardens and onto the pavement beside the Palace of Westminster.

Glancing up and down the road, which barely housed any traffic these days after the terror incidents that had occurred outside Westminster, he continued at his quickened pace until it was halted abruptly by a small object hurtling into his leg at great velocity. Reeling, he fell to his knees and watched as the dark-red liquid oozed down his leg, dripping hypnotically onto the pavement below. Reaching down he clutched at the wound and swore loudly. His eyes raked the skyline and the surrounding rooftops, but he could see nothing.

Distant screams started up around him, as his hands gripped the area where the bullet had hit him. He'd heard the metallic clang as it had hit the pavement behind him and that offered him some comfort. The bullet had passed straight through. That did nothing to dispel the pain that was shooting up the whole right-hand side of his body, spreading from impact area.

Gritting his teeth so hard that they hurt, he tightened his hold as his eyes began to slide in and out of focus. A moment later they accepted defeat, and the darkness engulfed him.

9

Ollie had to admit he was impressed. Having been rather dragged along to this talk, he found himself entranced by the guest speaker. Perhaps the setting was adding to the energy and atmosphere Sophia Blanchet was generating in the portrait gallery. The gallery housed world-class pieces of Victorian and more modern artwork, as well as the infamously eerie oil painting by Edwin Landseer *Man Proposes, God Disposes*, which depicts a doomed arctic expedition in which ravenous polar bears devour human remains against a backdrop of a wrecked ship. It had been based on a real expedition led by Sir John Franklin and his two Royal Navy vessels in 1845, during which Franklin and all 129 of his men had disappeared in the Northwest Passage in the Canadian Arctic.

It had become one of the great mysteries of the nineteenth century, and many rescue attempts had been launched in an attempt to find out what had happened to Franklin and his crew. In the year following the incident, some of the bodies were found by local Inuits, who believed the bodies to have shown signs of cannibalism, and although the Victorians at the time refused to accept this, it was later proved by the discovery of three more crewmen in the 1980s that this was correct.

The men aboard had been driven to the very limits of human endurance and had resorted to cannibalism in an attempt to prolong their lives.

The painting had taken on a grizzly existence of its own behind the macabre history that it depicted. It was said that one student had been driven to suicide after looking directly into the eyes of one of the hulking, ruthless polar bears that was depicted feasting on human flesh. Some students had claimed the painting was a curse that plagued those exams that had been held in the picture gallery, and in the 1970s, it reached the point where students refused to take examinations within the gaze of the painting – at which point, the decision was made to cover it during exam season. At that same time every year, a Union Jack had adorned the painting, shrouding it from the view of the students sweating over the exam papers in the sweeping splendour of the gallery.

Perhaps the words being delivered took on extra resonance and fear beneath the gaze of the painting. Yet that wouldn't give enough credit to the woman standing on the raised wooden stage at the end of the gallery. It wasn't just the words, or the manner they were being delivered in, but the frequent eye contact and the pacing around the stage.

Immaculately dressed in a tailored, dark-blue peplum dress, she stepped out from behind the podium once more. When she spoke again, her voice was calmer, less impassioned and almost melancholic, the French accent more evident: 'As the well-known Greek proverb says "A society grows great when old men plant trees whose shade they know they shall never sit in." But your ancestors, my ancestors, our parents and grandparents didn't take heed. They didn't think about the future. Instead, they repeated the mistakes of history. Humanity has never learned from its past, and it's all of us who'll pay the price.'

Blanchet paused her pacing, fixing her gaze on the third row of her audience, where Ollie was seated. It was as though those sad hazel eyes were looking directly into his soul, making a direct plea to his own humanity. 'Previous generations declared war on nature, and it's those generations and their ancestors who hold the power of governing the world in their hands. The power to change. Yet they're more interested in feathering the nests of themselves and their contemporaries.

'The world has been changed forever by the virus that affected every single one of us. Nevertheless, it's merely been yet another excuse to close their eyes to the greatest threat our world faces. For too long, climate change has been last on their lists of actions. So long in fact that nature has decided to strike back. The counter offensive is taking many forms: from devastating cyclones and landslides destroying what were often the poorest communities to wildfires ripping through millions of homes and claiming the lives of over 1 billion native animals in their wake.'

Ollie had rarely felt such a hush descend over a group of people, particularly students. Many of those who'd attended today had made the usual jokes about going to non-compulsory talks like this. But there was no scepticism now. The attention of all those present was firmly on the professor, who was now fixing her gaze on the rows behind Ollie.

When she spoke again, her passion radiated through the gallery. 'It's time to stand up for nature. It's time for a cultural and natural revolution. Without change, those same elites will continue to plunder and destroy. Take back the power and give it back to the world we're merely custodians of.'

It was with a large sense of responsibility that Ollie hoisted his rucksack onto his shoulder and made his way through the building several minutes later. His mind had been elsewhere ever since he'd seen the news about the shooting in the Brecon

Beacons. It so happened that the barracks backed directly onto farmland owned by some of his relatives. What if this really was the start of another outbreak? If so, then he should really reach out to them.

The spectre of climate change had now taken root in his mind, perhaps for the first time ever. As he took the steps down to the lower floor and entered the circular courtyard, Ollie ripped the mask from his face and breathed in the fresh air. Even that came with a pang of guilt.

He found Mike waiting for him, a characteristic excitable grin on his face. It was rare to see him without a smile on his chestnut features, which accompanied his bubbly personality, and this was just one of the things that endeared him to the girls on campus, along with his neatly trimmed black hair and beard and his easy gift of the gab.

He slapped Ollie heartily on the back as his friend approached beaming. 'All set for tonight?' he asked enthusiastically. 'What time are the guys arriving?'

Ollie checked the TAG Heuer watch on his wrist, which had been a present from his parents after his A level results. 'Any time after 6pm.'

'And there was me thinking you would have been tracking Emma's every move.'

After turning slowly to look at his friend, Ollie said two words.

To this, his friend feigned offence. 'Whoa! All right, mate. Chill out. I was just messing. Didn't realise I'd touched such a nerve.' Mike laughed, his black eyes twinkling. 'We were all surprised she agreed to come, to be honest.'

'And why is that?' As soon as he'd said it, Ollie was wondering why he'd asked.

Mike, as ever, didn't disappoint. With a rather malevolent grin on his face, he joked, 'Well, mate, she was never that interested, and you never exactly hid how you felt. I wouldn't say you were like a puppy following her around, but… it was a bit like that!'

'Cheers, man,' replied Ollie quickly, 'appreciate it.'

Emma would be there tonight. Her presence always made Ollie feel somewhat self-conscious. His friends told him that he changed when he was around her. The two of them had known each other since primary school, and although it seemed stupid to cling to the memory, they'd used to hold hands together in the playground and given each other presents on Valentine's Day. Their parents, of course, had found it all very cute, and he supposed it had been. And then they'd been separated. At least that was how Ollie had seen it at the time. Her parents had sent her to a different secondary school to his, but that hadn't stopped them remaining close.

Increasingly, he'd become nervous around her when they'd met up in later years. They'd been close friends, but he wanted more. He'd yearned to kiss her, but he didn't know how to go about it or how to talk to her about how he felt. That indecision and conflict had manifested itself in rather awkward silences and the occasional weird comment. They'd drifted apart, and although they'd retained the semblance of a friendship, by the time both had started uni, they'd barely spoken. The initial lockdown during the pandemic had changed all that. On Ollie's part, he'd found some comfort in speaking to her, as though she were slipping her small hand in his again, as they once had, and was squeezing it to reassure him. He'd realised just how fragile and short life could be and had wanted no more regrets.

Yet, despite all that, this would be the first time he'd seen her for almost three years. She'd wanted to meet sooner, but she'd been studying abroad in France for a year and remained there throughout the pandemic and beyond to complete the year. Now she was back in the UK. And his nerves were back as well.

The two lads continued walking under the arches of the courtyard that had originally housed one of the first colleges for women in the UK. They'd just crossed the centre of the quad and the rather haughty-looking statue of Queen Victoria that gazed down over the students admonishingly as though she disapproved of their various antics.

It was a well-versed cliché amongst the students, but the building really did bear a strikingly resemblance to the Hogwarts in his imagination from reading the Harry Potter books as a child, with its circular, red-brick towers, tall chimney stacks, and secret passageways hidden behind the richly carpeted floors and spectacular tapestries. The clock tower that adorned the northern face of the building was colloquially referred to as the 'Dragon Tower' due to the reptilian-shaped gargoyles that flanked the clockface.

Largely inspired by the Chateau of Chambord in the Loire Valley region of France, the building was Grade 1 listed and dominated the campus, even in the face of the newly purpose-built library that was its modern day equivalent and stood boldly facing its elder counterpart. The interior of the building was just as impressive as the exterior, with the corridors resplendent with creaking floorboards leading into the picture gallery or towards the ground-floor chapel, both of which were of equal beauty. The chapel was serenely awe-inspiring, with scenes from the Old Testament beautifully reworked on the understudy of the chapel ceiling, whilst the apse was loosely inspired by the creation scene in the Sistine Chapel – in this case, showing God pointing at Eve rather than Adam. Increasingly, Ollie had found it hard to find peace in the world, but the chapel instilled a calmness in him that had been hard to find elsewhere in the past two years.

The first couple of months of this uni year, essentially locked up away from their families and friends, had perhaps not helped, but in truth, Ollie had been relieved at the time that he didn't have to return home to face the reality of what had happened. It had suited him to be locked away in their uni house, unable to really go out or return home due to the risks of spreading the virus that had swept through the vast majority of the student population. Of course, he'd known that he'd already had the virus once before – how could he forget? – but it seemed it was possible to catch it more than once. Yet not even that had offered an escape route for him.

'*Oi, dickhead!*'

Mike's shout wrenched him back to his surroundings and he realised he'd been walking at an angle, cutting across his friend. They both laughed.

Mike said, 'I didn't realise me insulting you would make you go blind. You should be used to it after all these years! Or were you thinking about someone else?'

'Shut it,' retorted Ollie, smiling. 'I don't know what I did to deserve ending up at the same uni as you after spending primary and secondary school listening to your crap!'

'Admit it. You only chose this place because I was coming here.'

'As if.' Ollie grinned. 'You picked it after I said I had!'

'Nah, you've got that all wrong. Must be that memory of your playing tricks on you again – the same memory that thinks you have a chance with Emma.'

'You're getting close to the line, mate,' Ollie growled in a falsely aggressive voice, which his friend saw through straight away and laughed at. 'She's coming, isn't she? She can't hate me that much.'

'She doesn't hate you, man. You're just firmly in the friend zone.' Mike was laughing again, his chestnut features glistening in a sunbeam. 'You're wasting your time. I'm telling you, go for Grace. When has my advice ever been wrong?'

Ollie brought his hand to his mouth and affected a mock thinking expression. 'Er, what about the time you told me to steal that guy's shisha pipe, and he broke my nose just for trying to touch it?'

Mike laughed even harder, as Ollie's hand moved subconsciously to his suddenly fragile nose, as though the ghost of the punch had flitted across his face.

'Or when you told me to tell the bouncer I wasn't drunk, but I was working undercover and that's why he shouldn't chuck me out the club?'

'Exactly,' Mike stated with a chortle, 'top advice, mate.'

'I've still got the bruises from your "great advice",' Ollie scoffed. 'I think I'll just do my own thing.'

Mike stopped laughing and his face became mildly serious. 'Look, man, I'm just trying to help. We all know you struggle with girls. It's just a confidence issue, and I know just the thing that can help you with that.'

'I've told you before that I'm not interested.' Ollie, resolute, hitched his rucksack more firmly onto his shoulder. 'I'll stick with liquid confidence and see where that gets me.'

'Your loss.'

This was accompanied with a punch to the forearm, causing Ollie to chase Mike down past the prefabricated geography building. On eventually catching up with his friend, Ollie sent him sprawling by tripping him at the ankles, and then Ollie ran down the sloping campus as he heard Mike swearing loudly at him from behind. He glanced back at his friend, whilst still running forwards, and felt himself collide with a human-shaped figure. His back arched, and he dropped temporarily to his knees. Looking up, he felt his heart sink and the renewed sound of Mike's laughter only added to his embarrassment.

Without paying attention to where he was going, he'd run directly into Grace, knocking her backwards and sending the two books she'd been carrying crashing to the ground. Now he found himself on his knees looking up at her in what could be interpreted as the most cringe proposal ever. Despite the strange pose, Grace was smiling as she looked down at him, her eyebrows slightly raised.

Even at this angle, Ollie found her extremely attractive, with her silky olive skin, tapered waist, burnished complexion and flowing, black hair that hung to just below her shoulders. He was suddenly aware that his face had become very flushed and red. He got slowly to his feet, picking up her books as he did so and smiling rather sheepishly. Grace had a small button nose framed by delicate ears and arched eyebrows that soared over sweeping eyelashes. As ever, he felt himself entranced by her firmament-blue eyes and plump, heart-shaped lips.

He opened his mouth to speak, but he found that the words were trapped somewhere in his throat, and all that came out was a strange, strangled noise.

'Are you OK?' asked Grace, a look of concern appearing on her attractive features, her voice as light and dulcet as ever.

'He's suffering from a severe case of prickitis.' Mike had appeared behind Ollie, and he thumped his friend on the back.

'Hi,' Ollie said awkwardly and in a high-pitched voice that he didn't recognise as his own. What was wrong with him? His cheeks were still warm, and he found it difficult to meet Grace's eyes. Instead, he spoke to her feet, focussing on her black designer sandals. 'How are things?'

He chanced a glance upwards, and for a second, he was afraid she might think he was looking up the tightly fitted pencil skirt she wore. This was ridiculous. Steeling himself, Ollie looked up at Grace and saw she was wearing a rather amused expression.

Her tongue played around her lips for a second, moistening

them before she responded: 'Yeah, good. You didn't seem yourself in the seminar. Something on your mind?'

Again, it was Mike who replied, and Ollie cursed his friend silently. 'Probably worrying about the big night out tonight. You coming, yeah?'

If Ollie could have sworn in that moment, then he would have shouted the ugliest swear word he could think of.

'Night out?' asked Grace puzzled.

For once, Mike had shut up. He seemed to realise he'd put his foot in it.

Ollie forced himself to smile. 'Yeah, didn't I mention? Some friends of ours are coming to the uni tonight, and we're heading to the Students' Union. You wanna come?' He could tell from the slightly hurt look in her twinkling, blue eyes that she knew he'd concealed the party from her.

'Sure,' she replied eventually with a very forced smile. 'What time do you want me there?'

Ollie didn't know whether to feel relieved, embarrassed or both, but he tried to keep his smile as natural as possible as he said, 'About 8pm?'

Grace nodded rather stiffly. 'Cool. Well, I'll see you then.' And then she was gone, walking up a side path through the woods that sat at the bottom of the campus, the tops of the trees hiding the turrets of Founders Building from view.

Ollie watched her go, and not for the first time, regret scratched at his inside. He smiled awkwardly as she turned back to look at him, before disappearing into the trees. He knew what was coming and moved to pre-empt it. 'Don't start all right,' he said to Mike, swearing as he did so. 'Just don't start. I know.'

Mike raised his hands at the look Ollie shot him and imitated an American accent, 'All right, all right, all right.'

'Thanks, Lando,' muttered Ollie.

10

This is all turning into a bloody mess, thought Ben Viper as he strode down a side corridor of The Grid, a file clutched under his arm. *First Henderson, and now this.* He'd warned Aldwyn who would have been involved and deduced the identity of the sniper, but Aldwyn hadn't listened to him. He'd already seen the ballistics report, and – as expected – it showed that the same weapon used to kill Harold Morris had been used to gun down his boss. Ben had been right: their unit was being targeted.

It was at this moment that the pods slid open with a hiss, and Ben made an involuntary jerk forwards. Two people had stepped forwards into The Grid, but he had eyes for only one. He could tell at once that she looked shaken, her nougat-brown hair was dishevelled, two ugly bruises were already forming on her forehead, and dried blood was crusted around her nose and mouth. There was a rather empty look in those usually jewel-bright green eyes that concerned him more than the physical wounds.

At last, her eyes had located him, and Ben found himself unable to move for a split second before he regained his composure and swept across the floor towards her. For a moment, they looked at one another, and then he gave her a swift but telling hug. He tried to put a lot of unsaid apologies into that hug, and perhaps she understood, because when she pulled away, there was the trace of a tear in her eyes.

'How are you feeling? I've spoken to the doctor who examined you, and she says there's no lasting damage, but even so, you must be feeling shaken up.'

'What happened to patient confidentiality?' muttered Jackie, and that made them both smile. 'I don't appreciate being spied on, even if your friend arrived in time to save me.' She gestured at Zaf.

The other MI5 agent was smiling, however. 'If you don't want to be spied on, you've come to the right place. I think my soldiering days are over. You wouldn't believe the damage that training does to your knees. It turns out that spying fieldwork is much less intensive.'

Ben half smiled, but he couldn't meet his colleague's eyes. 'Thanks, Zaf. We're all gathering in the briefing room, and I'd like Detective Ambrose to join us.'

He saw a flicker of surprise cross Jackie's face momentarily before she nodded and made to follow him towards the briefing room.

On reaching the sliding door to the conference room, Ben slid it open to find a man seated at the end of the conference table in front of the TV monitors. He looked a lot paler than the last time they'd seen each other, and his close-set, deadened grey eyes seemed to have lost the last of their colour in the hours since they'd last sat opposite each other, but Aldwyn Haynes was already back at work. Ben should have expected as much from the moment he'd been told that his boss was out of surgery and the bullet wound to his leg wouldn't leave any lasting damage.

On closer inspection, Ben could see a pair of crutches propped against the edge of the desk, and the incident had done nothing, it seemed, to improve Aldwyn's mood, as he scowled at the entrance of his team.

When he spoke, however, there was a rather sarcastic edge to his voice. 'You'll forgive me if I don't rush to greet you all. Detective Ambrose, I'm glad you're able to join us. Aldwyn Haynes, section chief of this little band of ours.' The bullet wound seemed to have made his Yorkshire accent more pronounced. 'Please' – he gestured towards the chairs – 'be seated.'

Maya and Simon seemed to be temporarily lost for words as they lowered themselves into their seats, and Helen clicked her tongue in disapproval at her boss attending the meeting. Of all the team, she and Simon had known Aldwyn the longest, and they'd formed a close bond – as close as colleagues in their line of work could, of course.

'Ah, I see young Zafar here has been lax on all the details as usual,' said Aldwyn, spotting Jackie's gaze upon him. 'I had the unfortunate pleasure of being the target of a sniper earlier today. Strangely, given they must have had a free shot, they only hit my leg, and the bullet passed straight through above my knee. There will be no lasting damage. It seems that the bullet was merely designed to slow me down from reaching the Health Minister's flat in time. I assume we're all up to date with the supposed suicide of Hugh Palmer.'

They all nodded, but it was again Jackie who spoke. Ben couldn't help but smile to himself. She didn't seem at all fazed by her surroundings, although she was in the headquarters of MI5 for the first time, nor that she'd just been through a terrible ordeal herself. Her white blouse and smart pencil skirt were dotted with droplets of blood, but she seemed totally unperturbed. It was as if Jackie were working any other case as a detective, trying to piece together evidence.

'I don't understand what the Health Minister had to do

with all of this, and are you telling us that it wasn't a suicide?' she queried.

Aldwyn sighed rather heavily, his gaze at last found Ben's, and he nodded.

After rising from his chair, Ben rounded the table and stood beside his boss before addressing the rest of the team: 'I hope Zaf has briefed you on the identity of the man shot in Central London.' He took from Jackie's nod that the answer was yes, but he was conscious that he may need to elaborate.

'The truth is that Morris had set up a meeting with the Health Minister, Hugh Palmer, and was on his way to meet Palmer when he was shot by the sniper. Exactly why Palmer wanted to meet Morris, we don't know, but it seems clear there was some information he wanted to reveal to Morris, and we have to assume this was the reason why he was killed. Unfortunately' – he glanced at his boss, who didn't look up or meet his eye – 'we were unable to find out what Palmer knew about the meeting, if anything. He's now been found dead, a presumed suicide, with him being hanged from the bathroom ceiling. The boss was on his way to speak with Palmer when he was shot.'

'Whoever is behind Palmer's death was also responsible for shooting Aldwyn,' interceded Helen Robinson. 'Surely we should focus our efforts on tracking down the sniper who shot Aldwyn, which could lead us to the rest of the people behind this?'

'Touched as I am by your concern,' murmured Aldwyn, 'let's leave the saga of who shot Aldwyn for another time. There are more pressing concerns, and I don't think the shooter is our best lead in finding out about these people. They could be any sharpshooting assassin from around the globe who's been paid to do two hits in London. It's quite likely they know nothing about the wider plans these people have.'

Ben resisted the urge to contradict his boss, knowing that there was more behind his decision not to pursue the shooter for the time being. 'Simon has been looking into Private Stephen Faye, the man who tried to kill Detective Ambrose, and it seems he received a transfer of £100,000 into an offshore account held in his name last week.'

Simon wiped his spectacles hurriedly before nodding rather frantically. 'The money was wired through three back-routing multiple-SWIFT-code systems, but the whole thing wasn't especially elaborate. It didn't take much digging for me to find the account in the Cayman Islands and track it to the private or to trace the money. It seems that someone is making a joke at our expense. If you backtrace the money, it appears that Private Faye was paid from a Treasury account.'

'Given how tightly this Chancellor of the Exchequer likes to keep a hold of every penny, I highly doubt it,' Aldwyn grumbled darkly. 'They may inadvertently be giving us a glimpse into who's behind all this.' He paused and glanced briefly at Ben, who knew in that second that his boss would be revealing their shared suspicions to the rest of the team, but not yet, it seemed.

Instead, wincing slightly, he leaned forwards and gazed around at each person in turn before settling on Jackie. He spoke heavily, and there was a sour edge to his voice that left nobody in any doubt as to his personal feelings on the matter. 'It's been communicated from the PM that Private Stephen Faye will be buried with military honours, and the PM himself will make a speech expressing his condolences at the tragic loss of another member of the 1st Battalion Rifles. It's been decided that the scandal of him murdering the wife of his close friend and fellow soldier shouldn't be exposed. In short, the whole sequence of events at Senta Barracks will be covered up.

'Corporal Matheson died of a heart condition induced by over-intensive army training, his wife was tragically murdered by a member of the local community, and Private Faye was killed attempting to avenge her death. That's the story that will be reported to the press, and that's the sequence of events that the officers at Senta Barracks will have to swear to. I understand that the MOD and the Home Office are in discussion with a certain Major Pollard in an attempt to stop him resigning his commission over the matter. I'm sure we'll also share the sentiment of the major's stance if not the same naivety.'

Ben glanced at Aldwyn, who sighed rather heavily, a flicker of pain rippling across his ageing features.

Aldwyn said slowly, 'Ever since we discovered Corporal Matheson's route on the day he disappeared for a few weeks, Ben and I have the same working hypothesis.' The effort of speaking seemed a little too much for him, and he gestured for Ben to pick up the theory instead, which he did.

'If you recall,' he began brusquely, 'we tracked Corporal Matheson's car until he turned onto the A338, and then we lost him temporarily before picking him up again on CCTV refilling his car at a petrol station on the Salisbury Road. It was shortly after that when we lost track of him for good for three weeks. Wiltshire isn't necessarily the most obscure place for a military man to visit. It's a military county. In fact, it's home to nearly a fifth of the entire British Army, if they were all home at the same time. The army is by far the biggest employer in the county, and Salisbury Plain is home to the largest military training site in the country, where they can practise everything from tank manoeuvres to covert operations.

'It's commonplace to see military personnel around the sleepy villages that litter the county. You'll remember the large military presence that was deployed after the Novichok attack on a former Russian spy and his daughter in 2018. They were able to be mobilised in a matter of hours due to the mass of military personnel already stationed around Wiltshire.' He paused, aware that something rather sickening was tickling at the back of his throat. 'But in light of recent events, I suspect there was a more likely destination for Corporal Matheson.'

It was Helen who seemed to catch his meaning first. 'You don't mean…?'

Nodding his head gravely, Ben replied, 'Porton Down.' There were a few worried glances around the table, and he noticed Zaf had straightened in his seat, suddenly alert. 'Think about it: he vanishes into thin air for three weeks, then reappears after all that time, and finally ends up dying a few days later from a virus that shows signs of having been manipulated and tested with. Just a couple of miles away from where he disappears, there just happens to be the biggest scientific lab in the country. Not only that but a lab that has a history of testing all manner of weapons – chemical and biological.'

'Are you telling me,' Zaf began slowly, his expression harder than before, 'that they were testing this stuff on our own military? Is that what you're saying?'

Jackie looked alarmed too. 'British scientists tampered with a virus that killed tens of thousands of our citizens and tested it on Corporal Matheson?'

Ben held up his hands for calm. 'I'm saying it's a possibility. Just consider all the testing that Porton Down's been involved with in the past. Only a fraction of the truth has been made public. The scientific division of the MOD has worked semi-independently for decades, with very little reproach. Look at the information we have available.' Using the pointer clenched in his fist, he indicated the bank of screens behind him, on which the image of the three figures sitting around a table outside a café appeared once more.

'We've been able to identify all three of the men in this image, but we didn't know why they'd be meeting. Look at what we know about each of them and their recent activities: Harold Morris was involved in undisclosed work with the MOD, the soldier killed goes missing for three weeks in the area of Porton Down and, finally, Peter Vallance' – he motioned to the shortest and oldest of the three men, with his wisps of grey hair – 'the scientist who set up his own laboratories and was involved in tampering with and creating chemical and biological weapons, and then turned MI6 asset, who's been cosily working for the MOD in recent times. Where else would you place an eminent scientist like Vallance? Porton Down. Before his now-comfy retirement at a British university, of course.'

Realisation was obviously dawning on the faces of many of his colleagues, but Zaf still seemed sceptical. 'So our government has been authorising the testing of coronavirus strains at Porton Down? Testing on a soldier who then died. And then they've been covering it up ever since?'

'Loath as I am to come to the defence of the politicians,' Aldwyn interjected quietly, 'it's possible they had no idea what was taking place in those labs. I agree with Ben that it seems likely the strain of virus used on this poor corporal was tampered with and cultivated in our own labs at Porton Down. Whether he volunteered for the testing, we may never know, but it could be that he wasn't meant to die.'

'What we can say,' added Ben, 'is that Henderson and the people he's working for were most likely aware of this information. We have to consider the possibility that they've managed to get their hands on more of the virus cultivated at Porton Down, and they've been responsible for the deaths of anyone who may have been able to reveal the truth about what went on there. The deaths of the corporal's widow, the Health

Minister and Harold Morris were designed to slow us down in working out how this all started.'

Surprisingly, it was Jackie who spoke next, and it was the detective inside her that asked, 'Where's the third man, Vallance? If you're right, then he'll be targeted next, and he might be the only one capable of confirming what you think.'

'That matter is in hand,' responded Aldwyn. 'I know we've been pushing our MOD contacts as much as possible, and the fact we've yielded no more intelligence from them tells me that's a lost cause. We need to start thinking outside the box. That's why I'm so keen for Detective Ambrose to stay with us until the end of this crisis; we need some fresh eyes.'

At that exact moment, the doors to the briefing room slid open and a very nervous-looking woman appeared in the doorway. She was in her early twenties, with cropped black hair and curious brown eyes that spent most of her day darting across intelligence reports and unintelligible gibberish passed to her by GCHQ. It was unheard of for her to enter the briefing room, and her nerves were evident. In her left palm, she was clutching a small sheet of paper, which contained just half a dozen words.

'I'm sorry to interrupt, sir,' Lydia said, her eyes were fixed on Aldwyn, and there was barely a flicker of surprise to find her boss in the room just hours after being shot in the leg, 'but, um, the PM is here. He wants to see you in your office immediately.'

11

Ben Viper didn't feel the slightest bit uncomfortable as he stood by the door to his boss's office, watching the PM pace the small, scarcely furnished room. He'd declined the offer of a drink and had instead spent the past two minutes attempting to wear the plum carpet down to a few strands of fabric. Aldwyn Haynes limped into the room and rather collapsed into the leather-backed chair behind his desk; he gestured for the PM to take the seat opposite, which he also declined with a curt shake of his head. Both intelligence agents waited patiently for the PM to stop his pacing, which he did by coming to rest in a leaning position across the desk, his knuckles pressed against the sumptuous walnut surface. It was almost unheard of for the PM to make the short trip down the river to visit his domestic intelligence service.

It had been a difficult two years for the man in his immaculate tailored, blue suit, due to the significant divisions in his party as well as a large range of policy decisions they'd been forced to make a U-turn on. That had been before the pandemic, during which the government's handling of the crisis had been roundly criticised by anyone who hadn't been part of the decision-making group. There had followed mass anti-racism protests that had garnered so much interest and controversy. Yet, despite all of that, here he still was, leading the country through perhaps its most difficult period since the Second World War. There was much to be admired about the man's resilience, at the very least.

If they weren't able to get hold of this crisis, however, it would surely mean the end for him. The stories that had already begun to emerge in the press had undermined his decision to keep a lid on the situation at Senta Barracks. Perhaps it was desperation that had brought him to Thames House tonight, but Ben wasn't so sure.

'Firstly,' began the PM, breathing deeply despite his calm tone, 'I'd like to say how very pleased I am to see you still alive, Aldwyn.'

'Thank you, Prime Minister,' Aldwyn replied.

The PM's watchful, green eyes had narrowed somewhat. 'Whether you should be out of hospital so soon, I'm not so sure, but I understand you were insistent that you return to work. Ordinarily, I'd intervene, but we need our best people right now. And that' – he paused, as though trying to keep his voice under control – 'takes me to the question that's brought me here tonight. What the hell is going on?

'Since you've taken over the investigation, the situation appears to have escalated. The soldier's widow has been murdered down the road from Senta Barracks; my Health Minister has been found dead, supposedly suicide; one of our country's most senior intelligence officials has been shot outside the Palace of Westminster; and we appear to be no nearer to finding out who's behind these attacks.'

All traces of pain and apprehension were gone as Aldwyn met the PM's eyes. 'Regarding the shootings, we're still no nearer to identifying the shooter or how they've gained access to the rooftops of what's most likely a government building.'

Ben noticed his boss was avoiding his eye as he said

this, and he resolved to broach the subject at a time when a semblance of colour had returned to his boss's face.

'We're coordinating with all branches of the police, intelligence community and armed forces to find some answers, but so far we've drawn a blank,' Aldwyn confessed.

'I'm sorry, Mr Haynes, but that simply isn't good enough,' the PM interrupted (and Ben noticed immediately his switch to a more formal tone), 'I'm sure you can recall the mass panic that was triggered by a terrorist attack on Westminster Bridge. This was a shooting right outside the building that's a symbol of British democracy. The press is already having a field day, whipping the public into a hysteria we can hardly afford given the current situation.'

'I accept that we should have more intelligence on this matter,' Aldwyn responded frankly, 'but we don't at this moment in time. We have, however, identified a number of other individuals connected with this plot, and we have operatives in the field now.'

'And who are these individuals?' demanded the PM.

Ben could see his boss was hesitating, and he knew why.

It was in a rather more measured tone that Aldwyn Haynes continued: 'I think it would be better, Prime Minister, if you didn't know the exact nature of our operation until such time as we can give you a thorough briefing. The success of our operations relies on them being utterly secret.' It was obvious he'd chosen each word especially delicately.

The PM's eyes narrowed, and he turned to address Ben this time. 'Secrecy or not, I want a report from you into the possibility that Hugh Palmer was murdered. As for the leaks in the press, I may well be employing your services there too, but for now, I have my own people looking into them. Rest assured that they won't undermine your investigation.'

Both Ben and Aldwyn nodded.

'As to the threat of the virus, we've received no demands, and there are no signs of an imminent attack, are there?' asked the PM, returning his attention to the section chief.

'Nothing,' confirmed Aldwyn. 'There are no reports of an outbreak, and we've received no intelligence related to an imminent threat to the public. Security has naturally been increased around all government buildings and potential high-profile targets.'

'That's something I can tell the foreign ambassadors at least – although let's hope it's rather more successful than the increased security that didn't stop you being shot outside Westminster in the middle of the day.' There was a pause before the PM continued swiftly, 'I expect to be kept up to date. There will be another COBRA briefing tomorrow, and I expect you both to attend. I'd advise you don't tell the cabinet that you believe them to be indiscreet, even if that may be the case.

'I realise the pressures that we're placing on you and your team, but the country may not be able to withstand another wave of the virus, nor a large terror attack. Whatever it takes to find these people, do it. Any repercussions, we can deal with those another time.'

'Thank you, Prime Minister,' said Aldwyn, a ripple of pain evident in his Yorkshire accent.

The PM surveyed him shrewdly before his mouth creaked into a smile, as though it were a great effort. 'I always find a glass of single malt takes the edge off.' He moved to the leave the room, and Ben stepped to one side to allow him to pass.

On reaching the door, the PM turned suddenly. 'And Aldwyn, if you ever imply that I or my office are indiscreet again, then you'll be enjoying that enforced leave I've spared you from.'

Then he was gone, and the door swooshed shut behind him.

There was a brief silence before Aldwyn said wryly, 'Nothing like a politician lecturing us about secrecy. He did have one good idea, though.' Reaching down to the drawer beneath his desk, he withdrew a bottle of single malt whisky and rested it on the walnut surface before placing a crystal glass beside it. 'A perk of being the boss, I'm afraid.' He smiled at Ben. 'I need you at your sharpest. Talk to me about Porton Down.'

Ben crossed the room in a stride and seated himself opposite his boss, watching him grimace as the amber liquid disappeared down his throat. 'We know very little about the work that's done there. The MOD is more paranoid about security than the Kremlin. We've tried to get operatives in there undercover before, but they've never passed the MOD vetting. I spoke to a contact of mine who retired from the MOD last year, and all he could tell me was that they'd been conducting viral testing there in the aftermath of the pandemic, supposedly to help develop a vaccine. That was all he knew.

'As we appreciate, this wouldn't be the first time that Porton Down has tampered with a deadly strain of virus or disease. It deals with some of the world's most dangerous pathogens on a daily basis. Anything from anthrax to the plague, it's been studied there, primarily to develop means of fighting these diseases, but we both know that isn't where its remit ends. It's been responsible for testing chemical and biological weapons for decades, even after we ratified the Chemical Weapons Convention, notably in respect to sarin gas and other nerve agents. The work conducted there is often secret, even from the top levels of government, and the scientists there have a certain amount of autonomy with regard to the work that they conduct.

'During the pandemic, the labs there were commissioned to help work towards uncovering a vaccine for the virus, so we know they were looking into strains of the virus, and theoretically, they would have been manipulating and tampering with them in order to try to develop an effective vaccine. What we don't know – and the MOD is unlikely to tell us – is whether that's where Porton Down's remit ends with regards to the virus. It's possible that it's been developing a more lethal strain of the virus, perhaps just for research purposes. It also has a history of experimenting on servicemen and women. In the 1950s, the first human testing of sarin gas was conducted on servicemen.'

The section chief agreed. 'I personally find it a scary thought that a scientist as dangerous as Peter Vallance could have an element of free rein at our largest research facility. As to whether or not this was sanctioned research, we may never know. Whoever is behind this and why, they seem to be eliminating anyone who may have actively been involved in the development programme.'

'I concur. I suspect that, if the virus hadn't killed Corporal Matheson, then his friend Private Faye would have made sure he couldn't alert us as to what's going on. The only person they haven't yet got is Vallance himself. He may be able to provide us with some of the answers at least.' He paused, considering the man who had just the left the room. 'Do you think the PM will resign?'

Aldwyn eased back in his chair, grimacing as he took another gulp of whisky. 'If this virus gets loose or there's another attack, then he'll have no choice. Until then, he seems up for the fight. God help us if he leaves us in the hands of Seward Atley.'

Ben nodded once more, shifting slightly in his seat. 'We should have the latest report from the surveillance team following Atley soon. In this job, you learn that there's rarely such a thing as coincidence, and you met with Atley right before you were shot. Talking of which—'

At that moment, however, they were interrupted by the door swooshing open once more, and Maya Chowdhury hurried in, a folder clutched in her hand.

'*Haven't I told you to knock?*' winced Aldwyn Haynes. 'Even the PM has more respect for this office than you lot!'

'Sorry, sir. I mean, we have an urgent situation,' Maya gabbled rather hurriedly.

It was clear from the slight note of panic in her voice that something was wrong, and Ben got to his feet immediately. It had to be Henderson. They'd struck again.

12

Grabbing the bottle of fluorescent-purple liquid, Ollie clumsily poured out another eight shots into the double-sized shot glasses and swished his down his throat in one, before the others even had a chance to pick up their measure, savouring the sickly nectar. He shook the bottle; there couldn't be more than another shot left inside. He brought it up to lips and drained it before discarding the empty Sourz bottle into the laundry basket that had become a temporary home for the empties.

The wooden dining table was sticky with the various substances that had been spilled in the last hour, with an overturned plastic cup being the last remnant of the beer pong games that just ended. A music video was playing on the OLED TV that lay in the lounge area to the left, with two beaten-down, grey sofas arranged opposite. The rest of the open-plan area was a mess, despite Ollie's feeble attempts to clear up before the girls had arrived, and the smell of takeaway pizza hung temptingly in the air.

They'd already played a game of Cards Against Humanity before beer pong, but Ollie never found the answers funny until he was properly drunk. There was a way to go until he felt that sensation, but he knew it wouldn't take long, and he was partly drinking to avoid people's eyes. He found his gaze wandering towards Emma once more; she was leaning against the back of one of the sofas, laughing with Robbie, although she threw the occasional glance his way.

As soon as he'd received her text saying she was near the address he'd sent her, Ollie had felt his palms begin to become slippery with sweat. Those nerves had only intensified when he'd opened the front door and seen the tight-fitting Tiger Mist playsuit she was wearing. It showed off her figure perfectly, cutting off just below her hourglass waist and the light-pink fabric matched the pale-peach shade of lipstick she wore that served to entice him towards her plump lips. The lipstick aside, she wore little make-up, but she had a natural beauty all the same, with her pencil-thin eyebrows easing down gently to her beetle's-leg, black eyelashes, adding to the flowing, light-brown hair with a single blonde strand that hung loosely over her forehead, and brown eyes that seemed to radiate warmth.

As ever in her presence, he'd felt temporarily paralysed and became uncomfortably aware of how stupid he must look with his arms hanging uselessly by his sides. He frantically thought of a way to make them seem less awkward, but in doing so, he realised that his whole body felt tense and out of place. He'd only unstiffened as she'd smiled and leaned forwards to press her lips gently against his cheek in greeting. He'd barely noticed her friend, Anna, following her inside, as he'd stepped to the side to allow them in. As ever, her laugh was infectious, and he found himself captivated by it. He'd already received one swift punch to the ribs from Will for staring at her too long.

The pain had been made worse by Grace arriving shortly afterwards, as his eyes – like those of the other boys – had been drawn towards her when she entered in a blood-red, strapless peplum top complete with belt and tight-fitting, black leather leggings. Her elegant black hair was tied up in a bun, and she wore shimmery eyeliner that accentuated the constellation-like sparkling of her blue eyes. She too had planted a swift kiss on his cheek as she passed by, although he'd seen her eyes flash in a mischievous way that suggested she hadn't completely forgotten his oversight in not inviting her originally. He couldn't shake the feeling that his head was utterly scrambled, and part of him wanted to drink himself into unconsciousness to uncomplicate the situation for himself.

He was abruptly wrenched out of his thoughts as a figure came bounding towards him. Ollie's arm twitched, ready to adopt a defensive-block position, before he realised it was Mike.

'*Whoa,*' shouted his friend, '*easy mate. Don't take me out!*' He punched Ollie a little too hard on the arm, and Ollie made a mental note to pay him back for that one later. As usual, Mike was excitable, bouncing on the balls of his feet, although he inclined his head away from the overhead spotlights as though the light were somehow blinding him.

At that moment, Robbie joined them. Robbie was tall and clean-shaven with short, bleached-blond hair, and according to the girls at school, he was good-looking, with handsome, brown eyes and an athletic figure. He'd been one of the cleverest people in their year, achieving high marks in all the sciences and maths, which had earned him an offer from Cambridge, but he'd elected to decline it, claiming the place didn't have enough personality for him. He'd chosen instead to join University College London (UCL), largely on account of wanting to enjoy the London lifestyle to the max, and barely three days went by without him posting a video from some bar or another in Central London.

This wasn't the first time he'd been to visit Ollie at Royal Holloway University. The two of them had known each other for almost eight years, having been on the same bus route during their first year at secondary school, and they'd quickly

133

become really good friends. He was one of the people that Ollie always felt comfortable being around, and unlike some of his other friends, he was able to confide in Robbie. He was easy-going and great fun to be around, but he also had the talent of being of a good listener, and besides simply having a lot in common and having once played for the same football team, they'd listened to each other's problems in a way that wasn't possible with the others.

Having both chosen to study at the same uni, doing the same course in the field of media, Cap and Will had arrived together from Bristol in the battered Volkswagen Polo that Cap seemed intent on damaging beyond all recognition. Ollie wouldn't have believed it possible for its sides to be more dented than the last time he'd seen the car, but there was barely any red paint remaining on the left-hand side and a fresh crater in the rear bumper.

Although he'd never been as close to Cap as the other boys, they were still good friends, and neither would want to see the other annoyed. With his close-set, beetle-black eyes and watchful gaze, Cap had gained a reputation for being the peacemaker on nights out. Even so, you wouldn't want to mess with him; he was the most muscular of the friends, with broad shoulders and rippling biceps. He'd earned the nickname whilst stopping a group of guys from starting on Mike in a smoking area in a club in London, and when they'd refused to back down, he'd knocked one to the ground with a punch to the gut and the phrase 'I could do this all day.' Like his namesake, Captain America, there wasn't an aggressive bone in his body, but he was fiercely loyal to his friends.

'If you want my advice,' mused Robbie, gripping Ollie's shoulder, 'and remember this isn't me at my sober philosophical best here – you and Emma have had plenty of chances to make a thing of it. You've danced around each other for years, and neither of you have really gone for it. Maybe that's because it just isn't meant to be. You're different when she's around, you clam up and you're less fun. That's not the case with Grace. I've seen the two of you out together before, and it just works. You just need to be less of a prick and go for it.'

Twenty minutes later, and the advice still hadn't worked. Mike and Robbie grabbed him by the arm and frogmarched him away from the card game that was happening at the dining room table and into Mike's room at the end of the ground floor, just before the garden. Robbie shut the door firmly behind them once all three friends had crammed inside. It was a small room with a single bed pressed against the far wall and an even smaller desk squeezed along the opposite side, with the chair protruding from underneath it leaving little space between the desk and the bed. No carpet was visible beneath the myriad of discarded clothes and books and the broken guitar that lay strewn over the floor. There was a dirt-stained mirror hanging above the desk, which looked as though it hadn't been cleaned for years.

It was Mike who swore at him first, and Ollie noticed against that his friend's eyes were wider than usual, and he was sweating a little, although it wasn't the warmest evening.

Robbie laughed but echoed the sentiment. 'What the hell are you playing at, mate? What's with all the creepy smiles and weird silences?'

Ollie was caught between anger and amusement at the obvious frustration on their faces. They'd been down this path in the past, and even though he knew his friends had his best interests at heart, it always felt like they were digging him out of his failures and pushing him to be something that he wasn't. Why couldn't they just focus on their own evening? Why were they so obsessed with getting involved in his all the time? In the back of his mind, he knew there was only one way to shut them up, and he wanted to do it; he just found himself incapable. He didn't know why, but he certainly didn't need his friends highlighting his flaws to him and making him feel worse.

It was as though Robbie had read his mind. 'Look, man,' he said in a less exasperated and aggressive voice, adopting a more understanding tone, 'we just want to help you. You're a great guy, and there are two great girls who really like you.' He paused, a smile creasing his lips. 'I have no idea why they do, but for whatever reason, they like you over any of us.'

Now it was Ollie's turn to swear at his friends, both of whom laughed, although Mike's laugh seemed rather distant.

'Seriously, though, you just need to be a little more confident. Act the way you usually do when it's just the boys. Let us help,' Robbie offered.

This was something that Ollie had resisted for years and was something he'd told himself from an early age that he'd never do. But what harm could it do? Mike was excitable, bouncing on the balls of his feet; he pulled out the chair from underneath his desk and flung himself into it before reaching into the single drawer that lay beneath the middle of the table.

Robbie was rummaging inside one of the sports bags shoved onto the single shelf above the bed, which held the majority of Mike's clothes. He withdrew a Blu-ray DVD, *Kingdom of Heaven*. There was a certain irony to this that Ollie couldn't place, but he was sure Mike would make an awful joke out of it in a moment or two's time.

'Is this really necessary?' asked Ollie nervously. 'I'm doing fine, guys.'

Robbie was already laughing before Mike had even adopted his best and, in fairness, quite accurate Sean Connery impression. With his face rather screwed up and his mouth more pronounced than usual, he said, 'Losers always whine about their best. Winners go home and fuck the prom queen.'

*

Several minutes later, just as they were about to re-enter the living area, Ollie caught a glimpse of himself in the murky mirror. A few people had mentioned to him in the past that he was a difficult person to read with his emerald-green eyes capable of both radiating mischief and concealing emotion. They weren't implacable now, however; they sparkled with warmth and a tinge of regret that would pass in a few moments. He had closely cropped hair that was light brown with a few blond strands at the side – which were, like his slightly tanned skin, a remnant of a recent holiday – and had been swept to the left. Dressed in tight-fitting, black jeans and an open-necked, white shirt, he had to admit that he looked rather good, and the light stubble around his face made him look slightly older than his peers. Nevertheless, he found it curious that there was something in his eyes that even he couldn't decipher. With that realisation, Ollie left the bedroom, with the two others behind him.

Outside, rain was beginning to hammer down on the pavements and streaks of it were running down the window frame. As they reached the dining table that was sticky with alcohol, Ollie shouted for everyone to gather round it, and then he adopted a rather camp voice and addressed his friends, his finger pointed towards the window pane and the still-falling rain, 'Mr Gandalf, can't you do something about this deluge?'

Robbie responded instantly, assuming a passable impression of Sir Ian McKellen, 'It's raining, Master Dwarf, and it will continue to rain until the rain is done. If you wish to change the weather of the world, you should find yourself another wizard.'

Ollie joined in the laughter with his friends, noticing as he did so that the girls were all shaking their heads and rolling their eyes. To his surprise, his gums were tingling in an oddly pleasurable way as if they were being numbed to pain that didn't exist and his tongue flickered over them, enjoying the sensation. There was a light burning sensation in his nostrils, akin to that experienced at the back of the throat after a shot of tequila or sambuca. It was a very pleasant feeling, comforting in its own way. Even his tongue was becoming numb, and the back of his throat too was tingling in a way he'd never experienced before.

It was now time for them to head out to the Students' Union, and they left the house, though Ollie had darted into Mike's room a couple more times first. Once outside, Ollie found himself walking beside Emma. The rain had cleared and left behind it a slight haze in the sky. He noticed Grace was chatting happily with Mike in front of them, and he smiled to himself as Emma slipped her hand in his and squeezed it gently.

Leaning closer to him she breathed, and he felt the gentle touch against his neck. 'Grace is a great girl. I'm sorry for the way I've treated you over the years.'

And then she was gone, moving back towards the rest of the group. Ollie watched her go, her brown hair flowing behind her as she walked away from him once more. How many times had that happened over the years? He was so lost in thought that he nearly walked straight into the side of the gate that led to the back of the campus. He heard his friends laughing, and the sound was somehow amplified in the evening air, but something else caught his attention as he stumbled forwards. A sense of dread was creeping over him, and as he looked up to his left at the abandoned building where he'd seen the man earlier in the day, he noticed a jeep parked outside and a man climbing into the back seat.

There was something about the man that attracted his attention. It wasn't the same person he'd seen earlier in the day; this man was older, possibly in his late fifties or sixties, with just a few wisps of grey hair atop his head and thick-rimmed spectacles perched on his rather hooked nose, but it was his manner that attracted Ollie's attention. He was clearly exceptionally nervous, and he kept glancing over his shoulder and readjusting his glasses. In the back of his mind, Ollie was sure he'd seen the man somewhere before and wondered whether he was one of the university professors. As Ollie watched, the same man he'd seen earlier exited the building and moved across to the jeep, throwing a silver briefcase into the passenger seat before rounding the vehicle and opening the driver's door. He too was glancing nervously around him, and as his black jacket flapped slightly, Ollie was sure that, for a split second, he glimpsed a holster and pistol clipped to the man's waist. A moment later, however, the man had climbed back into the car, and Ollie felt himself being pulled up the hill by Robbie.

*

Royal Holloway University, Students' Union

After what seemed like an hour, Ollie was propelled back towards the ground, his feet hitting the dancefloor heavily, causing him to topple slightly on landing. He didn't even register the impact on his ankle as it shuddered slightly, his arm gripped firmly around Robbie's shoulder, the two of them bouncing up and down.

Minutes later, as he crossed the landing above the dancefloor, Ollie reflected that there was something different about tonight, though. He felt simultaneously calmer and more alert; it was a sense of self-assurance that he didn't normally have. Briefly, he shielded his eyes from the glare of the overhead spotlights. He suddenly felt a hand on his shoulder, and so he pivoted on the balls of his feet, instinctively dropping into a combat stance with his arm poised to strike out. The motion was too much for him; his head swam slightly, and he almost lost his balance as Mike's face came into sharper focus. His friend was already laughing, his black eyes clearly dilated as the now permanently positioned grin stretched into a laugh.

'All right, Jackie Chan, don't take me out. I'm here to help.' Mike was still chortling as he pressed something into Ollie's hand. He clapped Ollie on the shoulder, and then he was gone.

After hastily stuffing what Mike had given him inside the back pocket of his jeans, he made towards the unisex toilets that occupied the top level of the Students' Union. As he opened the door, a girl pressed past him, he felt her body up against his own, and then she was gone. It was a second before he registered that it had been Grace; he could tell by the scent that had lingered in the air and the fact that she'd allowed her hand to brush casually against the lower part of his body. The sensation had sent a tingle through his body, an electric charge that surged through him, and for a moment, he was sorely tempted to follow her. The glance she gave him was extremely suggestive.

A minute later, he'd left the cubicle and moved back out onto the landing. Glancing around him, his eyes focussed on the upstairs bar; as he was moved towards it, he spotted Emma sitting on her own on one of the long benches that were arranged around the bar. Although he'd been racked with indecision all day, he felt none of that as he changed course and walked confidently across to her. She looked stunning in her tightly fitting playsuit and pale lipstick, with her brown hair cascading over her shoulders. As he approached, she raised her head, and her face seemed to light up with a pleasing smile that made her all the more beautiful.

'I've been looking for you.' Ollie smiled as he lowered himself onto the bench beside her. 'How come you're up here on your own?'

'I needed a minute to take my feet off that sticky dancefloor,' she replied, returning the smile.

It was then he noticed the slight sadness in those brown eyes that had always entranced him. Acting on impulse, as though someone else was giving him instructions, although he was entirely confident it was the right thing to do, he slipped his hand over hers and looked into her eyes. She met his gaze for the briefest of moments, and he felt his self-assurance slip for that split second, but then she had her head.

'I meant what I said earlier, Ollie. I've treated you awfully over the years. I enjoyed the attention. I knew you liked me, and I played off that; that isn't how friends should treat each other.'

Ollie was growing increasingly aware of how hot it was in here, as well as how dry his mouth was, and he wiped his forehead with his free arm. Lifting his hand off of Emma's, he placed it on her cheek and moved her face around to look at him once more. He was surprised to see that the ghost of a tear was lingering on the end of her eyelashes. 'I always knew that, but there was a part of me that hoped you liked me too. I've been convinced that you actually did until tonight.'

Emma made to turn away again, her eyes racked with guilt and confusion. Suddenly, it wasn't just the drugs that were making him confident. He could see the truth written across her gorgeous face. That was the real reason she'd come here. She hadn't come here to tell him to move on. Like him, she simply didn't how to act. It had been so many years after all. Years of shared memories appeared to flash through his mind, and he was sure from the distant yet happy look that had unexpectedly flickered deep in those brown eyes that she was remembering them too.

With his hand still caressing the side of her cheek, he leaned forwards, never taking his eyes from hers. He'd never normally have acted so boldly. They were almost nose to nose now, and her pale lips seemed to glisten, tempting him, and he needed no further temptation. Their lips met and seemed to fit together like pieces of an intricate puzzle, her mouth melting into his, as their surroundings seemed to evaporate, leaving just the two of them. She tasted so good, as though she'd been lightly sucking a peppermint rather than drinking vodka all evening, and he pulled her closer, with his free hand finding her shapely waist. Her hand was in his hair, and he loved the feel of it, his insides squirming pleasurably.

After what felt like a lifetime, they eased apart from one another, both of them taking shallow, shaky breathes. Goose pimples had erupted all along Ollie's arms and at the back of his neck. Emma was looking at him rather sheepishly, biting her lip, and he couldn't resist pulling her into his arms once more. Their second kiss was even more passionate, and he allowed himself to linger on her mouth, feeling the warmth and tender caress of her tongue on his. Why hadn't he done this years ago? All those times they'd spent together at the park or the cinema or else at parties and school trips when he'd longed to tell her how he felt.

This time when they broke apart, they both laughed nervously.

It was Emma who said, 'I wish you'd done that years ago.'

'So do I.' Ollie laughed, allowing his tongue to brush across his lips, wanting to drink in every inch of her taste. 'I wish I'd had years of kissing you.'

Emma's eyes were twinkling as she replied, 'You still might.'

There was a rather awkward silence, and Ollie felt an urge to grab her arm and pull her out of the Students' Union and back to the house. Just as he was about to vocalise this longing, he heard a familiar shout of excitement from behind him and turned his head slowly, annoyed and amused at the interruption. He saw Robbie half jumping, half staggering towards them, his eyes slightly out of focus and a plastic cup full of dark liquid in his hand. He seemed delighted to have interrupted Ollie and Emma in what could have been an intimate moment.

It seemed as though Mike had managed to get himself thrown out, and they were all leaving. In hindsight, perhaps it hadn't been the wisest idea to compare the security guard to a Middle Eastern dictator, even if the similarities were there for all to see.

*

Although the first two minutes of the walk back down the sloping campus was spent happily abusing the security man and comparing him to tyrants from various sci-fi franchises, Ollie increasingly felt a sense of unease. He began to look nervously behind and around him, sure they were being followed or watched.

'Are you alight, Ollie?' came a voice close to him.

He jolted slightly before realising that it was Grace who'd asked the question. It took him a couple of seconds to focus on her concerned expression, but he didn't answer her. *Why would she ask that? Is something going on here behind my back? Are all of them conspiring against me?* It felt as though the world was beginning to crash down around him, and he was beginning to feel terribly isolated. He shook his head rather violently, hoping he could flick the feelings away, and hurried to get ahead of the group. His friends shouted at him and laughed as he moved a few steps ahead of them. He was alone, and he knew he'd get no help or support from any of them.

Everything happened in what seemed like slow motion to Ollie. He scratched irritably at his nose, fighting a sudden sense of anger quite unconnected with the waves of depression that were crashing around him. He heard Emma's voice call for him from behind, concerned first and then panicked. Then screams rent the air all around him. Cowering from the sudden noise, blurred figures flitted in front of his vision like angry, black bees; he felt himself seized roughly from behind, and something was forced violently into the small of his back. Fighting his churning emotions and the sudden urge to be sick, he tried to shake what must be an hallucination.

In front of him, other students – a scantily clad group of girls – were being dragged off the path that led down to the gate at the bottom of the campus by half a dozen men dressed all in black with desert boots fixed to their feet and Kevlar vests strapped to their chests. They had some kind of eyewear hung around their necks, but that wasn't what drew Ollie's attention. Even in his sickened state, his eyes were drawn to the somehow elegant assault rifles that they were using to force the girls forwards. He twisted round and saw, to his horror, that his friends were also being led onto the gravel that lay at the back of the derelict building that occupied the bottom of the university campus.

Reluctantly, he forced his eyes to look for Emma, and there she was, tears streaking what little make-up she'd worn, struggling desperately against the vice-like grip of the man pulling her effortlessly off the path. It took his own body several seconds to process exactly what was happening, and by the time he'd attempted to shake himself free of the man holding him, he was already at the back of the building.

He was shoved roughly around the side of the structure to where a metal fire escape was open. The screams of the girls and the angry, panicked shouts of his friends were gone, and he felt his own attempts to speak were cut off by the fabric glove that was clamped over his mouth. And then there was darkness and the loud clang of the door being shut behind them, blocking out the world.

13

His heart was racing, its desperate desire to break free amplified by the sudden situation, but his brain was moving incredibly slowly. Acting on impulse, he reached inside his pocket and slipped out his phone. He had perhaps a few seconds before the men were back or the lights were switched on. Careful not to make a sound, he slowly crouched down and eased the phone inside his shoe and beneath his foot before straightening up. It was incredibly uncomfortable, and he arched his ankle slightly to stop himself crushing the device or wincing at the pain in the ball of his foot.

It was then a cold voice spoke through the darkness: 'Silence.'

At these words, lights flickered on overhead, and despite them being dimly lit, Ollie shielded his fragile eyes from the glare, realising as he did so that his body was drenched in sweat. Finally adjusting to the light, he was able to look around him, and what he saw sent a shiver through his spine.

They were in a large, open room – rather like a derelict warehouse – with boxes and trolleys of disused books crammed into one corner, whilst broken desks and discarded chairs and chair legs were piled high in another. Ollie and his friends, along with the girls who had been ahead of them on the path, were in a ring in the centre of the floor – there were twelve of them in all. In a circle around them were a dozen men, identically dressed in all black, with holsters strapped to their waists that presumably contained pistols of some kind whilst the ugly muzzles of their assault rifles were pointed directly at the students. In the newfound light, Ollie recognised the headgear hung around their necks to be Pulsar night vision goggles, which were often used by the military – something he'd learned playing *Call of Duty: Black Ops*.

Glancing around at the men, he noticed certain similarities in the deadened, expressionless eyes and hard jawlines. All but one of the men looked to him as though they could be Eastern European. The other man looked as though he could be British, with thick, red-brown hair and a slim jawline, whilst his deep-set, milky eyes seemed almost supernatural. He alone of all the men was smiling – a self-satisfied smirk that flitted between each of the students in turn, completely devoid of pity – whilst his own assault rifle hung almost lazily by his side. He wasn't the man who'd spoken, however.

Another figure had stepped forwards. He looked younger and more handsome than the man with red hair, perhaps in his late twenties with closely cropped, light hair and close-set, hard, blue eyes that were as cold as ice. Whilst his chiselled lips and slender figure gave him the look of a dancer, there was a pale tinge to his cheeks that suggested the man lacked any warmth at all.

He spoke in a clipped voice with the faintest trace of what Ollie guessed was a Russian accent. 'We don't intend to impose upon your hospitality for very long. If you do everything we say, then you'll be free.' His eyes moved between the sobbing girls and raked over the thin material that clung to their bodies.

'Who are you? What do you want?' Robbie's voice was braver and stronger than Ollie was sure his friend truly felt.

One of the other men came towards them. Ollie made to move in front of his friend, but he was too late. The butt of the man's assaulted rifle had already made contact with the side of Robbie's head, sending him crashing to the ground howling in pain as blood trickled down his temple. The girls screamed, Mike swore, and Will and Cap hurled insults at the men as they crouched beside Robbie, looking at the wound. Ollie alone remained motionless, simply staring down at his friend without truly seeing him at all.

'Please,' the man who appeared to be in charge said in a silky voice, 'do not make this any harder for yourselves. Do not speak unless we require something from you.' He smiled rather coldly. 'I'm sure you can't be without brains. English universities are famous for choosing only the best after all. My name is Vladimir Conrad, and I am, you might say, your host for the evening.'

Why would he so blithely reveal his identity unless he means to kill us all? Glancing around once more, Ollie noticed a number of other things about the room they were in. Whilst this area may look like a warehouse, there were in fact two doors at the end of the square room, which seemed to lead off into a corridor, and he remembered that the building had once been used by the university for more than storage. Perhaps there were old seminar rooms or even a lecture theatre beyond; given the high ceilings and the look of the building from the outside, it was large enough to house several rooms.

'Take their phones,' ordered Conrad.

The men moved forwards, forcibly turning out the students' pockets. Will tried to resist, but he was shown the same treatment as Robbie before his phone was wrenched from his pocket as he lay on the ground. Ollie allowed himself to be manhandled by one of the men, wrinkling his nose at the man's putrid breath as he did so. He made no move to stop the man turning out his pockets or poking him hard in every area.

'Phone,' the man demanded in a thick Russian accent. Each syllable seemed like an immense effort for him.

'My family are Welsh. We haven't caught up with the twenty-first century yet.' Ollie was amazed to hear these words leave his own mouth and realised once again how dry it had become. The blow to the side of his head came as no surprise, and he staggered momentarily, a tunnel of black consuming his vision. He felt no pain, however; that would come later. 'I forgot to bring my phone with me, OK? I just left it at home.'

As the darkness faded from around his eyes, Ollie was able to make out the figure of Vladimir Conrad nodding curtly to the man that stood over the boy.

There was a curious smile on the Russian's face as he surveyed Ollie for a brief second, before continuing in his icy voice, 'We have, you might say, some business to conduct here, and then we'll be on our way.' He signalled for them all to move across the floor to an empty far corner of the room, which was just a few yards from the doors that led beyond.

Nobody moved until the rifles were used to force them to move their legs, and they stumbled across the battered wooden floor into the area the Russian had indicated. He smiled rather coldly and then spoke swiftly and quietly into the ear of the red-haired man, who nodded gruffly. A wave of desperation and exhaustion crashed over Ollie. There was still no pain from the blow to the back of his head, but a cursory check told him that his hair was matted with rapidly drying blood.

The red-haired man took several paces forwards, the same self-satisfied expression on his face, and on closer inspection, Ollie could see the toughened exterior and emptiness in those milky eyes. This was a man who'd sold his humanity long ago and with it any sense of compassion. Then the man spoke, and

Ollie detected a trace of a Northern Irish accent. He may have spoken differently to the others and didn't look physically alike, but in every other sense, he belonged amongst these hardened professional killers. Unlike the others, however, he seemed to be enjoying himself. He was taking pleasure in watching the students cower together in the corner of the abandoned building.

'Mr Conrad is correct; we have some business to attend to here.' He smirked, his gloved hand caressing the assault rifle hanging loosely by his side.

Whilst all his friends were transfixed in terror by the man standing before them, Ollie's eyes started darting around the room, and he noticed the Russian who'd called himself Vladimir Conrad, as well as half a dozen of the men, fixing the night vision goggles around their faces and pushing open another fire door opposite the one they'd led the students through. Then they were gone into the night.

There was no time to dwell on their disappearance, however, as one of the doors in the wall beside them was flung open, and two more men dressed all in black appeared, each of them dragging a figure behind them. Out of the corner of his eye, Ollie spotted there was a fevered, hungry expression on the face of the red-haired man as he watched these two figures thrown down at his feet. There were certainly not students, and Ollie recognised both of them immediately: they were the two men he'd seen climbing into the jeep earlier that evening from outside this very building.

At the time, he'd wondered whether he recognised the older of the men, and now he was sure that he'd occasionally seen him entering one of the science buildings on campus. He must be one of the professors here. There was mingled sweat and blood trickling down the side of his face, and one of the lenses of his thickly rimmed spectacles had been smashed, leaving them perched lopsidedly upon his hooked nose. There was no doubting the frantic terror in his eyes as he gazed up at the red-haired man and the others surrounding him.

'Please, I'll tell you anything. L-let me help you,' he stammered in a terrified, beseeching voice, and Ollie noted the harsh German tone immediately, having learned the language himself.

However, the red-haired man standing over him had let out a sharp laugh, like a bark, and focussed his attention on the second younger man, who was making no attempt to plead for his life. Like the older man, his short hair was tinged with crimson, and there was a deep cut in the sleeve of his jacket. He had a rather triangular face with a broad nose and small lips, whilst his light-brown eyes gave very little away, despite the obvious peril of his situation. As he had been earlier, Ollie was reminded of a soldier due to the man's muscular neck and arms and bulky torso, and there was a resolve in him that wasn't evident amongst the rest of the captives. He must have tried to fight the men off, as his knuckles were cut and bloodied.

There was a defiance to his voice as he looked up at the red-haired man and said in a rather gruff North London accent, 'I don't know what you're hoping to achieve here, Henderson, but you must know there's no escape. The campus will be surrounded within the hour.'

'Let's find out how little you know about our plans, but first we have the problem of what to do with Professor Vallance.' He jerked his rifle in the direction of the older man, who was cringing with his head slumped towards his knees. 'After all, he's just offered to reveal all his secrets to us. We both know how invaluable that information could be.'

Ollie noticed that the younger muscular man threw the professor a look of disgust before turning his attention back to the man standing over him. He opened his mouth to speak, but in the blink of an eye, Henderson's hand had flashed to the holster at his waist, withdrawn an ugly-looking pistol and fired twice. There was no sound of a gunshot, save for a short splutter, as the bullets hissed from the silenced weapon and buried themselves in the professor's chest.

The girls around Ollie screamed, and he heard a couple of his friends swear loudly. The men surrounding them raised their weapons in a threatening gesture for them to be quiet. One of the girls Ollie didn't know rolled over into the far corner of the room and began to retch, with the resulting liquid stream of yellow chunks splattering onto the wooden floor making more noise than the gun that had just been fired.

On turning his head slowly, Ollie saw the younger man hadn't even glanced at the professor's body, nor had he flinched as the gun had been withdrawn from its holster. It had all happened so quickly that there had been no time for anybody to react.

The man named Henderson was smiling down at the body of the man whose life he'd just ended. 'You see, John, the professor had no useful information that I didn't already have. We know his secrets – the important ones at least. There was no need to keep him alive. The same, I'm afraid, cannot be said for you. Make it easy on yourself and answer our questions.'

'Or what?' spat the younger man, 'you'll do what you did to Ben?'

For a split second, a flicker of emotion passed across Henderson's face, but it left no trace; when he spoke again, his voice was dripping with menace. 'Don't make the same mistake that your colleague made. This doesn't have to go the same way. You already have the deaths of enough children on your conscience, I think,' he added with a mocking sneer.

A flicker of some unforgotten pain rippled across the man's face for a moment, and there was a slight look of fear in his eyes as he glanced at the students. Henderson smiled once more as the hand still holding the gun moved lazily to hover over the group of students.

Ollie felt his heart pump even faster and wondered how long he could remain conscious given its desperate bid for freedom. Yet despite the crashing waves of emotion he'd experienced in the past hour, he found he was able to stare resolutely down the barrel of the gun that could so easily end his life and the lives of his best friends.

There was cold resentment in Henderson's voice as he said, 'You may feel differently when there are only two of them left.' He smirked.

As Ollie looked into the milky white of Henderson's eyes, he was left in no doubt what was to come. He fidgeted slightly where he sat in order to check that the phone was still hidden beneath his foot. That was the only remaining comfort he had available to him.

14

Rather than firing another a bullet, Henderson strode towards one of the fire doors. Ollie used the opportunity to turn to Emma and give her a brief but tight hug. Her tears had stopped, but her eyes were like petrified stone, unblinking in terror. Glancing around, he took in the state of the rest of the group. The girls they didn't know were huddled in a circle, crying silently, with two of them now having been sick in the corner. There was nothing he could say to comfort them, but he smiled encouragingly towards Grace, who returned it weakly. She alone seemed to be holding herself together, although he noticed that her arms were shaking slightly.

Will's wavy, black hair was buried in his hands, and his excitable eyes were obscured from the nightmare that surrounded him, whilst Mike had turned alarmingly pale and appeared to be on the point of vomiting. To his left, Robbie had propped himself against the plastered wall, his eyes sliding out of focus. Reaching out, Ollie slapped him hard across the face, causing his friend's eyes to snap back to the world, and then recoiled to avoid the retaliatory blow that was aimed clumsily in his direction.

As much as he tried to fight the impulse, his eyes were drawn to the motionless body of the older man lying just a few feet from him. He'd fallen face down on the floor, and his head was turned away from the students, but a pool of blood was seeping slowly from beneath his body, moving inexorably towards them.

And then Henderson swept back into the room, carrying under his arm a small briefcase. 'You're in luck, Mr Bromley,' he said, directing his words at the man a few feet from the students. 'We don't have a lot of time with you.'

By then, Henderson had reached the group and placed the briefcase on the floor. With a flick of his wrist, he motioned to two of the men dressed in black, who moved forwards and pulled John Bromley roughly to his feet. It was only then that Ollie saw the agent's hands had been tied together at the back, and the rope that bound him was drenched with blood.

Without warning, Henderson slammed his fist into Bromley's chest, causing the man to double over with a groan of pain, before dragging him across the floor, lifting him bodily and slamming him against the nearby wall. The air around Ollie was suddenly filled with incoherent screams, and his head began to swim with visions of his friends immobilised by fear; tears were streaking down Emma's face.

At that moment, Ollie noticed for the first time the ugly handle of a knife protruding from Henderson's belt. The man's hand tightened around the handle and the ugly blade was withdrawn from its sheath. The US Marine Corps bayonet was capable of puncturing aircraft aluminium and bulletproof vests.

Henderson made another inaudible hiss into the ear of John, who made no attempt to shake free of Henderson's grasp or answer the man. There was a grim resolution in John's face as his eyes found the blade.

Both he and Ollie watched transfixed as Henderson thrust out his hand, his face contorted into a snarl. Ollie looked on in horror as the knife was withdrawn, and blood began to gush from a vertical wound in John's chest and drip loudly onto the floor at his feet.

John clawed at the air, gasping for breath, before he collapsed into a pool of his own blood, his eyes widening in pain that he didn't seem to understand. His hand scrabbled hopelessly at the wood, his fingers darkening in his own blood, as he found his voice. 'Help me,' he rasped, taking several deep breaths. The composure that had characterised him a few moments before was gone, replaced by a longing desire to ease the agony that was clearly taking hold of him. John clutched at the wound in his chest.

When Henderson had lowered himself to John's level, the agent raised his head from the floor to look up at the man who had sliced his chest open just a moment before, and through the blood and bruises it was possible to make out a look of defiance on his face. 'Go to hell, Henderson,' he whispered, his voice displaying none of the pain that was etched across his features.

Henderson straightened, smiling mirthlessly, and turned back towards the briefcase, snatching it from the floor. His mouth still twisted in a cold smile, he approached the agent once more and lashed out with his foot; his boot impacted just above the knife wound in the man's chest. John grunted in pain as Henderson kept his boot pressed down on the gash, forcing the agent down on the floor. Blood oozed over his adversary's bootlaces, turning them scarlet in an instant. There was a moment of silence as both men looked at each other before Henderson shook his head slowly and lowered the briefcase to the floor at Agent Bromley's feet, flicking it open.

As Ollie strained his neck to see inside it, Henderson withdrew a pair of large headphones, not unlike those housed in music departments in schools around the country. Peering into the remaining contents of the briefcase, Ollie glimpsed a panel of high-tech-looking dials and buttons that he didn't recognise. After reaching down, Henderson pulled a blindfold from the briefcase. He forced the blindfold over the agent's eyes and ears, fastening it tightly at the back of his head, before placing the headphones over the top.

'There were people who trusted you, Henderson, but you betrayed them, and you sold out your country,' John chided.

'You think I betrayed this country,' spat Henderson, anger and resentment audible in his voice, 'but it's the other way around, my friend. My country betrayed me, or have they done such a thorough job at doctoring the MI6 archives that they didn't tell you that? If you want betrayal, then don't look to me.' With that, he turned a dial in the briefcase and smiled.

Ollie could make out the faintest whine from beneath the headphones as John began to twitch rather violently beneath the blindfold.

Stretching outwards in a desire for comfort, Ollie placed his other arm around Emma and pulled her tightly to him. The feel of her body on his made him feel safer, reminding him that there were people he cared about – people who were worth fighting for – and as he adjusted himself into a more comfortable position, his thoughts turned to his parents. They'd have no idea what was happening to him at that very moment, and the thought of them caused his eyes to glisten with hot tears. He hastened to wipe them away.

The faint whining sound had disappeared from the air, but it was apparent it was continuing to gain in intensity under the headphones. John's face was contorted in pain as he wrestled with the bonds tying his hands together, the colour slowly beginning to drain from his face whilst blood continued to drip steadily from the wound in his chest. And then the agent let out an awful drawn-out scream, a sound more terrible than anything they'd heard that night. It seemed to penetrate Ollie's skin, chilling his bones and causing him to shiver violently.

In a matter of minutes, John's face was blotchy and swollen, his features thickly obscured by blood, and his left eye completely closed as if in a prolonged wink. Blood was trickling from both of his ears. Henderson stared down at the pale and bloodied MI5 agent, who'd curled into a defensive ball, his body shaking in pain. The agent struggled to raise his head from the floor, and a spasm of recognition rippled across his face, as though he was seeing the group of students for the first time. He could do nothing except shake his head defiantly, and then he seemed to find the strength enough to croak, 'I'm not going to tell you anything, no matter what you do.'

Henderson seemed to consider him for a moment, before striding across the floor making for Ollie and his friends.

Acting on impulse, Ollie began to rise to his feet, but two of Henderson's henchmen stepped forwards, raising their guns in front of him.

For a moment Henderson paused, and he and Ollie looked at each other before the man hissed rather menacingly. 'Fine, you want to play the hero, boy, then I'll start with you.'

There was no chance for him to defend himself as the two men either side of Ollie moved behind him, forced his arms into a lock that he couldn't shake and pushed his head back towards the floor until it was level with that of John. A second later, he felt the jagged edge of the knife pressed against his neck and heard a cold whisper from above him say, 'Tell me, Bromley, or I'll kill the boy.'

Staring into the man's eyes, Ollie felt oddly calm. Perhaps it was the welcoming arms of death – which, in many ways, he'd longed to feel over the past year – or maybe it was the strange realisation that he trusted the intelligence agent who was a complete stranger and had been beaten half to death.

Nevertheless, he felt a spasm of panic as he heard the agent say perfectly calmly, 'If you kill the boy, Henderson, then it will be for gratification only, because I'm not going to tell you anything.'

There was a pause and then, to Ollie's very great surprise, he felt himself being released and thrust forwards onto the hard floor. Gasping slightly, he felt the place at his neck where the knife had been just seconds before. Evidently, Henderson had decided that Bromley would indeed not tell him what he wanted to know, even if he'd killed Ollie and all his friends.

'It matters not,' came the cold voice from above. 'Even if you were to make it out of here alive, you can't stop what we've planned.' Henderson paused before he said coldly to the agent at his feet, 'It's a pity that men like you and Ben waste your lives for something that no longer exists.'

Then he was gone striding away through the nearest door, and John was beckoned into the corner of the room, the circle of students closing around him before the men surrounding them backed off and busied themselves around a handful of duffle bags near the fire exit that Ollie and his friends had been brought through.

Ignoring the muffled whimpers from his friends, Ollie bent low to the ground on the pretext of feeling the wound to his head, whilst in reality, he was leaning close to John's ear, and muttered as quietly as he could, 'I still have my phone. Do you have someone we can contact?'

After a second of gazing into his eyes, the agent nodded slowly and then hissed in a barely audible whisper, 'Dial 1678. Wait for a moment then press 04. It will send a distress code to my colleagues. Don't let them see.'

A spasm of fear crept over Ollie's neck as one of the men looked over at them. Fortunately, the next second the man had returned to the work he and the others were doing with their backs to Ollie and the others.

'Leave the line open,' continued John in a barely audible whisper.

Feigning anguish, Ollie moved into a cross-legged position behind John, the agent blocking him from the men's view if they happened to turn. Under this cover, he eased the phone out from underneath his foot with difficulty and pressed 1678 swiftly, covering his head with his hands. Not daring to bring the phone to his ear, he waited a second then pushed down 0 and 4. There was a faint crackle and then a click. Ollie looked up at the agent, who nodded. He'd told Ollie to keep the line open, but the phone would disconnect immediately it was placed back in his shoe.

Dimly aware that his heart was hammering against the cage that contained it, Ollie reached down and carefully slipped the phone into his jeans pocket. At least he'd done something to help. Sweat was pouring down the side of his face, and he blinked the salt from his stinging eyes. His palms too were slippery with sweat.

Just then, Henderson strode back into the room. 'Before we leave here today, you'll be dead. And so,' he said in falsely warm voice, his smile lingered over Ollie and his friends, 'will be these shining examples of the current generation. Many of their friends out on the campus will die too, either alone in the accommodation flats or else gagging on their own vomit in the Students' Union. Perhaps one or two will have the immunity to survive, but they'll be exceptions.'

Behind him, Ollie felt Emma shaking, and his friends let out shouts that Henderson quelled with a look, whilst the group of girls began to whimper softly.

What does he mean 'immunity'? thought Ollie, his imagination racing.

'Henderson, you can't,' croaked Bromley feebly.

'Oh, but we can, John.' Henderson smirked. 'You see,

we've sent men out around the campus tonight, discretely placing aerosols filled with the strain of the virus that we've managed to acquire. Imagine the scandal when people learn that British students died because of a virus that was cultivated by their own Ministry of Defence. Perhaps this country might find the strength to change.'

Ollie watched in horror now as the men withdrew black gas masks from their duffle bags and placed them on the floor. A virus. No, it couldn't be. His head was spinning. *Please, not again.*

Henderson was holding a small electronic device in his hand, one no bigger than a TV remote control, which was blinking with green and yellow lights.

Agent Bromley tried to protest, but Henderson ignored him. Beside Ollie, Robbie tried to wrestle against the grip of the man searching him, and Mike was complaining. Yet Henderson's eyes found Ollie, as he sat cross-legged on the floor, his gaze fixed determinedly on the wall over the man's shoulder.

Slowly, like a lion stalking its prey, the man walked towards Ollie until he was standing right above him. 'Up,' came his cold voice, and Ollie had no choice but to comply.

He was surprised that his legs obeyed his instruction as they were heavily weighted with fear. Using his hands to push his body into action, Ollie clambered to his feet, feeling the menacing stare upon him. He tried everything to avoid Henderson's gaze as the milky eyes raked him; then Henderson's his hands began to search him roughly, finally settling on the bulge in his jeans pocket. Despite wanting to look anywhere else, Ollie raised his head and looked into the man's eyes. What he saw there was a curious malevolence unlike any expression that had appeared on Henderson's face until now.

'It seems you have a death wish,' he said in a low, menacing voice. Dropping his eyes to the phone's screen, he looked at the number that had been dialled and the connection that was presumably still going. 'See you soon, Ben.' Then he dropped the phone and brought his boot slamming down on top of it; a solidary spark emanated from the device as it splintered and broke apart. Henderson kicked the remains of Ollie's phone aside and considered the boy.

Ollie found himself shaking slightly as Henderson turned slowly to fix his milky eyes upon him. His eyes narrowed as they seemed to bore into Ollie's, making him want to recoil from the man's gaze. Nevertheless, he held his own despite the hammering of his heart and the sweat that dripped from his forehead onto the floor. He watched it fall, noting as he did so that the cut to his head must have stopped bleeding, as there was no crimson amongst the droplets of fear that hit the floor. Beside him, Emma was shaking worse than ever, and Grace had let out a moan when Henderson had spoken.

Without warning, the sleekly silenced gun was back in Henderson's hand, and he'd fired once, the bullet spat past Ollie in an instant. Screams and high-pitched cries rent the air and filled the hall all around him, piercing his eardrums and making him want to cower from the renewed horrors of the world. His head abruptly felt weighed down by a tonne of lead; he moved it slowly to look behind him once more, not wanting to see the result of his stupidity.

The group of girls had broken apart, with three of them crying hysterically, tears streaking their make-up, as they gazed down with glassy eyes at the girl lying between them. She alone wasn't screaming in terror or grief; she'd escaped the horror of her surroundings, and in many ways, she seemed almost peaceful. And then her eyes found him. Her hazel eyes had lost their fear and their emotion. They'd lost everything, and yet they seemed to stare accusingly through him. He felt in that moment they'd forever judge him, no matter what he did.

One of her friends had leaned down, trying to shake her into life, and Ollie felt his heart stop its relentless beating. The girl's body twitched for a final time, blood seeping from the round hole in her forehead into her matted, dark-brown hair and skin.

He was vaguely aware of shouting around him and knew that the voices belonged to people he cared about, but he was transported elsewhere. Suddenly, he was in a hospital car park, clad in personal protective equipment, and his mum was walking slowly towards him, tears streaming down her face. Now it had happened again. In a few hours' time, a mother and father would receive a call to tell them that their daughter was dead, and it was all his fault.

A second later, he was propelled back to the ground and his head hit the floor with a thwack that he didn't register. Nor could he respond to the frantic questions from his friends or Grace attempting to shake him into life. None of the words permeated the paralysing bubble of numbing pain that had engulfed him, as he stared unblinkingly into the eyes of the girl whose name he didn't know, beseeching her to forgive him, though he knew she no longer possessed the ability to do so.

A blinding pain exploded in his head, as Henderson's hand connected with the tough cranium protecting his brain. It was like being hit by a brick wall, and he felt every bone in his body rattle. He swayed on the spot, white lights exploding in front of his eyes, and then everything went dark.

15

Ollie had never been knocked out before, and he didn't much like the experience. His head was throbbing, and he felt like he was spinning in a never-ending Ferris wheel. Everything was blurry and out of focus, and there was a sour taste in his mouth. He attempted to get to his feet, but there was no strength left in his body, and so he fell back to the floor, his head ringing.

Groaning, he tried to lift his head, but the movement was too much for him, and he collapsed back onto the wood. His eyes slowly came into focus, and he saw his friends' faces materialise in front of him. He ran his tongue gingerly over his teeth to check they were all still there, which they were. He'd been surprised that the force of the punch hadn't broken his neck, as he'd instantly felt excruciating pain down his spine; all the nerves felt as though they were on fire.

Reluctantly, Ollie opened his eyes and peeked furtively around at the group of people huddled around him, but looks of disgust were nowhere to be seen. Instead, his friends were all looking at him with concern etched across their faces. His eyes bypassed them to the place where he knew the girl's body had lain. It had gone. Henderson's men must have removed it, but the streak of blood that had been left behind hurt Ollie quite as much as the girl's blank eyes, and the smell of it lingered over the group like blood in the water after a shark attack. The girl's friends were shaking silently, but the tears had stopped; perhaps they had no more tears left to cry?

Without knowing what he was doing or caring whether a bullet was going to thud into the back of his head, he crawled towards the girls, who looked at him in surprise. The nearest girl was short with a ginger pixie cut and her green eyeshadow and make-up were streaked down her face to her mouth and chin. She looked up at him with unseeing, blue eyes almost entirely obscured by tears that had yet to fall into her lap. There was no anger there, he was surprised to see.

Beseechingly, he reached out a hand and whispered, 'Please, I'm so sorry.'

To his very great astonishment, the girl showed no hesitation in grasping it, and a feeling of warmth seemed to flow up his arm at her touch.

'Help us,' she mouthed. The words seemed to act like a tonic that nothing else had done until that point.

Sitting up straighter, his eyes gradually adjusting, he noticed that many of the men who'd been busying themselves with the duffle bags were now standing close to his friends, their rifles raised. There were footsteps to his left, and he turned to see Henderson striding towards him, carrying the ugly knife he'd used to stab John Bromley. Fear gripped him so completely that he felt frozen as he stared fixedly at the knife, his heart hammering loudly inside his chest. He felt Grace seize his arm, but he smiled reassuringly at her and pushed her gently to one side, staring defiantly up at the man.

It seemed to take an age, but eventually, the man reached him, and Ollie struggled to his feet, the position lasting barely a second before Henderson slammed the back of his hand across Ollie's face. He staggered again, but he didn't fall this time, and he stabilised himself by balancing uneasily on the balls of his feet. John made to move forwards, but Henderson pointed the knife in his direction and then around at the surrounding students.

'If anyone talks, he dies, and then everyone else dies,' Henderson threatened angrily, and he lashed out again, knocking the Ollie backwards onto the wooden floor. 'Now, what's your name?' he asked. 'Tell me what your name is.'

Spitting blood from his mouth, Ollie realised there was no point in lying to Henderson. 'Ollie. Ollie Robson.'

Henderson seemed to consider him for a moment, a slow smile spreading across his face. 'Good,' he said quietly, and then turned away from him.

Ollie looked towards John in relief, but the next second Henderson had swivelled on the balls of his feet, slashing his arm violently through the air. The blood-stained knife disappeared briefly in a whirl of darkness.

There was a moment when Ollie was paralysed, fear and shock rendering every muscle in his body immobile. A moment later, however, he was left gasping for air, his breathing ragged as he clawed at the air with his hand, desperate to feel contact with someone. His white shirt was already soaked in dark-red blood. He hadn't felt the knife go in, but then the pain washed over him, along with a chill that lingered throughout his body. It felt as though the life was already beginning to drain from him.

There was screaming all around him, but Ollie felt somehow separated from it. This couldn't be happening to him. He felt arms catch his back as he dropped backwards, and then hands pressing against his chest. Yet he was removed from it all. It was as though he'd been transported to a different place – a quieter, safer place than the one he'd come from. There were no guns and no shouting.

Above him, he dimly recognised Robbie rising from the ground, shouting at a dark figure over him. The world in which he was safe from harm vanished as Robbie was forced over and then Henderson hit him too; Robbie fell next to his friend.

'Nice of you to drop by,' Ollie muttered feebly, and in spite of himself he began to laugh. There was a piercing pain in his chest, and he grimaced. Perhaps laughing wasn't the best idea.

Henderson had turned away from the group, evidently feeling he'd proven his point. Ollie inspected the wound to his chest, and he soon realised that he'd been very lucky because the knife hadn't penetrated deeply into his chest; rather, it had merely left a superficial gash in the skin. However, blood was still seeping from the cut, staining his chest red as it spread rapidly over the material of his shirt. He attempted to apply pressure to the cut, but before he could do so, he felt soft hands over his. Emma had interlocked her fingers over his and was pressing down on the wound, a watery smile on her face. Had it not been for her touch, he would have winced as they applied pressure to the gash, but the feel of her hand on his sent a spasm of warmth through his body.

The footsteps close by told him that Henderson had returned. 'Regretfully,' he said smoothly, 'it's time for me to leave you, but you'll be in capable hands.' He gestured to a burly, hard-faced man with black eyes and a thick jawline, his black hair receding at his scalp. He looked Eastern European or perhaps Russian. 'Dimitri is well versed in hospitality. He also has the pleasure of being in charge of releasing the virus.' Henderson hesitated, looking down at John. 'Did I not tell you before that I would kill you?'

'Then do it,' Bromley replied defiantly.

Surprisingly, Henderson shook his head slowly. 'You have exactly fifteen minutes on the timer in Dimitri's possession. Once those fifteen minutes are up, he'll detonate the cannisters holding the virus.' Then, the automatic rifle slung over his shoulder once more, he disappeared through the same door that Vladimir Conrad and his men had done earlier in the night.

Just a few seconds later, the world appeared to have been split apart in an explosion of noise, and the screams of his friends were nothing to those beginning to permeate through the windows from the campus outside. The noise had drawn everyone's attention, and in that split second, Ollie knew he had to act. He stood, and ducking low and ignoring the mutterings of his friends, he moved along the wall and darted through the door nearest to the group; he found himself in in a narrow corridor with more doors leading off and dirt-stained Perspex windows.

Looking desperately around him for another exit from the building, his eyes settled on a fire door at the far end of the corridor. He sprinted towards it, and had just placed his hands upon the rail to push it open when he felt an arm seize his throat from behind and begin to compress his windpipe. Reaching up instinctively, Ollie grabbed the arm and tried to pull it off him, but his adversary's grip was too strong. Gasping and spluttering for breath, he saw white lights pop in front of his eyes, and his surroundings began to fade into nothingness. He mustered all his strength, his face twisted in renewed determination.

He lashed out with his elbow, catching the man squarely on the chin. He spun round and drove the heel of his hand into his opponent's throat. The man collapsed at his feet, and Ollie looked down into the sallow face, feeling nothing but contempt and hatred. He was young and muscular, but his face was contorted with anger as he stared scornfully up at the student. Ollie reached down and grabbed hold of the man's semi-automatic pistol before slamming his fist down on the Russian's face, his hand barely a blur as it swished through the air. Moments later, the man lay unconscious at his feet.

Ollie had been twelve when his mother had suggested he try martial arts. A pupil at his school had been mugged walking home, so his mother had been fearful that the same thing might happen to him and had therefore signed him up for a ten-week karate course at the local gym. It had just saved his life.

Weighing the gun in his hand, he decided that he wouldn't use it. Nevertheless, it could still prove useful. Taking as much care as he could not to make a sound, Ollie eased open the fire door, went through it and dropped into a crouch on the soft ground below him. Shielding his eyes against the dimly flickering sun that was beginning to rise, bringing the world into a higher definition, he peered around him. Between the bushes that separated him from the main campus, he could see students running in all directions. A sense of panic had clearly set in amongst them. On glancing left towards the path that led to the black gate, he saw wisps of smoke curling into the sky. That was where the explosion had come from.

Then, across the student car park ahead of him, he caught a flicker of movement. Figures were stirring amongst the undergrowth opposite. What choice did he have but to hope? If he stayed here, he'd be found and killed instantly. If he turned towards the back gate, he may well run into Henderson and the remainder of his men. Running right and up onto campus would only lead him into the path of the aerosols that had been planted, and in any case, he'd be swamped by the crush of people.

After stowing the gun in the waistband of his jeans, he ran forwards, his head bent low in case of more explosions, zigzagging through the mass of students and heading straight for the undergrowth, where he hoped he'd find someone friendly. As he crossed the car park, he raised his hands in a defensive position and shouted, *'John Bromley sent me! I can help you.'*

As he reached the bushes, two figures dressed in combat clothing stepped out and pulled him forcibly into the undergrowth. Panting and with sweat dripping down his face, he found himself in a clearing amongst a thicket of bushes. There were three men dressed in camouflage gear lying face down on the ground with rifles pointing across the campus at the building Ollie had just escaped from. As he straightened up, he found himself face to face with two men who weren't dressed the same as the others.

They were dressed for combat, nevertheless, in black trousers and long-sleeved, khaki Viper base layers underneath bulletproof, black Kevlar body armour. They had semi-automatic pistols in holsters strapped at their waists, but unlike the men with rifles, they didn't seem to be fully equipped with assault rifles and knives. Nor were their faces disguised with face paint. Ollie looked between them. One of them was clean-shaven with spiky, black hair; wholesome, hazel eyes; and brown skin that hinted at perhaps a South Asian heritage. Remarkably, given the situation he found himself in, the man was smiling at Ollie.

However, the third man standing beside him, a few inches taller, was wearing a grim expression as he extended a gloved hand. 'Neil Carmichael. And your name is?'

There was something in his voice that made Ollie doubt the name he'd been given. The man was looking at him shrewdly, and the look in his eyes was always distrusting. He was in his thirties, fit and clearly relaxed, despite being in the midst of this situation. Of all the men, the clothing suited him best, but then this was a man who'd always appear well dressed. Despite his easy manner, there was something calculated behind the charm. His short, light-brown hair was slightly gelled at the front, and he possessed piercing, blue eyes that seemed to x-ray Ollie, examining him for any hidden details.

'Ollie,' he replied, trying to sound confident. 'I think I know your colleague, John Bromley.' It was clear to him that these men belonged to the same business as the agent he'd left in the building behind them. 'We were being held captive in that building over there.' The pain in Ollie's head was beginning to mount, and he tasted mingled blood and sweat in his mouth. 'They took us and your colleague captive, and killed another man' – he stopped as something painful rose in his throat – 'and a girl. They killed one of the girls.' His voice cracked.

After Ollie had quickly described the layout of the building, one of the men carrying rifles raised his left fist from the ground for Ollie to bump, which he did. 'The name's Wolf. Unlike these three, that's actually my name too,' he said with a slight North Welsh lilt to his voice, which Ollie recognised all too well. As he spoke, Wolf's eyes never left the scope of his rifle, which was fixed determinedly on the building opposite.

The men made their final preparations, and then – despite Ollie's protests – they left him behind as they slowly approached the building in a pincer formation. There were screams everywhere, but fewer students were running towards this part of the campus now. Smoke was still curling into the sky from the back gate. He watched as the men encircled the building and disappeared from view. *Can I really just sit here and do nothing?*

The agents had disappeared into the darkness as they rapidly approached the building. Darting between the undergrowth, Ollie crossed the car park swiftly. That was when the heavens opened and began to pour huge torrents of water down around him, drenching the leaves and ground in a matter of seconds. The smell of it filled his nostrils, and he blinked rain from his eyes. The sudden downpour had acted on him as a stimulant, clearing his mind.

171

He began to run, slipping and sliding on the freshly sodden ground, as the rain pounded down on him. His legs moved independently from his brain, drawing him closer to a danger that he was only dimly aware of. As he crept down the path, he saw that the gate had been blasted off its hinges. He felt sick as he turned the corner and saw the bodies of three men dressed in khaki, their assault rifles beside their sprawled bodies – yet more people who had died today. Their faces were charred and smeared with blood.

There had been one thing he'd omitted telling the men about: the gun he'd taken from the guard who'd tried to stop him leaving the hitherto abandoned building. He withdrew it from the waistband of his jeans and weighed it in his hand. Over his shoulder, he heard a rattle of machine-gun fire and paused, fearing the worst. Still unsure as to why he was doing it, he moved further down the path and out into the residential street that backed onto the university campus. He found himself coughing as thick, black smoke drifted across his face, clogging his lungs. The rain was obscuring his vision. At that moment, the rain and smoke seemed to drift away, just for half a second, and he found himself facing an empty street. He was too late. Henderson had disappeared.

Relief pounded through his body before it was flushed out by a sense of disappointment. *Do I really have a death wish?* He tried to shake himself, and then he heard, more distantly now, gunfire from up on the campus. Blood was beginning to pound in his ears as he turned and began to sprint back up the path, past the motionless bodies and into the area that surrounded the building.

Although the building was ringed with agents, their backs to Ollie, he noticed the fire door he'd left the building through was unmanned. On creeping towards it, he saw why. One of the soldiers lay motionless on the ground before the open door.

172

Steeling himself, Ollie moved towards it. As he reached the frame of the door, he peered around the corner.

The corridor was deserted, but the wall was riddled with bullet holes. After entering the corridor, he edged along it – pressing himself against the wall – until he reached the doorway that led into the main room where he knew his friends to be. Something had obviously gone wrong with the agents' plan, as they had hoped to extricate his friends without a full-scale shootout taking place, but as he peeked around the corner, his eyes were met with a hail of bullets smashing across the room.

The Russians had retreated across the hall towards a fire door, all the while firing at the open doorway through which the agents were attempting to enter the building. Meanwhile, his friends and John Bromley were pressed against each other in the same corner of the room as they'd been in before, their heads bowed, mercifully safe from the gunfire flashing around them. Leaning around the doorway, he waved his arms to attract their attention, and Robbie and Cap saw him immediately. Ollie was surprised that the agent hadn't tried to get his friends out through this corridor, but maybe he hadn't known it was safe and were afraid of drawing fire to the hostages.

He saw his friends as they began to scramble into a crouch and move towards the doorway. Grace was the first through the entrance, and she threw herself into Ollie's arms.

He enjoyed the feel of her body against his and breathed in her perfume before letting her go and urgently saying, 'Go,' as he gestured towards the fire door at the end of the corridor. He hesitated, wondering where to send them all. If Henderson was to be believed, a virus could be released on the campus any second. Sending them through the back gate, however, could lead them into more danger. He made a decision. 'Quickly. Head for the back gate. Don't look at the bodies. Get back to mine.'

She nodded resolutely, and they both managed a weak smile.

Cap and Robbie clapped him on the back as they passed, and Ollie relayed the same instructions to them, stuffing his front door key into Robbie's hand. As Emma followed them through the doorway, she kissed him on the cheek and said, 'Come on.'

He shook his head. 'Not until everyone is out. Go. I'll be right behind you.'

The group of girls scurried past him supporting Mike, whose eyes were out of focus and bloodshot. He opened his mouth to speak, but Ollie pushed him on after the rest of his friends. Finally, John Bromley staggered through the doorway, ducking his head low as a chatter of gunfire thudded into the wall behind him. For a moment, Ollie thought the man was going to collapse into him, and seeing the state of the agent sent a spasm of pain through the wound in his own chest. He clutched at it, the pair of them holding on to each other for support.

The next second, he'd fallen to the ground, unable to move any further, and there was a clang at the other end of the corridor as the adjacent door was thrown open and two of the Russians dressed all in black emerged, their faces obscured by grotesquely leering black gas masks. Simultaneously, the fire door they'd been making towards banged open, and Ollie looked up to see one of the men dressed in khaki and an intelligence agent framed in the doorway, their guns raised.

Dropping to the floor beside Bromley, Ollie was certain he was about to die. Bullets whipped through the air above him, and it was a miracle he hadn't been shot already, but that didn't stop him scrambling forwards on his knees, his head bent to avoid the hail of bullets. He wasn't going to leave the agent here to die, and he pulled John along with him. There had already been too much death today, and he wasn't going to watch any more. Then a bullet slammed into the floor at his feet, and he couldn't stop himself shouting out. There were several more shots and then silence. Ollie closed his eyes in acceptance as he heard footsteps move towards him, and then he was pulled to his feet.

*

They'd planned for the operation in the helicopter on the way · from Thames House, but the scene they'd walked into wasn't one that they'd been expecting. The team that had been tasked with approaching the building from the back entrance to the university campus had failed to call in after an explosion had emanated from that area. Seconds later, thick smoke had appeared from the area – thicker than the explosion would have caused. The men making their escape had set off smoke grenades that would have obscured the vision of the helicopter pilot circling over Egham. It would have been enough for them to make their getaway.

The crisp voice of Helen Robinson had crackled through the Chinook: 'Alpha team, make your final preparations for your approach to the campus. The latest thermal imaging suggests that one hostile has exited the target building and is making their way to the town through the back alley from the campus. Charlie team has already been dropped and will intercept. Sergeant Hiscock and his men from the Rifles have abseiled down at the entrance to the campus and are currently in the process of securing the main buildings.'

'Sounds like there won't be much for us boys to do,' Zaf had replied.

The strike team – consisting of a small team of SAS men led by Wolf, who'd commanded several operations under the section's directive in the past, as well as Zaf and Ben – would make their way from the playing fields to a dense patch of shrubbery across the car park from the building in which they believed Bromley and the students were being held.

In comparison to the SAS men, who were dressed in full combat clothing with tactical backpacks and C8 carbine assault rifles, the two operatives sent by Haynes were dressed in black trousers and long-sleeved, khaki Viper base layers underneath bulletproof, black Kevlar body armour. They did, however, have semi-automatic pistols strapped to holsters at their waists.

Ben and the others had been in discussion about whether to approach the building when the boy had come sprinting over to them, covered in blood and grime. It seemed as though some of the men had been left behind, with one of them in charge of a device that would trigger the release of the virus across the campus. They'd come equipped with gas masks on the helicopter, but they'd made a collective decision to leave them behind. If there was a chance of limiting the panic that would surely arise from this event, then it was a risk worth taking.

The boy had described the man in charge of the trigger, yet it was difficult to distinguish any individual. They could only have a few minutes left before the canisters containing the virus were detonated. The men had been expecting the agents' and soldiers' approach and withdrawn to a fire exit at the opposite end from the door that they'd entered by. Two of the SAS men had attempted to encircle the building, but they'd found themselves being repelled by their adversaries, who'd formed a defensive ring around the fire door. Fortunately, the captives hadn't been caught in the crossfire, and the SAS men were slowly picking off their enemies.

The battle had continued, and he'd watched as the

group of students and a man huddled in a distant corner had ducked low and began to scamper through a doorway to their right. He realised there must be another exit from the building. On their approach to the building, they'd spotted another fire door beside the one they'd used to enter the derelict structure. Motioning to the man nearest to him, Ben stepped away from the doorway and replaced the magazine in his Glock 19 pistol.

As he and Wolf withdrew from the others and fanned out towards the second fire door, they adopted a combat stance either side of the doorway and then leaned inside. As they did so, two figures appeared at the far end, both with their rifles raised. As Ben brought his gun round to fire, he noticed a glint of something in the spare hand of one of the men. He caught a glimpse of a thick jawline and receding, black hair beneath the gas mask as he fired two rounds at the man before ducking back behind the doorway; Wolf continued to fire his assault rifle.

The boy Ollie and a man were sprawled on the ground in the middle of the corridor, desperately trying to claw their way out of the firing line. Ben stepped back into the doorway, one eye closed as he concentrated fire on the figure to the left. A fear had crept into the back of his mind that he could activate the virus at any time. A bullet thudded into Wolf's shoulder, and blood sprayed into the air, splattering Ben's face. The SAS man ducked back, swearing grimly. After spitting blood from his mouth, Ben fired, his head bowed as bullets flew through the air above him.

Then he felt himself hurled backwards through the air, as two bullets slammed one after another into his Kevlar vest, sending him flying away from the doorway. His back crunched painfully onto the gravel path behind him, but he had the presence of mind to flip his body over so he landed upright on the balls of his feet, his gun still raised. He heard the first few shots he fired blind slam into the doorway, along with angry shouts from the injured SAS man.

As his vision cleared, Ben focussed his aim through the doorway, ignoring the bullets that whipped through the air and seared the tops of his shoulders. The first shot hit the man to the right in the throat, slicing through his windpipe, exiting his neck and disappearing into the undergrowth beyond. The man's body hadn't even begun to topple before the second and third bullets ripped through the oesophagus of his compatriot, who stumbled forwards, the device in his left hand still raised until his arm began to drop. Ben fired another shot and watched as it thudded into the man's forehead, spraying the walls and ceiling with an explosion of blood.

As Ben stepped into the building and pulled Ollie to his feet, Zaf rushed past him and began to attend to John Bromley, their missing agent. He grasped Ollie's shoulder briefly and steadied him before walking past him and across the corridor to where the two bodies lay.

The man he'd assumed to be Dimitri, the one in charge of the virus, had slumped forwards onto his front as the third bullet had thundered into his temple. Ben kicked him over and saw that the device in his hand was blinking. It was no bigger than a remote control for a TV. There was a timer that, as he watched, ticked over to zero seconds. A red light came on at the side. Were they too late?

'The timer is at zero. Repeat the timer is at zero,' he said swiftly, and then waited with bated breath for the response.

After what seemed like an eternity, Helen's crisp voice crackled through his earpiece: 'No reports of the virus being spread. Confirm the status of the trigger switch.'

Leaning down, Ben inspected the remote in the man's hand. A sense of relief flooded through his body. The man hadn't flicked the switch on the side of the device that presumably would have released the virus. They'd got to him in time. Raising his gun once more, he fired another shot in celebration.

16

The nightmare woke him; sweat was dripping off his clammy body. His head was pounding, and there was a dull pain in his chest from where the knife had slashed open his skin. Ollie pushed himself off the bed and moved quietly across his room, opened the door to the landing and crossed to the bathroom opposite. He brushed his teeth hurriedly, not wanting to look into the mirror, which he knew would reveal the same hollow, tortured expression he'd seen the morning before and perhaps would continue to see for the rest of his life.

Ollie knew he was lucky to be alive, but he didn't feel remotely lucky. He daren't close his eyes for fear of those images flashing through his vision once more. If anybody should have died back in that building, then it should have been him, he knew. Of all his friends and the girls that had been taken, he was the one who'd deserved to die.

*

As he'd been staggering from the wreckage of the building, he'd found the other two intelligence agents waiting for him, along with the SAS soldier Wolf, who'd been shot in the shoulder. He'd known that bodies must litter the ground around the building, but as he'd stumbled onto the path, he hadn't been prepared for the sight of the girl's broken body discarded in the bushes. Even now, he could taste the sick in his mouth that he'd expelled when he saw her.

The man who'd originally identified himself as Neil Carmichael, but whom he'd later found out was called Ben Viper, had pulled him away from the body. They'd tended to the wound in his chest, but he'd felt nothing – not even later when the doctors stitched the area. He felt nothing, just a hollow sense of emptiness. His parents had been waiting for him at the hospital, and the looks on their faces had triggered more pain running through him. Their tears felt more real than his own. They'd stayed with him throughout the examination, and Ollie had never before seen anything close to the concern on his dad's face.

Of course, Ollie hadn't mentioned to them what had taken place before the kidnapping. The back of his throat felt scratched and irritated, as though the lining had been ripped away, whilst his lips were both sore and numb. The next few minutes after the examination had passed in a blur, and he'd never be able to recall the conversation that had taken place with his friends, nor had he really seen their faces clearly. It was easier to recall the visit from John Bromley, who'd gripped Ollie's shoulder with a warmth that he hadn't been expecting. The agent still looked dreadful – his eyes and cheeks were swollen and bloodied, there were thick bandages underneath his jacket, and his left arm was in a sling – but he'd still managed a genuine smile on seeing Ollie.

Of all the friends and family to have visited or spoken to him since, this had been the one person whom Ollie had wanted to see above all others. It was difficult to explain why, but the experience they'd shared seemed to have created a strange understanding between them, and Ollie had felt able to speak to the agent in a way that he hadn't managed with anyone else.

'I can't stop thinking that I should have been killed,' he confided in Bromley after telling him of the guilt he felt for the girl's death and his inability to feel any emotion other than shame.

At this, the man had gripped his shoulder again and looked deep into Ollie's face with a knowing look that made him sure the agent knew exactly how he was feeling. 'You should be proud of how you acted, not ashamed. What happened to that girl was a tragedy, but it wasn't your fault. You saved all our lives. Remember that.'

The other agents – Ben Viper and the younger, possibly South Asian operative who introduced himself as Zaf – had been the next to visit Ollie, insisting on holding their conversation in the relative's room. Ollie's parents had wanted to join them, but Ollie hadn't wanted them to hear everything that had happened – not just yet.

He'd taken the two agents through everything that had happened from the moment he and his friends had been snatched. At one point, Ollie had the sense that Ben had been sizing him up, wondering how much to tell him.

Ben had continued. 'The thing is, Ollie, we haven't been able to find any trace of the virus yet. There weren't any aerosols. This raises the possibility that Conrad and his men were doing something else. Are you sure they said nothing that might imply where they went?'

Ollie had racked his brains, desperately trying to think of something, anything, that could help, but there was nothing. 'I'm sorry,' he'd replied, feeling as though he'd rather let the man down, 'but I don't think they said anything.'

When he'd finished recounting the events from his point of view, Ben had got to his feet and extended his hand to Ollie, a genuinely charming smile on his face. 'Thank you for all your help. You saved a lot of lives yesterday. Make sure you get some rest now. I'm sure we'll meet again.'

That had been a lie; Ollie knew that, as the two men had left the room, he'd see none of the agents again and he'd never know whether or not they were able to catch Henderson or the Russian, Conrad. *Why does that bother me so much?*

*

The lightly padding footsteps on the landing made him look round. There was only one good thing to have come out of the last few days. Ollie's parents had wanted to cancel their weeklong trip to the Lake District, but he'd insisted they still went. It had been in a very casual, offhand way that he'd mentioned this to Emma when she'd come to visit him in the hospital for a second time. Quite what had caused him to blurt out the invitation for her to stay with him, he didn't know, but here she was. Rather bleary eyed, she moved into the bathroom and put her arms around him, her naked body pressed against his.

Even without any make-up, she had a natural beauty that sent a tingling sensation through his insides when he saw her, with her flowing, light-brown hair and the single, lonely blonde strand that hung over her forehead, and those gorgeous brown eyes that seemed to warm even the coldest evening. She was smiling slightly groggily at him now, and Ollie found it impossible to look away. Somehow, the sensation of her arms around him was the best feeling he could have asked for, and at the same time, that very fact sent a fresh wave of guilt cascading over him. *How can I deserve this when others lie dead because of me?*

Breathing in her perfume, Ollie found himself succumbing to a happiness and warmth that he didn't deserve.

'What's wrong?' she whispered softly into his ear. 'You're really clammy.'

The truth was that she too had been twitching violently during the night, and Ollie had placed his arms around her to calm her once more. He didn't mention this to her, however. There was something else he felt he had to tell her now, before it might be too late. His nerves tingling, he looked down into Emma's face and said softly, 'I'm fine; it'll pass. I just need to tell you that I love having you here.'

To his surprise, her lips parted in pleasure, and he gazed into her brown eyes, finding it impossible to look away. They were almost nose to nose now, and her pale lips seemed to glisten, tempting him; he found himself unable to resist, and then their lips met. It was as though the sun was shining brightly down on the two of them, obscuring everything else from existence. All of a sudden, all the aches and pains and emotional scars left by the attack on the uni were extinguished, and they were entwined in a moment of affection that would endure. But then it was over, and it seemed to have lasted barely a second.

As their shining moment ended, Emma drew closer to him and whispered, 'I feel the same.'

He smiled, and then they were kissing once more, and it was the best feeling in the world to him. He never wanted to let go as he placed one hand on her back and the other in her sweeping, brown hair. Then she withdrew slightly and rested her head on his shoulder. As he held her close, he tried to shake off the unease that was stealing over him, despite the happiness he felt.

Then she released him, and he found himself lost for words, as he had been for years in her presence.

Luckily, Emma didn't seem to have the same problem, as she leaned forwards and kissed him gently on the cheek. 'I'm really glad you asked me round here,' she said softly, and the gentle smile playing across her lips made him wish he'd told her how he felt earlier. 'Especially as you have every Daniel Craig film available to watch,' she added in a teasing voice that made Ollie's eyes narrow slightly. Emma laughed at his reaction. 'Don't worry, you'll do for me.'

'Oh, thanks for the vote of confidence!' Ollie replied in mock indignation.

'I think I'm going to jump in the shower before you rugby tackle me back to bed.' Emma moved past him towards the walk-in power shower behind. 'Room for two, though…' she teased cheekily.

As sorely tempted as he was to follow her, Ollie wanted to clear his head. 'I'll rugby tackle you when I get in.' He smiled. 'Just don't go doing anything silly like putting too many clothes on whilst I'm out for a run.'

'No chance of that.'

The look in Emma's eyes made him regret his decision, even as he moved onto the landing and closed the door behind him.

As he stared out of the landing window, he could see his neighbour, Patrick, striding swiftly towards his house across the street. Ollie's neighbours had been given strict orders by his mum to check up on Ollie frequently to make sure that he was all right. They'd been very good friends to them ever since he could remember, and he liked them a lot, particular one of their two daughters, Steph, who'd inherited £4,000 from an aunt and, instead of investing it, had spent it all on a quad bike.

The quad bike itself was a road-legal all-terrain vehicle (ATV), and she'd taken Ollie out for a ride on it a few times. He could still recall the face of the man sitting in his Porsche as they sped past him on a quad bike. Ollie had been fourteen years old at the time, and he'd really enjoyed it.

Ollie crossed over to his bedroom and hurriedly pulled on

his running top and trousers before pulling a black half-zip training top over his torso and strapping his phone to his arm in a holder. He then extricated the matted headphones from beside his phone and untangled a pair. He left his bedroom and headed downstairs, taking the steps three at a time. He reached the hallway in a couple of seconds and stuffed his feet into his trainers before grabbing a front door key from the table in the hall.

As he unlocked the front door and pulled it open, Ollie settled on a playlist for his run. He selected it from his phone and tried to focus on the music as it began to beat steadily in his ears. Yes, the stab wound to his chest was only a minor slash, but they'd insisted that he take it easy. Even now Ollie could feel the thin stitches that ran across his chest being stretched, but he pushed the thought from his mind.

He closed and locked the door, slid the key into the holder on his arm, alongside his phone, then set off. Continuing to run hard on the main road, sweat began to pour off him, as memories swirled through his mind: Henderson raising the knife, the tear-stained faces of his friends, and the bullets thudding into the wall above his head in that corridor. He could feel the lactic acid building in his muscles, and he wondered how much longer he could keep running, but the pain hurt much less because it was helping to drive away the memories of the past few days from him.

Turning next to a small stream, he came to a decision: he couldn't keep running away. Emma didn't deserve that. He'd run off and left her on her own. He was being a coward, and she deserved so much better than that. *After all,* he realised, *she's been through the same experience as me.* He'd watched her lying curled up in a defence ball on that hall floor, with tears streaming down her face. She'd been terrified, but she wasn't running away from it. Instead, she'd decided to come and stay with him, and she'd tried to forget the things that had happened to her.

In fact, Emma had been brave – much braver than he'd been. She'd been forced to watch as people had been killed right in front of her and Ollie had suffered his chest being slashed open. How torturous the dreams she was having right now must be. Yet it was he who was feeling sorry for himself. Filled with a renewed determination and intent, he turned and began to run back the way he'd come, the pain in his legs vanishing into insignificance in the face of the task he'd now set himself. He had to take responsibility.

Ten minutes later, he re-entered the lane that led to his house, and as he jogged past an abandoned skip to his left, he noticed something that made him stop dead. There was a white van parked next to the side of his house, and although there were no identifying marks to distinguish it, he knew at once that something wasn't right. The van was parked right beside their house. There seemed no reason for it to be there. On closer inspection, he could see that the windows on the driver's and passenger's sides were blacked out. He could think of only one reason why it would be there.

Not pausing to think, he sprinted towards the house, an increasing sense of dread stealing over his heart. As he passed the van, he glanced inside it, but it was empty. There was no one in sight, and it was as though a deadly silence had descended over the whole neighbourhood. After fumbling to extract the key from his phone holder and get it into the lock, he finally managed to turn the key and push the door open; then he stumbled over the doorstep to find the hall deserted. He shouted for Emma, but there was no reply.

The whole house seemed still and quiet. Ollie stepped forwards, hardly making a sound as he crept towards the kitchen. As he neared the door, he felt his heart hammering against the inside of his chest and fear pulsated through every fibre of his body. Moving slowly, he reached out a hand and pushed at the door, which swung open silently at his touch.

Scared about what he'd find inside, Ollie walked into the room. It too was deserted. Breathing heavily, he retraced his steps back to the hall and turned right towards the lounge. Unable to take the fear any longer, he kicked out at the door and burst through into the room, but there was nobody there. He called out again with no response. Cursing under his breath, he ran up the stairs and began to search each room, starting with the bathroom, which – like every other room – was empty. He could no longer hold back the terror that had started to creep over him at the first sight of the van, and it engulfed him more completely than anything had ever done in his life.

He gave another shout, but there was still no reply. Frantically, he began to search the rest of the rooms until at last he reached the last room on that floor. It too was empty. A sense of desperation was filling him now, and as he glanced out of the window overlooking the driveway, he saw something that made his heart stop. There were two men in the middle of the driveway, and they were dragging a figure behind them. Ollie didn't need a second glance to know who that figure was. It was Emma. The back doors of the van were open, and even from this distance, he could see the fear in her eyes. Emma's mouth was obscured by a thick piece of duct tape, and her hair was dishevelled, but she still fought to throw the men off her.

The pain in his muscles forgotten, Ollie ran down the stairs and snatched at the front door. For a second, he fumbled with the door handle, but then the door was open, and he could see the scene clearly. Emma was already being bundled into the back of the van. One of the two men jumped in next to her, and then Emma's eyes found him as the doors were shut behind her. Although he was just a few yards from the van, Ollie could do nothing for her. The second man had thrown the doors shut and jumped into the driver's side of the van, and it was already starting to pull away. The sight of the tyres moving further and further away from him spurred Ollie into action.

With his heart thudding against his ribs, he sprinted across the lane to the gate that led to his neighbour's house. Vaulting the fragile metal gate, he ran towards the garage located at the far end of the driveway. After opening garage door, he headed straight for the back of the building. The garage was large with golf clubs and other sporting equipment strewn across the cold floor. However, it was the corner of the building that he headed to, where a huge, sleek, black quad bike sat. It was a four-by-four, road-legal Big Boss Quadzilla quad bike, and the largest physical size possible for a quad bike, so it could comfortably fit two people.

He grabbed a red helmet from a sideboard, jammed it on to his head and fastened it tightly. After being taken out for a ride on the quad bike by Steph, Ollie had gone home and researched the bike. He knew it had a 500cc, four-stroke, liquid-cooled engine and the brakes on this particular quad bike used hydraulic discs. After leaping onto the black seat of the Quadzilla, he quickly turned the key, which was conveniently already in the ignition, and the engine sprang into life. At once, Ollie felt the power of the machine shudder through him. He twisted the accelerator and gripped the handlebars as he felt the machine jolt him forwards. With his hands already slippery with sweat, he turned the handlebars and steered the bike out of the garage.

When he was out into the open, the roar of the 500cc engine filled his ears, and the wind rushed up to meet him, buffeting at the side of his face as he managed to steer the bike into the lane. Ollie couldn't see the van anywhere, and he couldn't suppress the fear that was creeping over him, so he pushed down on the accelerator with his thumb. In that moment, he realised the immense power this machine possessed. As he kept his thumb pressed down hard on the accelerator, he had to grip the handlebars tightly to keep himself on the seat as the quad bike shot forwards out of the lane.

The main road beyond was busy, but he didn't stop to check the traffic; instead, he burst straight out onto the main road, and as the front end of the quad bike surged out into the road, he had to twist the handlebars sharply to avoid colliding with a blue BMW that was speeding past him. The car lurched to one side to avoid an impact, and the driver jerked the steering wheel violently, eventually managing to regain control of the car. The sound of blaring horns filled his ears, but Ollie fought to keep his attention on the road.

He was staring transfixed at the cars in front of him, searching frantically for any sign of the van in which Emma now travelled, frightened and alone. With anger pulsing through his veins at the thought, he accelerated hard, and as he did so, he temporarily lost control of the quad bike, as his left hand slipped from the handlebars. As a result, the quad bike veered out of his lane for just a split second. Clawing at the handlebars, he tried to pull it back into the lane, but before he could do so, a car clipped the side of the quad bike, sending it veering off course. Although it was only the slightest of touches, he felt the machine beneath him shudder violently, and for one dreadful second, the quad bike threatened to topple over. Fortunately, Ollie wrenched the handlebars back in time, pulling it back into the right lane.

The driver of the car, however, wasn't so lucky, and out of the corner of his eye, Ollie saw the collision as the vehicle careered into another passing car. In that moment, he could see the fear in the driver's eyes as another car smashed into the back of the Audi, shunting it forwards with such ferocity that it threatened to spin further out of control. Ollie pulled the quad bike to the side of the road and brought it to a stop, staring unblinking at the crash he'd caused. He had no idea what to do for the best. He was faced with an impossible choice: either he stopped to help the drivers and risked letting the van get away, or he left the cars and continued to follow the van. Both cars had toppled over sideways and were lying on the road, and the underside of the Ford had left a trail of petrol in its wake. A little way to his right, a man had pulled his car to the side and was frantically talking into his mobile phone, and all the while, screams echoed from the vehicles.

He wanted to help them, but he had to find Emma. He knew that stopping was the right thing to do, but he couldn't bring himself to abandon Emma. Throwing the crash one last heart-wrenching look, he swung the quad bike back onto the road and pressed his thumb on the accelerator. *What if someone else had died as a result of what I'd done?*

The quad bike pushed ahead, and as it rounded a corner, relief flooded his body. He could see it. The van was just a few cars in front of him now.

Then, out of the corner of his eye, he saw a Range Rover screaming towards him out of a lane to his right. His already bruised finger was jammed more desperately onto the throttle, but he knew it was no good. Yelling in fear, he wrenched the handlebars to the left, just as the full force of the car slammed into the right-hand side of the quad bike. Then the quad bike was rolling, and Ollie screamed in terror and pain, as every single bone and organ in his body simultaneously felt as though it was being crumpled into a matchbox. His left arm broke his fall, and then his head slammed into the tarmac, as the weight of the bike collapsed onto his legs and all sound was obliterated around him.

Dully, he became aware that he was being brutally forced onto his feet, and then the dimly flickering light in front of his eyes faded for the final time, and the darkness consumed him.

17

As the custom-built Jaguar XJ Sentinel swept around Trafalgar Square and down Whitehall, Steven Houghton swore once more as he studied the newspaper headline in front of him. It wasn't in his nature to swear ordinarily, but he was already beginning to feel the strain that the last twenty-four hours had put upon the government. This story was the last thing they needed at a time when Houghton already suspected there were the beginnings of a coup against the PM. It was his job to ascertain whether it was true, who was behind it and how to neutralise it. Another party civil war was the last thing the country needed.

It wasn't that he had any particular sympathy for politicians; that was part of what made him such a good Cabinet Secretary. He wasn't a party man; he was a civil servant, and a damn good one. In the three decades he'd worked with politicians, however, he'd never faced a crisis like the last eighteen months. He would have gladly returned to the days of the Iraq War in terms of the difficulty it caused the government and special advisors.

Houghton had seen defeat in the PM's eyes a number of times in the past eighteen months, but he'd fought on. Indeed, he'd found an inner steel and resolve that many hadn't believed he possessed. It was the PM who'd initiated the policies that were slowly bringing the country back to a semblance of normality, and for that he should be applauded.

In the evenings, when Houghton returned from the corridors of power to his luxury flat in Fulham, he retreated to the comfort of a whisky bottle. Yes, he'd read memoirs and autobiographies, but the writing was blurred by the effects of the Macallan, of which he boasted one of the most extensive collections in the country. It was only in Downing Street that he truly belonged. He enjoyed his job, he had to admit, even in the darkest of times, such as the last eighteen months. Whether it was coercing backbench MPs to vote for a bill or being able to advise on and influence the biggest decisions facing the PM, he enjoyed the sense of power that the role brought.

The blacked-out Jaguar was passing the famous Banqueting House, where King Charles I had lost his head, and not for the first time, Houghton smiled at the irony. The man chiefly responsible for having the monarch executed was Oliver Cromwell, of whom a statue stood proudly outside the Palace of Westminster, despite the monarchy having swiftly returned to Britain after Cromwell's period in office. He wondered if any members of the royal family felt a sense of indignation that Cromwell still stood guard over the British government.

Houghton had been expecting the call, but that didn't make it any less of an unpleasant experience when it came through. The PM was angry, and Houghton knew he had every right to be. It had been Houghton's job to try to persuade the journalist Janine Crofton not to write any more articles regarding sensitive information and to find out her source. He had met her in a café in Butler's Wharf overlooking the River Thames, with the imposing Tower Bridge to their left, forming a perfect picture-postcard view with the Tower of London nestled humbly behind it and many of the city's skyscrapers looming above it.

She was the reporter who'd briefed the populace on the government's plans to cut meals for school children during the pandemic, as well as releasing a story that itemised the bill to limit wage rises for NHS employees. Both of those policies had been at a preliminary stage and were being pushed by Seward Atley and his cabal. They also happened to be two of the most unpopular bills proposed by the government, and the blame had fallen upon the PM, despite them being the design of the Defence Minister.

It was an open secret that Atley was resentful of the limited role he had in the cabinet. He'd lobbied for the position of Home Secretary, and the PM may have caved in to his demand had Houghton not stepped in. Keeping your enemies too close was foolish, in his opinion. Atley may have to be placated, but to give him too much power would have been a mistake. Yet, despite that refusal, Atley had found a way of instigating unpopular policies and undermining the PM. It wouldn't surprise Houghton if it were the Defence Minister himself who was feeding the press and using them to discredit the PM for policies that were actually his design.

Houghton knew his meeting with Crofton hadn't gone well, or not as well as he'd hoped, but he'd expected the journalist at least to keep her counsel for a day whilst she mulled over their offer. Bloody journalists. This was the problem with a society that demanded a free press. Sometimes, he wished that democracy wasn't so bloody awkward, yet that was the framework in which he operated. He'd known, of course, that this phone call was coming. The moment his own undersecretary had informed him of the article published by Crofton that morning, he'd been expecting the backlash.

'BRITAIN TURNS ON ITSELF: VIRUS ATTACK ORCHESTRATED BY DISILLISUIONED FAR RIGHT'

The armoured, custom-built Jaguar XJ Sentinel turned

into Downing Street after the black steel gates had swung open automatically to admit them. It was just over thirty years since this latest set of barricades had been erected, and Houghton couldn't help but smile to himself. Democracy. This had been Margaret Thatcher's idea of democracy: to shut herself securely away from the rest of the world. Given the events of the following couple of years, perhaps she'd been right to have them installed, but in reality, the gates themselves had become more of a symbol of oppressed democratic rioters than imposing leadership.

Moments later, the Jaguar came to a stop outside the iconic black front door that belonged to Number Ten Downing Street, in the middle of which glistened a letterbox engraved with the words 'First Lord of the Treasury' – the former title of the PM's office. Like many things surrounding Downing Street, however, it was just for show. The original door had been replaced in 1991 following the targeted IRA mortar attack, and this reinforced-steel replica had been made to look identical to the original. The head gardener still claimed to find fragments of broken glass from that explosion in the flower beds to this day, such was the devastation it had caused.

As ever, a gaggle of news reporters were arranged along the cobbled street, directing their broadcasts against the backdrop of perhaps the most famous door in the world. As the car door was opened for him and Steven Houghton clambered out, there was an excitable upsurge in chatter from the media present, and they pressed him for a quote on a range of matters. He merely raised a hand in greeting, hastily arranged a smile onto his face and walked forwards towards the door that had already been opened for him. He glanced briefly at the policeman stationed beside the door and rather grimaced at the sight of a Heckler & Koch MP5SF slung lazily over the policeman's right shoulder. Guns had always made him feel uncomfortable.

After taking a step forwards, he was greeted by the brightly lit corridor beyond the reinforced-steel door. It shut behind him with a snap, and with it, some of the weight on his shoulders lifted. It was as though the scrutiny of the outside world had been barricaded beyond the historic panelling and had thus now been silenced. He barely glanced at the paintings lining the walls, artwork that had been borrowed from a central government reserve, as his feet in their perfectly polished black shoes strode down the plush carpet beneath the glittering chandeliers that hung overhead. His grey suit and tie, heavily lined expression, and milky eyes seemed out of place in the brightly coloured hallways of power, but in fact, this was the environment in which he thrived.

Unlike most visitors to Number Ten Downing Street, he wasn't greeted by a member of the cabinet or an eager-to-impress intern. The few people he passed turned their heads briefly in his direction, but they made no move to welcome him. As he passed the grand staircase – which was perhaps the most famous aspect of the building's interior, due to the black-and-white portraits of former PMs that were placed in ascending chronological order up the stairs – he reflected on the location of this meeting. It was unusual for the PM not to hold a briefing of this nature in one of his private offices on the first floor. Indeed, it was rare for Houghton to bypass the staircase without making the climb.

He reached his destination and turned into one of the three state drawing rooms that occupied a large proportion of the building's ground floor. Built by the eighteenth-century architect Robert Taylor in the latter half of that century, the Pillard Room was predominantly used for hosting grand receptions or ambassadorial events. The plush Persian carpet in the centre of the room was an exact replica of the sixteenth-century original that was now housed at the Victoria and

Albert Museum in Knightsbridge. Several tables were arranged around the striking carpet as the room's centrepiece, with perfectly ironed, white linen draped across them, and dozens of wine glasses and cups for tea and coffee neatly lined up on top. Apart from half a dozen chairs dotted around the room, there was nowhere to sit, and as Houghton entered, he took note that the PM was leaning against one of the tables in a very casual stance, wearing one of his characteristic tailored, blue suits. That didn't bode well for anyone.

Another glance around the room told Houghton that he was the last to arrive, and he closed the door behind him accordingly. The other three people to have been invited to the meeting seemed more bemused by the change of venue than Houghton. The Home Secretary, Teresa Powell, was standing beside the marble mantelpiece and was clearly uncomfortable not to be sitting behind a desk; her legs were bent in a cramped position, and her sunken, brown eyes were irritable between her curtains of sleek, black hair. In contrast, Samira Patel, the Foreign Secretary, appeared concerned and a little nervous, her eyes darting between Houghton, the PM and the third man in the room.

Seward Atley alone seemed relaxed, almost bored. He too was leaning against one of the tables that lined the room, and he was smiling to himself as though he alone had just been told some very amusing joke. His piggy, hooded, brown eyes were watering, as ever, but he made no attempt to stop the flow. Like Houghton, his slightly crumpled, grey suit suggested a man out of his time, yet a shrewd political operator remained beneath the somewhat frail appearance. In this case, appearances certainly could be deceptive, and Steven had learned long ago to be careful around Atley.

'Nice of you to join us,' stated Atley with a smirk, directing his words at Houghton. 'The traffic from Putney at this time in the morning must be terribly irksome. Not very considerate of the PM to arrange a meeting so early; doesn't he know the Civil Service only work in the early afternoon?' He chortled to himself, but nobody else laughed.

There were no pleasantries from the PM, however. 'I assume you've seen it. More to the point, have you seen the hate-crime attacks throughout the country. There have been stabbings outside mosques in both Birmingham and Reading, and there are demonstrations and riots breaking out everywhere. The term "civil war" has never seemed quite so tangible in this country for centuries. The last thing we needed was the press triggering the unexploded bomb of racial divisions in this country at a time when we're trying to keep the people safe from a bunch of maniacs intent upon unleashing the next plague.

'We have enough to be dealing with at the moment. We already have environmentalists using the forthcoming storm as a pretext to hold a large-scale demonstration at the Thames Barrier, protesting that it needs upgrading, or London will become the new Atlantis, and now we have the prospect of demonstrations from both sides of the racial divide. What did you say to the woman? How did she get hold of this information? I thought she'd agreed to listen to our offer. Did you not seek assurances that there would be no more stories in the interim? I want to know who's responsible for this information getting to the press, and I want to know if any of you are to blame.'

'Isn't it customary, in these circumstances,' Seward Atley interrupted lazily, 'to order a Civil Service inquiry into the possibility of information leakage?'

'Goddamn it, Seward, for once can you try to show some loyalty. This is the sixth time in the last few months alone that Janine Crofton has released stories on sensitive policy decisions.' As if from nowhere, he unexpectedly produced a copy of the newspaper from a couple of days previously and threw it onto the centre of the Persian rug, so that the headline 'New Lethal Strain of Coronavirus Penetrates Britain' was clearly visible.

Houghton had been worried that he'd found the PM in a downbeat mood, but it seemed as though he was coming out firing. His green eyes were alert and angry, and he suddenly seemed younger than he had done for months and more like the man who'd served with the SBS in Libya and energised a fading political party with his dynamism and eloquent public speaking. The difference in just twenty-four hours was astonishing. Perhaps it was the impending arrival of the Chinese delegation, with whom the PM had been fostering close ties, that was the catalyst for this change.

It's amazing what some negative press can do, thought Houghton wryly.

'Forgive me, Prime Minister,' Seward Atley said abruptly, with a slight bite to his voice, 'but you surely can't be suggesting that one of us is responsible for this indiscretion?' His eyes had narrowed, and he was surveying the PM with a rather shrewd expression.

The response was immediate and blunt: 'I've made no such accusation.' The PM's green eyes flashed towards his Defence Minister. 'But it's a fact that you hold the great offices of state with the biggest departments. At the very least, you have the most resources to try to identify the source of the leak.'

'Even so, to categorically identify—' began the Home Secretary.

The PM was losing what patience he still retained and did not let her get further. 'I want to make myself perfectly clear. Between you, find out who was responsible for this leak, or so help me I'll have Aldwyn Haynes's team retrieve every call Miss Crofton has made in the last few months and get them to scour every CCTV camera in the country to trace her movements in the last twenty-four hours. Then we'll know the source of our leak. Please don't make me go down that route.'

'Perhaps you'd be better advised to ask Mr Houghton to lead the inquiry, given the fact he and this journalist appear to be on such good terms.' Atley was smirking again.

'I'm sure Mr Houghton did his best to discourage Miss Crofton,' said Samira Patel, perhaps seeking to defuse the situation. 'At least his loyalty in this room can't be questioned. That being said' – Atley and Powell turned their heads towards her – 'matters have escalated with this latest article. This story alone could be enough to bring down the government. We spent last night informing the ambassadors that the stories being published had zero truth to them, then we wake up to this. Our credibility is shot.'

'Remind me not to hire you as an entertainer for my son's birthday party,' quipped Atley. 'Governments have survived far worse.'

'Samira's right; our credibility is shot. We only have a few hours to turn this around. Now get out there and help us bring this government – and more importantly, this country – back from the brink.'

The other three politicians swept past the civil servant on their way out of the Pillard Room, Seward Atley sneering at Houghton as he snapped the door shut behind him.

Now it was just the two of them left in the room, the PM seemed to relax a little, his shoulders losing some of their tension and the aggression fading from his face. Indeed, he turned to the table and poured himself a glass of freshly squeezed orange juice from a jug that he'd presumably ordered to be brought down before the meeting had started, and he then offered one to his Cabinet Secretary.

The drinks poured, Landen Waverley rounded on the civil

servant. 'I assigned you the task of talking the journalist round, and now she publishes this story.'

There was a moment's silence before Houghton said calmly, 'I'll speak to her, Prime Minister. Today.'

'See that you do,' growled the PM. He drained his glass, replaced it on the table and stalked from the room.

*

Back in the car on the way back to his office, it took just a few minutes for Houghton to reach Janine Crofton, who it seemed had been expecting his call. In contrast to Houghton, who kept his tone deliberately abrupt, the journalist seemed in a particularly effusive mood – no doubt buoyed by her most high-profile article yet. Once again, however, she refused to meet him unless she selected the meeting place. There was a slight pause on her end of the line before she confirmed the location to him before ending the call.

As Houghton studied the nominated place a few moments later after a quick internet search, he frowned slightly before passing the information to his driver.

Pushing the location of the meet from his mind, Houghton reflected on the conversation with the PM. He thought to himself that threatening the journalist with legal proceedings wasn't the most diplomatic way to approach this problem. That being said, it was perhaps time to play dirty.

18

Ordinarily, this would have felt like a good morning to Jackie. She'd woken late to find Tiggy curled on the end of the bed at her feet, bleary eyed, and spent the next few minutes scratching him behind one ear. That was a first: her waking up before him. It was usually the heavy impact of his front paws on her chest or else the feeling of his wet nose against her own that stirred her from sleep. Perhaps it had been her late night, drinking wine on the sofa, that had worn him out, as he'd sat on her lap, making it difficult for her to reach the wine glass in which she'd sought refuge.

Tiggy made even the most boring programme on the TV interesting. If she had the remote in one hand and a wine glass in the other, he'd move forwards and nudge each of the objects in turn, impatiently competing for her attention. When she leaned her nose forwards, he'd reach up with his own and plant the usually wet tip affectionately against hers. She'd only owned Tiggy for a year, having yearned for some company during the pandemic, and she'd settled on him after viewing dozens of cats online.

There hadn't been a single moment since in which Jackie had regretted her decision. He really was a gorgeous cat, with his pointed, black ears and thin face, complete with a white smudge around his nose and long, white whiskers, as well as a white strip down his belly, which he displayed when he was particularly desperate for her attention. It took only the slightest tap on the sofa beside her for him to jump up with a little trilling noise that always made her smile.

In truth, she would have liked to spend the rest of the morning in her flat with Tiggy, such was her mood of late, but that hadn't been possible. She'd been summoned by the people who'd caused her such a dilemma. Jackie wasn't sure exactly why she'd been asked to attend Thames House once again. She'd thought this whole business was over. She'd followed the events unfolding at the university from The Grid in MI5 headquarters, and she had to admit she'd found the whole experience rather thrilling, if not terrifying. Helen Robinson, the senior analyst on Ben's team, had run point on the operation and advised the strike team on the positions they should take up before the assault, although Ben had taken final operational control from the ground.

The strike team approaching from the rear of the campus had lost contact with control soon after their arrival, whilst the team landing on the upper reaches of the campus had soon been met by a scene of utter panic, as there had been several explosions from the bottom end of the university. This was the point when Ben had launched his assault on the building, which had turned into a bloodbath. A targeted strike on the building had been ruled out because of the risk of civilian casualties, but even so, any assault was loaded with risk due to the structure's position on campus and losing one of the strike teams.

Strangely, Jackie had felt a sense of calm with adrenalin pumping through her body as she watched them approach the building from the camera mounted on the SAS men's jackets. Within seconds of approaching the building, they'd been met by a hail of gunfire, and it had seemed as though they'd be overwhelmed. The mercenaries, it appeared, had been expecting their approach and had retreated to the far end of the main hall, crouching behind an open fire door opposite the door through which the agents approached. When two of the SAS men had attempted to circle the building, they'd been welcomed with a flurry of bullets. The man leading the SAS strike team had been injured, whilst another had been killed.

Eventually, the imminent threat of the virus being released over the university had been averted, and that – Jackie had assumed – was that. But now she was being called back. There was conflict within her. Working closely with Ben had stirred up old feelings that she'd thought were long buried, despite the fact he'd clearly changed. The charm and composure were still there, but she'd noticed the cold calculation behind the smile. That had never been a part of him when they'd known each other before, and there was something else that troubled her. There was a shadowy nature to the attractive, blue eyes that hinted at what he'd been through. Instinctively, she knew it was unlikely he'd open up to her about what had happened, but she wanted to understand what had caused the change in him.

*

The storm that had been forecast for days had finally arrived, bringing with it a driving rain and intimidating, dark-grey clouds that obscured the sky. It hammered down upon Jackie, soaking every inch of her skin, despite the waterproof clothing she wore. The pavements were sodden and slippery, and she started as the first rumble of thunder crackled overhead, as though God were bracing the world for a dramatic announcement.

As she crossed in front of Thames House, Jackie took a deep breath and ran forwards into the building. Minutes later, having been signed in by security, she found the cylindrical pods sliding open to release her into The Grid, which appeared to be a hive of activity. There were people busying themselves between banks of desks – more people than Jackie remembered having occupied the floor.

The young analyst Maya Chowdhury was suddenly at her shoulder, juggling a pile of files in her hands and looking harassed. 'Detective Ambrose, lovely to see you,' she said rather absentmindedly, struggling to keep a hold of the folders in her arms. 'They're waiting for you in Mr Haynes's office. This way.' She gestured for Jackie to follow her.

Jackie did so, feeling increasingly nervous. *What could this be about? They've already made me sign the Official Secrets Act. What else do they want to discuss with me?*

When they reached the door behind which the section chief's office lay, Maya reached her hand out for the handle before withdrawing it as though scolded. With the files now stuffed precariously under her shoulder, the young analyst wrapped smartly on the door with her knuckles instead.

'Come,' came the command from within.

Looking rather relieved, Maya pulled the door open, and the files went tumbling to the floor. Jackie bent down to help her retrieve the reams of paper now strewn everywhere, as Maya wiped sweat from her brow and dropped to her knees frantically.

'In here, Detective, if you please.' There was no mistaking the gruff Yorkshire tones of Aldwyn Haynes, the leader of this department.

Her guilt alleviated slightly as a passing Simon Wynn-Jones began to help Maya gather up the papers, Jackie straightened up and stepped inside the office, closing the door behind her with a slight swish. It was the first time she been inside the office, and at first glance, she was surprised at just how plain it was, with just a sumptuous walnut desk in the centre, behind which the head of this section sat in a leather-backed chair, and a large wooden filing cabinet in the far corner. As ever, Aldwyn was dressed in a smart suit – today, accompanied with a red tie.

There was more colour in the face of the section chief today. Although no longer an attractive man – with his rather weathered skin and sagging, jowly cheeks – he emanated respect. There was something steely in his close-set, deadened, grey eyes that radiated leadership. There was a warmth in the smile he gave Jackie, however, as she entered his office, and he beckoned for her to take the seat opposite him. As she did so, she realised for the first time that they weren't alone.

Ben was there also, although he'd somehow managed to blend into the surroundings of the room. Dressed today in a black Belstaff Grove lightweight jacket – which was unzipped to reveal a crisp, white shirt beneath – and tailored, black trousers and black shoes, he looked perfectly relaxed, and his piercing, blue eyes seemed to lie dormant in a bedrock of ice. He too was smiling as she entered the room, and he inclined his head towards the chair, whilst he remained standing to the side of it.

'Thank you for coming back in, Detective Ambrose,' Aldwyn said gruffly. 'As you may have already gathered, I'm not really one for pleasantries, so we'll get right to the point, if you don't mind? We felt as though we didn't best utilise your abilities when you were last at The Grid. I want to remedy that. I'd like to keep you here on a temporary secondment until this crisis is over. Is this something you'd consider?' His voice was calm and even, but Jackie wondered if there was a flicker of concern in those deep-set, grey eyes.

'We all know you'll continue digging into this even if you aren't helping us directly,' Ben added wryly from the corner. 'This way, you won't be a pain in the arse.'

Jackie couldn't stop herself throwing him a warning look. She hastily tried to rearrange her expression.

However, Aldwyn had already begun to laugh. 'I don't think I've seen anyone give Ben that sort of look before; let alone get away with it. It'll do him good if you stick around. Far too confident for his own good, if you ask me.

'I don't need someone to help me take a piss or smile and nod at one of mine or Ben's decisions. If you don't agree with what we're saying, then put us straight – within reason, of course. Sometimes, you need a human element and someone with a bit of compassion. You lose that after a while in this job. Although it isn't just that. I've read your file.'

Haynes continued to eye her appraisingly. 'You're a dogged investigator. You don't let things go. That should have been evident enough when you went to Senta Barracks, but some of the cases you've worked on, whilst not being high profile, illustrate that you have extraordinary powers of deduction and instinct. To uncover the truth, you're able to piece together complex pieces of evidence that others would find obscure and irrelevant. That's why you're here. I don't believe we have the truth of this yet. So,' he paused, before holding out his hand, 'will you help us?'

There was no denying she was intrigued, and she wanted to see the case through to its conclusion. There was just the slightest doubt in the back of her brain, which she dismissed after a quick glance at Ben, who was smiling casually. Reaching out her hand, she shook Aldwyn's and said, 'I'll help.'

The section head waved his hand dismissively. 'Call me, Aldwyn. We aren't in the 1950s, and my knighthood seems to have gone missing in the post, so Aldwyn is fine.' He gestured at Ben, who moved towards the door and slid it open.

Jackie took that as her cue to leave.

As she stood up, Haynes added, 'One thing I'd appreciate.

Knock on the bloody door when you want to come in. And one of these days, Viper, you'll wear a tie.'

There was a dark look on Ben's face as he shot back, 'You know that's not going to happen.'

Jackie and Ben left the office together, and as they did so, their bodies touched briefly, and for a fleeting moment, memories of their time together flashed through Jackie's mind. Would Ben have felt it too? She expected not. She doubted whether he could even remember that life. He was too immersed in this world – the world she'd just agreed to stay in for a while longer.

He averted his gaze from hers until they reached the meeting room, the door of which he slid open. They entered the room, and he shut behind them before turning to face her.

'It's good to have you here, but I don't want you to feel uncomfortable,' said Ben brusquely. 'If we're going to work together, then we need to be able to deal with the past. I'm sorry for what happened, but I won't talk about it – at least not now. What's happening at the moment takes precedence over anything we had.' His expression softened, as Jackie raised her eyebrows. 'I know I treated you badly before. I'm not denying that.'

'Good,' replied Jackie shortly, 'because when this is over, you either owe me an explanation or you disappear from my life again. That's your choice, Ben.' She spoke firmly, and she meant it, but even she was surprised at how strong her voice remained.

He appeared to consider her for a moment. There was a haunted and conflicted look in his eyes that spoke to Jackie more plainly than anything he'd said to her in the past few days. 'We'll talk, and I'll explain what I can,' he said eventually, before taking a step closer to her and adding, in a softer voice, 'It really is good to be around you again. I'd forgotten—' He cut himself off, as though he were afraid he'd say too much.

That was another change in him, Jackie knew. He'd never have hesitated to show his emotions in the past, but then again, this was now the nature of his job.

Ben smiled, and the twinkle behind the eyes had returned. 'There are a few things you need to be made aware of. We have so far been unable to capture any of the other individuals who took part in the hostage situation at Royal Holloway University. The bodies of the men killed there have been identified, and they're mercenaries from the old Soviet states, with no known political affiliation. As you're now aware, thanks to our tabloid friends, the death of an ethnically diverse student has led to the country being on the brink of racial civil war. The pieces of the puzzle simply aren't making sense, and what happened at the university the other night has muddied the waters still further.'

'But there was no indication that Henderson shot the girl because of her ethnicity, was there?' Jackie asked confusedly.

Ben shook his head. 'None at all, but that's the perception. Only one of the captives wasn't white, and that was the girl who was killed. The optics aren't good, and in cases such as these, the optics matter more than the reality. For one thing, according to John, they detected the call the boy made to us by using a device able to identify phone usage in the building. If they have sophisticated equipment like that, then they could have easily had the means to block all mobile phone activity in the area, but they didn't. It's as though they wanted us to be alerted – or at the very least, they were more than happy for us to be alerted – to their presence at the university. That suggests it was more of a stunt than anything else.'

There was a troubled look in Ben's eyes as he paused briefly and looked directly at Jackie. In that moment, she found it impossible to look away.

'Then we come to the biggest issue of them all: the virus. The virus we believe was cultivated at Porton Down and could be used to kill thousands of people. Agent Bromley and the students held captive all give the same story, which is that Henderson told them he was going to release the virus across the campus in aerosols that had been positioned throughout the area. Yet we found no such devices anywhere. Of course, it's always possible they were incredibly well hidden, and we're yet to find them, but I don't think so.' He sighed and folded his arms. 'I don't think they ever intended to release the virus. I want you to work with Helen and Simon on this. Zaf will help too. Go over everything – and I mean everything – that has happened in the past few days. Identify anything unusual, anything that doesn't make sense. I need your eye on this.'

The door slid open with a hiss once more, and the spell of the moment was broken, as the younger agent Zaf entered the briefing room. 'Helen and Simon are waiting for you in the operations hub, Detective Ambrose. Would you like me to escort you there? It would be an honour.' From anyone else, the offer may have sounded patronising, but Zaf seemed unable to resist any opportunity to offer a compliment.

Rather ruefully, Jackie turned away from Ben, who looked as though he'd been robbed of the opportunity to say something he knew that he should have said long ago.

'I'll find it myself, thanks, Zaf.' She left the room, and as she passed him, she muttered, 'You'll just have to wait for that honour.'

'Not for too long I hope,' came the cheeky reply.

Jackie smiled as she closed the briefing room door on the two of them and headed across The Grid towards the operations area in which she'd find the two chief analysts for this section.

Ben watched her go with a slight feeling of regret. The last few days had conjured all sorts of emotions he'd thought long-since buried. Perhaps the rather painful truth was that he'd largely cut himself off from emotion, as consumed as he was by the world he inhabited. *How can you effectively carry out an undercover role as a ruthless arms dealer if you're worried about people back in the real world?* That was why there had been no meaningful relationships in his life since he'd joined the service. There had been moments and fleeting affairs, but he'd never truly committed to them – except, of course, the business in St Petersburg. That was another old wound he didn't wish to reopen; there were enough ghosts emerging in his life, it seemed. Even there, his role had required him to commit to the affair to a certain degree – although things had got out of hand, of course.

To commit was to feel, and to feel was to lose. That was why your very soul and the world in which you worked were shrouded from even those closest to you. It was more for their protection than your own. If they knew, then they would automatically become a target. It was more comforting by half to immerse yourself in aliases and secret identities. There was safety in the thrill of secrecy. Nevertheless, there were times when you were left pondering how unfulfilled your life could become.

Those thoughts had crept into his mind more regularly over the past few days, and he knew that, sooner or later, he'd be forced to confront them.

19

The pain woke him, stirring him from a dark reverie that was more comforting than the reality, despite the shadowy demons that had stalked his mind, clawing at his flesh. Then there had been the sinking feeling as stone walls surrounding him had contracted until they were tightening around his waist, slowly crushing him. It had seemed so real, with cold water gushing in around him, rising and creeping slowly over his body as the walls strengthened their hold on him, beginning to engulf him. Even that impending sense of death felt more reassuring than the truth to which he woke.

It felt as though his head had been wrenched from the rest of his body, as the white light cleared gradually. It took several moments for him to summon the strength to open his eyes; when he did, his eyelids flickered open tentatively, frightened of what they might find. Whilst his surroundings crystallised around him, Ollie twisted his neck, wincing at the spasm of pain that shot down his spine at the movement. *At least it isn't broken,* he told himself.

The same couldn't be said for his left wrist, which was hanging limply on the end of his arm. He tried to move instinctively, but at once, he wished he hadn't, as a blinding pain rippled up his arm. He knew instantly that it was broken, recognising the swelling that had already risen at the bottom of his hand. Gingerly, he brought it across to rest on his lap as he straightened his back against the solid surface around him, trying to blink the pain away from his head and wrist. On closer inspection, he had a deep gash in his left shin, from which blood was oozing – although the pain from the wound was being dwarfed by the other injuries he'd sustained. There were small cuts and grazes on his knees and arms, whilst his white running shorts were a dark red.

A stickiness on the left-hand side of his face told him that his cheek too had been cut open during the crash that had sent him spinning onto the tarmac. He was lucky the weight of the bike hadn't crushed him as it landed atop his body. *No, not lucky; I'll have to survive what's coming next.* That unnerving thought made him look around for the first time and take in the room into which his captors had presumably placed him.

He was surrounded by floor-to-ceiling banks of computer monitors and associated control panels, every inch of which was covered in complicated switches and dials. There were small letters printed beneath many of the switches, not that it would have helped Ollie identify a single one of them. Shaking his head slightly to clear an irksome black spot from his vision, he looked at the ceiling itself instead.

The smell of damp metal hung in the air, filling his nostrils with an unpleasant odour he couldn't shake off. Despite the relative expanse of the control room, the grey, metallic walls gave the place a sense of claustrophobia, as though he were trapped in a metal can that, at any moment, could be crushed. There was a large, red fire extinguisher by the door opposite him and a large, ugly-looking axe in a glass case in the far-left corner of the room, whilst a series of wires ran along the ceiling, covering every inch, and more loose fibres hung from a hole in the ceiling above a centre bank of monitors.

That was when a metal door at the far end of the control room clanged open, and eight people entered – three of which he recognised instantly. The Russian called Vladimir Conrad, who'd disappeared from the university before the SAS had shown up, was strolling at the back of the group. He seemed completely at ease, dressed in a pair of black Gorka Airsoft combat trousers and what looked like a navy cashmere sweater beneath a black Kevlar vest; a handsome Poljot Strela watch was strapped to his left wrist.

Then there was the man whom Ollie had dreaded seeing the most – Henderson – flanked by four henchmen, who were expressionless and battle scarred. Unlike the Russian and the men beside him, Henderson seemed to be enjoying himself. He was licking his lips as he entered, and his malevolent eyes darted from Ollie to the figure being dragged by the hair in front of the men. Emma, with her head hanging low, her light-brown hair matted and crusted blood from a cut just above her eye obscuring the left side of her face. She was dressed in a dark-navy boilersuit at least four sizes too big for her, and she grimaced visibly as her bare feet were dragged roughly over the metal floor.

Anger pulsed inside Ollie that he'd never felt in his life. He tried to rise to his feet, but he found at once that his body was in no condition to manage such a movement, and he collapsed onto the ground once more. Emma wasn't gagged, but nor was she looking at him or making any attempt to speak. Tears were streaming down her cheeks, causing the crusted blood to run afresh. Eventually, she turned her head to look upwards at him, and Ollie felt his insides wrench as he saw the pleading in her eyes. She expected him to do something, but he felt completely powerless to help either of them. Today, there was no beguiling twinkle in her eyes, tempting him back to bed, yet he still yearned to reach out and kiss her. Emma was cowering behind her hands, but Ollie was transfixed by the Russian, who remained expressionless.

Only then did Ollie realise who'd been dragging Emma. There had been no cat's-eye glasses and no pistol in a holster strapped at her waist the previous time Ollie had seen Sophia Blanchet. The elegant dress was gone too, replaced by jeans and an olive military jacket. Her hazel eyes weren't alive with passion but sparkling with malice as she'd thrown Emma to the floor. 'Surprised?' she asked, with no trace of a French accent this time.

The pain in Ollie's head was increasing. He didn't understand.

Clearly, that showed on his face, because the so-called 'professor' laughed. 'Men are so quick to underestimate women. I was sitting as close as I am to you now from the chief spook leading this so-called "investigation", and yet he failed to see even a glimpse of what I'm capable of. Instead, he was so quick to believe that my eagerness to come forwards was out of some simpering, pathetic spurned love. As ever, people see what they expect to see. He didn't expect an intellectual environmental activist to be a useful source of information. He expected to see a pining environmental sap incapable of initiative and manipulation. It's a lesson as old as time itself – and one that men seem unwilling to learn from.'

'But what are you doing working for them?' Ollie spluttered the words.

'Working for them?' Something resembling anger flashed across Blanchet's face for a second. Then, almost in a blur, she spun on the spot. Ollie didn't even see her withdraw the pistol, but mere moments later, two of the henchmen lay motionless on the floor, with blood seeping from holes in the foreheads. The other two men flanking Henderson started, withdrawing their own weapons, but Blanchet laughed. 'Relax. I just didn't need four of you to guard two teenagers.'

When she turned back to Ollie and Emma, her eyes were lost in darkness. 'You see, boy, power rarely resides where men believe it resides. I don't work for them. I don't necessarily believe in every aim of our organisation, but we have the vision to see we need change.'

'What are you planning to do? What do you want with us?' Ollie had tried to keep fear out of his voice, but he realised he'd been unsuccessful.

Sophia Blanchet smiled sadly. 'What did I tell you, Ollie? I hope you were listening. Nature has decided to strike back, but it can't do it alone. Your generation might one day hold the key to change, but it lacks the motivation. Or the example. Today, I give you and millions like you the incentive to act. To make peace with nature is to support it. And that means firstly striking at those who'd see it decimated for good.'

'People won't listen to you if you act the same as every other lunatic,' Emma said, pushing herself into a sitting position.

'We'll see,' Blanchet replied coldly. 'Fifty years ago, the world came together for the Stockholm Conference. Governments will bleat that action has been taken, but it's more lip service than true action. There's only one way to ensure world leaders and future generations bring the ambition and action needed to truly save our planet. That world order must be toppled. What good is one PM who believes in the fight if he's surrounded by those blinded by self-interest?'

And then Henderson was moving forwards, his hand sliding inside the pocket of his trousers.

'I'm afraid,' continued Blanchet, 'that it's time for me to take my seat for the performance of a lifetime. But you needn't worry. You'll be in very good hands.' And with one final malevolent smile, she was gone, striding away into the darkness.

Ollie tensed and reached out a hand towards Emma. 'It's OK,' he said in a low voice. 'I won't let them hurt you any more.'

217

Henderson laughed – a rough, humourless bark. 'We're not going to hurt your precious girlfriend. We have someone who'd like to speak to you.'

Instead of a gun, he withdrew a large, black object from his pocket, which Ollie recognised instantly as an old-style satellite phone that combat forces all across the world used. Henderson pressed a series of buttons as Ollie, grimacing as he did so, spat blood from his mouth, hating the aftertaste it left behind. Smiling as he did so, Henderson held out the satellite phone to Ollie, who hesitated.

Is this some sort of trick? wondered Ollie.

'Take it,' ordered Henderson. 'It's not going to blow up in your hand. If we wanted you dead, you'd be dead.'

Mustering the most defiant look that he could, although the effect was ruined by his expression of pain, Ollie reached up and took the phone. He weighed it in his hand for a moment before tentatively raising it to his ear. Before he did so, he glanced at the screen, but the number Henderson had entered wasn't visible. He could hear nothing but static at the other end of the line for a second.

As he waited, Henderson withdrew a pistol from his belt and pointed it at Emma. 'If you speak, she dies.'

There was a crackle of static for a moment and then a smooth, disembodied voice came through the silence. The silky smoothness of that voice sent a shiver through Ollie's body, as though it were being ensnared by the insidious hiss of a serpent. 'Young life and young love' – it felt as though an arctic wind was biting through Ollie's eardrums at the sound – 'so pure, but a business transaction, like all life. I must ask you not to speak. I'd hate to have to ruin our time together by ordering Mr Henderson to put a bullet in young Emma's forehead.'

Ollie's whole body tensed; he hadn't even realised he was doing it, but his hand was shaking, and sweat was beginning to drip down his forehead. The pain was building in his wrist from the effort of holding the phone up to his ear, and his heart was pounding at a speed he couldn't comprehend. Of course, the fear came from the situation they were in, but it was much more than that. That voice chilled every fibre of his body, making his very skin crawl, and yet he couldn't shake the faint feeling that he recognised it.

'I admire resourcefulness. It's made me what I am today,' the voice continued calmly, as though they were discussing the matter over a candlelit dinner. 'You have proved yourself most resourceful, and that's why I'm rewarding you with a front-row seat for what's about to take place today. You may be expecting this is the point where I spill all my plans and motivations to you in the certainty you won't be alive to repeat them.'

There was a pause, as though the owner of the voice were considering their next words very carefully. 'The opposite is true. My motivations are my own, and perhaps someday you'll learn them, but that is not this day. Today, you'll witness an event that will reshape the face of this world. You see, almost every politician and member of the public has become too short-sighted in looking around the corner for the next outbreak of the virus. That's all anyone has become concerned with, and they've lost sight of the bigger picture.

'Luckily for the world' – the voice paused once more – 'my friends and I have not. This is a day that will live long in the memory. You should count yourself lucky that you and your lovely young girlfriend have been chosen to witness it. I'm expecting something extraordinary, which is why I too have a front-row seat. Enjoy the show, Ollie Robson.' And then the line went dead.

Only then did Ollie realise he'd been holding his breath. He let it out with an almighty sigh, collapsing forwards slightly, as the phone tumbled from his hand and clanged against the metal floor.

In one sweeping motion, Henderson snatched it up and retreated several paces, speaking in hushed tones with the Russian, Vladimir Conrad. However, the other two men never took their eyes from Ollie and Emma, but Ollie stared back at them defiantly, trying to keep the mounting pain from his eyes. He felt his back slip down the control panel slightly, and he placed his hand on the floor to break his fall, his eyes watering in agony at the impact. One of the men laughed.

Although he wanted to do nothing more than pull Emma close to him, Ollie sensed that would only increase the danger she was in. Instead, he tried to keep as still as possible, as Henderson began to move towards him once more, the ominous clang of his boots against the metal echoing around the room. Then the man was standing over him again, and there was a cruel look etched around his mouth. He was enjoying himself, Ollie knew, in the same way he had done at the university.

'I'm afraid it's time for me and Mr Conrad to leave you. We're expecting company whom we must deal with before we depart.' He turned his smile upon Emma and reached out a hand to touch her face, but she recoiled from him. That only made his smile widen. 'How rude when we've come to know each other so intimately. Goodbye, my dear.'

Ollie barely even noticed him turn. His eyes had widened in shock and his heart seemed to have stopped beating as he looked at Emma. Tears were streaming silently down her cheeks, and she still seemed unable to meet his gaze. Anger coursed through him as he shouted the ugliest swear word he could muster. 'What did you do to her?'

Henderson turned; the smile was gone. 'We aren't savages, boy. You want to blame someone for the position she's in? Look at yourself. You left her alone, naked as the day she was born, days after a traumatic event.'

'Ollie, it's OK.' The sound of Emma's feeble, broken voice was more terrifying than the pain in her eyes. 'I'm OK.'

'It's not OK,' said Ollie through gritted teeth. He spat another ugly swear word in Henderson's direction.

The man remained unmoved. Behind him, Vladimir glanced down at his wrist and then around the control room, supremely unconcerned with the events taking place in front of him. Henderson, however, was looking at Ollie, and there was an emotion in his face that Ollie hadn't seen there before. What was it?

'You know nothing about me, boy, nor anything about the world you live in. How nice it must be to bury your head away from the world and go out drinking every night, ignoring the fragmentation of this country and many others around the world. Perhaps when we're done, you'll understand that change needed to be effected. You put the people in charge up on a pedestal – whatever they do must be righteous – but you don't know anything about what happened to me or what the people in charge are really like.'

'You're wrong.'

Ollie looked around in surprise.

Emma had forced herself into a sitting position and was blinking the tears from her eyes as she stared up at Henderson, a look of resentment on her face that Ollie had never seen before. 'You say we don't know anything about you, but I know that whatever happened to you doesn't excuse the things you're doing now. You just hide behind whatever happened as an excuse to kill and torture people. It's what cowards and bullies everywhere do. There are men like you in every war around the world,' she stated.

'I'm a coward,' said Henderson slowly, taking a step back towards Emma.

221

She remained unmoved, looking up at him resolutely. For a second, Ollie thought about lunging in front of her, so sure was he that the man would lash out.

Instead, Henderson smiled, his face contorted into an ugly, contemptuous leer. 'I hope you survive today, girl, so you can live the rest of your life with the memory of me burned into you.'

Then he turned on his heel, strode past Vladimir Conrad and through the metal door at the far end of the control room, and was gone.

The Russian, meanwhile, remained unmoved for several seconds. Ollie looked at him curiously, and their eyes met. Ollie had the strangest feeling that there was something like admiration in the man's eyes, and then he was gone too, leaving Ollie and Emma alone with the guards they'd left behind.

As soon as the door closed, Emma scrambled over to Ollie and rested her head against his chest as fresh tears began to stream down her face. After manoeuvring his injured wrist out of reach, Ollie pulled her in close to him, breathing in the smell of her. Feeling her body against his was the most comforting experience he could have wished for in that moment, yet he shifted slightly, ashamed of the impulse it had stirred beneath his clothes.

Emma was shaking in a way he'd never seen before. He remembered the words she had just spoken and, aside from what he'd felt when his dad had spent every day and night by his granny's bed as she lay in hospital, this was the proudest he'd ever felt about the actions of another person. He couldn't begin to imagine what she'd been through, but she'd stood up to Henderson in a way he hadn't been able to.

He knew the flirty girl she'd been was gone, though. Perhaps not forever – or at least he hoped not – but as he looked down on her now, with her body curled against his, he knew things would never be the same for either of them, even if they did survive this. His heart was racing, and he tried to think of something happier to calm himself down, but those happy memories appeared to have been consumed by the situation they were in. Would he ever see his parents again? That seemed unlikely now, and there were so many things that he knew he should have said.

'I'm so sorry they ever got to you or hurt you,' he whispered softly, stroking Emma's hair tenderly. He was on the point of apologising for his part in her being taken, but hearing of his own guilt and self-pity wouldn't help her now. 'I won't let them hurt you any more.'

She nuzzled her head into his chest as she replied in a low voice, 'I won't let them hurt you, more like.'

He couldn't help but laugh slightly at that. 'Emma,' he breathed into her ear, taking care to lift her head as gently as possible until she was looking into his eyes, 'where are we?'

As she told him, a strikingly cold tidal wave of realisation crashed over him. There was going to be a show all right, but they couldn't sit here and wait for it to hit.

20

'We've been through everything, Miss Ambrose. There's n-nothing hyere,' stammered Simon Wynn-Jones, pushing his spectacles up his nose until they fitted squarely over his narrow, green eyes as he finished playing the CCTV from around Admiralty Arch on the morning that Harold Morris was shot and killed.

Jackie smiled at the Welsh pronunciation. 'Where was it that you grew up, Simon?'

The technical analyst looked up in surprise at her words, as if he'd never been asked a question in this building that wasn't related to analysis before. Although Jackie guessed that he was in his late forties or early fifties, he had the nervous disposition of a newly graduated student at times; something that she found very endearing amongst the poker-faced and ruthless decision-makers that seemed to embody this building. Despite the fact that he clearly revered Aldwyn Haynes, for whom she guessed he'd worked for a number of decades, he was able to hold his own amongst the bigger personalities and make them listen to the point he wanted to make.

Talking about himself, however, was clearly outside of his comfort zone. For a moment, he busied himself at his keyboard. Scanned documents and more surveillance images flashed across the screen, and Jackie was left wondering if she'd ever get a response.

After several seconds, though, he turned back to her with a broadening smile upon his face. 'A breath of fresh air you are indeed,' he said warmly, his accent more pronounced than ever.

'I'm sorry,' replied Jackie, a little confused.

'That was how Mr Viper described you. A breath of fresh air, and a welcome one at that.'

'Did he?' Jackie was completely taken aback, and she turned to look through the doorway that led back into open-plan area of The Grid. Ben was standing at the nearest workstation, deep in conversation with John Bromley, the agent who'd been captured and tortured by Henderson and his men. The older man visibly bore the effects of that encounter, and the odd grimace of pain flitted across his face as he spoke, but it was Ben upon whom her eyes lingered.

'He's different around you,' observed the analyst.

Jackie snapped her head around, smiling.

'Ever since I've known him. Wonderful man, Ben, b-but er…' He paused, a slight stammer entering his voice, before he corrected himself.

Jackie narrowed her eyes, wondering what it was that Simon had been about to say.

'Anyway, you asked me where I'm from. I assume you want a more specific answer than just Wales, Detective.'

Jackie laughed. 'I wouldn't be much of a detective if I settled for an answer as vague as that.'

'And from what I've read, you're an excellent detective. How you managed to piece together the patterns of the East Croydon serial killer was incredible. I hope you don't mind me saying that I followed the case with interest.' His voice had suddenly become very excitable, and Jackie couldn't help but smile at how animated he'd become as he hastily pushed his glasses further up his nose.

Despite the fact she was smiling at Simon's enthusiasm for the case, Jackie was rather grateful when they were interrupted by the door swinging open and the handsome Zaf striding through it, a cup of steaming coffee in his hand. As ever, he was beaming, and Jackie wondered – not for the first time – whether any other expression would suit his features more perfectly than that smile. Even when he'd been stationed at Senta Barracks on the day they'd met, he'd oozed charm and been nothing but flirtatious.

'You remember what Mr Haynes said to us Simon?' said Zaf, a twinkle glittering in his hazel-coloured eyes. 'We can't spend our whole days flirting with the most beautiful woman in Thames House. Detective Ambrose needs to concentrate on cracking the case. She can't do that with you being a charmer.'

Jackie looked at Simon, wondering if he'd seem abashed or embarrassed. Perhaps if the remarks had come from any other colleague, he would have been, but the two men got on well. Instead, Simon was shaking his head as he turned to face the screen once more, and he couldn't suppress a laugh, although a response seemed beyond him.

'Perhaps you could learn a thing or two from Simon,' Jackie declared with a grin. 'Girls love a clever guy.' She was forced into a laugh of her own as Simon raised a fist in mock celebration.

Zaf stumbled backwards, clutching his heart. 'I'm not sure how many more of your interrogations I can take, Detective Ambrose. You must get so many false confessions from male suspects after just one interview with you. Prison must be preferrable to the pain you can cause.'

Jackie was saved the pressure of having to respond by the arrival of Helen Robinson, the senior analyst who was again dressed in a crisp blouse and skirt that seemed to characterise her. She looked every bit the professional with her long, blonde hair falling over her shoulders and angular, hazel eyes that almost glowered over her firmly pursed lips.

As she entered the room, she gave Zaf a mocking, disinterested look before speaking to Jackie. 'I hear you're helping us again.'

Her tone was deadpan and cold. Was this really the same woman whom Jackie had grown to like from her previous time in the building? It was as though she'd experienced a personality transplant overnight. Taken aback as she was, Jackie fought to keep her tone measured. If anyone in the station had spoken to her in that way, she would have had no hesitation in blasting back at them, but this was different. There were different pressures here, she had to remind herself. Helen was all business.

Jackie knew how to handle that, resisting the urge to add an edge to her voice. Jackie smiled. 'I've been going through the CCTV footage with Simon, but I want to focus on the men who were killed: the three men who met in that café. The people behind this had them all killed, but why? If John Bromley is to be believed, then they didn't even interrogate the scientist. They killed him without asking him any questions. Doesn't that strike you as odd?'

Helen's eyes narrowed slightly. 'Not if they'd got all the information they needed from Morris and Matheson already.'

'But as far as we know, they didn't question either of them.' Jackie's mind was racing as it always did when she became engrossed in a case. Her mind was a complex spiderweb of connections that she'd been unable to piece together so far, but she was sure there was something they were overlooking and just as convinced it had something to do with the three men who had been pictured together all those months before.

'If there never was any virus,' Helen said thoughtfully, 'then perhaps they were using the connection between these three as a smokescreen to keep us distracted from what they were up to. But they knew that, once the soldier died, we'd focus on that death and piece together the connection with the other two, so they used that to distract us by killing Morris, knowing it would lead us to the university to protect Vallance.'

Jackie shook her head. 'It's more than that. They made things harder for themselves by drawing your attention to the university. If they hadn't killed Morris, then there's a chance you'd never have sent protection to the university, which would have given them a clearer run at the place.'

'So why did they do it?' Zaf interjected curiously. 'Attention? We know they never had any virus to actually release, but by drawing our protection and attention to the university, they created the headline.'

'That's right.' Helen nodded. 'Right from the start, they've been misdirecting us, but their goal seems to have been to create mass panic amongst the public. By killing Morris and targeting Vallance, they made sure that the spotlight was on the university and that the national and international press would have first-hand accounts of SAS troops storming the campus. That all adds to the panic.'

Jackie stayed silent for a moment. What they were saying made sense, and they knew more about these people than she did, but even so there was a nagging doubt. What was it? 'You said Morris was on his way to a meeting with a minister?'

'Yes,' replied Simon, and he swivelled in his chair to face her. 'He was on his way to meet with Hugh Palmer, the Health Minister.'

That was it. That was what had been nagging at the back of Jackie's brain this whole time. 'So it's just a coincidence that Morris had arranged an urgent meeting with a member of the cabinet – a member of the cabinet who's since been found dead? If killing Morris was just about misdirection. and you have no evidence the people behind this had contact with or interrogated Morris for information, then isn't it strange he's killed moments before he's due to meet with Palmer?'

The two women eyes met each other for a second.

Jackie asked, 'So what did Morris know? Or what might he have heard that alarmed him enough to set up a meeting with the minister?'

'We know very little about what Morris did during his time with the MOD,' Helen replied cautiously. 'They mentioned that he'd been seconded to a couple of places during his time with them – to both the Foreign Office and the Environment Agency – but other than that, they weren't forthcoming, which isn't a surprise when it comes to the MOD.'

Something seemed to stir deep in Jackie's mind, but she couldn't grasp what it was that she was missing. A link to one of her own cases, perhaps, or to something else? There was something. She tried to retreat to the mind workplace she inhabited that sometimes housed answers or hitherto unreachable connections. Yet, this time, all she could see was darkness. *What's blocking me from seeing? Is it the stress and pressure of the situation?* That had never affected her in the past, but then the stakes had never been as high.

It was Simon who broke the silence, his Welsh lilt floating through the air. 'If we're exploring the possibility that it was something Morris heard that spooked him, then maybe we should examine the intelligence reports from the day before and the day of his shooting?' he suggested.

Immediately, Helen cut across him: 'Maya and I went through those reports. There was no significant chatter or information that could possibly have resonated with Morris.

Anyway, those briefings are for intelligence officials only, how would he have got his hands on them?'

Her sharp tone seemed to take the analyst aback slightly, but it was Zaf who came to his aid, saying seamlessly, 'A copy of those reports is sent to the MOD, and it may be that Morris was able to obtain one. I'll get Maya to bring in the files. Simon's right: there could be something there.' And with that he was gone, but he returned only a few seconds later.

Again, Helen smiled imperceptibly before apologising to Simon, who'd already swivelled in his chair to face his monitors once more and seemed not to hear her. Jackie watched their interactions over the next minute, as Helen walked over to Simon and whispered into his ear. Eventually, the two of them laughed, and Jackie couldn't help but smile. It was clear to her that the two colleagues shared a close connection, and she wondered how long they'd worked together.

At that moment, Maya bustled into the communications area, her arms full of files and papers.

'Jesus, Maya!' exclaimed Zaf, 'I only asked for the ones for the day of Morris's death and the two days prior.'

The junior analyst blushed scarlet at this and mumbled her apologies.

However, Helen was all business. 'Quite right too, Maya. Analysis and analytics are about being thorough. Now if I remember correctly, there was nothing within these briefings that we considered high priority, other than the extremist cell in North London, is that correct?'

Maya nodded, her fingers twirling through her shoulder-length, brown hair, which – according to Zaf – was a sign that she was always nervous in his presence. 'That's correct. Everything else was low level – the sort of intelligence we get on a daily basis. And then there was the request for extra intelligence staff from a couple of government bodies.'

'Which bodies?' Zaf was curious.

'The Nuclear Safety Commission and the Environment Agency, I believe,' replied Maya, rifling through the papers in her arms before they inevitably fell to the floor – at which point, Simon dropped to his knees to help her gather them up.

Jackie, however, was too busy looking at Zaf. The young agent, like her, had stiffened at Maya's answer. There was the connection. The morning she'd driven to Senta Barracks, there had been a call from the station about the body dragged from the Thames near Woolwich that morning. The Environment Agency. It couldn't be surely. She could feel her heart racing, as it always did when she was on the verge of cracking a case, but this time it was driven more by fear than jubilation. What if that was their target all along?

'Didn't you say,' began Jackie slowly, 'Morris was seconded to the Environment Agency?' She turned to look at Helen, whose eyes flickered towards her, understanding blossoming in her face.

'Yes,' the senior analyst replied quickly, 'he was seconded there in 2020 for four months.' There was a pause, a look of dawning comprehension and fear creeping over her usually impassive face.

'Did the MOD reveal what Morris did for the Environment Agency?' asked Jackie, not aware of her lips moving.

As Helen nodded slowly and revealed the information that Jackie had longed not to hear, Zaf wrenched open the door to the communications room and strode across The Grid, straight towards Aldwyn Haynes's office. The rest of them followed at a slower pace, Jackie hardly aware that her legs were moving her forwards. *Is this how success feels working here?* Cracking a case just meant a rush of fear and the certainty that lives were at risk. There was no sense of achievement.

Instead, two questions burgeoned inside her: *Are we right? And, more importantly, have we worked it out in time?*

21

As though from all around them, the screeching and grinding noises began. Ollie covered his ears to protect them from the shrill noise, knowing with an increasing sense of dread what they must mean. That also meant the controls weren't just being operated from this room, or else they must have been set to start automatically, as the two men left in the room with them hadn't even made a move forwards. Looking frantically around, he noticed that several of the control monitors in the far corner of the room had blinked on, whirring in a language that he didn't understand.

Neither of the men was paying any attention to the two of them now. He looked into Emma's eyes and saw that the fear was still there, but it wasn't as apparent as it had been before. Then he slipped further down the bank behind him, as her cries reverberated around the control room. As his eyes closed, leaving him in darkness, he felt the shudder of the metal floor as the men approached, the thud of their boots deafening him.

'What wrong with him?' came a gruff voice overhead in broken English.

'*Are you as stupid as you look?*' shouted Emma, and the distress in her voice was clear; Ollie could visualise the tears streaming from her eyes. 'Look at him. He needs help.'

There was a pause and then loud footfalls moving away until the screech of metal filled the air as the door at the end of the control room was wrenched open. A second later, it slammed shut, and Ollie sprang instantly to his feet, pivoting and slamming the heel of his shoe into the man's stomach, who reeled back, shock visible in his eyes. Without giving him a chance to react, Ollie dived forwards, trying to pin the man to the ground, but he knew immediately that the man was far too strong from him.

He felt himself pushed off the man's chest and lifted by the throat, and then he was flying through the air as the man propelled him across the control room. Ollie felt his back and already broken wrist slam into the room's steel wall, and he cried out in agony, screwing his eyes up as tight as possible to block out the pulses of pain emanating from the bottom of his arm, as it collided with the fire extinguisher stationed beside the door and knocked it onto its side. As he collapsed to the floor, he saw the man beginning to stride towards him, and he blinked rapidly to regain his vision, but it would be no good. He'd have no time to react before the man reached him. Then he saw Emma lurch forwards and kick the man in the back.

Fear seemed to flood Ollie's body, extinguishing the pain that had gripped it moments before. The man barely seemed to have noticed the impact, but as he turned slowly to face Emma, Ollie knew he had just seconds to act. Climbing blindly to his feet, he reached out with his injured wrist and hauled the fire extinguisher into his arms, biting down on his tongue so hard to stop himself shouting that blood began to swill around his mouth. He staggered forwards, just as the man raised his hand to strike at Emma, and with an almighty effort, he swung the metal fire extinguisher through the air with as much force as he could muster.

There was a thud followed by the cracking of bone, as it impacted in the man's back, sending him to his knees. There were simultaneous yells of pain, as the fire extinguisher tumbled from Ollie's grasp, and he cradled his injured wrist. Emma darted over to look at the damage, but before she'd reached him, the man grabbed her by the ankle; as he sprawled on the ground, he turned his face towards Ollie, a snarl of pure anger and menace upon it. He was an ugly man with a twisted, gnarly face, and at this proximity, Ollie could tell the man was older than he'd originally thought.

As he watched, paralysed by fear and pain, Emma was swung by her ankle until the man let go of her, and she flew into a nearby set of monitors. There was enough time for her to scream in fright before her head slammed into the metal console, and after the impact, she collapsed unconscious to the floor. Ollie scrambled back instinctively, jumping atop the nearest bank of monitors, hoping to give himself some semblance of higher ground against his opponent. His heart was racing, and he tried not to look at Emma's motionless body for fear of what he might see. *Please don't let her be dead,* an unbidden voice in the back of his head said over and over.

In a flash, the man had jumped up onto the monitors in front of Ollie and now he was brandishing an ugly knife, similar to the one that Henderson had used to slice open Ollie's chest at uni. It was the last thing he wanted to do, but Ollie spread his feet and dropped into a combat stance, biting back the pain in his wrist, knowing he had perhaps just seconds before the other man returned, and then it really would be over. And it wasn't just that. How long did they have to try to stop the deaths of potentially thousands of people?

The noises from outside the control room were getting louder and louder, as though metal was being wrenched free from some invisible hold. There surely wasn't much time left.

When had they initiated the process and how long did it take? His heart seemed to be beating harder and faster than it had ever done in his life, and the sweat began to drip down the side of his face as the man facing him waited, as though weighing up Ollie.

Then, so fast that Ollie had no time to react, the man took a step forwards across the monitors and lashed out with his heel, following through with a swipe of the knife. The blade missed Ollie's left eye by a matter of inches, but the kick found its mark, sending him crashing into one of the computer screens, which cracked and sparked beneath his weight. There was nothing Ollie wanted to do more than lie there and hope the pain would wash away, but he knew he had little time before the man and the knife were on top of him.

Springing onto the balls of his feet, Ollie was surprised to find that the man hadn't pressed his advantage. There was a lazy, self-confident smile on his face that suggested he believed this fight to be over already, and he was therefore not prepared for the roundhouse kick Ollie delivered to his midriff. As the man's knees hit the marbled work surfaces, Ollie jumped up and pulled further down from the ceiling the loose wires he'd seen after regaining his consciousness.

These wires were still connected to the circuitry in the ceiling, and Ollie relinquished the cables briefly to aim a powerful kick that connected with the man's face; he felt the man's nose break beneath his boot. Then Ollie stepped over him so he was directly behind the man, who was howling in pain. The knife had disappeared from his grasp. Grabbing hold of the wires once more, Ollie slung them around the man's neck and began to pull the cable close to him. Instantly, the man tried to get to his feet, but Ollie lashed out with his foot once more, hitting the small of the guard's back and forcing him back into a kneeling position. The man reached behind him with his hands and tried to grapple Ollie's legs.

With his feet planted to keep his balance on the work surface, Ollie took half a step back, just enough to be out of the man's reach. There was a scream of pain as the man's right arm was dislocated from its socket as he twisted it at an obscene angle in his attempt to throw Ollie off him. Then the man jerked his back, trying to find the gap between the wires and Ollie's body, but Ollie had pre-empted the move, stepping forwards once more to close the space. He pulled the cables back with all his strength, now closing his eyes against what he was doing, as the body before him began to thrash and the man's left hand clutched at his injured wrist.

Screaming in pain and with his tightly shut eyes full of tears, Ollie gritted his teeth still harder as the light began to pop in front of his eyes, but he still didn't relinquish his grip on the cables, despite every nerve ending in his body imploring him to stop the torment at the base of his arm. He felt one of his teeth splinter as he bit down, pulling the man's struggling body closer into him as the wires cut deeper into his neck. Then the flailing stopped, and Ollie felt the breath leave his body as he released control of cables, and the man rolled off the worktop and fell to the floor with a loud thud.

For a long while, Ollie stared down at the unmoving body with its grey eyes that had always seemed lifeless and had now rolled slightly towards the top of the man's head. His legs and arms were stuck out at odd angles, and there was a thick line of bruising around the man's neck. Ollie turned away, unable to look any more, and he somehow mustered the strength to clamber down off the monitors.

With his blood pounding in his brain, he made his way quickly over to Emma and felt her pulse with the hand that wasn't throbbing in almost unbearable agony. Relief flooded through him as he found what he'd feared was lost, and he dropped her wrist, instead scanning around him desperately before his eyes fell on the heavy-duty axe in the glass casing in the corner of the room. After striding across to it, he slammed his elbow into the glass and felt it smash open. He swore as several splinters cut into his skin, and he yelled some more as he lifted the axe from its stand and began to hobble across to the metal door.

He acted just in time. As he pressed himself flat against the wall of the room, he heard quick footsteps on the other side of the door, and a second later, it was flung open. He held his breath until the figure – who was shorter than the first man – had moved into the open part of the room, and then he darted out from behind the door, crouched down and swished the axe in a low, vicious swipe. The sheer savagery and power of the axe shocked Ollie, and he felt the brutal edge of the sharpened steel blade cut through flesh and bone with scary ease.

The pistol tumbled from the man's right hand, as he fell to the floor, blood splattering across the metal floor, and at the same moment, the axe tumbled from Ollie's grasp as he looked in horror at what he'd done. The smell wasn't something he'd been prepared for, but he had no free hand to cover his face. The man clutched the bleeding stump of his leg; abandoned beside its former owner lay his foot which had, until seconds before, been attached to his ankle.

The adrenaline and fear had taken over, and Ollie was acting on an instinct that he hadn't known he had within him. He stepped over the man and snatched up the pistol that he'd been scrabbling feebly for. As he pointed the gun squarely at the figure beneath him, he kept his eyes averted from the bloody mess. That meant focussing on the man's face instead, and he couldn't block out the screams and wheezing gasps of breath that echoed all around them. Not only was the man slightly shorter than his colleague, but there was more colour in his face, despite it draining away with every passing heartbeat. He had brown eyes the colour of chestnuts, and that fact brought a wave of emotion and memory into the equation that Ollie hadn't expected.

The man was staring defiantly up at him, but his eyes were swimming with pain. Somehow, some of the mercenary was gone. There was more human in him than there had been when he had stood like a stone gargoyle over the prisoners minutes before. There was no anger in his eyes, and no sadistic smile playing around his thin lips. In that moment, he was just a man who was in pain and scared for his life, and a man who knew that he was out of options.

Ollie knew how that felt. And without knowing why or how, he felt his own lips move. 'Why did you do this?' he croaked, and the voice that emanated from him didn't sound like his own.

A spasm of surprise mingled with pain crossed the man's face for a moment, then he replied, in poor, garbled English: 'Not like you.' His accent sounded Eastern European, although it was difficult to judge in which of the former Soviet territories he'd grown up. 'Save her.' Much to Ollie's surprise, the man gestured towards Emma with his head; she was beginning to stir from unconsciousness. 'Have time.'

The wrenching and screeching noises were reaching a deafening pitch now, and Ollie knew instinctively that could only mean one thing: their time was running out.

He was half expecting the man to strike out with whatever strength he had left, but he made no move towards Ollie. Instead, he pushed himself backwards, scraping his body across the floor, still clutching his mutilated leg and leaving a trail of blood in his wake. As Ollie watched, the man hoisted himself into the semblance of a sitting position against the metal wall before their eyes locked once more.

'Go,' the man rasped again.

Ollie found that both his hands holding the gun were shaking so badly that they amplified the mounting pain in his wrist, and his sweaty palms twitched as his index finger curled around the trigger.

'No,' said the man, but he wasn't pleading for his life; it was as though he were pleading for Ollie's. 'Go, save you both.'

Then, without realising why he did it, Ollie dropped his arm. The trembling and pain at his wrist seemed to ease as he lowered the gun and his arms to his waist. For several seconds, Ollie simply looked at the man on the floor, and then he nodded involuntarily. He was jolted from what seemed like a trance by a movement in the corner of his eye.

Without even being aware of her approach, Emma was suddenly by his side, and she clutched hold of his arm, before gasping, 'Oh my God.' Her eyes too had settled on the man on the floor before they turned to look at Ollie, who found himself unable to meet her gaze. 'What happened?' she asked, and then she swivelled around.

He knew she was searching for any sign of the other guard. The majority of his body was hidden from view behind the middle bank of monitors, but his mangled right arm was just visible where it protruded from underneath the worktops. Ollie reached out and grabbed her roughly, pulling her round before she could set eyes on the man.

'What are you doing?' she said in a startled voice, and she pushed him away from her. It was as though she were seeing him for the first time, as she took a further step away from him.

'Emma, I'm sorry.' Ollie didn't know what he was going to say, and he looked down at his own arm in disbelief. He hadn't meant to hurt her. He just needed her to understand. 'We don't have any time. We need to go now, and you need to trust me, please.'

She was still looking at him as though unseeing, her eyes slightly out of focus.

'Are you OK?' he asked. 'How's your head?'

'Remembered have you,' she snapped.

Ollie found he had no reply. He just stood there, feeling as though the world had been taken from him. Yet the remark seemed to have been the release of anger Emma had needed. Ollie looked down in shock, as she slipped her hand in his.

She breathed into his ear, 'Together. Let's go.'

And then she was dragging him towards the open doorway, and he didn't have a chance to look back at the man who'd been stirring by the frame and who had, inexplicably, offered him advice. Had that been his moment of redemption in the final minutes of his life? Would Ollie get such a chance?

22

Darkness had descended over London. The crackle of radios from the SBS crew was occasionally put into perspective by earth-shattering rumbles of thunder that seemed to cause the craft to temporarily lose control. Flashes of yellow lightning lit up the heart of the city as they glided through it along the Thames. London seemed unaware of the impending disaster, and Ben couldn't help but marvel at the beauty of the city that he had defended so many times yet never truly appreciated.

The floodlights from the Interceptor craft clashed with the bursts of lightning, causing a romantic golden hue to hang above the Gothic stonework of Westminster as they passed. On the opposite bank, the spectacular observation wheel named the London Eye was swamped with passengers, their silhouettes temporarily thrown into view. The lamps that lined the embankment shot bright bolts of light across the iridescent blackness of the water.

Water spray leaped high into the faces of the crew, as they crashed through the heart of the capital. This would once have been a familiar mission to the SBS men. Before the pandemic struck, they'd practised retaking the structure every year. But since the virus, the exercise had been abandoned. Although communications seemed to be operating as normal, the high winds were creating difficulties for the land team's approach.

Over the roar of the water and engine beneath him, the voices continued to crackle through Ben's earpiece. 'The land assault team will approach the Port of London Authority's Thames Barrier Navigation Centre on the south side, whilst you approach from the river itself,' he heard Aldwyn Haynes say gruffly into his ear. 'Walker is replacing Wolf in leading their strike team, alongside Zaf, and some of the men who served with Corporal Matheson are with them. Your approaches should be simultaneous and catch them off guard.'

Ben pressed the receiver earpiece deeper into his ear against the whip and roar of the river as he replied, 'Do we know if Henderson and Conrad are on site?'

'They've disabled the feed from the surrounding surveillance cams,' confirmed the nervous voice of Simon Wynn-Jones, 'and I've tried to hack into the surveillance inside, but my attempts are being denied.'

'We helped design and upgrade the bloody things,' Ben heard Haynes say angrily. 'What use is that if we can't access it ourselves?'

'It isn't as simple as that, sir,' responded the Welsh technician. 'There are hundreds of inbuilt safety protocols and firewalls, which are extremely complex to bypass, but that isn't the issue. Somebody else has control of the system and is stopping me gaining access.'

'I thought you just said there were hundreds of inbuilt protocols?' their boss asked curtly.

'Yes, sir, b-but... w-well,' stuttered the analyst, 'they seem to have bypassed them all. They have full control of the system. I don't understand how they've done it. It would take months of having access to the system, not to mention an incredible amount of processing power and hacking knowhow to be at the point where you could completely control the surveillance system at a level where it's ignoring its own inbuilt safety protocols for external interference. They have complete control of the Thames Barrier. If they lower the gates, then the city floods.'

Both Ben and Haynes swore simultaneously, as the boat crashed along over the slipstream of passing vessels.

Then it was Helen Robinson's smoother yet more-aggravated-than-usual voice that was crackling in Ben's ear: 'They had months. I managed to get in contact with a senior official in the Environment Agency. She told me they replaced almost their entire security team last year following an MOD assessment conducted by Morris. He told them that they needed to revamp their security staff and an entirely new team would be advisable. He even recommended a firm for them to hire the men from, and they came with a full security vetting and government endorsement.'

Ben's heart seemed to fall through the bottom of the boat into the mirky water of the Thames below. He shook rain and spray from his hair and spat river water over the edge of the boat. 'This is Henderson we're talking about. They've had control of the barrier for nearly eighteen months. They've already initiated the raising process, so we have to assume they have something more spectacular in mind than just watching London flood. In this storm, if they lowered the gates, then God knows how much of the city could flood. Yet they're raising the gates. We'll be at the structure in a few minutes, and we need to know what we're facing. Apart from Hiscock's assault team, have we got the other side of the river covered?'

'We'll have firearms with two SO19 teams there when you arrive. If Henderson and his men are still on site, then they'll be trapped,' stated Haynes. 'As for explosives, the site is checked monthly, and the gates are tested. If they were rigged with explosives, then it would have been found during the last sweep. Those security sweeps are done independently from the onsite security team; unless you think Henderson infiltrated them too?'

'They have something else planned. Check that the security sweeps have been talking place as normal. There's meant to be a test drill to recapture the barrier that takes place twice a year involving the SAS, but that hasn't happened for near two years now, with everything else that has been going on.'

'There's something else, Ben.' There was something in Jackie's tone that he didn't like. 'The boy who helped you at the university, Ollie Robson. He's missing and his girlfriend is too. It seems as though he was involved in some kind of collision, and there are eyewitnesses who claim that he was carried off in a white van.'

Ben swore again; his mind was calculating as the boat crashed down over a bump on the river, yet his balance remained. 'Without confirmation that the two of them are there, we can't alter our strike plan. There's too much at stake. We have to strike hard and fast.'

He knew that Jackie would be the one to object, and she proved him right: 'But they'll get caught in the crossfire. Ben, you can't.'

'We don't have a choice. This is the best chance we have to secure the facility and potentially save hundreds of thousands of lives, not to mention the damage to the country's infrastructure. There's no choice to be made here.'

Before the detective could reply, however, the boat curved around an almighty bend in the river, and as they did so, Ben's attention was caught by a sleek Interceptor craft speeding past them at a pace only they were entitled to be doing on the river. At about thirty feet in length, hunkered low to the water, in its signature metallic-grey colour, it was slicing along the Thames at a tremendous pace. Ben recognised the boat immediately. It was a Fast Interceptor Craft, often adopted by the SBS for stealth missions, which he could well have found himself on for this mission, except it was heading in the opposite direction.

He turned to the SBS commander beside him, whose head was also directed to follow the course of the boat as it sped away from danger. It wasn't possible to make out any figures on board it, but that wasn't unusual. The accommodation on the craft was typically housed within the enclosed cockpit, whilst the forward cabin was shrouded from sight too.

The commander grasped the radio at his breast and spoke rapidly into it, before looking up at Ben. 'Not one of ours, sir.'

Ignoring the gabbled scenarios from Simon in his ear, Ben cursed inwardly. It looked as though Henderson had once again made his escape just in time. There was no doubt in Ben's mind who was onboard that vessel. They didn't have enough boats out on the river to split their attention by following the craft. They had to remain focussed on stopping whatever impending disaster was lying in wait for them once they rounded the final bend of the river on their approach to the site.

After wrenching out his earpiece, Ben flipped open the mobile phone he'd extracted from his body armour and pressed two buttons before holding the phone to his ear.

Within a second, John Bromley answered: 'Ben.'

'John, I need you to try to track a Fast Interceptor Craft that passed our position thirty seconds ago. I need Simon focussed on the prep for this assault and the schematics of the structure.'

'Henderson?' John asked in his typically blunt manner.

'Do what you can. I expect it will vanish without trace soon enough.'

'Will do.'

Ben went to disconnect the call, but then he heard the MI6 man add gruffly, 'Good luck out there.'

'Keep your eye out for the 6pm news.' It was with a wry smile that Ben replaced the phone in the zipped breast pocket of the body armour that he was wearing.

Then, as they traversed another bend in the river, the structure came into view, and with it an almighty crash of thunder that reverberated through Ben's bones. The torrential rain wasn't able to wash away the tension mounting inside him as lightning crackled overhead, illuminating their destination and seeming to charge his very soul. This was truly being alive. This was what invigorated him the most, and the danger was a major part of that.

After reaching down to the radio hooked into the Fortis armoured vest he wore, he quickly changed the frequency and immediately heard the rarely-so-serious voice of Zaf. In truth, Ben would rather have entrusted the strike team to another's leadership, but Bromley was in no fit state to lead such an operation, despite what he might tell them, whilst Wolf also remained out of action. It wasn't that Ben didn't trust Zaf – quite the contrary in fact, having taken Zaf under his wing and overseen his promotion to field operative – but it was clear this had been years in the planning. That made him uneasy about what Henderson and his men may have lying in wait for them.

'Zaf, are your men in position?' he asked, keen to keep any tension from his voice.

He comforted himself with the knowledge that the young field agent was surrounded by experienced soldiers. Although Sergeant Hiscock seemed a rather robust individual, he came with an exemplary army reputation, whilst it was clear that Zaf had built up a rapport with the younger Corporal Dawkins. Naturally, all the men had been vetted before being approved to join the SAS soldiers and Zaf on this operation, but their determination to avenge their colleague had been a factor in Aldwyn Haynes allowing them to assist.

'Affirmative; we're moving towards the navigation centre now. Are we clear to proceed?'

Through his earpiece, Ben detected a slight quiver at the end of Zaf's final word. It only served to heighten his own mounting feeling of trepidation, which he dispelled swiftly. This was Zaf's first operation of this magnitude, but Ben had no such excuse – albeit, this time, the stakes seemed rather more tangible.

Peering through the downpour, Ben focussed his eyes on the Chinook circling above the navigation centre on the south side of the river. In his mind's eye, he could visualise figures zipping down towards the ground on a rope dangling from the helicopter. In reality, he could make out nothing through driving rain. Ben turned to the commander beside him and looked around at his team, who all nodded. The boat was slowing now, as it approached its destination.

'We're coming up on the structure now and will begin our disembarkation imminently,' confirmed the SBS commander from beside him, and Ben heard the words echoed through his headset. He'd worked with Phillips before and knew the man was exceptionally good at his job. He didn't have the biggest personality in the world, but that hardly mattered.

'You are a go. Repeat, you are a go, strike team,' said Ben, raising his voice to be heard as the thunder crackled deafeningly overhead and boat's engine coughed abruptly to a standstill. He resisted the urge to wish them luck. That would do nothing but sow seeds of doubt in their mind.

The men beside him were checking their own suppressed C8 carbines and Sig P226 handguns, which were in holsters attached at their waists, beside the HK P11 underwater pistols. This unusual weapon was unique to the SBS. Designed by

Heckler & Koch, it fired five high-velocity darts per magazine and could be used to engage underwater targets up to fifteen yards away. Propelled by solid rocket fuel, the firing system made the P11 virtually silent above water and was often used by the SBS to neutralise sentries as they emerged from the water. Strapped to each of their wrists was a Cabot watch that had been tailored specifically to the SBS's needs. Being water resistant up to 330 yards, the black physical-vapour-deposition (PVD) casing was durable even in the harshest climates that the regiment operated in.

There was no talking between the SBS men, who merely exchanged glances and nods. A couple touched the cap badge on their sleeves, which displayed their unit's motto: 'By Strength and Guile'.

They'll need both today and a lot more besides, Ben thought.

After turning away from the special forces troops, Ben checked his own sleek, black Glock 17 semi-automatic pistol, testing the safe-action trigger system that was the weapon's signature. Pressing the trigger down, Ben began to disassemble the gun with a sense of *déjà vu*. This wasn't the first time he'd approached such a structure on a boat alongside members of the SBS whilst testing this exact weapon. He could only hope this operation was more of a success than that particular previous mission. As one of the standard-issue weapons used in the Thames House armoury, Ben had a fondness for the Glock 17 that went back many years and wasn't merely due to the 9mm Luger firearm being one of the easiest and quickest to use, although such advantages were critical in situations like the one facing him now.

He was on the point of muting his own microphone embedded into his vest when he heard a rattle of gunfire echoing through his earpiece and from the riverbank to his right. On looking up, he was able to discern a slight orange haze, which often accompanied a hail of bullets, rising from the control room that adorned the bank of the Thames. A split second later, there were panicked shouts and more gunfire, then a crackle of static before an eerie silence began to emanate from the navigation centre.

The silence seemed to drag on, and Ben felt his heart rate climb ever higher. He dared not change frequency and hear the panicked questions and murmurs from those back in Thames House. 'Zaf,' he said quite calmly, listening intently for any response. Nothing. 'Zaf.' Another crackle of static. Still no response. 'Sergeant Hiscock, Walker, Zaf, report.' Only silence came through in response. Then, echoing from both the riverbank to his right and through is earpiece, Ben heard a single loud crack of a semi-automatic round being fired.

Gesturing to the men beside him, Ben gripped the Glock 17 in his hand, weighing it in his palm. It was little wonder that the weapon was favoured by military and law enforcement personnel around the world. It seemed to add no weight to his arm and as he checked the magazine to ensure the optimal seventeen rounds were housed inside, it was like having a reassuring old friend accompanying him.

23

Thames Barrier Navigational Centre, south bank of the River Thames

'Zaf, are your men in position?' The words had crackled through the storm like a sharp clap of thunder.

The Chinook was circling briefly above the recognisable structure below, and Zaf had allowed himself a moment to marvel at this feat of civil engineering. It had become one of the capital's most striking landmarks. Stretching over 570 yards across the river, the nine stainless-steel piers were an enigmatic sight. From the air, Zaf could see the water lapping against the ten raised steel gates between the piers, and amidst the howl of the storm, he thought he could see the faintest movement of grinding machinery.

By the time they'd reached the site, the hollow gates had already started their journey upwards, and they watched from the sky as the gates emerged from the Thames, water falling from them back into the river. The rising sector gates that usually lay flat on the river bed to allow traffic to pass through the barrier had been rotated, using the yellow hydraulic cylinders, and moved into the closed position, creating a steely defence for London. That would usually be enough comfort in the face of a storm and tidal surge such as this, but not today.

The orders were being relayed through the earpiece in his right ear, and they couldn't be clearer: regain control of the barrier at all costs. London was in the midst of a tidal surge that had made its way in from the North Sea, and the barrier was the capital's main line of defence against devastation from such a surge. This was what it had been designed for. Surges happened twice a day with tides from the North Sea driving water past Southend, right through the heart of London and out the other side, as far as Teddington in its south-western suburbs, but the storm that had been forecast for days had chosen this moment to strike.

Below them, the mass gathering of miniscule dots that were environmental protestors was being ushered further away from the riverbank and the strike zone. Some were dispersing, but others were pointing in the direction of the Chinook. Zaf stared out down the river. Seeing London from this vantage point was special, but the sight of Greenwich and further in the distance the recognisable landmarks of Westminster made the enormity of the situation even more real. How many lives and how much infrastructure were at risk if the river were to flood?

Of course, the barrier had been designed with the purpose of preventing such an event ever happening. Its origins lay in two severe flooding events that had affected the capital. The first had been the Thames Flood in 1928, which had caused thousands to become homeless, as well as claiming the lives of fourteen people. It had been the second incident, which had occurred in 1953, that had prompted the complete rethink of London's flood defences. In that year, the North Sea Flood, caused by a heavy storm, led to severe flooding in the Netherlands, Belgium, England and Scotland. Sadly, more important than the 300 people who had lost their lives had been the cost of the damage. In the UK alone, it had cost the equivalent of approximately £5 billion pounds in today's money.

By the mid-1960s, experts had abandoned the customary plans to simply increase the strength and height of the river walls. The solution concept was a simple one, although it was not simple to execute: a flood barrier with movable gates would be built across the Thames. Remarkably, from when construction began in 1974, it took just eight years to become operational. That it was still in operation today was testament to that feat of design and civil engineering.

If it were to fail today, then it would take us all down with it, Zaf thought grimly.

*

As they'd boarded the Chinook thirty minutes earlier, Zaf had exchanged a brief conversation with Corporal Dawkins. Under the command of Sergeant Hiscock, a small group of soldiers from the 1st Battalion Rifles would again be part of the strike team. Dawkins had hesitated when he moved towards the Chinook, as the twin blades had begun to slice through the air above it. Perhaps it had just been as simple as a pause to reflect on the operation that they were undertaking, but Zaf suspected it was more than that.

'You don't have to do this, Adam,' Zaf had said to him, pausing on his own way towards the chopper, as he fastened the semi-automatic pistol to his waist. 'You've done your bit.'

The look that Dawkins had given him had been as cold as ice. 'Ross sacrificed his life to expose what was going on and stop these people. You're not keeping me off that helicopter.'

It hadn't felt right to contradict him about his friend, but the truth was that they still didn't know how Ross Matheson had been involved in all of this. Instead, Zaf had clapped him on the shoulder and said, 'Gives them another pretty face to aim at other than mine, so I'm happy.'

'Don't flatter yourself, Zaf. I'm not giving my life to save a spook.'

*

The memory had brought a small smile to Zaf's face. The two men had hurried towards the helicopter together and been helped aboard by the humourless Sergeant Hiscock. Zaf wasn't sure even now what to make of the man. He'd only spent a day serving alongside the Rifles, but those brief hours had been enough to tell him that he didn't like Hiscock one bit. Despite that, he was here and he'd insisted on being involved in the operations to halt these terrorists.

Even arseholes can have a sense of honour and integrity, Zaf thought dryly.

Pressing the earpiece further into his ear, he raised his voice to shout above the roar of the storm. '*Affirmative, we're moving towards the navigation centre now. Are we clear to proceed?*' As he spoke, the Chinook momentarily lost its battle with the elements and dropped several feet towards the ground. Whilst clinging on to the side of the cabin, Zaf felt his stomach lurch uncomfortably, and he grimaced at Corporal Dawkins, who was gripping the bottom of his seat tightly.

'You are a go. Repeat, you are a go strike team.' Ben's voice was clear and calm, as though he were sitting right beside Zaf in the belly of the Chinook. At the sound of those words, Zaf felt something clench inside his stomach, no doubt the nerves he'd been trying to hold back, but he wasn't going to let Ben down. The anger he'd felt towards his mentor had already dissipated. He had a job to do, and he sure as hell was going to do what Ben had taught him.

Before he'd even finished motioning to the rest of the men, the sallow-skinned Sergeant Hiscock had grabbed hold of the fast rope and disappeared from sight, with two of the men in his command following suit. It was just Zaf and Adam Dawkins left in the cabin of the chopper now. The dark skies were closing in above London, creating an oppressive claustrophobia and blocking out all light. Through the gloom, Zaf could make out the corporal's boyish features, and for a second, the two of them looked at each other.

Then the young soldier rose from his seat and extended his arm to Zaf, who used it to pull himself onto the swaying cabin floor. The pilot was fighting to keep the Chinook balanced, and they had just a few seconds before he'd have to pull up. Dawkins was several inches shorter than Zaf, and it was clear that he too was worried about what lay ahead. As they reached the door of the cabin, Zaf deliberately kept his eyes averted from the ground beneath them.

The corporal said quietly, 'For Ross and Amelia.'

With that, the two men exited the helicopter and descended the rope.

Zaf's feet hit the ground hard, and he winced as he felt a slight crack in his right boot. There was no way he was going to let Sergeant Hiscock see that. The sergeant had never got over Zaf's deception at Senta Barracks and would relish the opportunity to remind him again that spooks weren't soldiers. It seemed as though the military had a complex when it came to intelligence officers, even if they were meant to be on the same side.

After slinging the SA80 rifle from his soldier, Zaf crouched low and surveyed their landing point. It was exactly as they'd planned. They'd been dropped in a patch of open fields just between Eastmoor Street and the river. There was distant shouting, and Zaf took that to be the thousands of protestors who had gathered by the barrier earlier in the day. It sounded as though they were continuing to be steadily moved away from their location, as he had seen from the Chinook. He took the opportunity to scan the rest of the area. As he did so, Corporal Dawkins landed beside him without so much as a sound. 'Show off,' he muttered under his breath.

Diagonally across from them, crouched in formation with their assault rifles raised, were Sergeant Hiscock and the other three members of the Rifles who had joined the strike team, as well as three members of the SAS team that Wolf had commanded. Today, they were being led by a grim-faced Glaswegian by the name of Walker. Zaf somehow doubted this was his real name, particularly as the man had suggested they call him Johnny instead.

In contrast to the perfect physical specimens of the SAS men, Zaf would have recognised Hiscock's figure even if he hadn't been the designated leader of the other soldiers. Even when in a crouching position, his back was stooped and arched like a stone gargoyle. The memory of the man's nickname at the barracks brought a slight smile to Zaf's face. Hiscock signalled to the pair of them.

Glancing nervously over his shoulder, Zaf ducked down and ran across the sodden grass, feeling his boots squelch in the ground. As they approached, a gap opened up in the line behind Hiscock, and Zaf and Dawkins darted into it. The six men behind them had turned their backs and trained their weapons in the opposite direction. Zaf knew the area had been cleared of the public prior to them landing, but he hadn't expected it to be so still.

Thunder rumbled overhead, and Zaf found himself twitching involuntarily. The rain was pounding down upon them, seeping through their specially designed clothing. The soldiers didn't so much as flinch. They were totally still, tensed and ready to spring into action. In contrast, Zaf's legs were already beginning to cramp. He forced himself to concentrate on the figure of Hiscock in front of him. Despite the man's grotesque posture, there was a relaxed poise to the way he held his frame.

Just as he began to take several deep breaths, Zaf felt a hand on his left shoulder. A feeling of mingled reassurance and embarrassment surged through his upper body. Keeping his breathing even, Zaf tried to relax his diaphragm as much as possible. After several seconds, he felt the tension in his back ease, and he relaxed, leaning forwards ever so slightly. With that came the confidence he needed to whisper into Hiscock's ear, 'Time to move, Sergeant.'

There came a curt nod of the head in response. At the best of times, Hiscock was a man of few words. Operationally, it seemed, he preferred silence. The sergeant took his right hand off his SA80 rifle and clenched it into a fist, extending it away from his body, before creeping forwards. Evidently, the men at the back had sensed the order, as they followed behind as Zaf and Dawkins trailed after Hiscock, their weapons still covering the rear of the strike team.

In a compact line, they moved through the park, raising their rifles occasionally to survey the buildings above. There could be a sniper hidden in any one of the surrounding apartments, and they were sitting ducks. As it was, however, everything remained quiet and still, except the steadily falling rain. They moved quickly through the streets, edging closer to the river's edge all the time. Eventually, as they turned off Unity Way, the Port of London Authority's Thames Barrier Navigation Centre came into view, with the building set to the side of the barrier beyond.

As they edged nearer, Zaf found himself looking around more frequently. He kept his eyes averted from the river and what was happening there. This was where his concentration needed to be. They'd expected an ambush or at least to find the navigation centre guarded by Henderson's men, but there was no one in sight. There was a car park to the rear of Unity House, and there were several modest-looking cars stationed there. Two of the men behind Zaf darted forwards and moved between the vehicles, shining their spotlights through the soaked windows, whilst Corporal Dawkins edged away from the main group, heading towards an area of bushes to their right.

Within seconds, all the men had signalled that the area was clear. Blinking rain from his eyes, Zaf focussed on the rear of the building in front of them. There was a fire escape to the right-hand side of the building that looked as though it had firmly been closed. To the left side of the building, there was a flight of concrete steps leading up and out of sight, presumably looping round to the front entrance of the navigation centre.

The concrete steps led to a blind corner, and the positioning made Zaf all the more nervous. He hesitated and then motioned to Hiscock. 'You and your men take the fire escape. Walker and I will approach the building from the front. If we need backup, we'll radio through.'

'Take Dawkins,' replied Hiscock at once, without a flicker of emotion on his face. 'He'll do more good for you than me.'

At these words, Zaf thought he saw a ripple of anger pass across the corporal's face for a moment. Then it was gone, and he was nodding firmly. In truth, Zaf was grateful for the extra backup. He watched for a second as Hiscock briefed his men and then led them across the tarmacked car park towards the fire exit. Walker was already assembling the SAS troops, who'd begun to check their C8 carbines – the Canadian assault rifle that was the regiment's preferred choice. Zaf found his eyes lingering on the water dripping from the ends of the sleek, black muzzles.

It wasn't until Zaf felt a clap on his shoulder and caught a passing wink from Corporal Dawkins as he moved past that he took action. Unlike the rest of the men, he wasn't wearing tactical gloves, and he could feel the SA80 rifle slipping slightly in his hands. His palms were slippery, not only with rainwater but with sweat too, he realised. He lifted his hands off the rifle, one at a time, for just a second to wipe them on the black combat trousers he was wearing.

In that second, he felt suddenly vulnerable and found himself glancing around nervously. Taking a deep breath, he gripped the SA80 once more. Walker and his SAS men were lined up at the foot of the concrete steps, with Corporal Dawkins just behind them and Zaf at the rear. The SAS leader was looking at Zaf, and there wasn't a shred of emotion on his face; this was a man ready for battle. Zaf could only imagine how he must look in comparison.

After taking in another deep lungful of humid air, Zaf nodded at Walker and crouched low as the SAS man raised a hand towards Hiscock and his men, who were all across the car park. Then he was moving up the concrete steps that were sodden with rain, the rest of the SAS men and Dawkins following in close formation. Zaf's leg hovered in mid-air above the first step for a fraction of a second. As it did so, there was an ear-splitting crack of thunder overhead, an ominous sign of what was about to happen.

Ben, he knew, would be waiting to see that they'd successfully raided the control room before he led the SBS men onto the barrier itself. He couldn't risk moving in if Henderson had snipers ready to pick them off from the navigation centre. That reminder was enough to push him forwards, behind the troops. Each step added an extra jolt to his increasing heartbeat. When he reached the top of the steps, he stopped with his back flat against the brick wall of the building, and Dawkins signalled for him to wait. Ahead of them, the SAS men had moved around to the front of the navigation centre, aiming to catch any of the terrorists off guard.

Ahead, he could hear the sound of hurried footsteps, then came a slight crack before a loud bang. There were two shouts, but no sound of weapons being discharged. That only made Zaf more uneasy. Thirty seconds of silence followed these noises, then another incoherent shout. They must have signalled to Dawkins, as the corporal nodded his head at Zaf, turned the corner and took another few steps around the side of the building. Zaf followed, feeling uneasy as he lost the security of the building wall at his back. The steps led to a raised concrete platform that was much wider than the narrow stairwell they'd traversed thus far. It stretched back and out of sight towards further platforms that overlooked the river. As Zaf climbed the final few steps, he found Corporal Dawkins standing beside a now-open side door that had been kicked in by the SAS soldiers.

There was a bitter edge to the corporal's eyes as Zaf moved past him into the navigation centre. The control room itself was an odd oval shape with a sweeping, curved glass front that looked out over the Thames Barrier and the river itself. The windows were streaked with rain, and there was an unpleasant smell that hung in the air as he stepped forwards. In front of a bank of monitors that stretched the length of the window were three black leather swivel chairs. Walker was standing beside the nearest of the three and caught Zaf's eye before turning the seat to face him.

Zaf had known from the back of the heads slumped to one side that the men and women who worked in the control room were dead. That didn't make their blank, lifeless eyes any easier to see, however. Zaf touched the earpiece in his right ear, re-engaging the connection to the other units. He'd just opened his mouth when there was a flurry of loud cracks from the doorway. Before he'd completely turned his body, something thudded into his right leg, and he felt a searing, white-hot pain jolt through him.

Squinting through the pain, he watched one of the SAS men beside him crumple to the ground in a cloud of red vapour that exploded from his body. Behind him, Walker was shouting something incoherent before a shallow grunt told Zaf that he too had been hit. The pain took Zaf, and he dropped to his knees, turning his head as he did so. Now only one of the SAS soldiers was still standing, his carbine pointed through the open doorway and cartridges thudding into the floor around him.

With all instinct deserting him, Zaf followed the line of the man's rifle. Adam Dawkins was still upright, his back pressed against the wall beside the doorway leading out of the navigation centre. Beyond it, Zaf could make out three men with their own weapons raised. They were dressed in combat gear and appeared to have stepped over the body of a fourth figure as they approached the doorway. Zaf recognised the hunched figure of the man at the front at once, which was what made him finally reach for his weapon.

The SA80 had tumbled from his grip, and his hands slipped clumsily over the clip to his holster, as he frantically tried to withdraw the semi-automatic pistol that it contained. Bullets flew through the air around them, and there was no means of escape. There was a splintering noise above them as the glass panel of the control room was peppered with gunfire. Several seconds later, there was a deafening crack and glass rained down onto the floor of the control room, bringing with it the howl of the storm and a driving, vertical rain.

The SAS man beside him was shouting something he couldn't hear, as Zaf finally withdrew his weapon and tried to make for the relative cover of the swivel chairs. It was just as he reached the nearest chair, trying not to look at Walker's unmoving body, that there was a deafening rattle of gunfire and the final SAS man still standing was blasted off his feet.

His body was propelled backwards and landed atop that of his commanding officer. There was fear and confusion in the man's eyes and maybe accusation. Zaf tried to drag his arm up and bring the gun around, forcing his gaze towards the doorway as he did so. Corporal Dawkins had ducked out from behind the doorway, his gunfire hurling one of his regimental colleagues backwards through the air.

Zaf squinted, trying to aim his pistol around the corporal, but he couldn't get a clear line of sight at Hiscock and his men. There was an ugly spitting sound, and Dawkins too dropped to the floor, swiftly crawling behind the safety of the doorframe and staring imploringly at Zaf. Pain spasmed across the soldier's face and Zaf again saw a look of accusation in the man's eyes.

It was enough to spur him into action. Ignoring the hail of bullets that smashed into the control panel above his head, Zaf threw himself out from behind the chair. In one fluid movement, as he slid across the floor, he took aim and fired three shots. The final man supporting Hiscock crumpled, but the sergeant was just a couple of steps from the doorway now, and Zaf's eyes were drawn to the deadly muzzle of the weapon pointing directly at him.

In vain, Zaf tightened his finger around the trigger and watched as the bullet thudded into the man's vest. The second bullet missed him altogether. Sergeant Hiscock had reached the doorway now, and Zaf was finally able to make out the expression on the ugly, contorted face: bitter resentment. Well, Zaf could understand those emotions.

Hiscock smiled humourlessly, and through the howl of the rain Zaf heard him shout, '*I'm sorry it had to come to this.*'

Even as Zaf watched the man's finger tighten on the trigger and knew that there was no hope, he fired the Glock until it clicked uselessly in his hand. Before the bullets had made their way across the control room, however, Dawkins had thrown himself out from behind the doorway, his own SA80 rifle clutched in his hand. There were two loud, simultaneous rattles of gunfire as Dawkins and Hiscock came face to face. Both men staggered, and Zaf was horrified to see his own bullets whip past the corporal's shoulders, only just missing him. The two soldiers fell backwards through the air, almost in slow motion, each other's fire peppering their adversary. As their bodies hit the ground, there was an ear-splitting crack of thunder, timed almost as a commemoration.

Clutching his bleeding leg, Zaf dragged himself along the blood-soaked floor of the control room, grimacing at the pain from both the wound and the loud whine of static in his ear. The doorway was littered with the bodies of the SAS men that Hiscock and his soldiers had gunned down, their limbs sticking out at odd angles and their eyes unfocussed. He managed to haul himself across to the lifeless figure that was sprawled across the narrow entrance, his head resting against the doorframe. He might have been asleep.

They might not have known each other long, but there had been an instant bond and respect between him and the man he looked down on now. The boyish features and light-brown hair were flecked with blood, and the corporal's eyes held a far-away look. Zaf had known there was no hope from the minute he'd seen the bullets rattle towards Dawkins' body, but that didn't make his lack of a pulse any easier to find.

From the moment they'd met, it had been clear to Zaf that Dawkins felt a level of responsibility for what had happened to the Mathesons. Zaf knew Ross Matheson had been his closest friend from the regiment, and his wife Amelia had been on her way to meet Adam the night she'd been killed. In some small way, Dawkins killing his fellow officer Private Faye to save Jackie's life had begun to heal that guilt, but his insistence that he be on the strike teams for the university raid and this mission were proof it hadn't been enough. After leaning down, Zaf slowly lowered the soldier's eyelids. He hoped Adam would be able to find some peace now.

With pain spasming up the right-hand side of his body, Zaf spared one bitter glance across at the bodies of Hiscock and his fellow traitors, who were spreadeagled several paces from the entrance to the control room. With an almighty effort, he used the doorway to pull himself to his feet, taking a second to balance the majority of his weight on his left leg. Staring around, he saw that the photo hung over the control panel, which depicted the Queen's visit to this place for the barrier's opening in 1984, had been shattered. Broken glass was scattered across the floor of the room, and the frame lay on the surface of the control panel.

On ripping his earpiece free, he relished the momentary stillness and quiet as the static whine fell to the floor along with the earpiece. The relief lasted barely a second, as far-off screams of terror broke through the cacophonic roar of the river behind and the storm that was lashing rain down upon them. In that moment, the shock of what had happened kept him rooted to the spot. He was paralysed by his own brain and body, which refused to obey his commands to leap into action. He found himself glancing back towards the doorway of the control room and felt a single tear begin to roll down the side of his face.

After wiping it away along with the rainwater, he reached down, tore open a pouch attached to his belt and withdrew two items. After flipping open the mobile phone, he limped across to the console and scanned it rapidly. Simon had told him what to look for. There were several ports jutting out from the control panel. Zaf located the one designated by a green strip beneath it, and then he thrust the other device into the port. It looked no more obscure than an everyday USB stick.

At once, several of the dials along the control panel

blinked on. Using the panel to steady himself, Zaf scanned the overhead monitors, squinting through the rain that was now driving directly into his face. The majority of the monitors had been blown apart by the gunfight, but two appeared to be largely intact. After placing the phone on the work surface, Zaf pressed two numbers. The phone didn't ring, but there was a metallic click before a voice he recognised at once answered.

'Zafar, what's your status? Viper has stormed the barrier. We lost contact with your team.'

'I'm good, boss; thanks for asking,' Zaf responded with a grimace. 'We had some complications, but I'm in the control room. Is Simon there?'

'Yes, I'm here, Zaf.' (Oddly, Zaf found the analyst's voice more comforting than that of Aldwyn Haynes just now.) 'I'm working on the override. I'm trying to regain access to the system's main firewall. It appears as though they've not only gained control of the system themselves but created further firewalls to prevent us regaining access.'

'Can you shut the entire thing down?' Haynes asked bluntly.

'If I do that, then London floods. I can shut it down, but only at the same rate at which the gates were raised. Although individual gates were designed so that they could be raised in ten minutes, closing the whole barrier usually takes ninety minutes. There was, however, functionality built in to speed up that process in the event of an extreme emergency. They've activated that protocol, which was why they managed to raise the gates so quickly. If I close them at that speed, it will send a tidal surge up river that could flood everything up to and beyond the Houses of Parliament.'

'They're 200-feet-wide gates that weigh more than 3,000 tonnes each, for Christ's sake,' snapped Haynes. 'There must be a way to deactivate them.'

'Raising those gates and that weight in a compressed time wasn't without risk. We still don't know what their intentions are, but if I shut down the barrier at that speed, I could create a much worse scenario.'

'There's £200 billion pounds' worth of infrastructure at stake here, and that's before we even get to the lives at risk. There are thousands of people in the red zone near the barrier and thousands more on the Tube that could be flooded. We need to find a way to regain full control.' There was a measured authority to Haynes's voice, but Zaf knew that he'd be getting pressured from above.

Zaf glanced around the control room, his eyes pausing on the body of Corporal Dawkins. The rain and wind was buffeting into his face through the shattered window.

'Zafar,' interjected Aldwyn, 'are all the hostiles down? Is there no sign of any more of Henderson's men?'

Zaf didn't need to look around the navigation centre again. He didn't need to see the bodies of the SAS men or Adam Dawkins. 'They're down, sir. No sign of anyone else. Are you in contact with Ben and the SBS men?'

There was a pause – just for a fraction of a second. 'When we lost contact with your team, he led them onto the barrier anyway. They encountered resistance. As far as we know, they're still fighting their way through Henderson's men.'

'Any sign of the boy?' Zaf knew Ben wouldn't want to dwell on his fate. Besides, if anyone could look after themselves, then it was Ben Viper. *He wouldn't have hesitated to draw his weapon,* he thought bitterly, before dismissing the thought from his mind.

'Nothing,' replied Jackie Ambrose. 'There's a possibility that—' The detective never got to finish her sentence.

'Zaf, you need to get out of there immediately.' It was Helen Robinson who'd interrupted, and for once there was emotion in her crisp tone. 'There has long been a radar system operational along the river to detect certain threats that might target the capital. Our radar has just picked up two torpedo-shaped objects entering the Thames Estuary, moving at high speed. They'll reach the barrier in a matter of minutes.'

24

Not the best weather for a date. That was what Robbie had thought that morning as he exited the Tube at Greenwich and looked miserably into the grey sky above. He hadn't intended to use the umbrella himself. It was more a gentlemanly gesture to protect Anna than anything else. Yet, as he waited by the *Cutty Sark*, which looked as though she were riding the seas once more, his resistance folded. It was one thing trying to look macho, but it was quite another to look like a drowned rat.

The station had only got wetter the further he'd travelled from the platform. People riding the escalators down had shaken off their umbrellas and shrugged rain off their hoods and shoulders. There had been a strong smell of damp. As he'd reached the top of the escalators, he'd cursed as his feet began to swim in dirty water.

Now outside, the rain pounded down onto the umbrella, the sound reverberating around him like a bass drum. It was coming down like a curtain, hissing like an angry cobra as it hit the pavements. Robbie blinked rapidly, watching the water run off the edges of the pavements and cascade onto the ground around him. It was already seeping into his shoes, and he swore as he flicked them outwards, smiling at what his friends would have said if they'd seen that particular move. Ollie would doubtless have made some joke about him being the worst tap dancer in the country.

Perhaps he should have told Ollie that he was meeting Anna. After all, she was Emma's best friend. He resolved to drop Ollie a message tomorrow. It might be too soon for a double date, given the circumstances, but it might kick his mate into action. That was a conversation Robbie knew he should already have had with Ollie – even more so given recent events. If he weren't careful, his friend was going to let guilt and misery ruin his life.

That thought was interrupted by a jolt of surprise, immediately followed by the instinctive reaction to laugh. Anna was hurrying towards him through the monsoon, her shoulders hunched in a yellow raincoat and her face running with mascara. Taking a deep breath and trying to hide his smile, he squelched his way towards her, extending the umbrella aloft to cover them both. She gratefully hurried beneath it, and they briefly found themselves huddled against one another. There was an awkward silence, and then Anna giggled nervously. Robbie felt it was now safe to smile. Maybe this wouldn't be such a rotten date after all.

*

Really, thought Carol Weston as she stared out of the window of the care home in Woolwich. *After this crappy day, I'll have to travel home in this crappy weather. Can't the universe give me a break just for one day? Just an evening would be nice.* It wasn't that she hated her job. On the contrary, there were times when it couldn't feel more rewarding. But not right now. Going home to an empty flat and voicemails from her solicitor listing another of her husband's divorce demands was making her hate this job. Maybe she should spend her weekends walking alpacas? That might cheer her up.

There were some patients you grew to like more than others. Any carer will tell you that isn't true, but they're lying. They all had their favourites, and Farida Chowdhury was one of Carol's. She was in her eighties and had suffered from multiple sclerosis for over a decade, but she didn't seem to let that get her down. Only recently had she lost her vision completely. She'd simply used it as an opportunity to slap her daughter Maya on the backside and plead lack of sight.

It was Farida Carol had just left, and the old woman had managed to put a smile on Carol's face even after the hellish week that this had been.

She'd heard the rain lashing against the window and insisted that Carol take her outside for a dip in the Thames, so long as they didn't tell Maya about it. 'You must have some armbands in this place,' she'd wheezed at Carol.

'If I get swept up in the storm, I'll be sure to swim a few lengths for you, Mrs Chowdhury.' Carol had laughed as she'd closed the door to the old lady's room.

Judging by the state of the windows, that comment seemed less of a joke now. Carol hated getting cabs in London, and not just because she couldn't afford it. She spent all day indoors in musty corridors and rooms, and her own flat wasn't much better. The travel time had always helped her clear her head. There was a quaking rumble of thunder overhead, which made her jump a little. Sod it. She'd add the taxi receipt to the divorce settlement.

*

Further along the south bank towards Woolwich, Steven Houghton was in a very bad mood. It was bad enough that

Crofton had made a fool out of him with those headlines. Now she wanted to humiliate him by watching his suit cling to him like some shrivelled, elderly waxwork. As ever, the journalist seemed completely relaxed at her choice of location. Doubtless her expensive raincoat was keeping her perfectly dry in the storm.

She could have at least booked an indoor table, he thought bitterly.

What he'd give for a glass of whisky just now. Instead, he had to pretend to play nice with a smarmy journalist who'd outmanoeuvred him and who now seemed thoroughly delighted with herself.

'Are you angry with me, Mr Houghton?' asked Janine Crofton. 'I do hope I haven't caused any friction within Whitehall. It would be a shame if any illustrious careers were ended prematurely.'

'I'm pleased to hear you consider your own career illustrious thus far, Miss Crofton.' Houghton hadn't meant to be so abrupt, but he wasn't in the mood for her games. 'That knowledge will no doubt be of some comfort to you when you're writing column inches for *Surrey Pond Life* magazine.' He was pleased to see a flicker of shock flit across her face for a second. 'How about we dispense with the adolescent jibes and cut to point – what do you want?'

The journalist had opened her mouth to respond, but Houghton's attention had been diverted. Overhead, he could see a Chinook. He was sure of it. He would have recognised the distinctive rotor blades anywhere. From his seat, he was facing in the direction of the Thames Barrier, and although visibility was virtually non-existent through the driving rain, he knew that silhouette hovering above the point where the barrier must be. A streak of lightning flashed above them, but unlike those around him who screamed in shock, Houghton concentrated his gaze.

The lightning lit up the grey sky momentarily. It was as though a director had signalled for lights up, and the stage was illuminated at once. In that fleeting flash of light, the shadow of the Chinook was clearly visible, suspended impossibly in the air above the Thames Barrier. As the screams and shouts of passers-by faded, there was a second of silence. Just a second. But in that moment, Houghton thought he heard the faint wail of sirens and klaxons. It might just be his imagination filling in the blanks, but even so, something was wrong.

*

They disembarked the Interceptor craft at the pier nearest the south bank, landing lightly on the structure. The rain was torrential now, and they bowed their heads from the onslaught as they circled the pier, checking for any sign of Henderson's men. There was nobody in sight. Thunder cracked through the black sky above them, and for a split second, Ben mistook it for a merciless rattle of gunfire. In truth, he was more comfortable in a storm of bullets than in the tempest that seemed to be closing in around them, with the darkness continuing to descend over them all. He hadn't seen anything like this before.

Ben knew the layout of the piers by memory now. The barrier comprised nine metal-hooded piers and two abutments that supported the ends of the structure. Glancing towards the bank, Ben thought he could make out whisps of smoke curling into the air above the navigation centre. He peered towards the control room, but he couldn't make anything out through the driving rain. Blinking rapidly, he gestured towards the SBS commander, who nodded at the thick reinforced-concrete hull of the pier.

This structure had been built to withstand all but the worst-case scenarios. It had been designed to be bombproof, although that hadn't been truly tested. When a 3,000-tonne dredger hit the barrier in 1997, the ship sank. The barrier only lost a ladder. It seemed incomprehensible that Henderson could find a way of undermining its defences, but Ben knew the man well enough to realise this wasn't just a power move.

The rest of the SBS men had joined them, having completed their sweep of the pier. Built into the hull was a heavy-duty steel door. They knew it would take two of the SBS men to open it. The grip provided by their tactical combat gloves would help them prise open the weighty gate that led down into the belly of the pier. Two of the soldiers moved forwards and wrenched at the door, whilst the rest of the men trained their weapons on the structure. Ben aimed his own carbine, which the commander had insisted on giving him before they disembarked the Interceptor, feeling it slide a little beneath his grasp.

As the door was pulled open and the rain clattered down onto the metal hull of the pier, creating an echoey bubble around the SBS men, Ben kept his gaze focussed on the hole that had appeared. The SBS commander took a step forwards and shone the flashlight attached to his weapon into the darkness. He nodded and climbed onto a thin metal ladder that led inside the dense hull of the pier, his rifle hoisted over his shoulder, whilst two of his men lay flat on the surface of the pier, pointing their flash-lit weapons into the darkness.

The commander barely made a sound as he alighted at the bottom of the ladder. Two more of the SBS men followed swiftly. Then it was Ben's turn. He glanced around as he reached the open shell of the pier. Lightning flashed violently across the sky, and for a moment, distant Greenwich was illuminated, the Royal Observatory standing guard over the maritime borough below. It might need such protection today.

This was a unique position. Standing atop the pier, Ben looked down on the huge gates that were protecting London from the tidal surge that had swept in from the North Sea. Water was lashing against the gates, rolling up the mass of steel before crashing back down into the river. When raised, the main gates stood as high as a five-storey building and as wide as the opening of Tower Bridge. From astride the hull of the pier, Ben could appreciate the sheer scale of their defensive blockade.

The mass of water was clear to see. The threat of the capital being flooded had never seemed so real as it did now. There had been plots against the barrier in the past – one of which Ben had handled personally – but he'd never been forced to set foot on the structure, let alone in the midst of such a storm. The threat was real enough.

The storm had been predicted for days, and the barrier had been tested in advance of it arriving. They'd known it would be required. And in the early hours of this morning, the satellites and coastal stations had all confirmed what would hit the Thames Estuary. The three-foot-high surge coupled with high tide, strong winds and an already high river meant only one thing: without the barrier, London would flood. If just one of the gates were to open, it would produce a surge of water so powerful that the reinforced walls of the embankment and the abutments would be overwhelmed.

There was another sharp crack of thunder overhead, and Ben holstered his weapon. Reaching out, he grasped hold of the steel ladder and began to lower himself into the belly of the pier's hull. His eyes needed little adjustment to the gloom, given the comparative darkness of the world outside. As he descended, however, he was slightly taken aback by the pine interior that was affixed over the pier's ceiling. He hadn't expected to find that beneath the world's second-largest flood-protection structure. He wondered vaguely if the same were true of the Delta Works Oosterscheldekering in the Netherlands.

It didn't take long to reach the bottom of the ladder, and Ben jumped lightly onto the concrete floor. The other SBS men had formed a small circle, their flash-lit weapons trained in all directions. They'd descended onto a small walkway that led off in two directions. As with everything else designed for the Thames Barrier, there was a backup. They hadn't just built one tunnel to allow engineers access to the piers; they'd built two.

The tunnels had often been used for training by the emergency services, but they'd been forgotten in the past couple of years. Glancing around, Ben could see why the narrow confines of the passageways would make a good place for training. They were surrounded by miles of steel-ringed piping and large, compressed cannisters affixed to walls. A red steel door lay open to their right, whilst the darkness stretched to their left.

A faint, musty odour pervaded the air. Ben had expected to hear nothing beneath the pier, but the rage of the storm was as palpable below as it was above. Thunder echoed through the tunnels and off the coloured conduits that laced around bulkheads, seeming to reverberate around them. There was no sign of anyone, but Ben thought he heard distant shouting and then an unmistakeable rattle of gunfire. It rebounded down the tunnels, moving steadily towards them until the sound appeared to be right above them.

The final two members of the SBS team had landed beside Ben. All of them had their weapons ready and were in a combat stance. Ben walked slightly across the concrete floor until he was standing beside the SBS commander. 'We have to find out their plan. Our first priority is preserving the barrier. If it fails, the city floods. If you find the hostages, get them out with one of your men. The tunnels are probably the safest way off the structure.'

The commander nodded, his face grimly resolute. 'They aren't taking London down without a fight, Mr Viper; I can assure you of that.'

'Stay on comms,' replied Ben.

Turning on the spot, he beckoned for two of the SBS men to follow him and set off left down the passageway. The oppressive darkness of the tunnel began to open up as the flashlights atop their carbines illuminated the gloom, revealing more twisting pipes. The pine cladding had disappeared now, replaced by a low, vaulted concrete ceiling that closed in around the men as they made their way slowly and quietly along the passageway. The further they walked, the more the sound of the storm seemed to fade.

There was still no sign of any guards. Then, as they rounded a corner in the tunnel and heavy droplet of water fell onto Ben's forehead, they stepped into a hail of gunfire. Framed in the centre of the tunnel were three bulky figures, all holding semi-automatic rifles that spat a frenzied volley of bullets towards them. Ben ducked back behind the bend in the tunnel as bullets rebounded off the metal bulkheads above his head and slammed into the concrete walls.

The two SBS men had retreated too. One of them, Ben noticed, was bleeding from a wound in his upper right shoulder, but other than that, the three of them had remained miraculously unharmed. They knew their attackers would soon be advancing around the corner. They couldn't allow themselves to be pinned in this narrow stretch of open tunnel. As it was, the bend in the passageway was affording them their only cover, but they'd have to leave that safety behind.

Ducking low beneath a long stretch of intricate steel pipework, Ben flung himself round the corner in the passageway. Immediately, bullets twanged into the steel and thudded into the floor at his feet. It was difficult to distinguish individual gunshots, but the bullets sliced through the air with alarming speed, forcing Ben to roll sideways to avoid them. He fired on instinct, spreading his shots evenly throughout the place where he knew the three men had been standing. There were shouts and grunts of pain, and he watched as two of the figures crumpled to the tunnel floor.

Beside him, one of the SBS troopers was blasted backwards by a cluster of bullets. His head slammed into the concrete wall of the tunnel, and he rolled to the floor, unmoving. Ben continued to fire. The bullets disappeared into the darkness with the merest flashes of orange. Something slammed into the pipework a hair's breadth above his head. He could make out a hulking silhouette moving through the shadows.

The man was rounding the corner now, and Ben retreated, still crouching and hoping that the darkness would conceal him, noticing as he did so that the other SBS soldier lay spreadeagled against the opposite wall. He pressed himself against the wall beneath the pipework, focussing on the approaching thud of the footsteps. Then, as the first black boot came into sight, he darted out from beneath the pipes and lunged at the man.

The move had taken the mercenary by surprise. He either hadn't noticed Ben squatting beneath the steel conduits or had assumed he was out of ammunition and therefore easy prey. Ben smashed his hand down on the man's wrist, knocking the ugly sub-machine gun out of his hand, and at the same time, tried to pull his own weapon around. But the mercenary reacted in time to lash out at the carbine, sending it flying out of the agent's grip. Ben didn't wait for the gun to hit the floor. He was already moving, slamming an elbow into the man's chest and pulling him into a tight headlock.

The mercenary struggled ferociously, and Ben found himself unable to hold on. After releasing the man, he scrambled for the sub-machine gun lying just a few feet from him, but his attacker got there first. The mercenary tried to bring the weapon to bear, but Ben lashed out again and followed through with a roundhouse kick that broke the man's nose in an instant.

He tried to take the advantage by moving forwards, but the man blocked his attack easily.

Their limbs flashed with alarming speed, the moves performed with expert precision and their bodies moving like lightning, but the relentless kicks and strikes met only skilled defence. It was a stalemate. Ben withdrew his Glock, but when he did so, he found it instantly dislodged from his grasp and sent tumbling into the darkness around them.

The two of them broke apart, with Ben taking the opportunity to regain his breath. The mercenary snarled, flecks of blood flying through the air from his broken nose.

'There's still a way out for you,' said Ben calmly, wiping blood and sweat from his forehead. 'You can still walk away from this.'

The mercenary opened his mouth in a twisted smile, but he never had a chance to speak. Ben flew at him, pinned him to the floor and brought his fist down on the man. The mercenary tried to react, attempting to twist away from the agent's attack, but Ben had been expecting the move. He grabbed the man by the throat and brought the edge of his hand crashing down on the man's temple. Ben scrambled to his feet, as his adversary writhed on the floor in agony, and the agent kicked out at him twice more.

Remarkably, the mercenary found the energy to pull a knife from his pocket. He swiped it through the air, narrowly missing Ben's throat and causing him to reel backwards. Another lunge with the knife forced the agent to jump aside. He aimed a kick at the mercenary, but his foot found only thin air. The man had moved aside with amazing speed, managing to avoid the MI5 agent's attack, before lashing out with a back kick that caught Ben across the eye, causing him to fall backwards, temporarily blinded in agony.

Capitalising on his advantage, the man threw three jackhammer punches that caught Ben full in the face. His back was slammed into the object beneath him, and he grimaced in pain. Ben lay on the floor exhausted, clutching his nose. He watched as blood trickled from the wounds on his face into the pool around him.

Static whined in his ear for a moment, then the frantic, nervous voice of Simon Wynn-Jones crackled into life. 'Ben, we have two torpedo-shaped objects entering the Thames Estuary, headed straight for the barrier. The footage from the cameras along the river walls isn't conclusive, but we think they're some kind of submersible device.'

'They'll reach the barrier in a matter of minutes,' added the harsher tone of Aldwyn Haynes. 'Our best guess is they're going to attempt to blow the structure or at least part of it. You need to get out of there now.'

Then came another voice; one that seemed to take Ben back ten years: 'Ben, are you there?'

Blinking blood from his eyes, Ben looked up at the menacing darkness above him. Slipping his hand beneath him, he gripped the object wedged into his spine. He thought he could make out a smile on the indistinguishable features looming over him, but Ben was already rolling, freeing his arm and pulling the trigger of the Glock. The bullet hit the man full in the chest, and he looked down in surprise. Red tinged the blackened canvas as blood began to spread steadily across his vest, and he pitched forwards onto the floor. Ben struggled to his feet, grimacing at the dull pains across his body.

With every movement requiring a painful effort, as he forced his aching limbs upright. Numbly, he pressed his finger against his ear and said, 'They'll be the former SEAL submersibles that went missing recently. They'll have packed them full of explosives. My guess would be that they're going to try to blow one of the outer gates on either bank. It'll create a flow of water that will flood the bank, but not enough to flood the entire city.'

'But why—?' began the Welsh analyst.

Ben cut in: 'They could open the gates now. They have control of the barrier. If they wanted to, they could let the city flood. Whatever their reasons, they don't want that. They know that we know they could do it. My guess is they'll create a spectacular explosion to destroy part of the barrier. What are our options?'

'Or they could open a gate and allow the submersibles to pass through the barrier,' interjected Helen Robinson. 'If that's the case, then we can't rule out any number of other targets. They could position the submersibles besides the Houses of Parliament or the SIS Building to name just two. The hacking of the barrier could be a cover to allow the submersibles through.'

'It's a possibility. Everything with the barrier could be a diversion, but at the rate those submersibles travel, they would have needed to start the process of lowering a gate already. That hasn't happened yet.'

As he spoke, he was already running down the tunnel in the direction they'd been heading. He could hear voices drifting down the passageway towards him.

As he ran, Aldwyn's voice crackled through his earpiece. 'The Thames Barrier Sentry system would usually stop anything like this getting through, but it's offline. They have control of that too. We could set off the electromagnetic pulse built into the river wall as a safeguard. It will fry any electronics and disrupt communications within two and a half miles.'

'Then do it,' said Ben at once. 'Stop these things before they reach the barrier.'

'It's not as simple as that. It will take out everything electronic within two and a half miles. That could include the barrier, and the backup generators may not activate in time, not to mention life-support systems in hospitals and whatever aircraft are still airborne. The risk is too great. We can't even get an exact radar lock on the submersibles, meaning it could all be for nothing.

'At this point, Simon has no reasonable expectation of regaining control over the barrier's systems. We've started evacuating emergency personnel into the tunnels beneath Greenwich and other at-risk areas. Parliament has been evacuated into the bunker. Without knowing the amount of explosives being carried in the submersibles, we can't be sure of the damage they'll do. If you're right, and they elect to blow up one of the outside gates, then the flow of water will be less catastrophic. Isn't that right, Simon?' Aldwyn could have been giving an after-dinner speech, so calm was his tone, but Ben knew that even his boss would feel the enormity of what could be about to happen.

Aldwyn continued, 'If they successfully manage to blow the gates on the north bank, City Airport will be submerged in a matter of minutes. The Victoria Docks, Canning Town and much more will be flooded soon after. If only one gate is destroyed, then the water will funnel through that gap, and the pressure will force the water over the bank. That initial surge will be enough to reach and submerge much of the Docklands. It would have been much worse if they'd chosen to blow it an hour ago.'

'What if they blow the south bank?' Ben wasn't surprised to hear the fear in Maya Chowdhury's voice.

There was a pause, and Ben could well imagine the looks being exchanged in Thames House.

'Assuming the last recorded position of the submersibles is correct, they'll be on course to hit the south side of the barrier. That would cause a flow of water that would overwhelm the abutments and embankment wall. Assuming the latest data is correct, Woolwich and Greenwich would be flooded minutes after impact. The surge is likely to continue upstream until it hits the bend in the river by the Blackwall Tunnel. Again, it's likely that the Docklands, The O2 and numerous Tube stations would be flooded shortly afterwards.'

Ben knew all too well the reaction those words would have caused in the Thames House briefing room. Maya, he knew, had a personal loss at stake. Her mother's nursing home would likely be submerged by any breach of the embankment wall along the south bank. He also knew that he wouldn't be hearing her voice through his earpiece for the remainder of this mission.

*

Lights flickered feebly in the dim passageways. There was a trace of damp in the air, but Ollie's senses had adapted now, and his nose no longer recoiled in distaste. The sirens continued to blare overhead, yet they didn't permeate the focussed bubble that had settled around him. Nothing else mattered except getting out of here. The voice that had spoken to Ollie might have told him they'd survive, but Ollie had seen the look in Henderson's eyes. The men weren't going to let them live.

The absurdity of the situation still nagged at him. This couldn't be real. The news channels for the past two days had done their best to hype up the incoming tidal surge from the North Sea. This was exactly the type of event that the barrier had been designed to prevent. Was their plan to not raise the gates and let London flood? No, he'd heard the hydraulic whine and the sirens. He'd seen the YouTube videos. They were both signs that the gates were being raised.

They had to act as though this was their only chance of survival. Gripping Emma's hand reassuringly, Ollie squinted through the gloom. They'd stepped into a long passageway that stretched left and right beyond his field of vision. Leading off were a series of corridors, their destinations unclear in the oppressive darkness beneath the river. In any other circumstances, Ollie would have thought it was a privilege to be here. How many people could say they'd been beneath the Thames Barrier?

Fighting back a slight smile at the thought of exploring the myriad tunnels, Ollie thought hard. His natural inclination was to make their way as far along one of the passageways on either side until they hopefully reached a stairwell leading up to either bank of the river. If Henderson had found a way of controlling the barrier, however, then the banks of the Thames might not be safe at all. Having said that, if these passageways flooded, then they'd die a horrible death. But they shouldn't flood. They'd been built to withstand flooding. The cynic in him told him not to trust that fact either.

There was another option. He'd read something about the tunnels that existed beneath the Thames Barrier, or else watched a programme on it. The barrier was designed to be bombproof, and in the event of the National Grid failing, there were three backup generators that could keep the barrier in operation for a month. Fascinating, but currently useless information. What about the tunnels? He was sure they could theoretically lead them to safety, but for the life of him, he couldn't remember the details.

Increasing the pressure on Emma's hand, he looked at her. Even in the intense darkness, he could make out her lips slightly parted and the scared but resolute look in her eyes. 'Right or left?' he asked with a slight smile.

There was a pause as Emma hesitated. 'I don't know. You choose.'

Ollie laughed in spite of himself. It was a release of tension more than genuine humour. 'I don't think we have time to do rock, paper, scissors for it.'

'We picked a fine moment to have our first domestic,' Emma replied with a slight edge to her voice that made Ollie smile all the more. 'Left, but if we die, I'm blaming you.'

Grinning, Ollie led her down the passageway. Although they moved quickly, he was careful not to make too much noise. As they approached the first alcove in the tunnel leading off to their left, however, he stopped still. He could hear footsteps moving up the corridor towards them, echoing ominously off the tunnel walls. Gesturing to Emma, Ollie flattened himself against the tunnel wall, closing his eyes as he felt the cold damp of the surface against his shirt.

The footsteps were moving closer now, and Ollie could feel his heart hammering against his chest. He tensed his body as the sound reached a crescendo. Any second now. The tip of a black shoe appeared in the corridor, and as it did so, Ollie pushed himself off the wall and lunged at the figure. Instinctively, his hands grappled the machine gun clutched in his hand, the outline of which was just visible in the gloom. Clawing at the man's hands, Ollie forced the gun upwards. It went off. The rattle of gunfire reverberated around them, and for a split second, Ollie expected to feel the white-hot sting of the bullets pierce his body. But it didn't come.

The hulking figure was too strong for him, and Ollie could feel the butt of the gun being forced back down at him. Meanwhile, the man's free hand had found his throat. He spluttered as the grip tightened around his airways, and he was lifted into the air. In a final desperate attempt, he flailed out with his right leg and heard the grunt of pain as he made contact with the man's midriff. He found himself falling back towards the ground, and he strengthened his grip on the rifle. With an almighty effort, he wrenched it free from the man's grasp, but as he hit the tunnel floor, the impact caused the weapon to tumble out of reach into the darkness.

Water dripped from the pipe, landing painfully on his forehead. The man had paused, and Ollie knew why immediately. He tried to shout out a warning, but the words died in his throat. Instead, he watched helplessly as Emma sprinted towards the man, swinging the rifle like a club. In what little light there was in the passageway, Ollie saw amusement turn to blotchy anger on the man's face, as the rifle slammed into his knee. There was a dull crack, and Ollie's eyes widened in terror as Emma was lifted into the air and thrown into the darkness, screaming. He heard her hit the floor, and as she did, her scream died.

Anger pulsed through Ollie's body, re-energising him. There was little time to react. The man had already turned his attention back to him. Grimacing in pain, Ollie rolled to one side, narrowly avoiding the man's attack. He jumped to his feet, blood pouring from the various wounds on his body and one hand clutched to his chest for support. He swayed momentarily on the spot, and then lashed out with an elbow that he expected to catch the man around the chin, but which only found his defensive block.

The mercenary had reacted with surprising speed, and he spun through the air, easily avoiding the boy's follow-up punch. Then he twisted round, planted his left foot and swung his right boot around to catch the boy around the back of his head. Ollie crumpled, blood trickling slowly from his broken nose into his mouth. Through the cascade of blood covering his eyes, he saw the man withdraw a pistol from the holster at his waist.

However, the man didn't fire. He seized the boy by the throat and pulled him to his feet, so that they were face to face, staring into each other's eyes. The man's eyes were black and pitiless. Ollie tried to put as much contempt and hatred into his gaze as was humanly possible, but he had to react fast to avoid the butt of the pistol, as it swung through the air towards him. He ducked and punched his fist up into the man's throat. He heard the man spluttering and gasping for breath behind him, but he was already moving, pivoting on the balls of his feet and sending a roundhouse kick into the man's chest.

The sound of cracking ribs brought a slight smile to his lips, as he spat blood from his mouth and strode forwards. The pistol hit the passageway floor as the mercenary doubled over in pain, clutching his chest, but Ollie was already snatching it up. The man was slow to react, and Ollie seized the opportunity to bring the weapon crashing down on his opponent's temple. The man crumpled immediately and was unconscious before he hit the floor, but Ollie had already turned and was running into the darkness.

It didn't take him long to find Emma. She was lying spreadeagled in the middle of the passageway several feet away from where she'd been thrown. There was a small pool of blood mingling with the water on the floor around her head. For one horrible moment, Ollie thought he'd lost her, as he slipped his hand in hers and felt her wrist. There was no pulse. Taking a deep breath, he leaned up and listened to her chest. Relief flooded through him, as placing his head against her chest had seemed to stir her into movement.

Ollie couldn't take his gaze from her eyes, as he watched them blink back to reality, looking confused. He tried to shake off the feeling that had just sent goose pimples over his arm. If he were going to die, then he'd want his final moments to be looking into those eyes. That wasn't going to happen, though. He watched, his mouth incredibly dry, as Emma felt the back of her head and then looked up at him.

'Don't think I didn't feel you against my chest. If you could control yourself until we're out of here, I'd be grateful.'

Looking back down the passageway to hide his smile, Ollie replied, 'If you didn't keep making a habit of trying to save my life, then it would make it easier.'

As his gaze returned to her face, Ollie saw a sudden intensity in her eyes. He wanted to look away or take a step back, but they held him frozen in place.

'Never.' That one word was enough to make him shiver in the darkness. That moment seemed to stretch on until Emma broke the spell, every syllable spoken slower than normal. 'We should probably try to move.'

'Yes,' said Ollie, snapping out of the moment, and holding out his hand for her grab. As he pulled her to her feet, their bodies were pressed together momentarily, their eyes boring into each other's again. The breath seemed to leave Ollie's body, and the oxygen evaporated from his brain. He swallowed, feeling how dry his throat was. 'This isn't the time,' he said, still unable to look away.

Emma squeezed his hand, and Ollie closed his eyes at the pressure, feeling it echo through his body.

'Let's earn that moment by saving each other one more time.'

'There are bound to be more of them around. We'll have to be careful.' Ollie gripped the pistol in his sweaty right palm and smiled grimly. 'Ready?'

Nodding at each other, they both smiled, turned and headed back down the passageway. When they reached the unconscious figure, Ollie hesitated before leading Emma down the darkened corridor the man had appeared from. Water dripped more frequently now from the pipes above them. A thought stirred in Ollie's mind, and he scanned the ceiling. There was a complex interlocking pattern of steel-covered piping that ran along the top of the passageways. Could they be concealing explosives? Surely not. They'd need miles of the stuff to blow a structure on the scale of the Thames Barrier.

They reached a steel door, but Ollie's attention was drawn to a sign above it. An arrow indicated that the passageway led to upriver access, piers 1–7 and the north abutment. A faint musty odour was mingling with the damp now and crawled into his nostrils. There had been silence since the sirens had stopped and the mechanical noises had ground to a halt. Now, however, he could hear voices echoing from unseen parts of the barrier. Were they drawing closer? It was impossible to tell. Then, unmistakeably, there was a rattle of gunfire. Ollie stopped dead in his tracks, but there was nowhere for them to go.

'Trust me?' he asked, turning to look at Emma.

The smile that he loved so much flickered across her face. 'Always.'

Gripping her hand still tighter, Ollie ran forwards, following the direction of the arrow. The tunnel seemed to widen as they turned a corner, and light became visible at the end of the passageway. As they sprinted past yet more twisted steel bulkheads, he was able to make out a red steel door that stood ajar. Any hope that had flickered inside him was extinguished immediately, however. Standing in front of the door were two burly figures, both holding Uzi sub-machine guns.

The teenagers skidded to a halt in the middle of the passageway, panting hopelessly, both of them looking around frantically for any means of escape. There was none. They'd been spotted, and the Uzis were already trained on them. Ollie's eyes were drawn to the weapons. They seemed to emanate death and suffering. His eyes wide with fear, Ollie came to a decision. He was going to die anyway, so why not die fighting. He balanced himself on the balls of his feet, ready to attack. He didn't know what he was going to do, but he might be able to cause enough commotion for Emma to run for it.

'You'll have a second. Run,' he whispered out of the corner of his mouth, trying to slip his hand from hers.

Emma merely gripped it even tighter, and he heard her breathe defiantly into his ear, 'I'm not going anywhere.'

It was that pressure he closed his eyes to, not the sight of the men's fingers curling around the triggers. He returned the pressure, bracing his body for what was to come. There had been so many moments in the past year when he'd thought about this moment. He'd thought that it would be a relief, but he felt only anger and bitterness. Then it came. The gunfire. The sound of death. The death rattle.

No, there was no rattle. Instead, four clearly defined separate cracks reverberated off the steel piping and the concrete walls of the tunnel. His head moved from side to side, subconsciously trying to follow them to track down the sounds. It was several seconds before he accepted that bullets hadn't pierced his body. Beside him, he could hear Emma gasping for breath, and he felt her hand drop away from his. *No, please no.*

Fear made him open his eyes once more. Emma was crouching on all fours, sucking in the damp air, her face hidden in shadow. He thought she might be crying, but there was no blood. Confusedly, he turned his head back towards the centre of the passageway. He stared in disbelief, as the two mercenaries began to fall slowly to the ground until their bodies hit the concrete with a dull thud. Ollie watched them fall in astonishment as he realised how close he'd come to death. The relief he'd expected to accompany his death washed over him at the realisation he was alive. A complex mix of differing emotions engulfed him, and he released them via a short, sharp laugh that sounded more like a bark.

It took a second for Ollie to register the figure now walking through the doorway of the adjacent red steel door. Only as they drew closer out of the darkness did he recognise they were the MI5 agent Ben Viper. His light-brown hair was flattened and tinged with blood and sweat, and the piercing, blue eyes that shone out of the gloom were deadly serious. His mouth and nose were obscured by congealed blood and some of his swagger had gone.

Having said that, when he reached Ollie, he clapped him on the shoulder and laughed. 'Looks like you've had the whole situation under control. Don't suppose you found a way to stop London being flooded whilst you were at it?'

Ollie felt the corner of his own mouth twitch a little, but he could only muster a shake of his head.

Ben, meanwhile, was smiling at Emma. 'Quite the boyfriend audition, huh?'

'I think I saved him more than he did me,' replied Emma.

Ollie winced as she aimed a light jab at his left arm. Now that they appeared to have been saved, the adrenaline was subsiding, and with it, the pain in his wrist and head was steadily increasing.

The MI5 agent had laughed at that, but his face was now concentrated. 'We need to move,' he said after a second, pointing at the door through which he'd come. 'We don't have very long. The terrorists are going to blow up part of the barrier. If they succeed, then these tunnels will be flooded minutes after the explosion. We need to get to the north pier now and onto the bank.'

All three of them began to run, and as they did so, Ollie heard Ben speaking rapidly.

'Phillips, you and your men need to make for the north pier immediately. We're all out of options. The only hope London has is that this structure can withstand the blast. If it can't, then the south bank and the southern-most piers will be flooded instantly. The water will overwhelm the tunnels too. You have to make for the north side of the structure now.'

Fear and tension were pounding through Ollie's brain once more. 'What will happen to the city?' he asked breathlessly, as they passed yet more steel bulkheads and coloured piping.

Ben glanced back at him as they ran. His expression was calm, but there was something else in those blue eyes that Ollie hadn't seen there before. 'We can't be certain, but if they succeed, thousands are at risk.'

Ollie felt the pressure tighten on his hand and glanced at Emma as they ran. Her cheeks were pink, and her eyes were slightly red, but he didn't see the fear he'd expected. Not the fear that was causing his heart to hammer painfully inside his chest. *This can't be happening. It must be a hoax designed just to spook the government.* The thought faded as soon as it had materialised. He'd spent enough time in these people's company to know they weren't playing games.

Ben was speaking again as they ran, presumably issuing frantic instructions to his team. 'It's too late for a full-scale evacuation, but get as many people to high ground as you can. The tunnels might be safe for important personnel, but the Tube won't be safe for the rest of the public. Get as many to the top of the Royal Observatory at Greenwich and other elevated areas around Woolwich and Greenwich as you can. If they blow the south bank, those are the areas with the highest population densities that are certain to be flooded.'

As they turned sharply down another passageway, Ollie glimpsed an overhead sign. They were nearly at the north pier. As the gloom in front of his eyes began to clear, he saw another large, red steel door. The MI5 agent was several paces ahead of Ollie, and he wrenched open the door with a grunt of pain. As it was forced open, Ollie saw a tunnel bending back the way they'd come. This place really was a maze.

Relief flooded through his body, extinguishing the pain and tension that had gripped him. There was a metal ladder in front of them and the MI5 agent was already clambering onto it. In a flash, he was moving up the metal rungs and disappearing into the darkness above. Ollie turned to offer help to Emma, but she'd already placed her foot on the bottom-most rung and was beginning to climb. Unable to suppress a smile, he waited until she was a quarter of the way up and then grabbed hold of the ladder.

It was as he did so that he heard a panicked shout from up above. The words were lost in the descending darkness, but he didn't need Emma's accompanying panicked urgency to know he needed to move. Whatever Henderson and his men had planned, it was on the verge of happening. Wincing at the renewed pain in his wrist, Ollie quickened his pace as he scrambled up the ladder. As he moved higher, a circle of light opened up above him. He brought his arm up to shield himself from the glare.

It was only as he moved closer that the light began to dim. Then the smell of London and the river filtered down the ladder and filled his nostrils. He was nearing the top of the rungs now. A shadow passed above him, and he saw Ben's looking down on him. The man's face was calm, but Ollie noticed the agent's eyes darting back and forth. As Ollie climbed the final few rungs, the light adjusted, and he glimpsed the sky above them. It was just as dark and bleak as the scene below – a blackened canvas of ominous clouds.

As Ben helped him off the ladder and his feet landed on metal, a loud rumble of thunder echoed around them. Ollie blinked rapidly, taking in the rest of his surroundings. He couldn't quite believe what he was seeing or where he was. He was standing on a metal platform with a large hull-shaped steel structure in the centre. Turning around, he saw the rest of the platforms behind him, with the yellow hydraulic systems and the gates that defended London raised. He'd never expected to find himself here.

He felt a hand slip into his, and the next second he was being pulled across the platform to a gangway that led across to the riverbank. Before he followed the other two, he turned back. He'd never stopped to appreciate before just how immense the Thames Barrier really was. Stretching across the river, it was an intimidating piece of engineering. Seeing it now, he felt his confidence rise.

There was a shout from behind him, and Ollie spun round. Ben was gesturing frantically at him to follow them off the pier, but the agent's gaze was focussed on the river itself. Ollie began to move, but as he reached the end of the pier, he followed Ben's stare. In slow motion, his head swung back across the barrier's structure, but this time, his eyes dropped to the river. For a moment, he was unable to see what the agent could possibly be looking at.

Then he remembered what Ben had told them, and his gaze moved over the river towards the water that was lapping against the furthest pier. Even beneath the gloom of the darkening sky, he saw it. Amidst the consistent flow of water, two streaks were scything beneath the surface and heading straight for the barrier. Ollie began to stumble backwards, but he couldn't pull his eyes away from the water. They were hurtling alongside one another in parallel, and their dead-accurate movement could mean only one thing.

Ollie felt his ankle slam into steel and heard a yell from behind him. He lost his balance and fell backwards. For a second, his head and shoulders flailed in mid-air, before the lower half of his body slammed down onto the edge of the pier. He cried out as pain rippled through his back. The top half of his body was now suspended over the edge of the platform. For the first time, the roar of the river beneath him drowned out the storm above.

It was then that he felt the structure beneath him shudder violently. His whole body felt as though it were being propelled temporarily into the air, as the Thames Barrier itself seemed to vibrate. Then an ear-splitting crack rent the air, which was more terrifying than anything the storm had produced. In the distance, sparks leaped into the air, almost feebly at first like the early flickerings of a firework display. They were beginning to dim when orange flames rose imperiously into the air. Ollie gazed up in wonder as they grew taller and climbed to meet the darkened sky. As the two pillars of flame met, there was an explosion of colour that threw the horror of what had just happened into stark focus. There was no longer a black canvas to hide behind. The flames had mingled with the cloud to bathe the barrier in a catastrophic blaze of colour.

Acting on instinct, Ollie hauled himself to his feet. Dread had cast the pain aside from his body for now. He knew he had to move, but he couldn't pull his eyes away from what had and was continuing to happen. The southern-most pier had been blasted apart, as well as the non-navigable gates that bordered the bank of the river. The steel structure was mostly still intact, but the explosion had been enough to blast a hole between the south bank of the Thames and the nearest gate. That small opening was all the river needed to take its revenge on the defences that had been built to repel it.

They were in perhaps the only safe position on the northern bank. The monster headed straight for the gap on the opposite side of the river, surging through it with alarming speed. The enormous volume of water suddenly unleashed mercilessly tore over the south bank before it crested and sloped towards them. For a second, Ollie thought he was dead as spray and saltwater filled his eyes. He felt the power of the river surge past him, but when his vision cleared, he saw it had evaded them by mere yards. Having been carried away in the midst of the wave, he glimpsed the yellow of the hydraulic gates that had been blasted apart from the furthermost pier.

The water had gushed over both banks further up the river. The cheer force of it had flipped containers beside the barrier into the air, before it engulfed the nearby factories and warehouses. Their roofs collapsed instantly, the screams of those inside muffled by the roar of the river. Ollie watched in awe and terror as the water swept inland. He saw people desperately rushing towards tower blocks or else trying to scale fences in their vain attempts to escape the oncoming doom.

Shackled all these years, the river gleefully took its revenge. It surged towards The O2 arena, the domed structure imperious on its bend in the river. There was a flash of lightning overhead, coupled with an almighty gust of wind, which caused Ollie to sway violently. It caught the back of the rising wave, whipping it up into a venomous cobra ready to strike. Its jaws snapped down over The O2 with an ear-splitting roar of triumph. Those waiting desperately to board boats upriver never stood a chance.

There was a crunching sound from beneath his feet. Ollie blinked water from his eyes and spat it from his mouth. But before he'd realised what was happening, he felt a strong grip on his arm, pulling him unceremoniously off the pier and into the air. It was only as he was hoisted into the air and carried away by the rope descending from the Chinook, his eyes still transfixed on the wave now crashing through the Docklands, that he realised tears were mingling with the river water.

25

A few miles away, in an office in Harbour Exchange, Lucy Stiles stared at the screen in front of her eyes without really seeing it. Her eyes were out of focus. It had been another long day in which she'd achieved nothing. That was the pattern, the routine she'd slipped into. Was this all life had planned out for her? She was stuck in a job she had no interest in and was unable to use the law degree she'd worked so hard to get. Of course, it was as much down to her as it was the environment that surrounded her.

Despite being cut off from her family back home to a degree, Lucy had never felt alone in London. That was until the past two years. Her thriving social life had been disrupted due to the pandemic, and it had hit her mental health in a big way. Being confined to a basement flat with her girlfriend for weeks on end had been tough. It had taken months for the cracks to appear in their relationship, but once they'd started, it had been impossible to repair the fractures that had been created.

Lucy had tried to reconnect with her once the second lockdown had eased, but it had been too late. The toxic ending to their two-year relationship had been enough to destroy the self-confidence she had left. Having been forced to move out of the flat in the middle of the pandemic, she'd been forced to take a spare room in a shared block just a few minutes' walk from work. *The cost alone is enough to make anyone miserable,* she thought bitterly. Now that things had begun to return to normal, she no longer had a friendship group to fall back on. Her deteriorating mental health had driven them all away. Not that Lucy could blame them.

The city she'd grown to love now felt alien to her. Though she'd previously relished any lunch break or weekend as an opportunity to wander through the streets, she now kept her head down as she moved from destination to destination. Mostly, this was from the block where she lived to the office and back again. She no longer enjoyed walking through Canary Wharf. Indeed, she barely even noticed the hustle and bustle of it these days. On the rare occasion she did venture onto the Tube, she didn't even register the renewed crowds of people. Nor did she understand the occasional stares she got. That was until she stepped out the other side and realised she hadn't worn a mask at all.

Her enjoyment in all things had faded. Where she'd once enjoyed walking the short distance towards the footbridge and stopped for food from the trucks just before it, now she barely ate during the day. In those moments when the hunger became unbearable, she merely took the lift down to the reception and walked the short distance to the overpriced sandwich bar opposite the building. After purchasing something to eat, it was back to the lift and up to her desk once more.

There was an understanding from her colleagues that she didn't want to engage with them. They'd long since given up inviting her to the bar after work or out at the weekend. Lucy didn't mind. They seemed nice enough, but she just couldn't connect with them. In truth, she found it hard to connect with anyone these days. It was as though the lights had been switched off, and she was waiting for something or someone to switch them back on.

Dully, Lucy stared out of the huge glass window beside her. She was on the fifteenth floor, suspended high above the Docklands Light Railway trains that rattled beneath. Ordinarily, she had a view that most people would be envious of. The toughened-glass windows were the perfect lens to the River Thames beyond, as it snaked its way around the impressive structure of The O2. On a clear day, it was easy to make out the Thames Barrier behind, but today, the only sign of it came from dimly flickering lights that Lucy knew belonged to the barrier. It wasn't possible to make out anyone climbing The O2 today, and the Emirates Air Line Cable Car that carried people to it had been suspended.

The skies above London were a dark, ominous grey, and the windows with their huge panes of glass were streaked with rain. The day had been punctuated by frequent rolls of thunder and flashes of lightning that temporarily bathed the city in light before retreating into the gloom once more. By squinting, Lucy could make out a sleek boat rounding the bend in the river. It curved around The O2 and streaked off past her. *That was odd,* she thought vaguely. The Thames Barrier had been fully closed due to the storm and tidal surges. It was all over the news. Maybe the boat had come from somewhere else.

Just as she turned back towards her screen, there was an almighty crack that made her start slightly. *What is it with this weather?* It certainly seemed to be a reflection of her mood. There was nothing more she was going to achieve today, she knew that. But heading outside wasn't exactly an option either. She could perhaps order a taxi to pick her up right by the front door.

As she considered this possibility, Lucy returned her gaze to her depressing lens on the world. The dark clouds were sunk low over the city, obscuring the tops of the buildings. Even if they had been running, it would have been impossible to make out the cable cars shuttling people across the Emirates Air Line. A flash of light crackled across the grey canvas for a moment, and in that split second, Lucy saw something that made her climb to her feet.

No. I must be mistaken. It couldn't be.

The brief flash had illuminated the Thames Barrier in the distance and the river beneath it. In that moment, Lucy had thought she'd seen the river rising into the air like a hissing cobra and flowing over both banks of the Thames. It wasn't lightning that revealed the terrifying truth this time. As though it were glorying in the terror it had created, the storm had parted to give itself a front-row seat for what was unfolding. The break in the cloud was accompanied by a sliver of sunlight, allowing the Docklands to bask in a yellow haze.

That glow revealed the horrifying truth. The river had come alive. No longer held back by the gates that protected London, it was writhing and surging over the banks, sweeping aside all in its path. Lucy pressed her hand against the window, barely registering the shouts of her co-workers as people rushed to see what was happening. The water snaked into the air as it reached The O2 before diving through the domed structure. Lucy watched as it surged out the other side and crashed back into river.

There was a brief union before the roads nearest the bank, with their flats and houses, were enveloped by the gushing water. Her eyes still transfixed by the leaking dome of The O2, which seemed to sag like a deflating hot air balloon, Lucy saw small dots being carried away into the depths of the merciless river. She realised dully that the dots were people. Their lives had been snatched away in the briefest of moments.

Gasps from further down the office caused her gaze to

drop. The river had surged not just through the lower levels of buildings but across roads too, and the chaos was clear to see. Two cars on the road nearest their building had collided, whilst a bright-red double-decker bus lay grotesquely on one side, like a pig with its trotters pointing sideways. As Lucy watched, the vehicles were born aloft by the wave, and the bus slammed into a shop. The customers and workers alike had already scattered from the building, but they weren't quick enough to escape the ferocious power of the water.

*

Those scenes were replicated throughout the city. At Woolwich, Steven Houghton's attempts to convince the journalist to move fell on deaf ears. Exasperated, he stood up and began to stride purposefully along the riverbank. He knew something was wrong. Instinct told him to run. So he did, the unfamiliar movements causing his breath to become short almost instantly. He glanced back and his eyes widened in horror.

He'd registered the increased panic and screams around him, as people sprinted past. Bodies stumbled and fell, whilst others pushed their way frantically away from the edge of the bank. That wouldn't be enough to save them. What Houghton had seen had paralysed his heart; its rhythmic beating was no longer palpable within his chest. Time had stopped too. It was as though everything was temporarily suspended in a bubble. That was until the water breached the river wall defences and took his feet out from underneath him. The scream died in his throat, as water flooded his lungs and the sheer force of the river lifted him into the air before crushing him beneath its weight.

Just a few minutes later, the water poured beneath the *Cutty Sark*, and the power of the river ripped it free and carried it aloft for a while before consigning it to its depths. The irony was lost on everyone as the water swept through the national maritime museums and colleges, threatening the hill that led up to the Royal Observatory, before respectfully retreating back towards the body of the river. Robbie and Anna had attempted to run further inland, but there hadn't been enough warning. Hand in hand, they were lifted bodily into the air and propelled over the railings that ran along the riverbank, before being swallowed whole by the relentless wave.

As the initial surges of water eased, the screams were slowly being replaced by sirens and tears. Woolwich, Greenwich and the Docklands were submerged, as were many of the Tube stations. Many had hoped they'd find sanctuary beneath the streets, but they were sorely mistaken. They huddled together, their scared faces upturned to the ceiling, as loud booms heralded the arrival of the water.

The ceilings came crashing down, along with an avalanche of water that erupted into the confined spaces. There was panic everywhere, and their screams echoed off the subterranean walls around them. The force of the torrent hurled people onto the tracks. Some were spared drowning by the impact of arriving trains, which were also soon engulfed in water. The lights flickered and died; the only light now was provided by the sparks of the destroyed commuter trains. Water surged in the darkness as people tried frantically to escape, but the river pursued them without mercy until it swallowed the screams in their lungs and pulled them down into its depths.

Thankfully, the river eventually had its fill, but not before it had wreaked havoc throughout that part of London. It wasn't just the infrastructure or the thousands of lives that were snatched away in an instant. It was mental scar it would leave behind for generations. It could have been worse, of course. Had all the gates failed, then the surge could have extended much further inland and upriver, wiping out large swathes of the city. In truth, they'd been lucky, but that wasn't what would be remembered. The unthinkable had happened: London had been flooded.

26

The mood was unlike anything Jackie had ever experienced. Everybody seemed to be in a state of shock, other than perhaps Ben, whom she knew was putting on a brave act of collected calm, as though nothing had happened. The chatter that she'd come to expect from The Grid had died; no intelligence briefings were frantically being convened between colleagues nor was Simon Wynn-Jones hurriedly analysing fragments of surveillance material.

Their boss, Aldwyn Haynes, had spent much of the time since the devastation attending emergency COBRA meetings at Whitehall, and he had rarely been seen within the walls of Thames House from the moment that the first wave had hit. On the one occasion that Jackie had glimpsed Haynes, she'd noticed at once that he'd discarded the crutches and was walking with barely a trace of a limp – although, from the twisted look on his face, every effort seemed to cause him discomfort. It was a show of strength to his team, she knew, as well as a message to his superiors.

In truth, Jackie didn't know why she was still here. She supposed it had become a routine. In the immediate aftermath of the devastation, she'd been asked to assist the first responders, but she'd been told in no uncertain terms by Ben that it wasn't going to happen. It was a sign of the shock and numbness she was feeling that she'd made no move to argue with him. That was most unlike her. Instead, she'd continued to travel into Thames House each day, although she could no longer face the Tube or the walk to the building. Both routes were littered with people fearfully discussing what had taken place and looking around themselves gingerly, wondering whether or not it was safe to travel.

For the first time in her professional life, she'd taken taxis from her flat to a short distance from the building – just far enough away to disguise her exact destination. She couldn't bear to meet the eyes of any of the members of the public for whom the exact details of what had taken place and why were a mystery. That fear was something she shared to a degree, but the extra knowledge she had made it unbearable to be in the presence of those feverishly discussing what had taken place.

She'd also found it difficult to speak to her family about what had happened, and each phone conversation had ended rather abruptly, after having confirmed she was safe. The fear in the voices of those she loved was something that she'd been expecting, but Jackie had felt detached from it. For all they'd known, Jackie might have been out walking that day or investigating a case and been caught in the middle of the desolation. Yet she couldn't relate to how they felt. She wasn't able to tell them that she'd watched the whole thing unfold on a bank of computer screens in the office of the British Secret Service. There was nobody she could speak to about how she'd felt watching the waves envelope London, or about how her heart had temporarily seemed to stop beating and she'd gripped the back of Helen Robinson's chair for support.

It had become a haunting habit, with her walking slowly round The Grid all day aside from the odd briefing, in which very little was actually spoken. Ben had attempted to keep up everyone's morale, but it was impossible. There was anger, yes, but that was tempered by the reality that there was no avenue of revenge or retribution open to him, given how Henderson and the Russian, Conrad, had seemingly disappeared into thin air, and the people behind them were still to be unmasked – particularly the woman who appeared to have masterminded this.

The evenings in her flat had become as torturous as the days spent reliving what had happened in Thames House. It was impossible to turn on the TV without being reminded of what had taken place, and so Jackie sat in silence. She'd tried to read a book, but the words blurred into one, and even the wine tasted bland in her mouth. Tiggy, of course, could sense her mood and had tried to wake her from it by nuzzling his mouth against her nose whilst sitting on her lap, and looking up at Jackie with those green eyes that had so often melted her heart. Yet it was with little enthusiasm that she ran her hand over the top of his head. The truth was nothing was sinking in.

That day, as she sat at a desk at Thames House, there was a sudden movement next to her and Jackie was startled to see Ben was standing beside her. She'd been so lost in her own thoughts that she hadn't noticed him approaching. He seemed rather amused at what she imagined was a shocked look on her faced and tried to remedy it.

'May I borrow you for a minute?' he asked, his perfect blue eyes smiling at her.

Jackie nodded, avoiding his gaze, and followed him to the door of the small technical suite that was usually occupied by Simon Wynn-Jones but was temporarily empty.

Ben stood to the side to allow her through first and gave a slight bow that Jackie tried not to smile at, before he closed the door behind the pair of them and turned to face her. 'I'm not going to ask how you are,' he said rather abruptly, although the smile never left his face. 'That's not my style of management, and there are people you can speak to. If that's what people in my team need, then I encourage them to seek out any help they need.'

'Your team?' asked Jackie. She was surprised to hear that her voice was rather broken, and she realised she couldn't remember the last time she'd spoken.

Ben showed no sign of reaction. 'Yes, my team. My recruitment policy is rather unconventional, but we need good people now more than ever. You've impressed a lot of people with your work here.'

'Have I surprised you?' quizzed Jackie, raising an eyebrow.

That garnered a flicker of a smile once more. 'Not in the slightest, but then I've followed your career more closely than you could ever have imagined, Jackie.' He cleared his throat, as though he'd temporarily forgotten himself. 'I can promise you'll be chronically underpaid and underappreciated, but those are things you should be used to already. If you die in service, then your family will get very little by way of compensation, but you'll have your name inscribed on a lovely memorial wall across the river. How does that all sound?'

Jackie wasn't sure why she was so taken aback. She was even more unsure as to why she couldn't tell whether she wanted the job or not. 'What makes you think I'd give up being a detective?' she asked, rather more aggressively than she'd intended.

'Who said I was asking you to?' replied Ben, his piercing, blue eyes locking on to her own, as he held her gaze for several seconds. 'I'm asking you to put those skills to greater use. We need different people here, people with the mind of a detective, but also people that can remind me...' He stopped himself. '... remind us, of the human side. I must warn you that I'm not used to people turning me down.'

'And I'm not used to people telling me what to do,' responded Jackie at once, feeling her lips spread in the first true smile she'd worn in days as she watched Ben in turn.

Perhaps it had that effect, because Ben nodded slightly. 'Take the job, Jacks,' he advised in a serious tone that she hadn't expected. 'If we'd had you on board from the start, then this might never have happened. We need you here, just as much as you need to be here.'

She opened her mouth to respond, but Ben raised his hand to forestall her.

'You can go back to solving murders, and you'd make a difference to people's lives, but you can make a difference on a bigger scale, and you can see this through to the end. Help us find these people.'

Jacks. He'd called her Jacks. There had been too many emotions stirred up in this building that had temporarily been smothered by the sheer enormity of what had happened, but just for a moment, those emotions threatened to seep through once more. She knew it was what she wanted. Ben was right; she'd struggle with the regret if she walked away now and returned to the force. Her own feelings could wait. There were far greater things at stake, and Jackie tried to shake her head clear of the fog.

There was another aspect that Ben had perhaps suspected but had deliberately avoided. Yes, she'd been the one to begin to put the pieces of the puzzle together, but it had been too late. There was the smallest part of her that felt responsible for what had happened. If only she'd worked it all out sooner. If only she'd been given the time. Ben was right again; they needed her here, and next time she'd make sure she had no regrets.

*

As Ben left the suite, he allowed himself the ghost of a smile. Jackie would accept the offer – of course she would – but he knew he'd have to redefine the boundaries of their relationship again. He couldn't speak to her about what had happened a decade ago, and he'd have to make that clear. Her reappearance in his life had been a complication he'd never expected, and it had stirred up uncomfortable feelings that he'd thought long since lost. That was something he'd have to deal with, and quickly, in order that it didn't interfere with the work at hand. Nevertheless, as he strode across The Grid once more, he couldn't help but feel a sense of relief.

It had no doubt been a symbolic target, despite the seeming lack of environmental agenda. Several eco-terrorist groups had already come forward claiming to be responsible for the attack, stating that it had been done to shock the governments of the world into action to combat climate change by taking away the inadequate flood defences of London. There was no basis for any of their claims of responsibility. Only one of their messages rang true, which was that the government and its intelligence and enforcement agencies had become transfixed on the issue of a weaponised virus, and in doing so, they had become blind to other threats.

The cylindrical pods that allowed access to The Grid suddenly hissed open, and Helen Robinson strode in, dressed in a characteristically pristine violet blouse and white skirt. She was older than she looked, Ben knew, with her long, blonde hair swept over her shoulders and angular, hazel eyes that were extremely attractive. Were it not for the fact that she never seemed to drop her crisply professional persona and her light-pink lips were permanently pursed in disapproval, Ben would have found her good-looking. Her mouth twitched in greeting as she saw Ben and moved towards him, her stiletto heels barely making a sound across the floor, despite expectations to the contrary.

'I have what you asked for,' she said matter-of-factly. 'The autopsy was inconclusive as to the cause of death, but he suffered significant internal bleeding. As you know, there was no CCTV in the surrounding alleyways, so the police have nothing to go on. The case will remain unsolved. You know how they treat matters like this.' As she spoke, she slipped a thin, brown folder from her stylish, blue handbag, before closing the clasp handle once more. 'Unless of course you're intending to give the case to Miss Ambrose.' Her tone hadn't changed, but even so Ben detected the trace of a jibe.

Ben opened the file she handed him, and glanced at its contents. Snapping the file shut, Ben looked up at her. Helen was an extremely difficult woman to read, even for him. He'd learned that over the years. Yet he'd noticed she'd become snappier in the days leading up to the attack on the barrier and that had only intensified since. Pressure affected everyone, it seemed, even the consummate professional Helen she was. He noticed a slight crease was forming between the eyebrows above her angular eyes, and was there perhaps the faintest trace of a smudge to the blusher she'd applied to her cheeks?

'Just being nosey,' he replied, holding up the file, 'thanks for this.' At that moment, he noticed the briefing room door had been slid shut. He glanced swiftly around The Grid, taking note of every individual who was visible, before striding briskly towards the room. In one fluid movement, he slid the door open, stepped inside and closed it behind him once more. Inside, he found John Bromley, as he'd known he would.

The two men had worked with each other on and off for a couple of years, and it had been Ben who'd recommended to Aldwyn Haynes that they bring Bromley over from MI6 for a longer stretch. There was little humour in the North Londoner, with his triangular face, broad nose, small lips and light-brown eyes that gave little away. It was his physique that told the world who he really was, or had been. His muscular neck, wide shoulders, strong arms and bulky torso pulled back the curtain to reveal the soldier he'd once been before joining the intelligence community. Ben knew the full story behind John's switch, but he'd never broached the subject with him. It must still haunt him to this day, he knew, and likewise, there were plenty of demons in Ben's past that he wouldn't want others quizzing him about.

Even so, Ben wondered whether the events that had taken place at the university had stirred up memories the man had tried to repress. John wouldn't be human if it hadn't triggered a certain reaction from him. It was clear he was still feeling the effects of what had happened, and not just physically – although those scars were plain for all to see. His chest was heavily padded beneath the loose-fitting, collared shirt that he wore, and his face was ugly and blotchy with a yellowy-green tinge around his eyes and cheeks. His eyes seemed to have retreated into freshly dug, sunken sockets, and the rest of his face seemed permanently tensed in a highly defensive expression.

The two had spoken little since the attack on the Thames Barrier, just long enough for Bromley to inform him that the SBS boat Ben had suspected was carrying Henderson had been swallowed by the water.

After dropping into a chair at the side of the conference table, Ben slid the file towards John. 'Lance Bombardier Will Hughes; 5th Regiment of the Royal Artillery. Served with distinction for twelve years, including a tour of Iraq and two tours of Afghanistan.' As he spoke, he noticed John hadn't moved to open the file and his face was resolutely expressionless. 'You served together in Afghanistan, didn't you?'

John looked at him blankly. 'Yes, I knew him.'

'He was with you when—'

'Yes,' said John abruptly. 'When we got home, Will took it hard. We lost touch.' It was as though his face had been glazed to remove any flicker of expression from it, his eyes sunk low in their darkened sockets.

Something was wrong here. Ben knew John's file, but he was aware of what wasn't in the file too. The two men had been more closely linked than John was making out.

With his own face smoothly unreadable, Ben nodded and said simply, 'I'm afraid his body was found by the police a few days ago. They aren't sure what the exact cause of death is, but his lifestyle can hardly have helped. He was found dead not far from our North London safehouse; in fact, in one of the nearby alleyways.'

No reaction. Not even a flicker. 'Hardly a surprise,' John muttered darkly. 'He should have turned his life around.'

Ben felt his own eyes narrowing. 'Sometimes, it isn't as easy as that for people. There was something else.' He paused. 'The post-mortem revealed a large amount of internal bleeding, which may have ultimately led to his death. It's all in the file.'

There was still no reaction or move to open the file from John.

Ben got up to leave. 'It was probably some thug trying to make himself feel harder than he was or looking to make himself feel better. There's little active CCTV in the area, although there's some near Camden Market, but nobody of interest was seen heading towards the alleyway. The police won't be pursuing it – hardly a surprise there.'

As he walked past Bromley once more, he saw John's eyes dart briefly towards the file and away again. 'Thanks for telling me, Ben. Do his family know?'

Ben stopped with his hand on the door. 'I'm not sure.' He nodded towards the file. 'Perhaps some of the details require your attention. I'm sure they'd be grateful for a visit from his former army colleague, no matter how little you might have known one another.' He detected what was perhaps a ripple of anger pass across his colleague's face, and then he opened the door, went through it and slid it shut behind him.

27

Maya stared at the empty shell of the building that had been the care home her mother had spent the last moments of her life in. It hadn't truly sunk in yet. Maybe it never would. Or perhaps it would on the day she was allowed to finally visit the site. Closing the tablet, Maya looked around the hotel room that was now her home. Her flat had been within the flood zone, and the surrounding area had been thoroughly devastated. Even though her flat was high enough to be safe from damage, there was no means of getting to the building itself.

That was the story for much of Greenwich and Woolwich. They'd been directly in the path of the tidal surge that had broken free of the Thames Barrier's defences. The waves had swept through the care home building, ripping apart anything or anyone unfortunate enough to be in their path. Some had been swept into the maelstrom, and others had been crushed beneath the weight of water or collapsing plaster. It would be weeks, maybe even months, before they uncovered all the bodies. Until then, she couldn't even say a proper goodbye.

Maya had spent most of her life in the areas of London the surge had devastated most. There had never been a part of London she wasn't allowed to go before. That was the case now, however. Greenwich and Woolwich were desolate wastelands, with thousands of people displaced from their homes. The Docklands had been torn asunder too, although mercifully, the tidal surge had eased before it had swept away the entire financial district. As it was, the rail network had been obliterated and countless streets cordoned off. The whole district had been isolated, and those non-residents who had worked there had been told to work from their homes.

There were still moments when it didn't feel real to Maya. Moments when she allowed herself to dream it had never happened at all. Then another news report showing the flooded Tube stations, their ceilings collapsed and leaving huge craters in the streets, would flash onto the TV. She'd heard many liken the devastation to the Blitz. Those comparisons had, of course, angered others, sparking heated debate and antagonism amongst an already fractured society.

Maya closed her eyes, remembering the images from the news last night that had torn at her heart. The mother wading out through the retreating water to find her daughter's body floating in the park near the flats where they lived. She wasn't alone. Thousands were mourning the deaths of loved ones who'd been caught in the midst of the greatest natural disaster of the twenty-first century to date. The impact of which would echo down the generations.

Vigils had been held, not just across the UK but throughout the globe. The world once again united in grief. Except, of course, it wasn't. There was a public face of unity, but in truth, it was more divided than it ever had been. Just last night, Maya had attended such an event in Battersea. She'd joined the hundreds of others as they raised their phone lights to the sky in a tearful tribute to those who had been lost. As a mark of respect, lights across the country had been switched off for two minutes, plunging the population into solemn darkness, so the only lights in the sky were those held aloft by the ones who'd been left behind to mourn.

The emergency and armed forces had acted with exceptional speed in closing off the worst-affected areas. Sirens were never far from the eardrums in London, yet their sound was diminished as though they too were dampened by the water that had flooded the streets of the capital. Even those Tube stations and lines that were unaffected by the flood were as empty as they'd been during the early days of the pandemic.

Maya had been in London in 2007 during the terror attacks that had ripped through the Tube in a similar way to the river, except the surge of water had claimed more lives than the deadly bomb blasts. At the time, her mother had been working near King's Cross, and cold panic had flooded through the young Maya. There had been no mobile reception in operation, but one of her teachers had managed to get hold of her mother's building to reassure Maya that her mother was safe.

As a teenager, the attacks had profoundly affected Maya. She'd been heading for a career in medicine, but that day changed everything. She and her mother had travelled to Russell Square to see the messages left on the bouquets of flowers in memory of those who'd died. The two-minute silence a week later had somehow made her feel part of a shared community. From that moment on, she'd been in love with London and its people. The attacks had undoubtedly influenced the career path she'd taken now.

Nevertheless, today, she was as helpless as she'd been as a teenager that day. Despite the job she had, there was nothing she could do. They hadn't been able to stop this from happening. The job was about saving lives and protecting their capital city. But they'd been totally out-thought. Nobody had seen this coming. Maya felt infinitely more alone than she'd done in July 2007. Her mum was gone, and that loss would always be with her. It was more than that. She'd wanted to make a difference. That was why she'd taken the job she had, but it all seemed to have been for nothing.

There were reminders of their failure everywhere. Whether it be the images of the *Cutty Sark* being ripped free and carried into the Thames before being crushed beneath the water, the remnants appearing only briefly, as the nineteenth-century wood snagged on the roof of The O2 arena. Or else the water threatening to climb the hill up towards the Royal Observatory before retreating back to the river's edge.

The river itself was littered with debris, ranging from destroyed vessels to the ruins of buildings that had lined the banks of the Thames. Maya had watched on the news as the PM had visited the wreckage of the barrier itself, whilst plans were being made to bring the Royal Yacht *Britannia* out of retirement to carry the sovereign to the site of the destruction. It might seem like nothing to some, but Maya knew that image would bring hope and strength to some of the population. It was what they needed right now.

As for Maya, what would she do next? She ran her fingers through her shoulder-length, brown hair, glancing down at her chest. It felt strange not to be dressed up during the day. Her routine had involved doing her make-up and making herself look smart before beginning the commute to work. Instead, the pencil skirts and blouses were gone, replaced by a black All Saints hoodie and leggings. Although the outfit suited her and had often been worn in the evenings, being dressed in it during working hours made her shudder slightly.

It was then that words she'd heard long ago echoed in her mind, as though they'd been sent forwards from the past: *'There are millions of people in the world who'll never have the opportunity to make a difference. So if you're ever privileged enough to have that opportunity, then you owe it to the world to make it count.'*

Tears slid silently down Maya's cheeks as she remembered the words her mother had spoken to her just after her dad had died. Maya hadn't fully understood the meaning behind those words, but now she knew generations of her family had been deprived of opportunities to have a say or the chance to make a difference. That was still happening across the world. Maya was lucky enough to find herself in a privileged position compared to them. No matter how hard it might be, she couldn't waste that.

*

As Ben shut the door to the briefing room behind him, he noticed that the glass behind which Aldwyn Haynes's office lay was darkened, meaning nobody could see in. Snatching up a thinner file from the nearest desk, Ben hesitated for a moment. It seemed as though today was a day for difficult conversations. It was times like this that he missed being in the field. That was where he felt the most in his element – making swift decisions and adapting to what was facing him. Even so, this was part of his job.

Aldwyn Haynes scowled instantly. 'Do none of you bloody people know how to knock?'

Ben was often allowed a pass where this was concerned, but it seemed as though today wasn't one of those days.

Taking the seat opposite his boss without invitation, Ben surveyed him for a second. In any ordinary job, the man facing him would have been prescribed bed rest for several weeks. He looked paler and thinner; his receding, mousy-coloured hair was flecked with strands of grey; and there were deep bags beneath his close-set, deadened, grey eyes. His sagging, jowly cheeks seemed to have darkened in colour too, and as he watched, he saw a spasm of pain pass briefly across the man's face.

'I assume you didn't come in here just to see whether or not I've kicked the bucket yet,' growled Haynes.

Ben smiled, but he didn't respond.

'Well, seeing as you're here…' Haynes stretched his back against his chair, grimacing as he did so. He slid open the drawer beside him, withdrew a bottle of single malt whisky, rested it on the walnut surface and placed two crystal glasses beside it. Aldwyn poured the amber liquid into both glasses and slid one across the desk towards Ben, before leaning back in his chair and taking a deep gulp from his own glass, smiling satisfactorily as he did so. The whisky seemed to breathe a little colour back into his face as he frowned across the desk at Ben.

'Tell me about your source: Ivanovic. The one who kicked this whole thing off. He told you the threat was the virus, did he not?'

Ben nodded, picking up his own glass and taking a sip, after first placing the file between the two of them. The liquid burned the back of his throat, but he liked the smokiness it left behind in his mouth. 'That's right. He set us on the path to the virus, in effect, just before the death of Corporal Matheson. Shortly after that, he went missing. He hasn't been seen at his work since, nor has he attempted any form of contact with us. Either he's disappeared—'

'Or he's been disappeared,' growled Haynes.

Ben took another gulp of whisky, feeling the liquid warm his insides and allowing the smoke to drift behind the back of his teeth, enjoying the sensation. 'Talking of sources, we appear to have been played by more than one individual. Miss McKinnon or Professor Blanchet – or whoever the hell she is – suckered us good and proper.'

The woman who'd attended climate-change conferences alongside government ministers had turned out to be much more than anyone had expected. It would appear their services own background checks had failed, and they were still trying to uncover the truth. After contacting the Direction Générale de la Sécurité Intérieure (DGSI) in France, they'd confirmed the identity she'd given at the university – that of Professor Sophia Blanchet. Born in 1986 in the suburbs of Lyon, she'd lost both her parents at the age of five whilst they were on holiday in the Philippines. They'd been caught in the Mount Pinatubo eruption and typically died.

A young Sophia Blanchet had been relocated to a foster family in Paris and had thrived, achieving a first-class degree in environmental science from the Sorbonne. A glittering career had followed. Yet there were gaps in the file – periods of disappearance. It would appear Blanchet had somehow managed to balance multiple lives. Ben doubted Professor Charlene McKinnon was her only other identity. Nevertheless, the legend that had been created for McKinnon was virtually watertight. She'd had help.

This hadn't been Ben and Aldwyn's first debrief following the events that had culminated with half of London being submerged. They'd both been summoned to an emergency session of COBRA in the immediate aftermath, at which much of the emergency action planning was taking place. Only once those plans had been discussed had the conversation moved on to the failure of the intelligence services to stop the attack. The blame had been placed squarely at their door for failing to gather the adequate intelligence required to stop the attack.

A video had been released to all major news outlets around the globe depicting the chaos of the flooding, as well as recent natural disasters. What had followed was a display of coal and nuclear power stations, deforestation, sub-continent roads full of trucks, and lastly, markets in China. *Nature has had enough. The war has just begun.*

It hadn't just been Aldwyn, however, who'd faced questions. Both the DG of MI5 as a whole (Dame Nicole Brennan) and the chief of MI6 (Sir Jocelyn Bower) had been berated. Their only defence had been that none of their informants, sleeper agents or wider contacts had hinted at there being any attack planned on this scale, although Aldwyn Haynes had honestly – but perhaps unwisely – admitted there had been a threat made against key structural targets in the UK. This, however, had been marked as low priority due to both it not being significant chatter and the heavy focus on a virus threat.

There had, in truth, also been numerous reports of incoming cyberattacks directed at big British business. Those had failed to materialise, but there had been a cyberattack with a different target. Simon Wynn-Jones, as well as a host of specialists from various departments, had been unable to regain control of the barrier's operating system, which had rendered their attempts to thwart the attack hopeless. They'd realised the true intention of the plot too late.

'It's not only your source who's disappeared,' continued Aldwyn, gulping down the remainder of his whisky and refilling his glass. 'The body Detective Ambrose recalled being pulled from the Thames near Woolwich has been identified as one Phillip Mulhern who, until recently, worked in the Navigation Centre for the Port of London Authority. He may have been an insider helping Henderson and his men. He was reported missing two weeks ago. The coroner has concluded that he was forcibly drowned before his body was put into the water.'

In spite of himself Ben, smiled slightly.

'Have I said something funny?' asked Haynes, his own tone rather amused.

'Not funny, no, but interesting.' Ben drained the rest of his own whisky and, without thinking poured himself a new glass, noticing his boss's raised eyebrow as he did so. 'They had no need for this man, Mulhern or whoever he is. We know very little about the people behind all of this or what their true motives were. I doubt very much it was to draw attention to climate change or just to prove how fixated we all were on the virus threat. But I think we've just learned something about them.'

'And what's that?'

Ben put down his glass. 'Remember what Ollie Robson told me about the voice at the end of the phone? Whoever it was told Ollie and Emma that they were going to survive, even though that was never their intention. Talk about it being the hope that kills you,' he muttered. 'He wanted to give them that hope and then watch them die. He watched the whole thing. He told Ollie he had a front-row seat.'

'So he's a sadist?' asked Haynes. 'It certainly sounds like it. Watching thousands die and delighting in giving the condemned hope, only to watch them die. Deranged, by the sounds of it. A sadist and a deranged eco-terrorist.'

'More than that – they enjoy the power. They enjoyed the fact they were one step ahead of us the whole time; they even left us a clue with Mulhern's body, knowing that we wouldn't be able to piece it together in time. Arrogant, certainly; sadistic, yes; but they couldn't resist showing off just how far ahead of us they are. As for Blanchet, I wouldn't call her deranged. Passionate, clinical and ruthless, yes.'

'What good does that do us?'

'Chances are they'll do the same again. Drop hints in plain sight of what their next plan is. They won't be able to resist the temptation to show off just how powerful they are. We just need to spot the pattern. From now on, every piece of intelligence gets over analysed on The Grid in case it gives us a clue about what's coming next, because one thing is for certain

– we're a long way from their endgame, whatever that may be. Even if we'd worked it out a few hours in advance of their attack, what could we have done?'

Haynes raised an eyebrow. 'Begin evacuating the poor sods who drowned, for a start.'

'An evacuation of London on that scale would have caused complete chaos and been a shambles. Yes, we could have attempted to evacuate London. We could have deactivated their explosives. We'd have saved some lives, but ultimately, they still had control of the barrier. People would still have died.'

'So you're saying we have a leak in this department?' Haynes demanded in an accusatory tone.

'It doesn't have to have been someone in this department. The whole of COBRA was kept up to date with our progress. For God's sake, the media got hold of classified details! This operation was essentially played out in the National Theatre, and Christ knows who was in the auditorium!' Ben paused before continuing exasperatedly, 'Or for that matter, who was backstage. The cabinet, the whole of MI5, MI6, the Met and the entirety of the armed forces have been given some level of access during this operation. Any one, or any group, of them could have let something slip or been working with these people from the start.

'They've second-guessed every move we've made, even the decision to have members of Matheson's unit involved in the operation. They either knew that the MOD and the major would push for it, or they had a hand in the decision-making. More worryingly, they knew we'd go along with it. Then again, there's a chance it was a happy coincidence for them that Hiscock was with us that day, but everything seems to have been so well planned out. And that brings me back to their little stunt at the university.'

Aldwyn smiled. 'Don't let the politicians hear you refer to it as a "stunt".'

'I keep coming back to one thing: what was the point? Yes, they wanted to create panic by taking over a university campus where the majority of students haven't been vaccinated and threating to release a new strain of the virus that's more lethal. They succeeded in creating panic. It makes sense that they chose the university where Vallance worked. A stunt. That's what they'd have us believe it was.'

'Like you say, it worked. It created panic, exposed some of what's going on at the universities, created a firefight with our men for the world to witness and heightened the threat of the virus. Seems a well-executed plan to me.'

'On the face of it, yes – but they also knew that, once we'd searched the campus, we'd realise there was no virus. The bluff would only last so long. We know now that Henderson and his men never had their hands on any of the virus. Corporal Matheson was killed because of the experiments at Porton Down, and they never kept significant stocks there. However, it doesn't explain one crucial bit of testimony. The Russian, Vladimir Conrad, took a few men and left the campus long before we showed up. I had Simon look into the area surrounding the university for any anomalies. I wasn't sure exactly what I was looking for, but he came up with this.'

Ben leaned forwards and tapped the file before flipping it open to reveal a black-and-white Ordinance Survey map of a plot of land. There were several structures helpfully annotated on the map, which identified the place as Egham and the surrounding area of Englefield Green in the Runnymede borough. The largest structure outlined was that marked as the Royal Holloway University, which was a sprawling mass of buildings and fields encompassing both sides of Egham Hill.

'What am I looking at?' asked Aldwyn, although Ben knew his boss had already taken in every inch of the image in front of him.

'All the buildings and structures have been accounted for,' said Ben. 'Everything looks as it should do with nothing out of place. This is what the people are meant to see.' He reached across the desk and turned the paper over to reveal another image, this one in colour and clearly taken aerially. It showed the same area as the Ordinance Survey map, though the buildings were brought to life more by the colour the image was imbued with.

Haynes raised an eyebrow. 'I assume I'm missing something here.'

'The images look the same. Nothing out of the ordinary.' Ben smiled and retrieved a second piece of paper from the file and placed it on the table. The third image showed a ground-level schematic of a section of the Egham area, including any foundations dug into the earth depicted in grey. He watched Haynes's eyes dart across the image before settling on a building located on Cooper's Hill Lane in Englefield Green. The image showed not only the structure of the building but also a grey mass beneath the centre of it, which was rectangular in shape.

'Those aren't part of the foundations of the structure,' observed Aldwyn.

Ben nodded. 'It's a bunker hidden beneath the Air Force Memorial. A Ministry of Defence bunker dating back to the development of the memorial itself. We know that, in the aftermath of the Second World War and particularly later during the Cold War, the MOD built hundreds of bunkers across Britain, as well as several across Europe. They housed everything from munitions to plans for military operations.

'The dimensions of the mass captured in this image fit with the typical size of an MOD bunker. I had Simon analyse the dimensions. We thought it may be a Soviet silo built by one of their sleeper agents during the Cold War, but they were typically dug much deeper into the earth. Besides, this bunker seems to have been built prior to or during the construction of the memorial itself, making it too early for Soviet involvement. You have to admit the beauty of the idea. It wouldn't be unusual to see service personnel around the site. They could be visiting the memorial. They even got the Queen to open it. I doubt Her Majesty was aware of what she was standing on at the time, mind you.'

Aldwyn smiled. 'Ingenious. I assume you've checked it out?'

'I sent a team over to the site this morning. Conrad and his men tidied up after themselves fairly well, but several centre slabs of marble had been dislodged, which conceal an underground entrance to the bunker. Whatever the MOD had housed there had been taken, however. They checked the bunker for traces of nuclear or chemical radiation, but they found none. Whatever was in there, it had been kept in a stable state.'

Haynes let out a low whistle. 'The information must have come from Harold Morris. He gave them access to the barrier and would have been capable of locating the information regarding MOD bunkers for them. He had sufficiently high-level MOD access for him searching for those sites not to be flagged to his superiors. Did Maya's contact give any indication as to what was in the bunker beneath the memorial?' He leaned back in his chair once more and sipped his fresh glass of whisky.

'No indication at all, although I'm not sure he has the clearance for that information. Knowing of the existence of the bunker is one thing, but the details of what's stored in these MOD bunkers is classified and restricted to those at the very top.'

Aldwyn didn't speak for a moment as he replaced his

whisky glass on the table, half of the amber liquid still swilling around the handcrafted tumbler. Then he said, very carefully and deliberately, 'That's a very serious allegation, Ben. Let me look into this.' He was looking at his senior intelligence officer with a highly suggestive expression on his face, which Ben understood at once. Both men nodded, and Haynes smiled slightly before he asked, 'Speaking of Maya's contact at the MOD, how is Maya herself holding up?'

'As expected,' Ben said, reflecting on his brief conversation with the junior analyst the day before. He knew there was little he could say that would truly console her. The loss had been personal and more real for her than anyone else in the team.

His boss nodded in an understanding manner. 'She'll need time. However, given the issues we're facing, if she isn't up to returning to work soon, we'll need a replacement.' There was no room for sentiment here. 'At least in the short term.'

'I understand. I'll speak to her again. If she doesn't feel up to returning to work, then I have a replacement in mind.'

'On quite the recruitment drive at the moment, aren't you? Well, if that's all, then I need to check in with the DG,' said Haynes, gesturing towards the door.

Ben didn't move.

'Unless there's something else you want to discuss?' A slight frown had joined the other lines stretched across the section chief's face as he surveyed his senior intelligence officer.

Ben inclined his head, smiling slightly. 'There is one thing.' He paused, fixing his gaze resolutely on his boss, searching for any sign of a reaction as he began. 'During the siege, Henderson told Bromley that he'd been betrayed by the service; he even hinted that the MI6 archives had been altered to conceal the truth about what happened in Israel and Tehran.'

There was not a flicker of a reaction. Haynes remained totally still, his expression smoothly impassive and inscrutable.

Those close-set, grey eyes seemed to have retreated further into their sockets, like a hedgehog curling into a defensive ball, but other than that, it was impossible to read anything in his face. When he spoke, there was no emotion on display, and his Yorkshire accent was more pronounced than before. 'Colton Henderson is perhaps the single worst post-war British-intelligence traitor. You, of all people, don't need me to tell you that. Lies and deceit are his ways now.'

There was a long silence during which Ben continued to study his boss's expression. It was almost impossible to gauge when their section chief was lying, so well versed in it was he, but Ben couldn't shake the feeling that he wasn't being told the whole story here. What Aldwyn said about Henderson was true, but he hadn't addressed the allegation that Henderson had made. 'So it isn't true? What happened to me in Tehran and everything he's done since, they have nothing to do with him feeling that he'd been betrayed?'

Aldwyn leaned back in his chair, eyeing Ben rather shrewdly before chuckling slightly. 'I can't claim to know how the mind of a traitor works. He may have felt slighted, betrayed even, by the service because of some sense of paranoia. Men like him see enemies everywhere. They don't trust anyone because they can't even trust themselves.' He reached forwards and snatched up his whisky glass before adding in a sombre tone, 'If there was something else, Ben, I'd tell you. If there was some information I could have offered you to help you make sense of what happened in Tehran, don't you think I'd have told you?'

A warmth had returned to Aldwyn's eyes, and Ben knew his boss had never given him a reason to doubt the man. He'd always been straight with Ben and always supported him. Haynes had taken a personal interest in Ben's recovery from the events in Tehran, and the two of them had become close. He was Ben's mentor, and they were a good team. And yet, as

Ben nodded, rose from the chair and moved across to the office door, a feeling nagged at him. He looked back to see Aldwyn watching him, his expression inscrutable once more.

No matter how close their professional relationship might be, Ben had always known for a fact that there would always be secrets between them. It was the nature of their work, and Aldwyn had been in the game a lot longer than him. It would be just like Henderson to try to weave mistrust between them all and to spread discord into their investigation, but Ben had been in intelligence long enough to trust his instincts. Sliding the door open, he resolved to do some investigations of his own. There was more to Henderson's history with the service than he was being told, and he was going to find out the truth.

28

They met by the statue of King Alfred the Great at the bottom of Winchester. The dazzling sunshine reflected off the parked cars and flashed into people's eyes, causing them to bring their arms up to cover their faces. The usually tranquil Abbey Gardens to their left was full of people striding along the pathway that separated two large lawns ringed with beautifully coloured trees, leading off into a rose garden. Behind them, couples walked hand in hand along the Weirs Walk, the sunlight glinting off the River Itchen. The door to the pub on the corner of Bridge Street swung open and laughter drifted through the air. It was a perfectly idyllic Saturday afternoon. Not at all what Ollie had been expecting.

Yet what had he been expecting? Everyone to be locked inside their houses, hiding away from the world? No, that was just how he felt. Life, he knew, would always win out. There was still the odd masked face amongst the crowd, but people had slowly learned to deal with the post-pandemic world. It had taken a while, and there was still unease and the odd furtive glance as someone passed close to you on the pavement. Maybe that would never go away. He wondered what this same scene would have looked like a week ago when the rumours of a new outbreak had been swirling. Would people still have swarmed up and down the cobbled streets, stopping at every market stall they passed? Perhaps not, but life was winning out.

On the uni campus, there had been worried, frantic conversations about what another pandemic would mean in light of those media stories, but it hadn't stopped any of them descending on the Students' Union for a party. That wouldn't have happened a year ago or even six months ago. Then, the stigma and the paranoia and the obedience had been at their highest. Ollie remembered the eerie feeling he'd experienced sitting on the Tube on the way to Shoreditch during the peak of the virus. The memory sent a shiver down his body even now. The desolate, almost empty carriages. Those few onboard had been glancing nervously at the other passengers and assessing the gap between them. There had been a solidarity there too, with weak smiles and nods exchanged with strangers, as though they were trying to convince each other that it would all be OK in the end.

Was this the moment they'd been smiling in hope for? For a time when, just days after thousands had lost their lives in London through a terrorist attack, they could all be out as one. The British public in defiance – one of the most unfailing and binding characteristics of the country. If ever there was a chance to show the world that the British weren't scared, it was now. He tried to shake the memory from his mind as he waited for Emma to arrive, but on the Tube that day, he'd felt as though he'd been drenched in icy water.

The people he'd nodded and smiled weakly at that day would likely have been on the Tube for legitimate reasons. He remembered squirming as an exhausted woman in her forties wearing an NHS lanyard had smiled at him. She'd looked emotionally drained; no doubt having spent a long shift fighting to save people from that deadly virus. Stay at home and protect lives. What a mockery he'd made of that by travelling to a party with his friends in Shoreditch. How selfish and pathetic had that been? He'd known it at the time. His reaction to the woman's smile had stirred the guilt inside him.

Yet he'd continued anyway. Maybe he and his friends had thought they were superhuman. He remembered them discussing it, assuring each other that they'd be fine. What harm could it do them anyway, even if they'd caught it? And what were the real chances? It had been on the journey back two days later that he'd listened to a doctor on the radio urging people to abide by the rules and stated that, by disobeying them, you could inadvertently be killing people. It had been a tough – even harsh – thing to say, but it had struck Ollie.

The words had rocked him, but in the end, he'd convinced himself that everything would be OK. *My parents and family wanted me to come home. They wanted to see me, and they knew it would mean breaking lockdown. That must surely mean it was OK?* That was what he'd told himself, and so he'd gone home when he knew it would mean coming into contact with a vulnerable person whom he loved. He'd been too selfish and too arrogant to stay away. Look what it had cost. It hadn't stopped there. By not keeping his mouth shut, he'd caused the death of a fellow student and put Emma in harm's way. He knew everything that had happened to her was his fault.

It was then he saw Emma climbing out of the passenger side of a blue Ford Mondeo that had pulled up in front of the bus stop. As she closed the door, Ollie glimpsed the smiling face of Emma's mother, whose flowing, light-brown hair and pencil-thin eyebrows were identical to her daughter's – although without the single strand of blonde that hung over Emma's forehead. He was surprised to see her mother was waving at him, and he raised his hand clumsily, unsure how to respond. He saw Emma smile slightly, as though the gesture had been amusing.

'She's not the Queen you know,' she said as she walked towards him, and Ollie was surprised to see the warmth and slight twinkle in her polished-amber eyes.

'I stopped short of curtsying,' Ollie replied awkwardly.

There was a moment's silence when they simply looked at each other. Ollie was taken aback by just how radiant she looked in her yellow cotton dress, which seemed to flow over her body seamlessly and was tied around her waist with a thin belt. She was wearing the same shade of pale-peach lipstick she had done on the night of the kidnapping, and he remembered how drawn to her he'd been. The truth was that he still was, but he wouldn't allow himself that yearning. There was a deep-purple bruise in the corner of her forehead from where she'd been thrown into the monitors inside the room where they'd been held.

'Shall we walk?' Emma asked hesitantly.

Ollie realised that he'd been staring at her without saying a word. He nodded, and the two of them began to walk up the cobbled High Street. The first two minutes were filled with a silence that was torturous for Ollie. They passed a bar that he'd booked for the two of them after leaving college. He'd thought that the unique and inventive cocktails and the dimly lit underground room would impress her. Maybe it would have done, but he'd never worked up the courage to invite her.

Memories swirled in his mind, and none of them particularly pleasant. As they walked, he found that their surroundings only added to his sadness. The market was as busy as it always had been, and there were some boutique shops that had survived the pandemic. Some, however, had never been able to reopen. Their shop fronts lay abandoned, the council unable to find businesses willing or able to replace those that had perished. In comparison to many cities around the country, Winchester had been able to survive largely intact, but even here there were lingering signs of what the virus had cost.

He was surprised to see Emma smile as they passed the man on the cheese stalling proclaiming aloud to the public. The brash, confident voice seemed somehow out of place to Ollie, as though it didn't belong in the wake of everything that had happened. The seller must have spotted her smile too, as he beckoned her across for a free sample. Emma merely laughed and raised her hand slightly as they walked on. Ollie glanced back to see the vendor feigning a broken heart, and he was shocked at the surge of anger he felt. *What's the matter with me?* He'd ordinarily be laughing along too.

'Do you want to grab a coffee or something?' he asked tentatively, trying to inject some normality into himself. He glanced nervously towards Emma and then away again quickly, afraid to meet her eyes.

'I'm more of a hot chocolate kinda girl,' replied Emma softly. There was something reassuring in her voice that made him peek at her once more.

'I can work with that.' He managed a hesitant smile.

As they turned left into one of the many narrow side alleys that lined Winchester High Street, Ollie felt his left hand brush lightly against Emma's right hand, and he closed his eyes at the touch. He looked down at the place they'd made contact, feeling his palms begin to sweat. Emma was looking down too. At the same moment, they both raised their heads and looked at each other. Their faces were almost touching, and Ollie found himself sucked into her gaze. There was a strange, slightly confused glint in her eyes, as though she was hesitating over what to do next.

His body almost acting on auto pilot, Ollie found his hand coming up to rest against her cheek. Emma closed her eyes at his touch, and when she opened them once more, a single tear had formed in her left eye. Ollie began to lean down when he suddenly found himself shunted to one side. Without realising it, they'd both stopped in the entrance to one narrow side street. As he was barged into, Ollie was knocked forwards and into Emma. He reached out and put his hand on her shoulder to stop himself knocking her backwards. As he did so, their eyes met once more, and Ollie saw a slight shadow ripple across the brown irises, and he let go of her at once, not even registering the muttered grumble of complaint from those passing them.

There was another awkward silence for a few seconds before Emma smiled uncertainly and began to walk further into the side street. They passed an attractive timber-framed building dating to the sixteenth century on their right that was one of the pubs in the city to have survived the pandemic. There were people standing around outside the door with plastic cups of beer and wine merrily enjoying the sunshine. Ollie glanced over his shoulder back through the passageway and to the Buttercross, which was also adorned with people chatting happily to one another, atop the lower level of the Perpendicular monument which depicted people associated to Winchester, including of course Alfred the Great. Perhaps it really was just him incapable of happiness.

'Do you want to grab a table or find somewhere else to talk?' asked Ollie, his mouth exceptionally dry, as they approached the nearest coffee shop and the queue in front of it.

'Seems a shame to waste the weather,' she replied, and he was surprised to see that she was smiling once more. 'Let me get these,' she added as they joined the queue.

'No chance,' he said at once, rather more snappily than he'd intended. 'I wouldn't have let you pay for anything on our first date normally,' he added quickly, forcing a smile on to his face, 'so there's no chance I'm letting you now.'

'Well, as first dates go,' Emma declared with a smile, 'you're already winning for bringing the weather.'

'What can I say?' Ollie found himself laughing in spite of himself. 'Call me Helios.' *Why did I say that? What an idiot,* he thought to himself, and he opened his mouth to apologise, but he found Emma laughing at him.

'Don't ever apologise for being a geek.' And in a fleeting gesture that took him completely by surprise, she leaned up and kissed him on the cheek. 'I love it.' Her lips were so soft against his skin and her touch seemed to breathe fresh life and confidence into Ollie that he hadn't been expecting. 'I'll see you by the cathedral,' Emma said rather sheepishly.

He watched her go, walking through the gates that led into the grounds around the impressive cathedral building with its imposing west front and great fourteenth-century triple porch and Gothic window overlooking the hordes of people gathered on the lawns beneath it.

Winchester Cathedral itself could be seen from the hills surrounding Winchester, and it served as an imposing visual landmark for the city. It also boasted the longest nave and the greatest overall length of any Gothic cathedral in Europe. On the north side of the building, it was still possible to make out the foundations of the Old Minster traced in brick, whilst the interior of the cathedral was beautifully adorned. Ollie had visited the place several times with his parents when he was younger, and although he couldn't remember many of the details, the fabulously crafted chantry chapels had remained in his mind. They'd been built by powerful bishops, whose souls were said to inhabit them, and daily masses were held in them. It had the most chapels – seven – of any cathedral in England, which was said to be a reflection of the city's great power and wealth between the fourteenth and sixteenth centuries in which they were built.

Having paid for and collected two hot chocolates, Ollie walked through the gates, flashing a smile at the old couple on the bench nearby who were shielding their eyes against the sun. The grass around the cathedral was full of people: small families having picnics or kicking a ball between them; couples lying down and kissing; and groups of friends drinking and laughing raucously. It all still felt very alien to Ollie. He couldn't relate to any of it.

As he spotted Emma standing by the corner of the cathedral that led through to the cloisters where the Christmas markets were usually set up, he adjusted his grip on the drinks, feeling his palms beginning to scold slightly. Ollie kept his head down as he walked through the crowds of people, not wanting to make eye contact with anyone. The entrance to the cloisters was adorned with a stone archway, and as he walked beneath it towards Emma, he was seized by the urge to pull her close to the wall.

There was no ice rink at this time of year. Instead, there was a huge marble water feature that had been erected in the middle of the cloisters, with the sound of the running liquid between the godly figurines creating a sense of tranquillity. Ollie was reminded of the rose garden located not far away, and he reflected on how peaceful a place Winchester truly was. There were two couples on the benches that ringed the water feature, and Ollie made to walk towards the vacant third bench, but Emma slipped her hand in his and began to lead him past the water fountain.

They walked for nearly fifteen minutes; Ollie enjoyed the feel of Emma's hand in his. *Is this what it's like to have a normal relationship?* he wondered. He kept the happiness that he felt at bay, knowing what this all meant. It wasn't until they reached the banks of the River Itchen in the fields that ran behind Winchester that Emma beckoned him towards a bench nestled beside a bend in the river that snaked around two large meadows. The water glistened like diamonds in the reflection of the sun's rays, and wildlife chirped all around them.

'Not a bad spot for a date either,' said Ollie rather hoarsely, his mouth very dry.

Emma smiled rather sadly, but she still retained her grip on his hand as they lowered themselves onto the bench. Neither of them spoke for a minute, nor did they look at one another.

'I'm sorry for how I treated you, Ollie. All those years I knew you liked me, and I led you on. You didn't deserve that.'

'It's only leading me if you didn't feel anything for me.' Ollie turned to look at Emma, who continued to stare out over the meadow. 'I was fine with that,' he continued, not understanding where the words were coming from. 'Thinking that you didn't like me back. I mean why would you? You were the cleverest, hottest girl in the year. I was just some nerd who spent his evenings writing fan fiction. What hurts more now is knowing that you do like me. I'd convinced myself that being too pathetic to ask you out was fine because you'd never have said yes. But there was a chance, wasn't there?'

Slowly, Emma raised her head, and he was surprised to see that tears were gleaming in her brown eyes. 'I always enjoyed attention,' she said in a hollow voice, 'and look where that got me. I didn't see what was right in front of my eyes the whole time. That's what makes this so hard now. You don't deserve this. I don't deserve you.'

It was as though a dark cloud had passed overhead. Ollie felt his jaw clench and his body tense. He bit down hard on his tongue, fighting against the impulse that was welling inside him. 'I think it's the other way round,' he suggested, tasting the bitterness in his mouth. 'The things I've done.' He paused, momentarily unable to go on. 'You need to get away from me.'

To his surprise, he felt Emma tighten her grip on his hand, squeezing it until he looked at her once more. Silent tears had begun to fall from her eyes, and she hurriedly wiped them away, a blazing look on her face as she said firmly, 'You're a good person, Ollie. Don't doubt that even for a second. What happened wasn't your fault. This isn't your fault.' Her voice faltered before she went on. 'Do you remember the first time that you ever held my hand?' she asked with a watery smile.

He turned to look at her, surprised, but before he'd opened his mouth to respond, she answered: 'I do. We were seven. We were playing some game; I can't remember what it was called. But I tripped and fell onto the concrete. You remember how hard that playground used to be. My knee was bleeding, and I was crying like the princess that I am. The teachers tried to help, but I pushed them all away.' Emma laughed, her eyes lost in memory. 'I was such a brat. I wouldn't let any of them touch me. I just kept crying.'

It had once saddened Ollie that he could remember very little from his early school days, but the memory stirred within him as vividly as though it had happened the day before. He could remember looking down at her tear-streaked face, not unlike he was now. The memory stung the back of his own eyes.

'Nobody could get near me.' Emma was still smiling as she attempted to dry her face. 'You remember what you did? We didn't know each other, but you walked across the playground and held out your hand to me. You didn't say anything; you just smiled at me.' Emma swallowed deeply and the smile died on her face for a moment. 'You calmed me down and made me comfortable in a way that nobody else could. That hasn't changed from then until now. I took your hand then, and I didn't ever want to let go of it.'

Ollie found it difficult to get the words out, as he bit back the emotion that was rising in his throat. 'You used to look for me at lunch, and we'd hold hands for the whole hour.' It was a happy memory tinged with the gut-wrenching truth of where they were now.

'I felt safe with you, and I always have done. No matter what has happened. I still feel safe with you.' She placed her hand against his cheek, and it seemed to breathe life and strength into him to fight back the tidal wave of feeling that was threatening to overwhelm him. 'That won't ever change, Ollie.'

He longed more than anything to lean over and kiss her. Emma, it seemed, had succumbed to her tears, and she turned away from him to look out over the meadow. For a minute, the only sounds that could be heard were the river lapping over the debris that littered its edge and the joyful chirping of the birds overhead.

'When do you leave?' he asked eventually in a hollow voice.

Emma didn't ask how he knew. 'Tomorrow. You do know it's not forever, right? Just a couple of months. I just can't be here right now. You understand that, don't you?'

Ollie nodded. 'I'd want to get away from here too.' He hadn't meant to sound self-pitying, but he noted how miserable his voice was. 'I wish you'd never come up to my uni. None of this would have happened to you.'

There was a slight hint of her old teasing nature behind the tears as Emma gripped his hand and said quietly, 'You wish we hadn't spent that time together at your place?'

Ollie looked at her confused. 'But everything else. It happened because you came to mine—'

'And I wouldn't change that decision for anything,' interjected Emma, her eyes swimming with tears now. Black mascara was running slowly down her cheeks, but she was still in control. 'I wish we'd made that decision sooner. I loved being at yours.'

As he looked into the brown eyes that he was so attracted too, Ollie was shocked to see the genuine warmth in her eyes as she spoke. There was sadness and pain in her eyes, but love also. That took him aback.

'I wouldn't swap what happened for never having spent the time with you. It's the happiest I've felt for years.' Emma reached up with her free hand and placed it against his cheek once more.

He closed his eyes briefly at her touch, and then stared out over the winding river, but he couldn't prevent hot tears spilling from his eyes.

'It's the only time I can remember truly feeling myself,' she whispered. 'You're the only person that has ever made me feel that way. From the day that you took my hand in the playground until now.'

He knew what he wanted to say, but he couldn't begin to form the words. It was taking all his effort to fight back the pain he was feeling.

However, it was again Emma who found the strength for speech. Her breathing was slow and controlled, and he imagined that she was steeling herself to say something that he wouldn't want to hear. 'I just need time. After everything that happened, I have to learn to deal with it—'

'And you can't do that around me,' finished Ollie, trying to inject some positivity into his voice. 'I understand. I just never thought it would come to this.' There was a cloud descending slowly in his mind, creating an oppressive darkness that blocked out the brilliant sunshine. 'I never thought that our first date would also be our last,' he added, allowing the misery to seep in.

Emma's face was streaked with tears as he looked back at her and reluctantly met her eyes. He could see the pain there, and that held him back from asking the question that had plagued his nightmares of late. They were sitting so close together that the smell of her perfume filled his nostrils, its floral aroma enticing him closer to the nape of her neck. Ollie took the moment to take in every single inch of her, from the shape of her body to the nose and lips that he loved so much.

It was as his gaze returned to the beauty of her eyes that Emma said softly, 'This isn't over for us.' She paused before adding with a nervous smile, 'Our second date is just on ice.'

Ollie could see the truth hidden in her eyes. He couldn't look away. There was an intensity to her gaze that just held him. He shivered slightly, but there was no cold. He allowed the sensation to travel down his body. How easy would it be to succumb to these feelings?

Their eyes never leaving each other's, Emma leaned forwards hesitantly. The tips of their noses touched, their eyes boring into one another. Ollie could feel his heart beating faster against his chest, the anticipation washing away the pain that had filled his body. Emma moved her head slightly, her eyes giving away her intention, as their lips brushed gently against one another. Ollie closed his eyes at her touch as their lips pressed together, softly at first, before he parted her slightly shaking lips, the action sending tremors along his nerves and kick-starting them into life. For the next few seconds, the clouds in his mind lifted and the sun blazed down upon them once more, obscuring all other feelings and memories from existence.

It was the most perfect feeling in the world to him. Ollie never wanted to let go as he placed one hand at her back and the other in her sweeping, brown hair. It was as though Emma had peeled back his soul, and it was a moment he'd been waiting for his entire life. The pain and loss were gone, replaced by warmth and love, which had been waiting to blossom inside him, hitherto suppressed by the trauma he'd experienced.

It was over all too quickly. Emma withdrew slightly, and the spell of the moment was broken as she placed her head on his shoulder, looking out over the meadow. Ollie held her close to him whilst he watched a robin flutter gracefully onto the arm of the bench beside him, its red breast gleaming in the sunshine. Hopping on its tiny, black legs, it cocked its head from side to side before looking at them with curious eyes. Then, in a sweeping motion, it burst into song and rose aloft, quickly lost amidst the backdrop of the golden sky. Ollie knew he would always cherish that moment, as he watched it disappear and drew Emma closer to him, breathing in the fresh summer air and smells, and hoping it would never end.

29

The shadows shrouded the two faces from the view of any passing members of the public, not that there were any. This meeting place had been chosen particularly carefully. Neither man would want to be seen. Indeed, the shorter of the two men wouldn't have arranged the meeting at all had he not been 100 percent certain that his presence here couldn't be traced. The two of them had met on just a couple of occasions in the past. It was best to keep their direct contact to a minimum, but today's meeting was as much a celebratory one as it was strictly business. At least that was the case for the man who kept his face averted from that of his companion.

'You do realise they'll come looking, don't you? They won't stop investigating until they know who was behind this attack. You've painted the ultimate target on your back,' the other man said in an uncharacteristic display of nerves.

A smirk flitted across the hidden features of the man who'd arranged the meeting; he then responded with an ice-cold silkiness to his voice that sent a slight shiver down the neck of his companion: 'Our backs, don't you mean?' As the other man began to bluster a response, he continued smoothly, 'It's lucky that we have the people who control them. We can monitor everything they do and shut them down if they get too close.'

'Don't you think that would create suspicion? We don't want them to realise just how far this goes. I'm sure my interference has already been noted. You can't expect to destroy half of one of the world's most prominent capitals and there not be any repercussions.' As they passed briefly beneath the spotlight of the moon, it was possible to make out the crumpled, grey suit that the second man was wearing.

'But why not? The only people who are aware of my involvement and those of my associates are you and a select group of others, and we're friends. Friends don't betray each other's confidences, do they? And we are friends, aren't we?'

The other man swallowed, the index finger of his right hand scratching absentmindedly at the back of his scalp. A bead of sweat suddenly appeared at his temple and dripped down his forehead. 'Of course, we are,' he replied, although his voice had lost some of its composure.

'That's reassuring to hear,' the shorter man responded softly, his tone swiftly becoming more dangerous as he continued, 'because if I were to find out that were not the case, then I'd have no hesitation in ordering your entrails to be forcibly removed, burned and hung from the top of that precious parliament building you still claim to serve.' A sanguine smile had slithered into place on the man's face, and his tongue seemed to flick through his teeth as though they were the fangs of the most lethal serpent.

'I… I am an appointed representative of the people…'

The other man gave a horrible, menacing laugh that seemed to carry on long after he recommenced speaking. 'You're my representative. Appointed by me. Chosen by me. Owned by me. And need I remind you that you aren't the only such privileged person in this world? I like you, I really do, but don't mistake my friendship for weakness or equality. Do not presume to tell me how to run matters operationally again, or I shall be forced to terminate our friendship prematurely – and I really would hate to do that.'

There was silence that followed these words – a cold, fearful silence – ultimately broken by another shorter, more pleasant laugh. 'But friends shouldn't have to speak this way. You've done well. Ensuring the journalist and poor Mr Houghton were in exactly the right place was a masterstroke. A journalist betrayed by her source rather than the other way round has a certain poetry to it, don't you think? We're all set to implement the next phase of our operation. The goods have been flown out of the country on the next leg of their journey. I trust that you won't be experiencing any more pangs of democratic conscience between now and their release?'

The other man cleared his throat, trying to regain his composure. 'Of course not. Everything is ready at our end.'

'Excellent, then all we have left is to tidy up some loose ends.'

'Loose ends? You mean Haynes's team?' A smile had returned to the other man's face, as though he were within reach of a prospect that had delighted him for years.

'No, no; Aldwyn and his team will be invaluable in the months to come. We're by no means finished with them – at least not all of them. No, I'm referring to certain individuals who were previously left alive to suit our goals. You need not concern yourself with such matters. Now I've taken up enough of your time, I think. You have a city to rebuild and a public to reassure.' With a passing smirk, the man disappeared into the gloom.

It wouldn't have been possible for anyone to track his movements in the minutes that followed. It was as though he blended seamlessly into the darkness, and his strides caused barely a ripple across the surface of the city. His expensive, shiny, black shoes made hardly a sound, and his black Italian-woven-cashmere trench coat rippled in the cold night air.

The sound of the rail network reached his ears, and there was a slight twitch at the corners of the man's mouth. He was passing through some of the less redeveloped parts of London now, crossing between salubrious alleyways and darkened side streets, but this didn't seem to concern him in the slightest. As he turned another corner, he came within sight of the undulating brickwork arches that supported the trains that thundered along the tracks overhead. There was no break in his stride as he moved purposefully towards the middle archway and slipped beneath its shadow, finding the hidden doorway that had been opened for him by one of his associates minutes beforehand. Before he entered, the figure withdrew something from the inside pocket of his coat and brought it up to his face.

A couple of moments later, he stepped into the large, open-plan area that now housed nothing except several discarded desks. This old KGB substation housed beneath this arch had long since been abandoned and fallen into disrepair. Anything of interest had either been removed by the last members of the KGB to have used the building or had subsequently been stripped by the British intelligence services in the hope of acquiring any information on their Russian compatriots. There was nothing present now that gave any insight into the area's former masters or the activities that had taken place here.

As he entered the building, the old-fashioned lamps overhead flickered in time with the final few trains of the night that rattled overhead and seemed to cause the building beneath them to shake. In the moments when there was silence overhead, it was possible to discern a slight hiss from the overhead sprinkler system that now appeared to emit only a whisper of vapour in its old age. In the centre of the room, which looked as though it were an abandoned warehouse, stood a small man with watery eyes, whose face was horribly disfigured. The acid had burned away his short, black hair, exposing his black eyes in their hollow sockets and disguising the man's real age.

The lamps themselves illuminated the figure in the centre of the room, but kept the newcomer in the shrunken shadows, his face and features concealed from Vasily Ivanovic. Nevertheless, it seemed the outline of the man's physique alone had been enough to spook Ivanovic. He seemed confused and glanced around him nervously, as though expecting someone else. 'Where's Mr Conrad?' he asked in heavily accented English. 'I deal only with him.'

The other man had stopped at a distance from the Ukrainian and was surveying him with an amused expression. Slowly, leather gloved hands were withdrawn from the pockets of the expensive coat and were brought together in exaggerated clapping.

'What is this?' said Ivanovic angrily. 'Who are you?'

The words seemed to have an effect, as the clapping ceased at once. 'I'm your benefactor, Mr Ivanovic, come to congratulate you in person. Vasily Ivanovic,' he said with an icy smoothness that sent an ominous chill through the air, 'the master spy who fooled the British intelligence services. Is there nobody you wouldn't betray, Mr Ivanovic?'

Red blotches of anger had appeared on the Ukrainian's face now, and he took a threatening step towards the man, his finger raised, before he seemed to think better of it, and he lowered his hand.

'Remembered who you're dealing with?' the man suggested with a smirk, his voice slightly muffled.

'I want what I owed.' There was as much fear as anger in the Ukrainian's voice now. 'What you asked... I did it. Never... I never asked who you were.'

'Your services have certainly been useful, but how long would it be before you betrayed our organisation too? The list of those you've deceived grows longer, Mr Ivanovic, and I'm afraid I'm far too careful a man to ignore such a track record.'

Instinctively, it seemed, the Ukrainian seemed to realise all of a sudden that something was wrong. He took several blundering, hasty steps forwards until the shadows shrouding the other man parted. Fear bulged instantly in Ivanovic's eyes for a moment, and he opened his mouth, perhaps to shout, but the sound appeared to die in his throat. His bottom lip began to tremble and very abruptly began to splutter uncontrollably, his hands coming up to grasp at his throat.

The fear had turned to horror in his eyes now, which were becoming steadily more bloodshot. Vasily Ivanovic fell to his knees, as the first rivulets of blood began to seep from his nose and mouth down the disfigured face now twisting in agony. He clawed in vain at his own throat, his fingers desperately attempting to tear it apart, to stop this torture. His screams of suffering never made it to his mouth as his limbs began to shake, and he shuffled pathetically across the floor. Ivanovic scrabbled fruitlessly for a final time at the coat hem of the man, who took one step backwards out of his reach, his striking different-coloured eyes glinting hungrily from beneath the military-grade MIRA Safety gas mask.

Then the Ukrainian pitched to one side, his body twitching uncontrollably and with foam and blood mingling into thick bubbles at the corners of his mouth. It was as though every nerve ending in his body was firing at the same time, and the ever-feebler instructions from his brain were being ignored. All the while, the taller man stood over him, a feverishly excited look just discernible beneath the gas mask that was protecting him from the same fate as the excruciating one that Vasily Ivanovic was experiencing.

Finally, it was over. The large fingers stopped scratching uselessly at the concrete flooring. The piggy eyes lay bloodshot and weeping, face down on the floor, and the man's rather podgy figure was curled awkwardly like an upturned foetus on the ground. There had been tears in the final seconds of his life, as much due to pain as the fear of what was to come. Almost as though they had known instinctively that their work was done, the not-so-derelict sprinklers stopped their lethal hiss, but the sound seemed to carry on as the man muttered in a voice icily similar to that of the sprinklers: 'Consider your contract of employment terminated, Mr Ivanovic.'

30

Ollie sat alone on the bench in the corner of the cemetery. His mind was a blur of emotion and memory that he was struggling to control. Rain lashed all around him, both a sickening reminder of recent events and also a striking personification of his own feelings. *Is this my punishment? I've been searching for over a year for a way to pay my penance for what had happened during the pandemic, and is this it?* He'd expected to feel relief when that moment arrived, not pain such as this.

The grief wasn't his alone. It was nothing to that the parents of the girl killed at his uni would be feeling right now, nor that of Robbie's parents. He hadn't found it within himself to be able to lift up the phone to speak to them. *What does that say about me?* He knew he should hate himself for that cowardice, but he felt only grief and loss.

The world had been changed by what had happened, but he found he didn't much care about the devastation inflicted on London. He was numb to the wider sense of loss that the country felt, in comparison to what he'd lost personally. Robbie would have understood what he was feeling, just like he'd understood the guilt that had haunted Ollie for over a year, but Robbie was gone where Ollie couldn't reach him. He couldn't help but feel that he'd failed to value their friendship. *I always took it for granted, but did I make the most of it?*

Indeed, he couldn't truly comprehend the fact that he'd never again be able to speak to his friend, although he knew Robbie was gone. He hadn't seen the body, but the voicemail Robbie's parents had left on the home phone had been enough to confirm it. The fact that his friend's mum had been unable to keep her emotions together long enough to finish the short message was proof enough. He'd known long before then, in truth, from the minute he'd seen the water crashing backwards from the barrier.

Had it not been for the fact that both of them had lost their lives in the event, Ollie was sure Robbie would have considered the excitement of the moment his most successful date ever. That brought a thin, watery smile to Ollie's face in spite of himself, and he looked up into the steadily descending rain, embracing the stinging impact of the droplets on his tear-streaked cheeks. He couldn't stop himself laughing regardless. The involuntary sound that emanated from him was swallowed up in the noise of the wind and rain that was whipping through the graveyard. *What's wrong with me?* Then, unbidden, he saw clearly the expression Robbie's face would have worn if he could see Ollie now – sodden and sitting alone in a cemetery – and he laughed even harder, uncontrollably for several minutes, and the release of emotion seemed to create a bubble around him through which the rain couldn't permeate.

He found himself wondering what his friend would have said to accompany his incredulous look, and that created a renewed fit of laughter that died suddenly in his throat. *'How have you let Emma slip through your fingers again, you prick?'* That was what he would have said.

Would he have been right? Was letting her walk away a mistake? It was too much to imagine the time they'd spent together in his home, and so he shut off his mind to the image of her naked figure walking across the landing towards him. He tried not to feel the press of her body against his in bed. Tears tumbled from his tightly shut eyes, and pain built in the back of his mouth from his clenched teeth. That time had been some of the happiest moments of his life, but he'd known that he didn't deserve them. He'd proven that by leaving her alone. Everything that had happened to her from that moment onwards was his fault, he knew. She hadn't said it, but he'd seen some of the accusation in her eyes when they'd last spoken.

There was no question that she was better off without him. Yet in spite of himself, her words came to the forefront of his mind. She'd believed in him, despite what he'd done, and she'd told him to forgive himself. As he squinted through the rain at the small headstone that lay in the corner of the graveyard and the name etched into it, he was reminded of another person he'd let down who'd believed in him. And he loved them both. Their opinions must mean something, or else he was disrespecting them. There might come a time when Emma would need him again. Would he let her down again, just as he'd done his granddad? No, that was an insult to them, as it was to his friend, if he let her walk away from his life altogether. For now, it was the right thing to do. She needed time to heal, but that didn't mean there was no future for them.

There were still people who loved him and believed in him, despite the self-loathing that he felt. For the first time he felt as though that was something he wanted to combat, not embrace. He knew too much had happened for that to be a smooth process, even before he got to the two bodies that he'd left in the barrier control room to doubtless be crushed by the sheer force of water that descended upon them. One had already been dead before that impact – killed by him. That knowledge was nothing compared to the other pain he felt. Indeed, strangely enough, it was the fate of the other man whom he'd left cradling the bleeding stump of his leg that added to the turmoil preventing him from sleeping at night.

The man was a killer, Ollie knew. If he hadn't wielded that axe in his hand, then the man wouldn't have hesitated to kill both Ollie and Emma. Yet as the gun had tumbled from his grasp and he'd felt the pain and seen the horror that Ollie had inflicted on him, it was as though the lost years of humanity had returned to him in that moment. How curious. It had been Ollie who'd been temporarily paralysed by the shock and revulsion at what he'd done. Had it not been for the man's insistence that he move, and Emma regaining consciousness, then they might have shared a tomb together.

Oddly, Ollie found it difficult to watch the news reports of what had happened with any kind of perspective. There was shock, yes, at the images of parts of London submerged and of the Thames Barrier that had been rendered useless. The pictures, though, didn't do justice to what Ollie had experienced. They felt like two disconnected events: what the news showed had happened and what had actually taken place for him on the barrier. The personal aftermath was what hurt more. He knew he should feel some of the gravity of what had taken place. The country – the world even – had been changed, and so many lives had been snuffed out.

It was as he rapidly blinked the raindrops from his eyes and stared straight ahead at the gravestone of his granddad, who he'd so admired, that he became acutely aware of a shrill noise in the air. It was almost indistinguishable from the howl of the wind, but as he squinted his eyes in concentration, the sound appeared to become more pronounced. It was coming from the ground at the foot of the gravestone, where an hour before, Ollie had placed a bunch of flowers that were now little more than brightly coloured mud.

Clambering off the bench and trying in vain to shake the rain from his hair and face, Ollie scanned the ground around him. It was the ringing of a mobile phone. He was sure of it. *Has someone dropped their phone whilst they were visiting a relative's grave?* It was possible, but as he dropped to his knees, cradling his right wrist, which had been plastered and now hung in a sling, Ollie's suspicions were confirmed. The sound was coming from directly in front of him – the patch of sodden earth that covered the foot of his granddad's gravestone.

Not for the first time cursing his decision not to wear gloves, he carefully moved his hands over the muddy earth. For several seconds, his hands met nothing, but then, beneath a slight mound of damp ground, his fingertips hit something solid. He dug his left hand into the earth, grasped it and wrenched it free triumphantly. He was on the point of straightening up when he returned his attention to the ground and carefully smoothed it over, before giving a slight nod up at the gravestone.

Now the phone was in his hand, Ollie knew it had been planted for him to find. Very few people tended his granddad's grave, and the phone had been covered by earth, indicating that it hadn't simply dropped from someone's pocket. Hesitantly, Ollie got to his feet and brought the phone up towards his left ear. Instinctively, he knew the voice he was about to hear. What other reason could there have been for the cloak-and-dagger approach?

There was no mistaking the silky-smooth familiarity of that voice, even though he was sure it was being distorted somewhat, perhaps in an attempt to disguise the true identity of the man on the other end of the line. When questioned about the voice he'd heard whilst being held at the Thames Barrier, Ollie had told the intelligence agents that he was certain it was a man's voice. Despite the individual's attempts to mask his voice, the deeper pitch and languid manner of speech made Ollie certain that it was a man. He could glean little else from the words that now drifted smoothly into his ear.

'Congratulations on your continued survival, young Master Robson,' said the voice in little more than a silky whisper.

The sound sent a shiver of fear down Ollie's spine, and he closed his eyes to the memories that the voice elicited.

'I must admit I was surprised to watch you escape the Thames Barrier alive.'

Perhaps it was the memory of Emma standing up to Henderson in that control room, and Ollie wishing he'd done the same, but he found himself interrupting the man who'd seemingly controlled his destiny. 'I bet you were,' he said, and much to his surprise, he found that the anger inside him was cool and controlled. 'Especially after telling us we'd survive and to watch the show. That was all some sick game to you, I suppose?'

There was silence for several seconds, but Ollie felt no fear at the consequences of his words. Indeed, he even mustered a laugh at the response that now hissed dangerously through the receiver. 'I warned you before not to interrupt me.'

'There's nobody here to hold a gun against my head today.'

'Not today perhaps,' the voice continued menacingly, 'but your time will come, and you'll remember this conversation. You're half-right in my motivations for telling you and lovely Emma that you'd survive. I can only imagine the fear you felt when she told you where you both were. I'd expected you to cling to that sliver of hope that you'd be spared right up until the final moment.'

'Lucky for us, then, that I didn't trust a word you had to say.' Ollie wasn't sure why he felt compelled to keep speaking, but he felt a sense of intrigue. *Who is this man and why had he taken the time to speak to me when his plan has succeeded?* 'Why call me now?' he said, echoing his internal thoughts. 'You won most of your sick game. You destroyed London, killed thousands and have nearly forced the PM to resign, but you chose to pick up the phone to me. Why?'

A shallow, cold laugh came from the receiver. 'You undervalue your role in all this, Ollie. London and the barrier: that was largely business. You and I, though, that was and remains personal. You interfered in our business, and that means you're now part of our drama, Master Ollie.' There was a calculated edge to the voice, as he continued, and Ollie couldn't help but wonder what the true reason was for this call. 'Our paths will inevitably cross again. There's nothing quite as infuriating as unfinished business, and that's what we have now. However, I must warn you not to seek it out, or it will be those around you who will suffer. You've seen we can get to anyone, anywhere, at any time we choose. Wait patiently until your time comes. Until then, I wish you better fortune than you've endured thus far.' With that, the line went dead.

Ollie slowly lowered the phone from his ear, overthinking every motion. As he did so, he noticed that the call had come from an unknown number. He knew the conversation had been meant to scare him, but in fact, it appeared to have done the opposite. *He's blown up the Thames Barrier, for God's sake, and submerged half of London, whilst supposedly having watched the whole thing unfold first-hand, so what is it that's making me smile?*

For all his smoothness and calculated calm, the man had taken the time to call him. It seemed as though Ollie's survival had got under his skin. He'd made this personal, and that meant there was a chink in this man's seemingly infallible armour. Spinning on the spot, Ollie threw the phone into the air and brought his right foot round to volley it into the dark thicket of trees that bordered the cemetery, a satisfied grin spreading across his face.

Epilogue

Death and fear had become daily companions during the pandemic. People had become fixated with the press briefings on the virus, waiting with bated breath to hear how many people had fallen victim to it in the last twenty-four hours. What did that mean for everyone else? The months without freedoms stretched on. It took up the entirety of the news reels, so it was impossible to escape it.

Behind the scenes, chaos ensued. There was no serene leadership who had a plan prepared for this eventuality. The backbiting and leaks that had come out after the pandemic were evidence enough of that. If half the stories were to be believed, then it was nothing short of mayhem. In the ensuing bedlam, the focus was understandably all on the virus and how to tackle it. The usual processes of governing were largely discarded.

Of course, it would be wrong to say no other policies were contemplated or that other threats weren't considered. But to a large extent, these were downgraded in terms of priority. There were checks that were ignored, and searches and sweeps that weren't conducted. Even when the pandemic was more under control, the wheels took longer than they should have to move again. Eyes were taken off areas where they were needed. That would come back to bite not just the UK but also the world as a whole – everyone would suffer.

The images of swathes of London submerged by water would haunt a generation. Were those images alone enough to inspire change across the world? They could be the catalyst to reignite the passion that had been demonstrated over the past eighteen months.

As always with humanity, the pandemic had brought out the best in society. In the UK alone, sums raised through charity funding for health organisations in the first few months of the outbreak vastly outweighed government expenditure in the health system for the previous three years. There were heroic tales from veteran servicemen and from the most vulnerable in society, as well as some of the wealthiest, in support of the health workers who were fighting daily against an unrelenting adversary. Weekly demonstrations of appreciation became entrenched, and despite the challenges they faced, doctors and nurses were overwhelmed by the displays of gratitude and admiration afforded them by the wider public.

Ordinary people suddenly seemed more empowered to stand up for social issues, with incidents around the globe sparking worldwide anti-racism protests. Unlike those that had preceded it, however, this movement was to attract support on a scale never seen before, forcing governments to look seriously at the racial divide that remained in society. Although tentative steps were made to heal some of the wounds that had lingered for centuries, there were those whose bigotry stunted their country's response to movement; however, unlike in the past, the protestors didn't shrink away from those in power but continued the struggle, giving hope that real change is achievable.

It was that spirit and humanity that would be key to the struggles ahead. Without them, the world had little chance of combatting what was to come.

As the aircraft curved and dipped down towards its final destination, the cargo that had been unearthed from beneath a memorial in Surrey, England, began its final descent into Syria.

About The Author

Tom, a Jersey-born wordsmith with a flair for history and a penchant for espionage, is finally unleashing his literary prowess upon the world with his debut novel, *Blood in the Water*. This long-anticipated gem is not just a standalone book; it's the first instalment of the thrilling Wolfhound series that promises to keep readers on the edge of their seats.

A proud Welshman at heart, Tom's connection to his heritage shines through in his writing, proving that he can wield a quill just as deftly as he can cheer for his favourite sports teams, despite the constant heartache that brings! With a degree in history tucked under his belt, he crafts narratives that are as rich as a well-aged cheddar and as exhilarating as a last-minute goal. Prepare to dive into the pages of his work, where history meets intrigue, and thrills lurk around every corner.